KILL or be KILLED

IMAGE COMICS, INC.

Robert Kirkman — Chief Operating Officer
Erik Larsen — Chief Financial Officer
Todd McFarlane — President
Marc Silvestri — Chief Executive Officer
Jim Valentino — Vice-President
Eric Stephenson — Publisher
Corey Murphy — Director of Sales
Jeff Boison — Director of Publishing Planning & Book Trade Sales
Chris Ross — Director of Digital Sales
Kat Salazar — Director of PR & Marketing
Branwyn Bigglestone — Controller
Susan Korpela — Accounts Manager
Drew Gill — Art Director
Brett Warnock — Production Manager
Meredith Wallace — Print Manager
Brian Skelly — Publicist
Aly Hoffman — Conventions & Events Coordinator
Sasha Head — Sales & Marketing Production Designer
David Brothers — Branding Manager
Melissa Gifford — Content Manager
Erika Schnatz — Production Artist
Ryan Brewer — Production Artist
Shanna Matuszak — Production Artist
Tricia Ramos — Production Artist
Vincent Kukua — Production Artist
Jeff Stang — Direct Market Sales Representative
Emilio Bautista — Digital Sales Associate
Leanna Caunter — Accounting Assistant
Chloe Ramos-Peterson — Library Market Sales Representative

IMAGECOMICS.COM

Standard Cover, ISBN: 978-1-5343-0028-6
DCBS Variant, ISBN: 978-1-5343-0204-4
Newbury Comics Variant, ISBN: 978-1-5343-0205-1
Midtown Comics Variant, ISBN: 978-1-5343-0206-8
Dragon's Lair Comics & Fantasy Variant, ISBN: 978-1-5343-0207-5
Forbidden Planet/Big Bang Comics Variant, ISBN: 978-1-5343-0208-2
Convention Hardcover Variant, ISBN: 978-1-5343-0261-7

 Publication design by Sean Phillips

Volume One

Ed Brubaker
Sean Phillips
Elizabeth Breitweiser

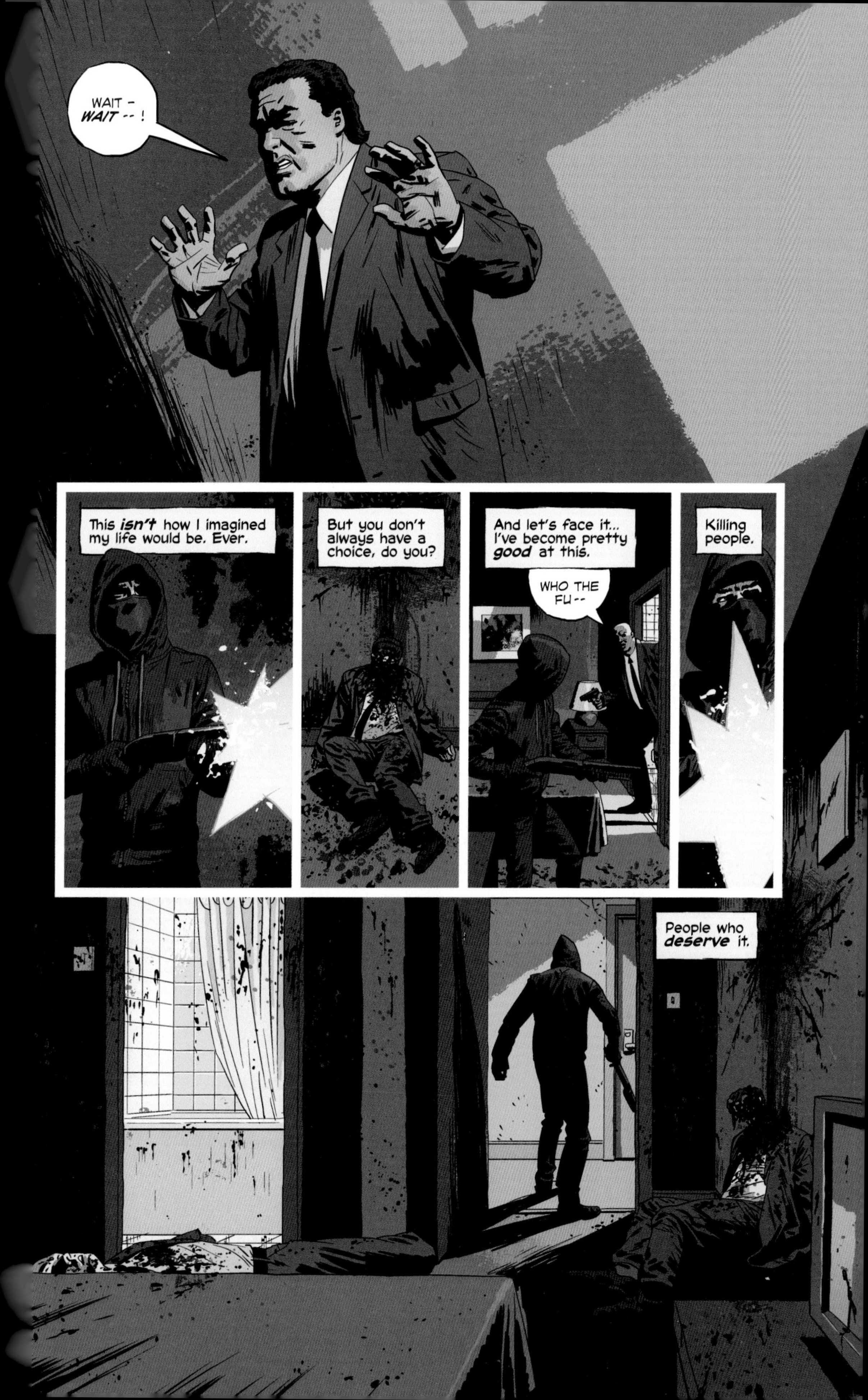
WAIT -
WAIT -- !
This isn't how I imagined my life would be. Ever.
But you don't always have a choice, do you?
And let's face it... I've become pretty good at this.
WHO THE FU--
Killing people.
People who deserve it.

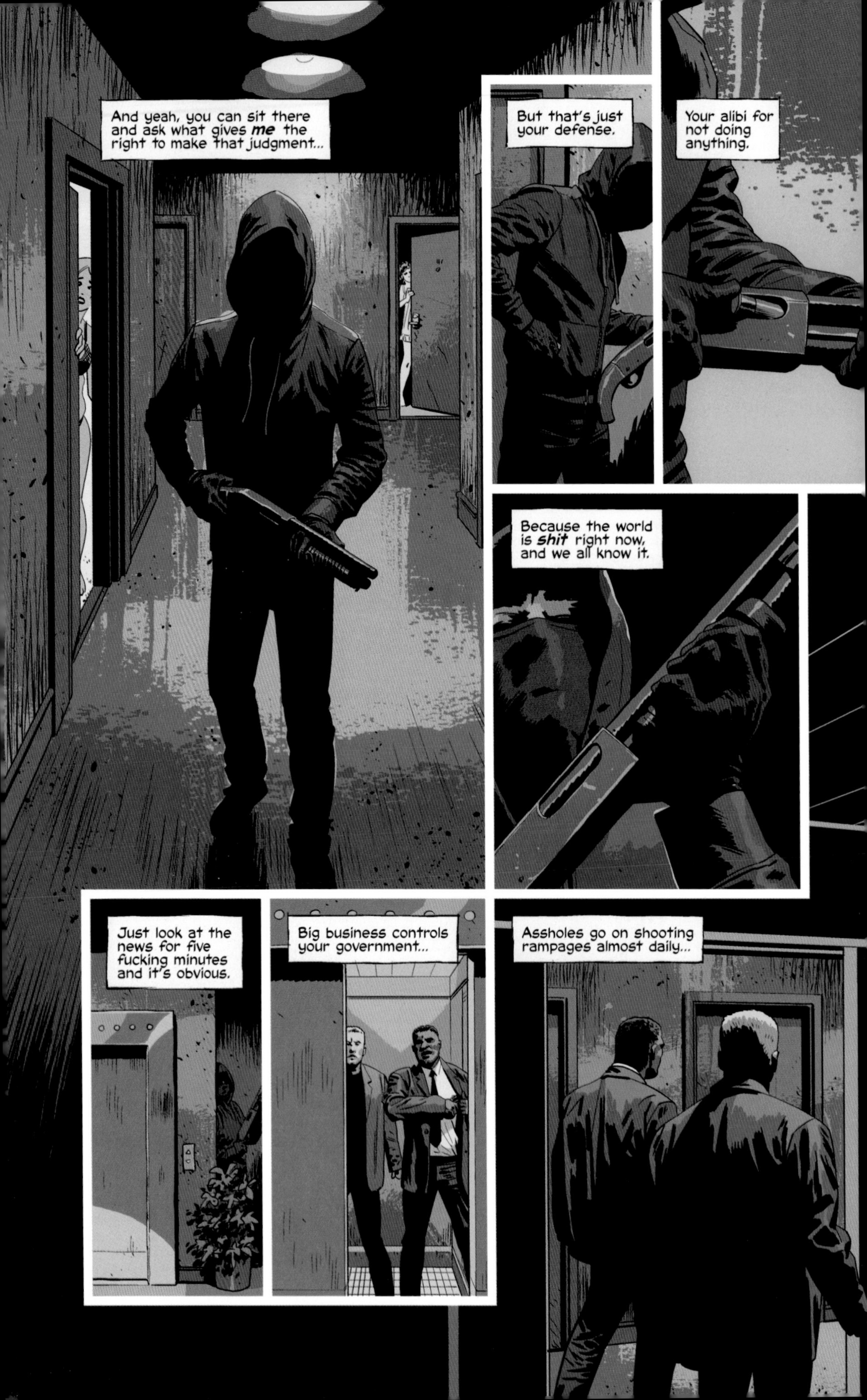
And yeah, you can sit there and ask what gives *me* the right to make that judgment...
But that's just your defense.
Your alibi for not doing anything.
Because the world is *shit* right now, and we all know it.
Just look at the news for five fucking minutes and it's obvious.
Big business controls your government...
Assholes go on shooting rampages almost daily...

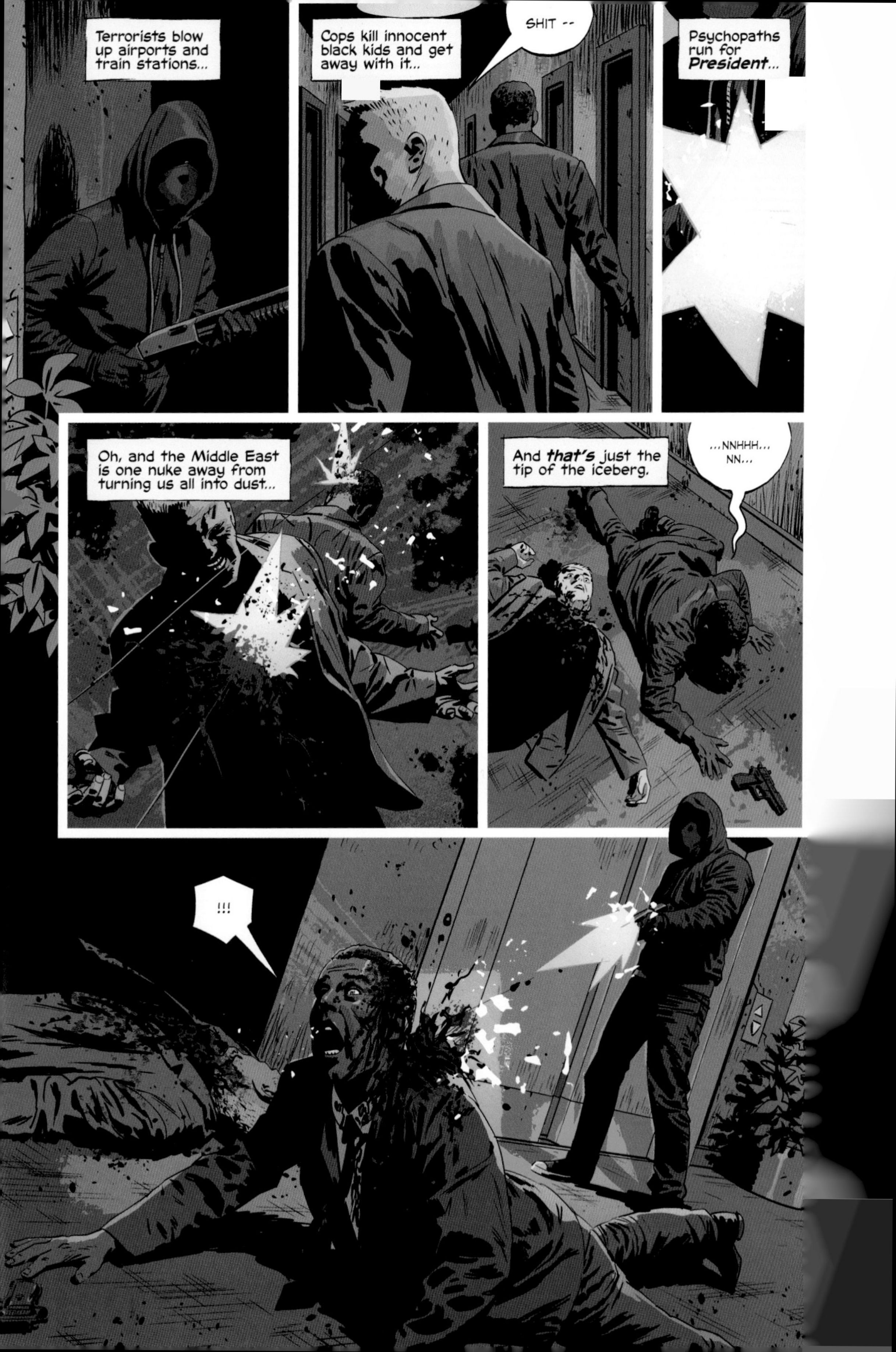
Terrorists blow up airports and train stations...
Cops kill innocent black kids and get away with it...
SHIT --
Psychopaths run for *President*...
Oh, and the Middle East is one nuke away from turning us all into dust...
And *that's* just the tip of the iceberg.
...NNHHH... NN...
!!!

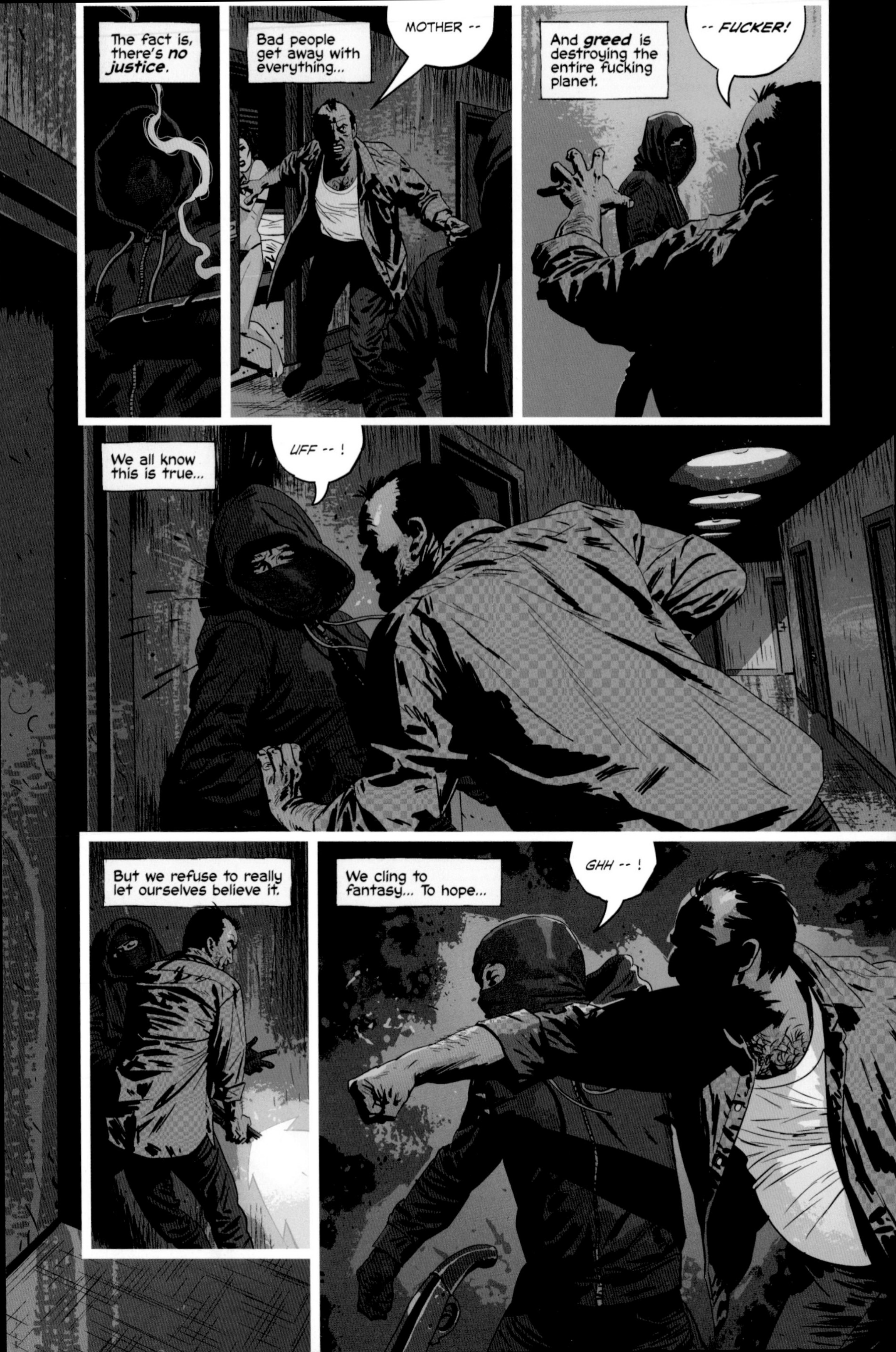
The fact is, there's **no justice**.
Bad people get away with everything...
MOTHER --
And **greed** is destroying the entire fucking planet.
-- FUCKER!
We all know this is true...
UFF -- !
But we refuse to really let ourselves believe it.
We cling to fantasy... To hope...
GHH -- !

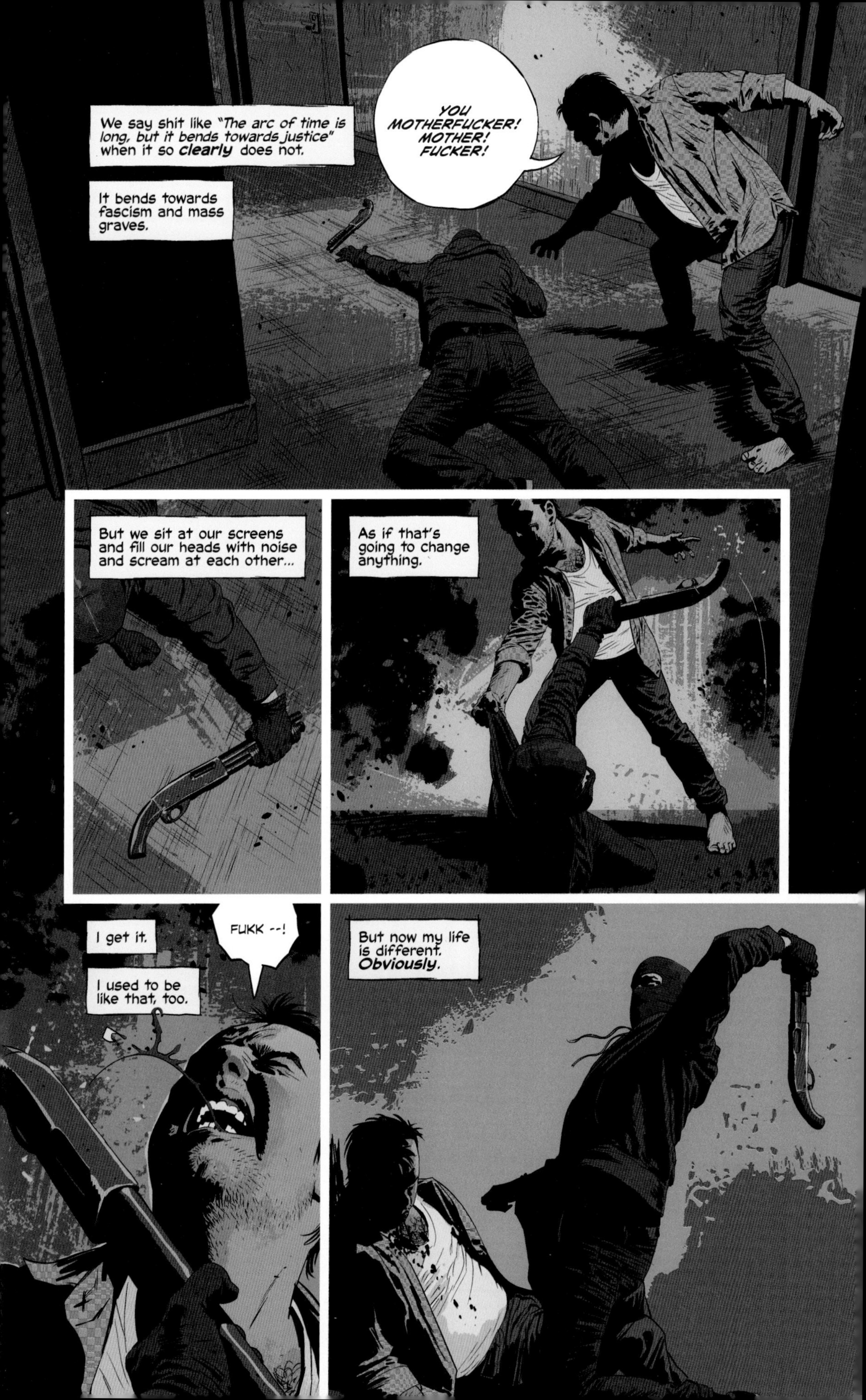
We say shit like "The arc of time is long, but it bends towards justice" when it so clearly does not.
YOU MOTHERFUCKER! MOTHER! FUCKER!
It bends towards fascism and mass graves.
But we sit at our screens and fill our heads with noise and scream at each other...
As if that's going to change anything.
I get it.
FUKK --!
I used to be like that, too.
But now my life is different. Obviously.

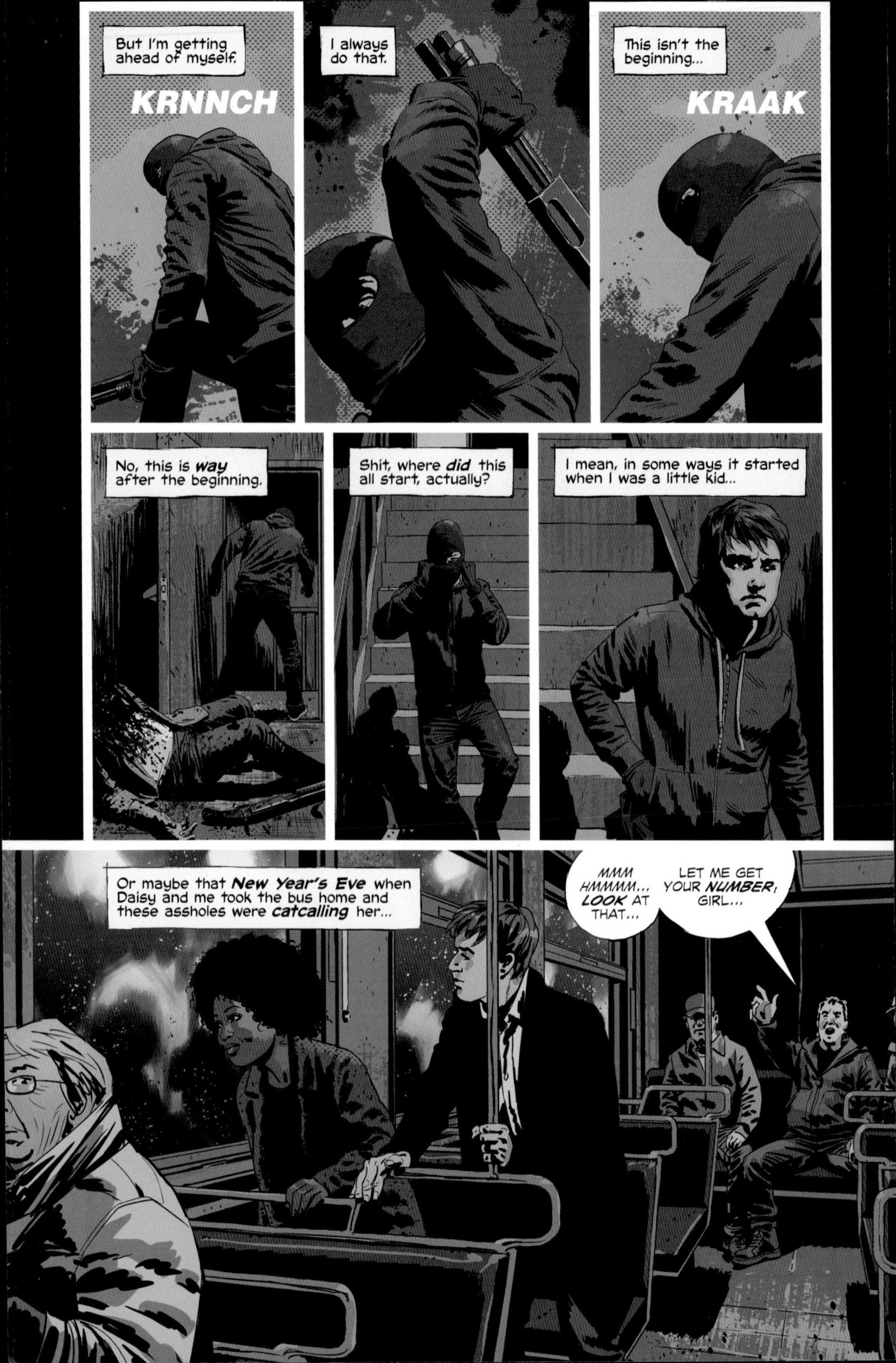
But I'm getting ahead of myself.
KRNNCH
I always do that.
This isn't the beginning...
KRAAK
No, this is *way* after the beginning.
Shit, where *did* this all start, actually?
I mean, in some ways it started when I was a little kid...
Or maybe that *New Year's Eve* when Daisy and me took the bus home and these assholes were *catcalling* her...
MMM HMMMM... *LOOK* AT THAT...
LET ME GET YOUR *NUMBER*, GIRL...

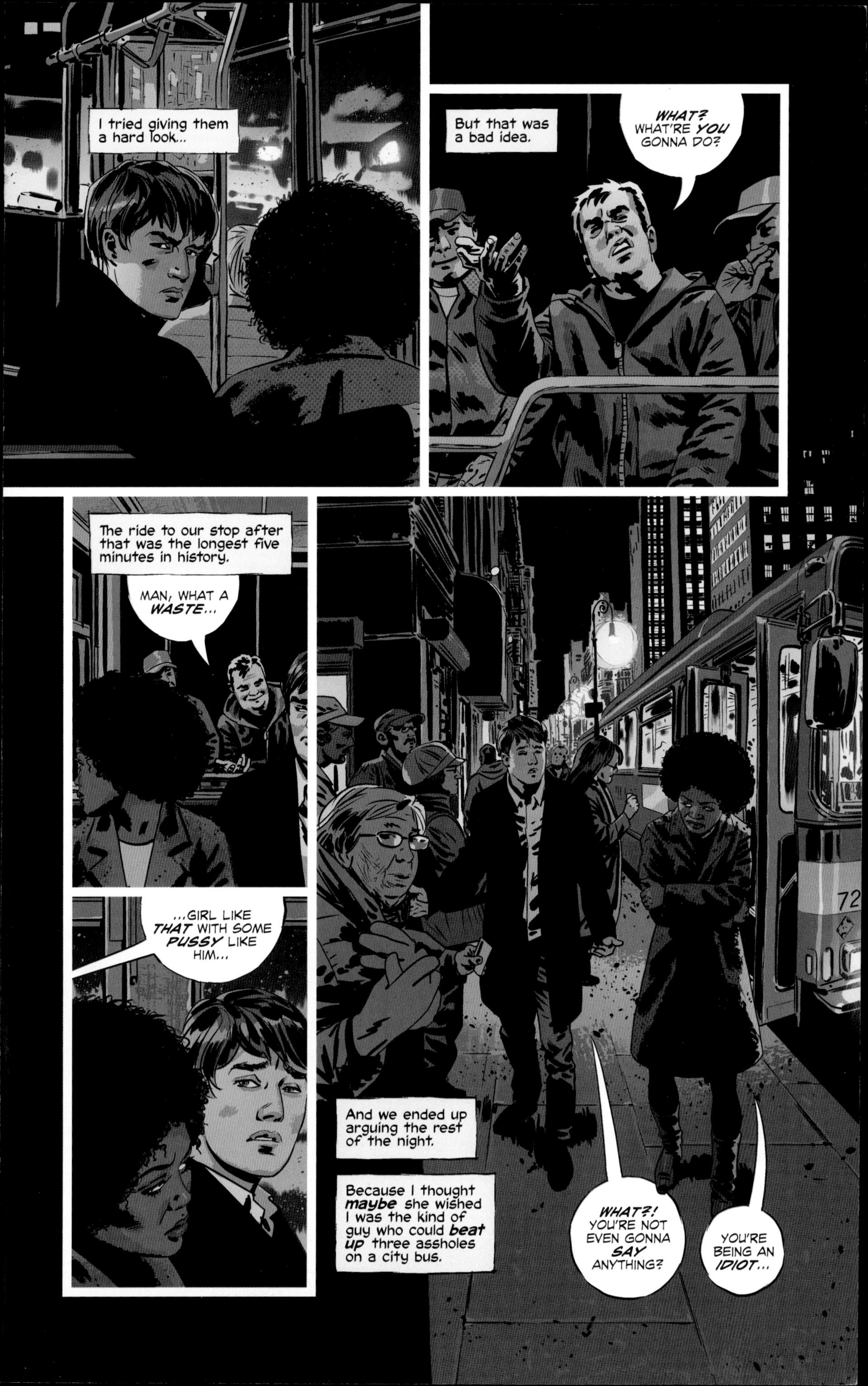
I tried giving them a hard look...
But that was a bad idea.
WHAT? WHAT'RE YOU GONNA DO?
The ride to our stop after that was the longest five minutes in history.
MAN, WHAT A WASTE...
...GIRL LIKE THAT WITH SOME PUSSY LIKE HIM...
And we ended up arguing the rest of the night.
Because I thought maybe she wished I was the kind of guy who could beat up three assholes on a city bus.
WHAT?! YOU'RE NOT EVEN GONNA SAY ANYTHING?
YOU'RE BEING AN IDIOT...
72

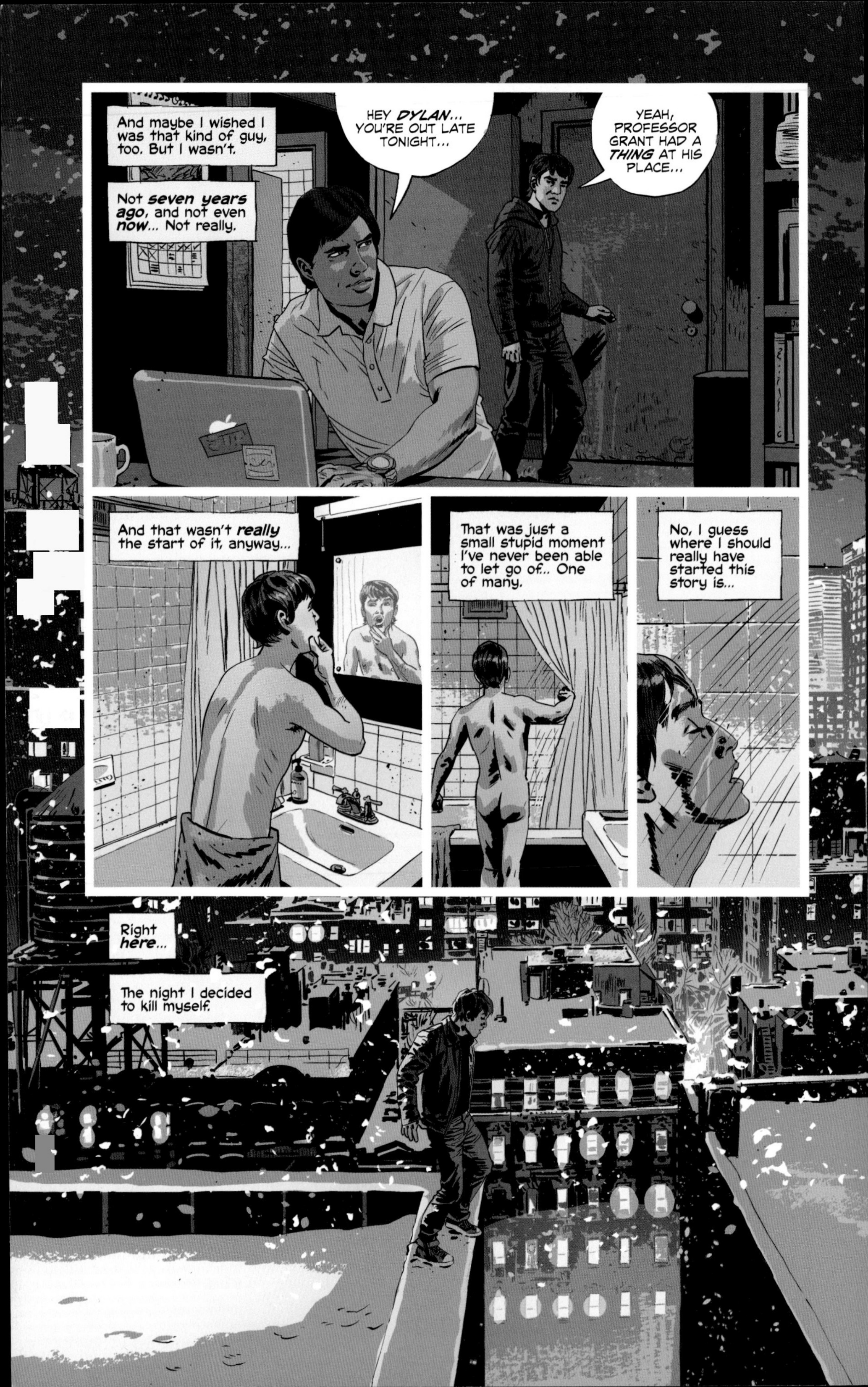
And maybe I wished I was that kind of guy, too. But I wasn't.
Not seven years ago, and not even now... Not really.
HEY DYLAN... YOU'RE OUT LATE TONIGHT...
YEAH, PROFESSOR GRANT HAD A THING AT HIS PLACE...
And that wasn't really the start of it, anyway...
That was just a small stupid moment I've never been able to let go of.. One of many.
No, I guess where I should really have started this story is...
Right here...
The night I decided to kill myself.

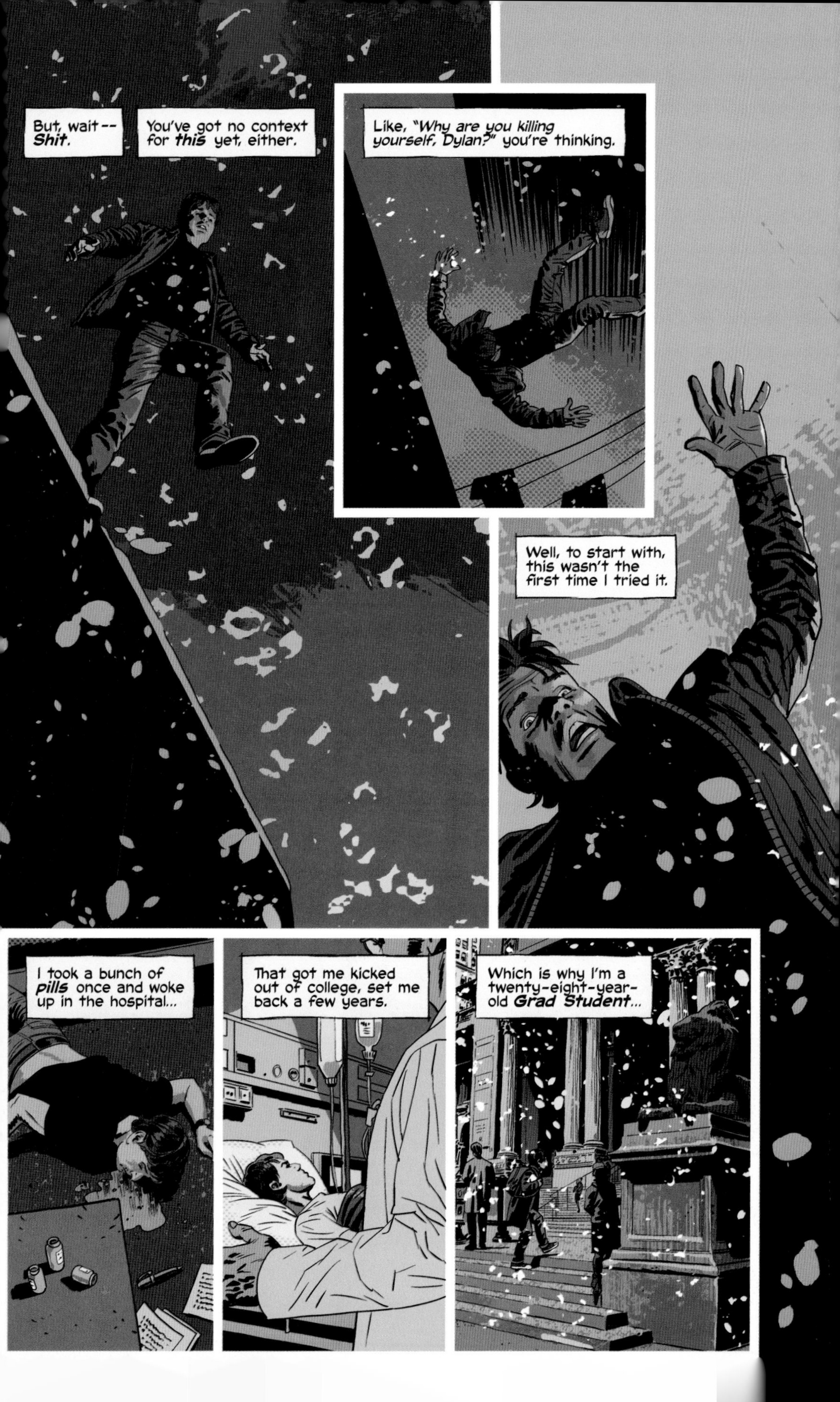
But, wait-- Shit.
You've got no context for this yet, either.
Like, "Why are you killing yourself, Dylan?" you're thinking.
Well, to start with, this wasn't the first time I tried it.
I took a bunch of pills once and woke up in the hospital...
That got me kicked out of college, set me back a few years.
Which is why I'm a twenty-eight-year-old Grad Student...

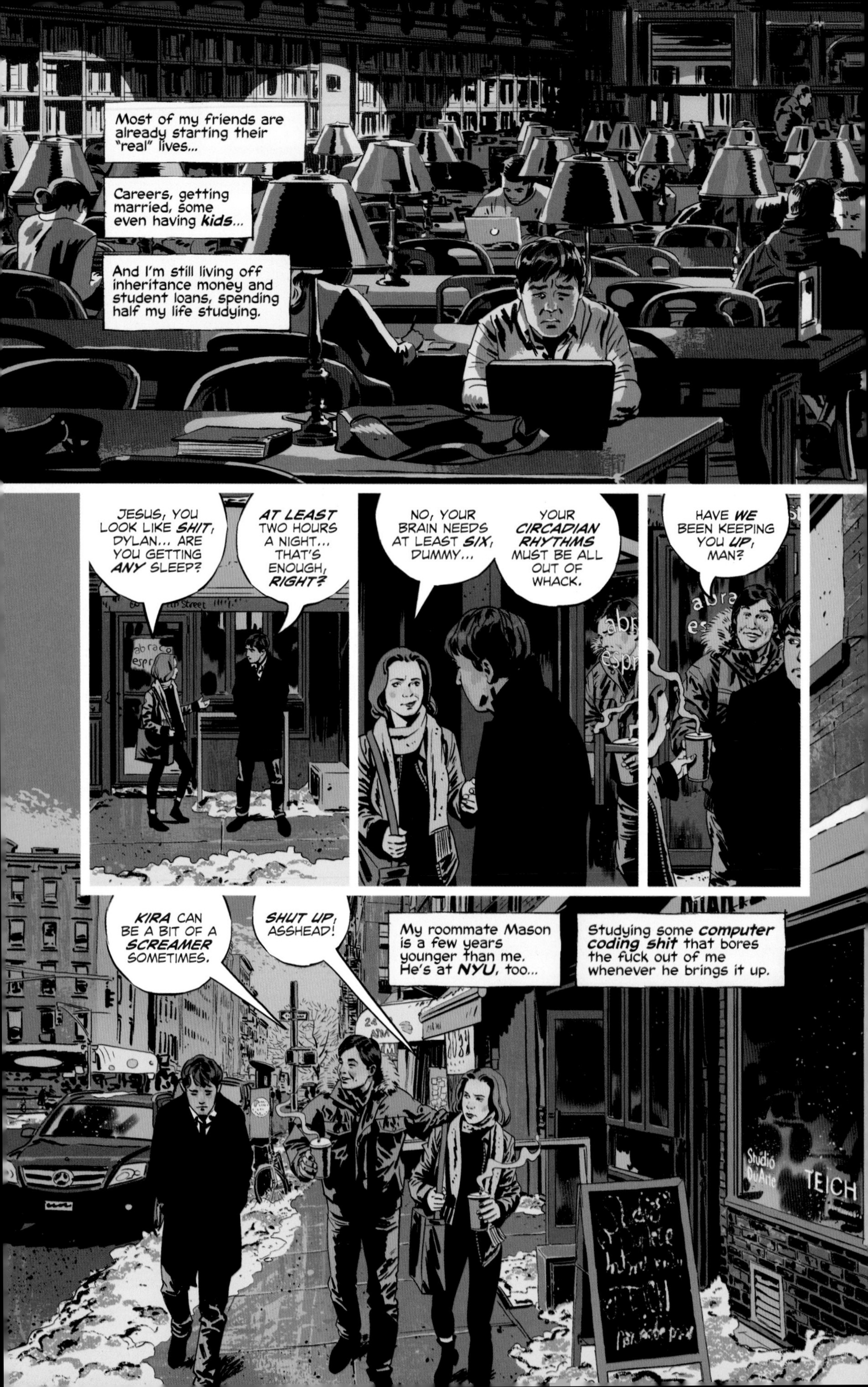
Most of my friends are already starting their "real" lives...
Careers, getting married, some even having **kids**...
And I'm still living off inheritance money and student loans, spending half my life studying.
JESUS, YOU LOOK LIKE **SHIT**, DYLAN... ARE YOU GETTING **ANY** SLEEP?
AT LEAST TWO HOURS A NIGHT... THAT'S ENOUGH, **RIGHT?**
NO, YOUR BRAIN NEEDS AT LEAST **SIX**, DUMMY...
YOUR **CIRCADIAN RHYTHMS** MUST BE ALL OUT OF WHACK.
HAVE **WE** BEEN KEEPING YOU **UP**, MAN?
KIRA CAN BE A BIT OF A **SCREAMER** SOMETIMES.
SHUT UP, ASSHEAD!
My roommate Mason is a few years younger than me. He's at **NYU**, too...
Studying some **computer coding shit** that bores the fuck out of me whenever he brings it up.
Studio DuArte
TEICH

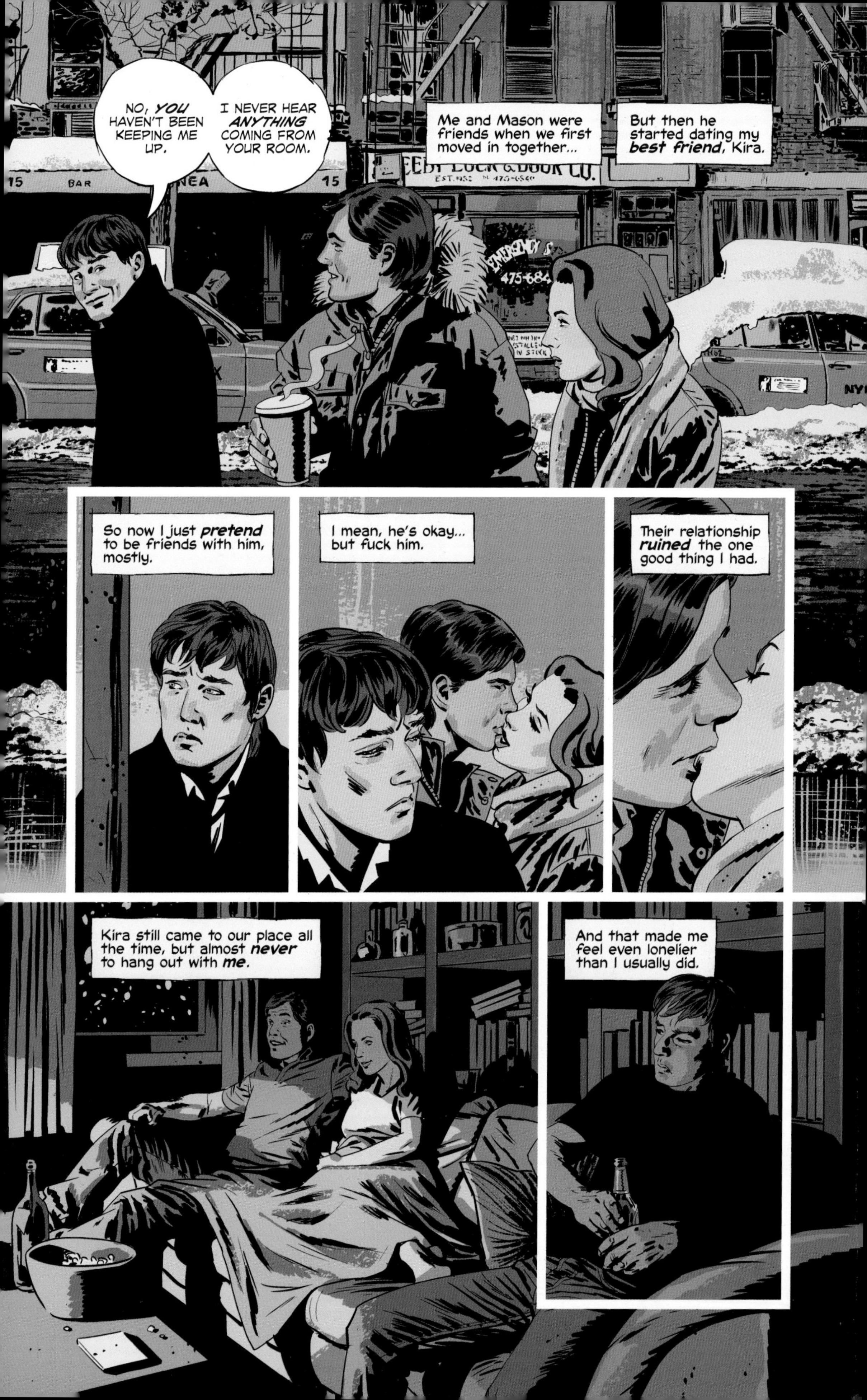

NO, *YOU* HAVEN'T BEEN KEEPING ME UP.
I NEVER HEAR *ANYTHING* COMING FROM YOUR ROOM.
Me and Mason were friends when we first moved in together...
But then he started dating my *best friend*, Kira.
So now I just *pretend* to be friends with him, mostly.
I mean, he's okay... but fuck him.
Their relationship *ruined* the one good thing I had.
Kira still came to our place all the time, but almost *never* to hang out with *me*.
And that made me feel even lonelier than I usually did.

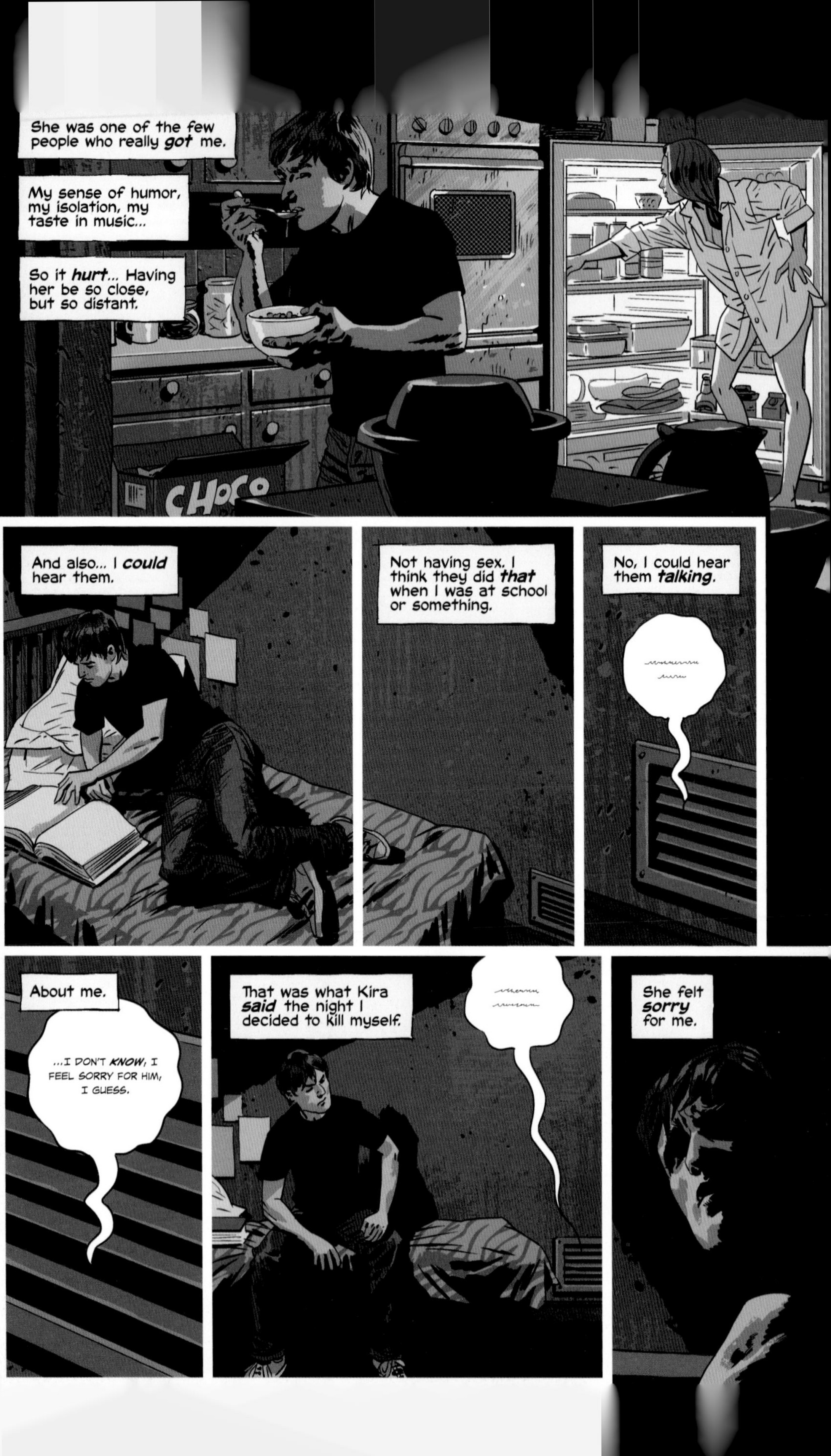

She was one of the few people who really got me.
My sense of humor, my isolation, my taste in music...
So it hurt... Having her be so close, but so distant.
CHOCO
And also... I could hear them.
Not having sex. I think they did that when I was at school or something.
No, I could hear them talking.
About me.
...I DON'T KNOW, I FEEL SORRY FOR HIM, I GUESS.
That was what Kira said the night I decided to kill myself.
She felt sorry for me.

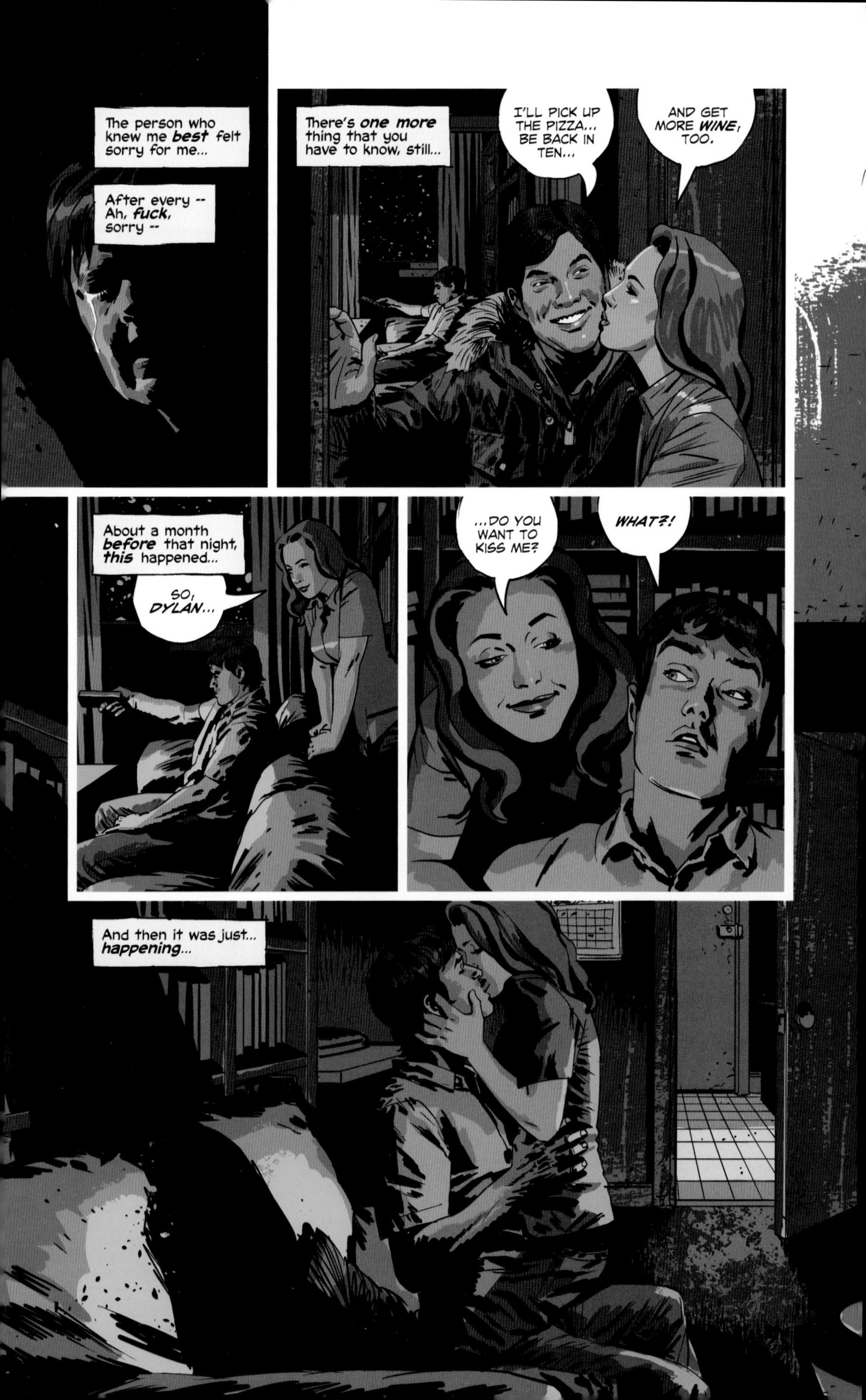
The person who knew me *best* felt sorry for me...
After every -- Ah, *fuck*, sorry --
There's *one more* thing that you have to know, still...
I'LL PICK UP THE PIZZA... BE BACK IN TEN...
AND GET MORE *WINE*, TOO.
About a month *before* that night, *this* happened...
SO, *DYLAN*...
...DO YOU WANT TO KISS ME?
WHAT?!
And then it was just... *happening*...

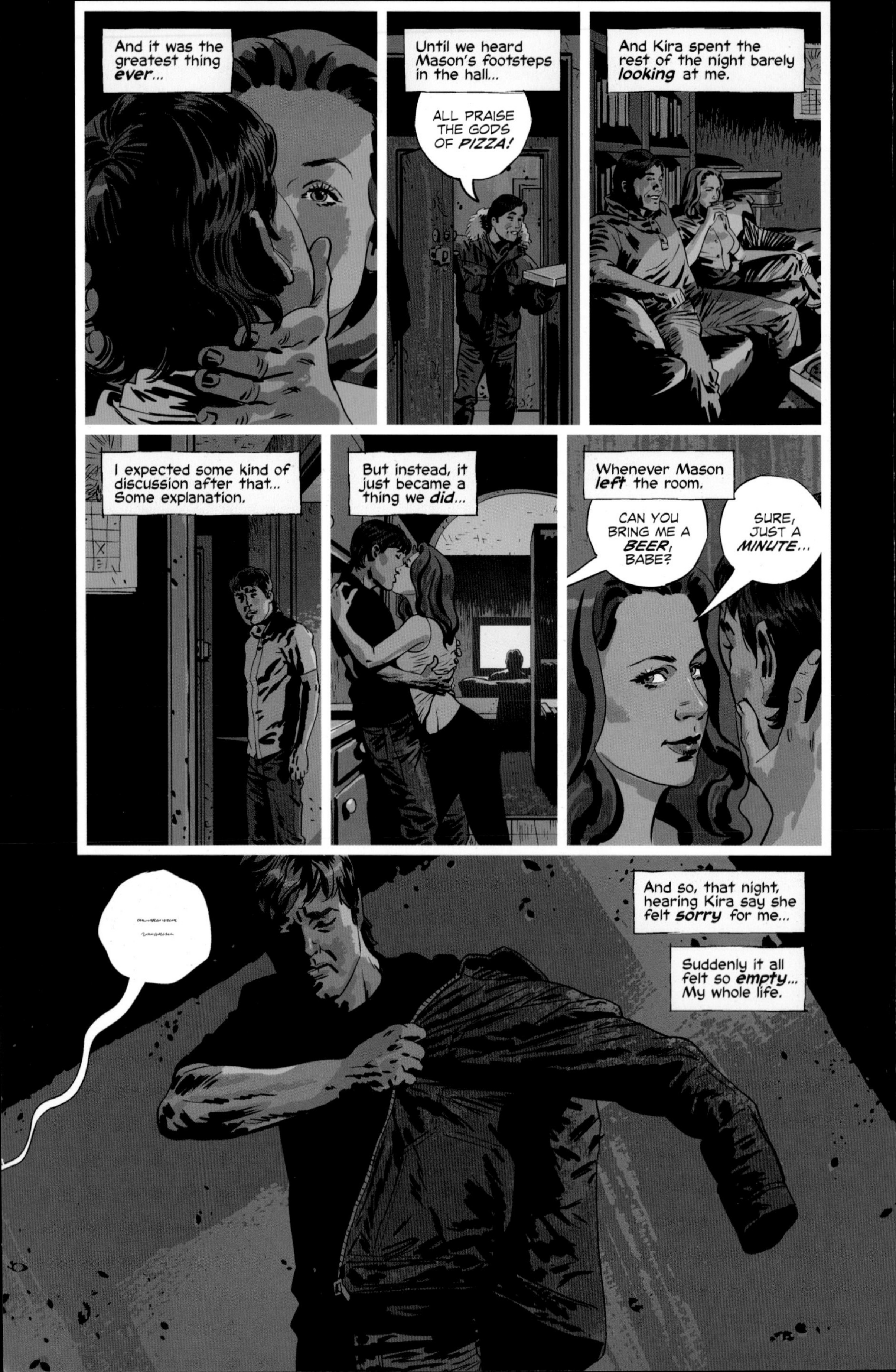
And it was the greatest thing *ever*...
Until we heard Mason's footsteps in the hall...
ALL PRAISE THE GODS OF *PIZZA!*
And Kira spent the rest of the night barely *looking* at me.
I expected some kind of discussion after that... Some explanation.
But instead, it just became a thing we *did*...
Whenever Mason *left* the room.
CAN YOU BRING ME A *BEER*, BABE?
SURE, JUST A *MINUTE*...
And so, that night, hearing Kira say she felt *sorry* for me...
Suddenly it all felt so *empty*... My whole life.

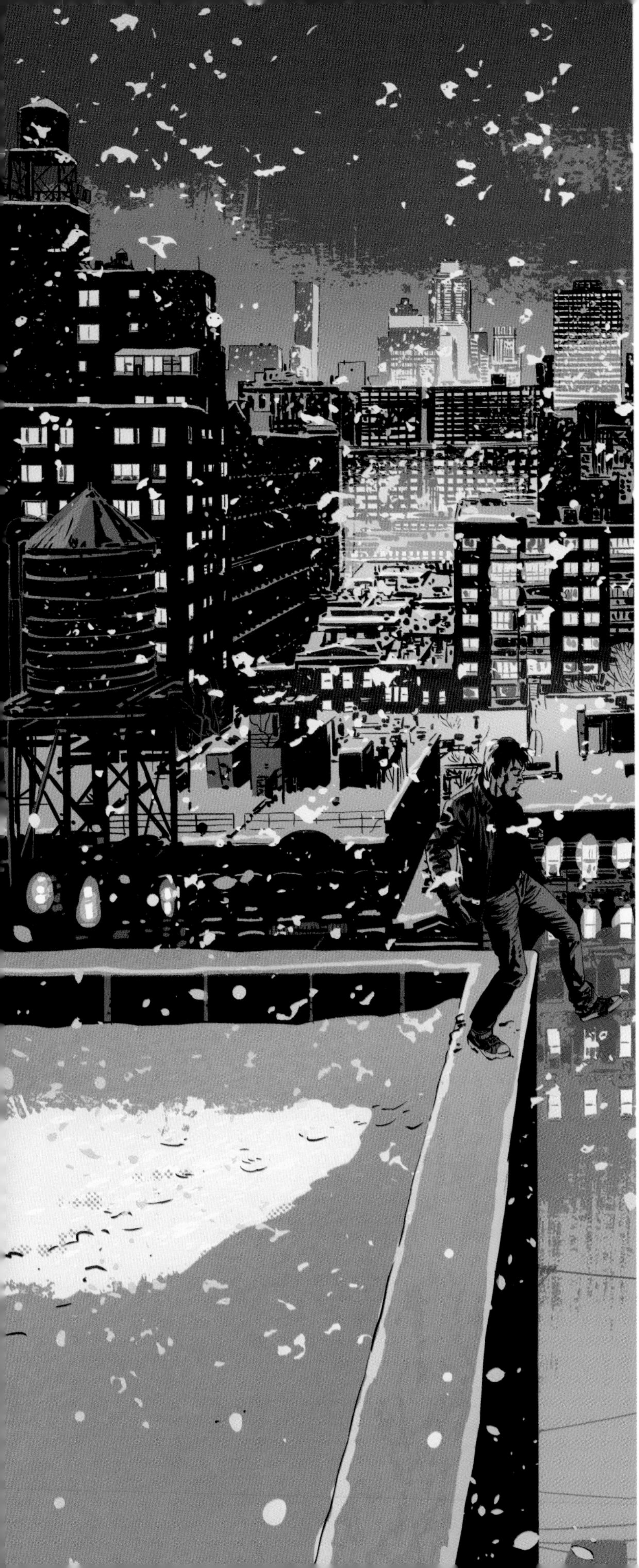

I'd been thinking she was going to break it off with Mason... And Kira and me would become some kind of couple.

But that wasn't what was going on.

Those kisses were the ***death throes*** of our friendship...

She was giving me what she thought I'd been waiting for, but it was her voice I wanted more than anything... Not her charity.

At that moment, nothing mattered... I felt like the only person in the entire fucking world...

Like I could scream for ***hours*** and no one would ***ever*** hear it.

So I said "fuck it" and went up to the roof to kill myself...

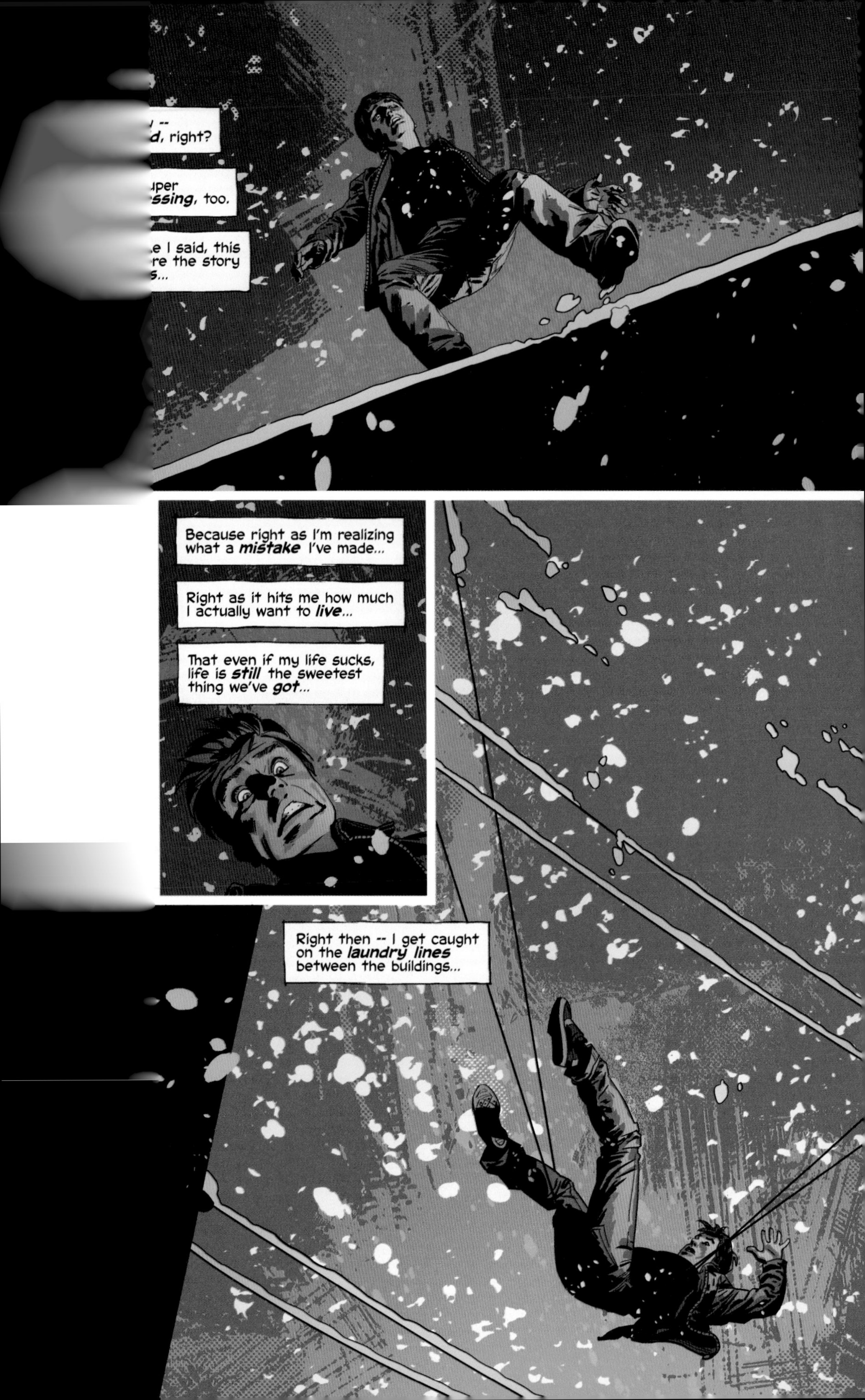

right?
too.
I said, this
the story
Because right as I'm realizing what a *mistake* I've made...
Right as it hits me how much I actually want to *live*...
That even if my life sucks, life is *still* the sweetest thing we've *got*...
Right then -- I get caught on the *laundry lines* between the buildings...

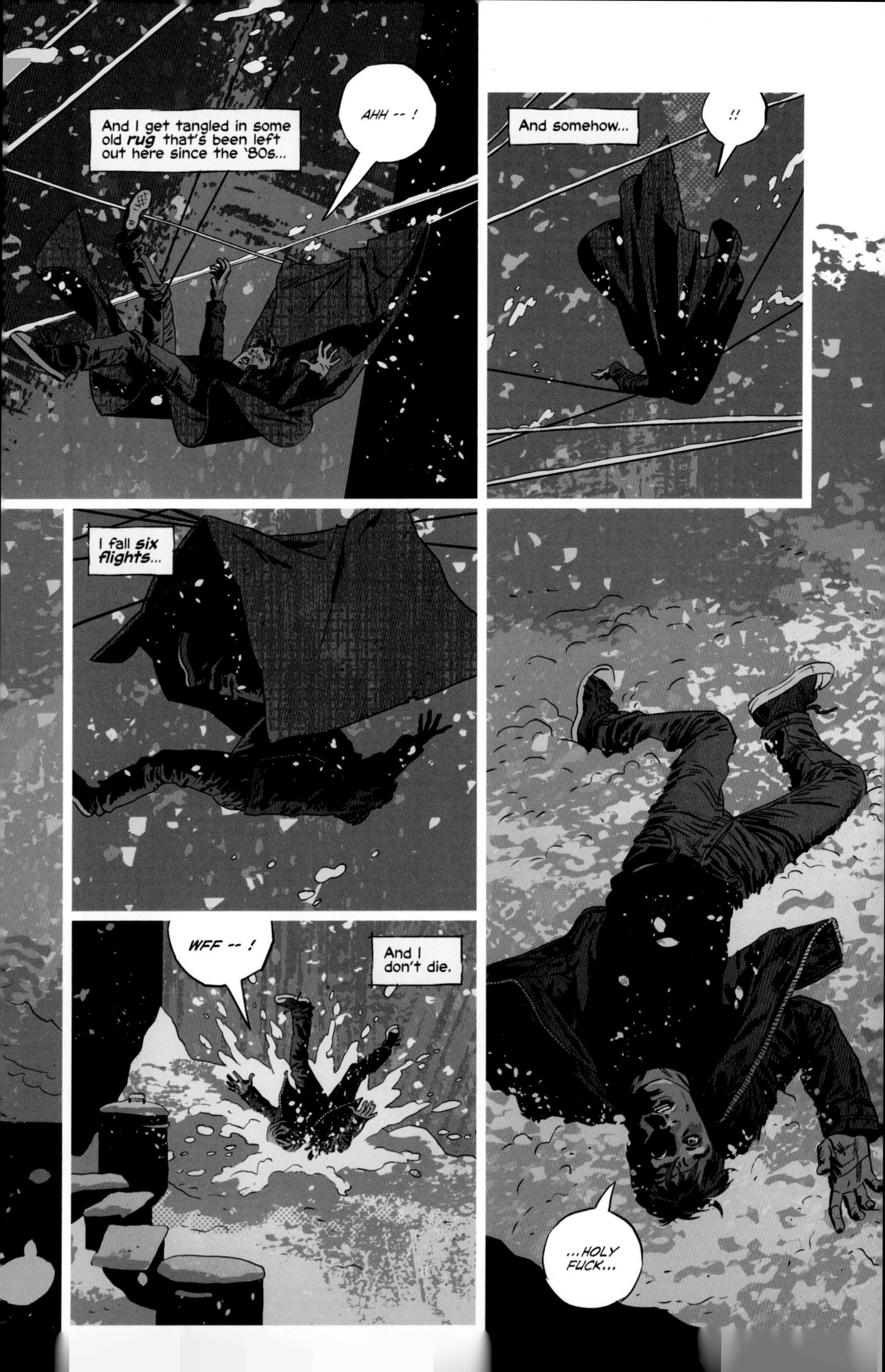
And I get tangled in some old rug that's been left out here since the '80s...
AHH -- !
And somehow...
!!
I fall six flights...
WFF -- !
And I don't die.
...HOLY FUCK...

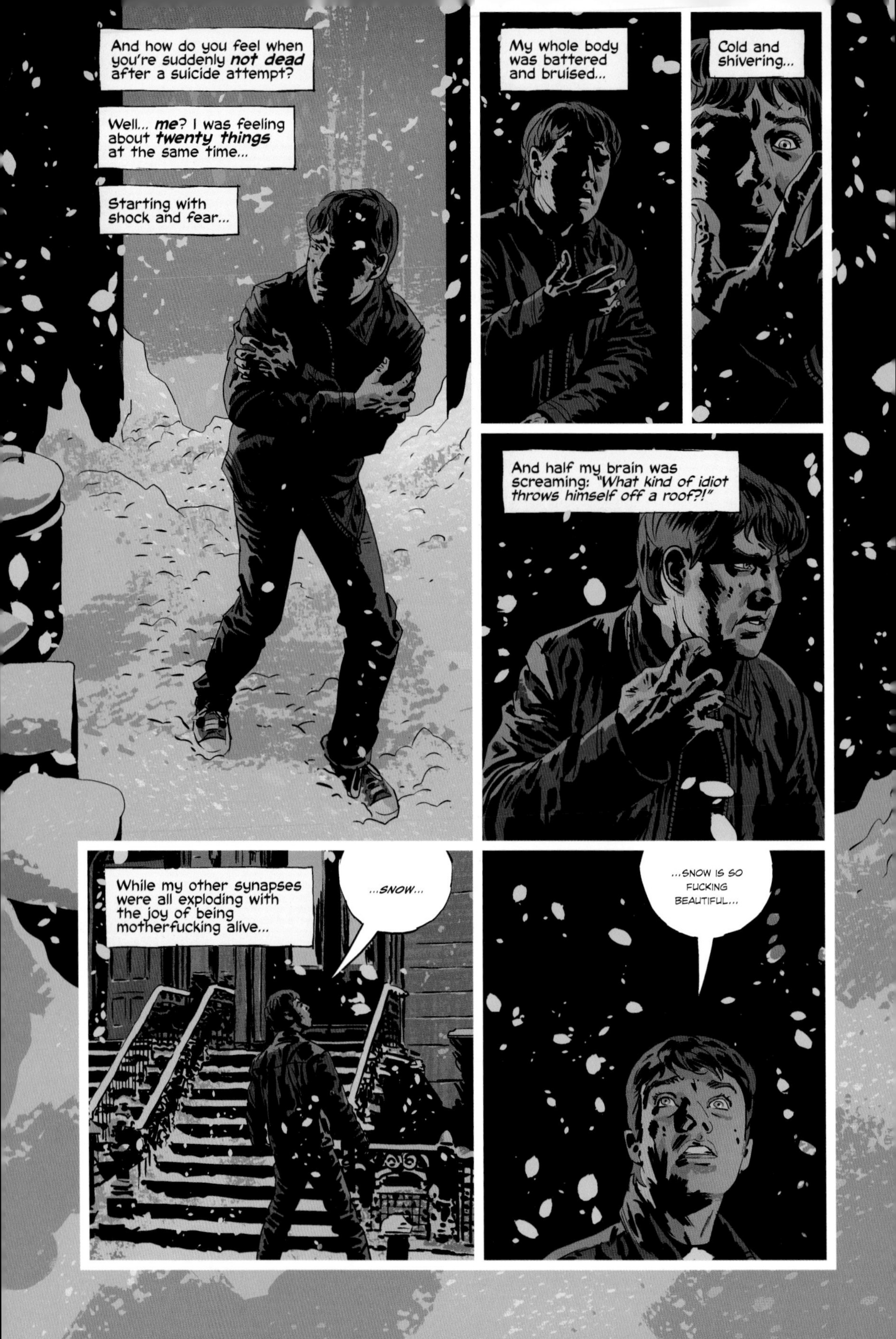
And how do you feel when you're suddenly **not dead** after a suicide attempt?
Well... **me**? I was feeling about **twenty things** at the same time...
Starting with shock and fear...
My whole body was battered and bruised...
Cold and shivering...
And half my brain was screaming: *"What kind of idiot throws himself off a roof?!"*
While my other synapses were all exploding with the joy of being motherfucking alive...
...SNOW...
...SNOW IS SO FUCKING BEAUTIFUL...

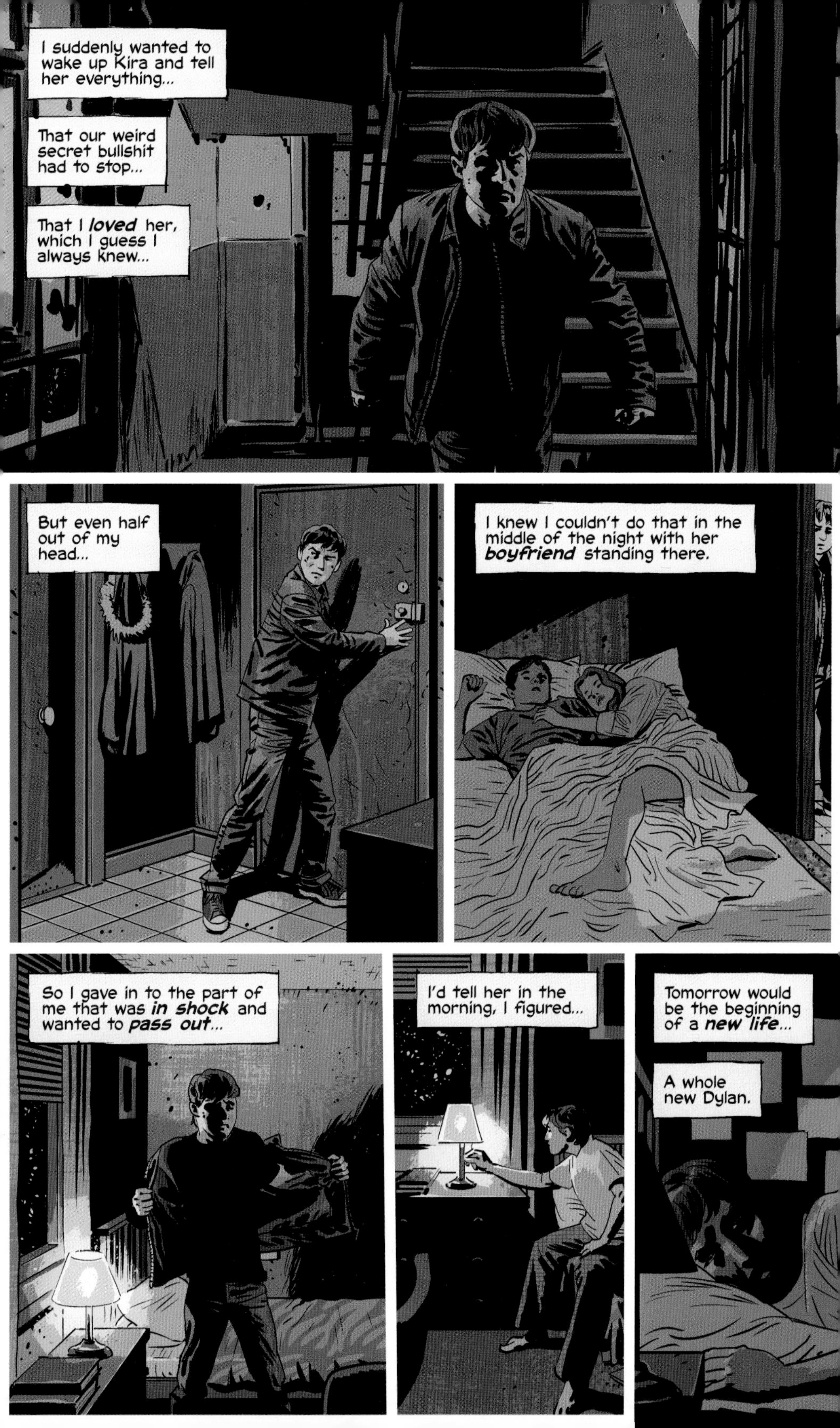
I suddenly wanted to wake up Kira and tell her everything...
That our weird secret bullshit had to stop...
That I loved her, which I guess I always knew...
But even half out of my head...
I knew I couldn't do that in the middle of the night with her boyfriend standing there.
So I gave in to the part of me that was in shock and wanted to pass out...
I'd tell her in the morning, I figured...
Tomorrow would be the beginning of a new life...
A whole new Dylan.

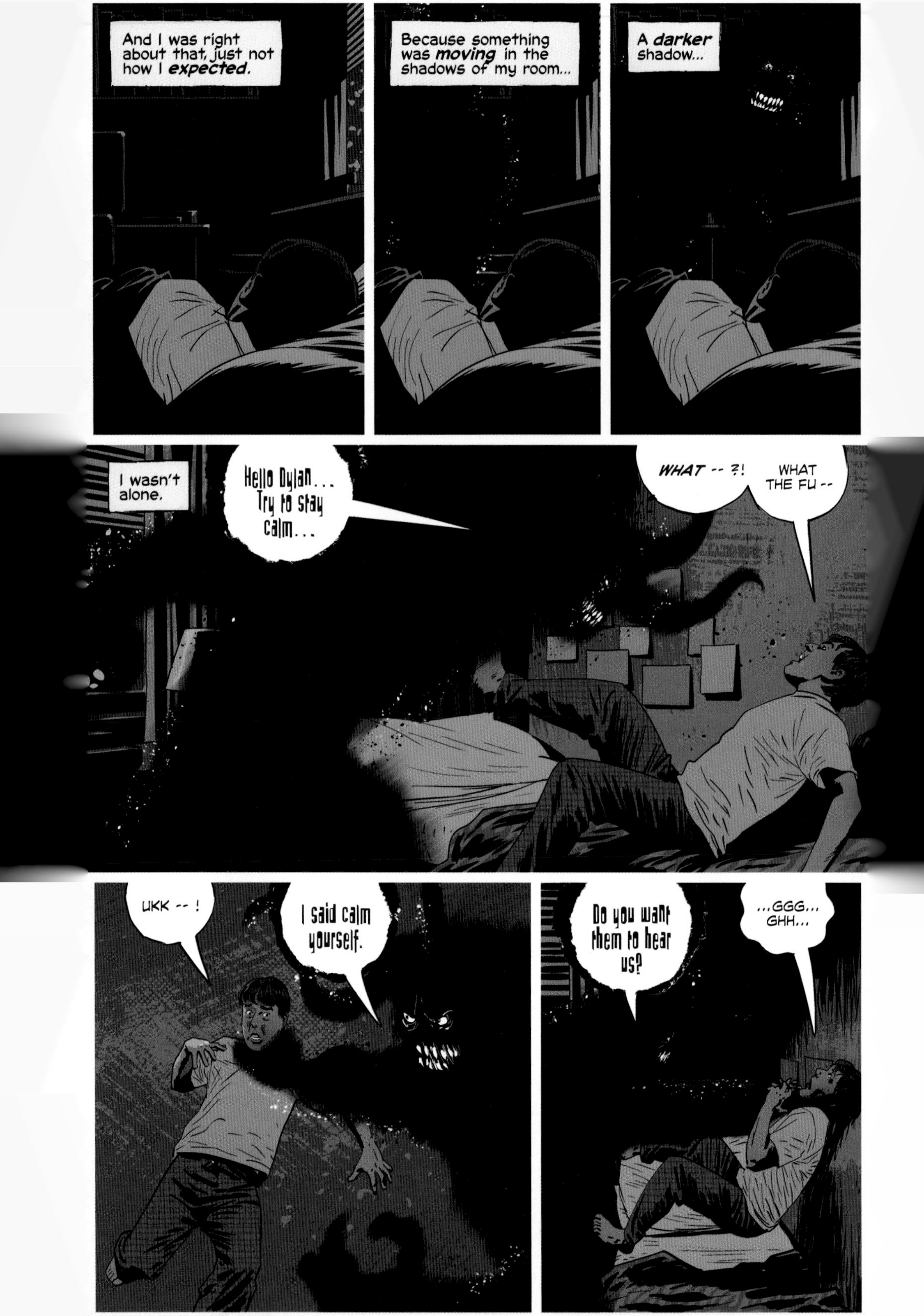
And I was right about that, just not how I *expected*.
Because something was *moving* in the shadows of my room...
A *darker* shadow...
I wasn't alone.
Hello Dylan... Try to stay calm...
WHAT -- ?!
WHAT THE FU --
UKK -- !
I said calm yourself.
Do you want them to hear us?
...GGG... GHH...

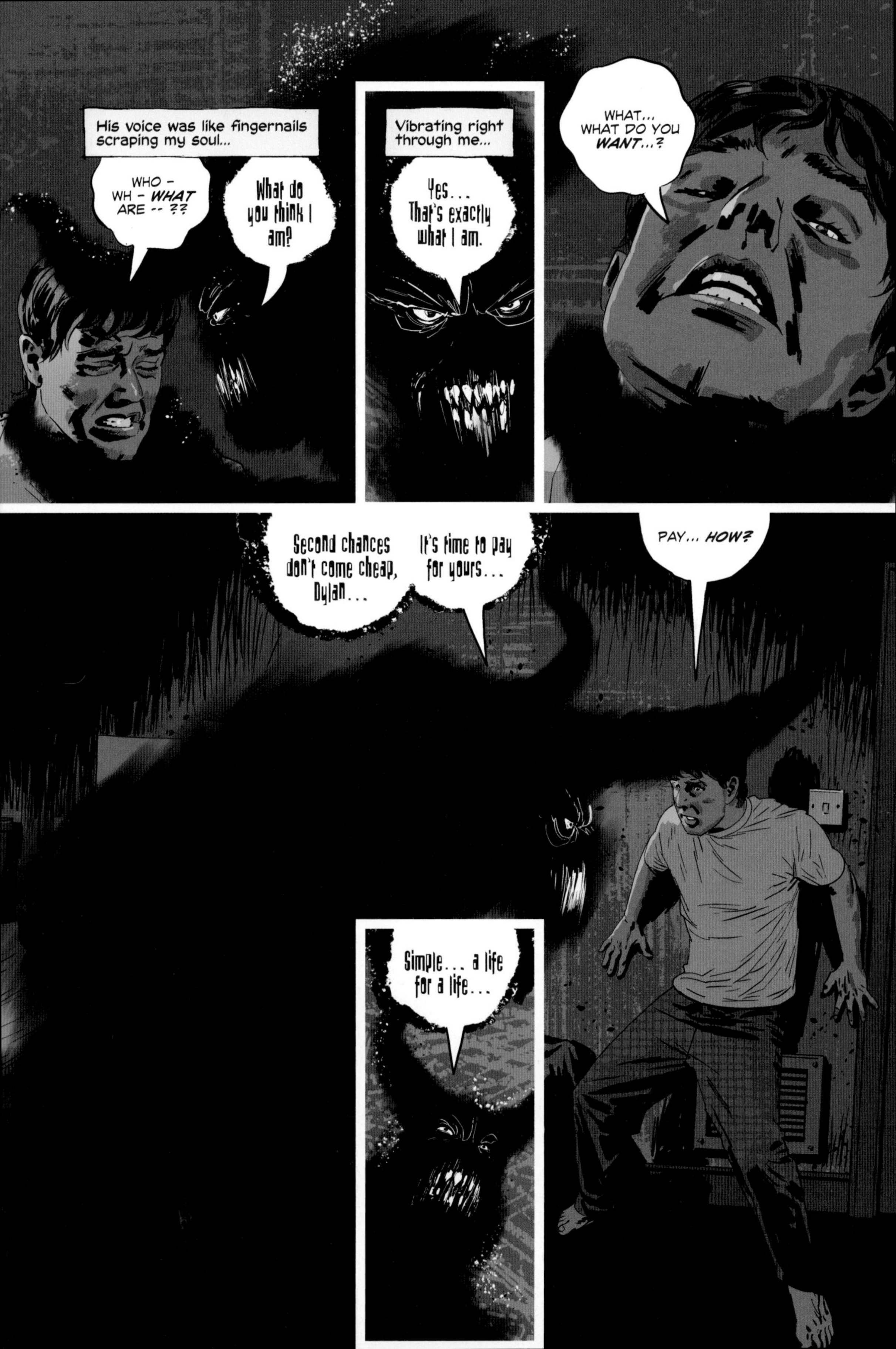
His voice was like fingernails scraping my soul...
WHO - WH - WHAT ARE -- ??
What do you think I am?
Vibrating right through me...
Yes... That's exactly what I am.
WHAT... WHAT DO YOU WANT...?
Second chances don't come cheap, Dylan...
It's time to pay for yours...
PAY... HOW?
Simple... a life for a life...

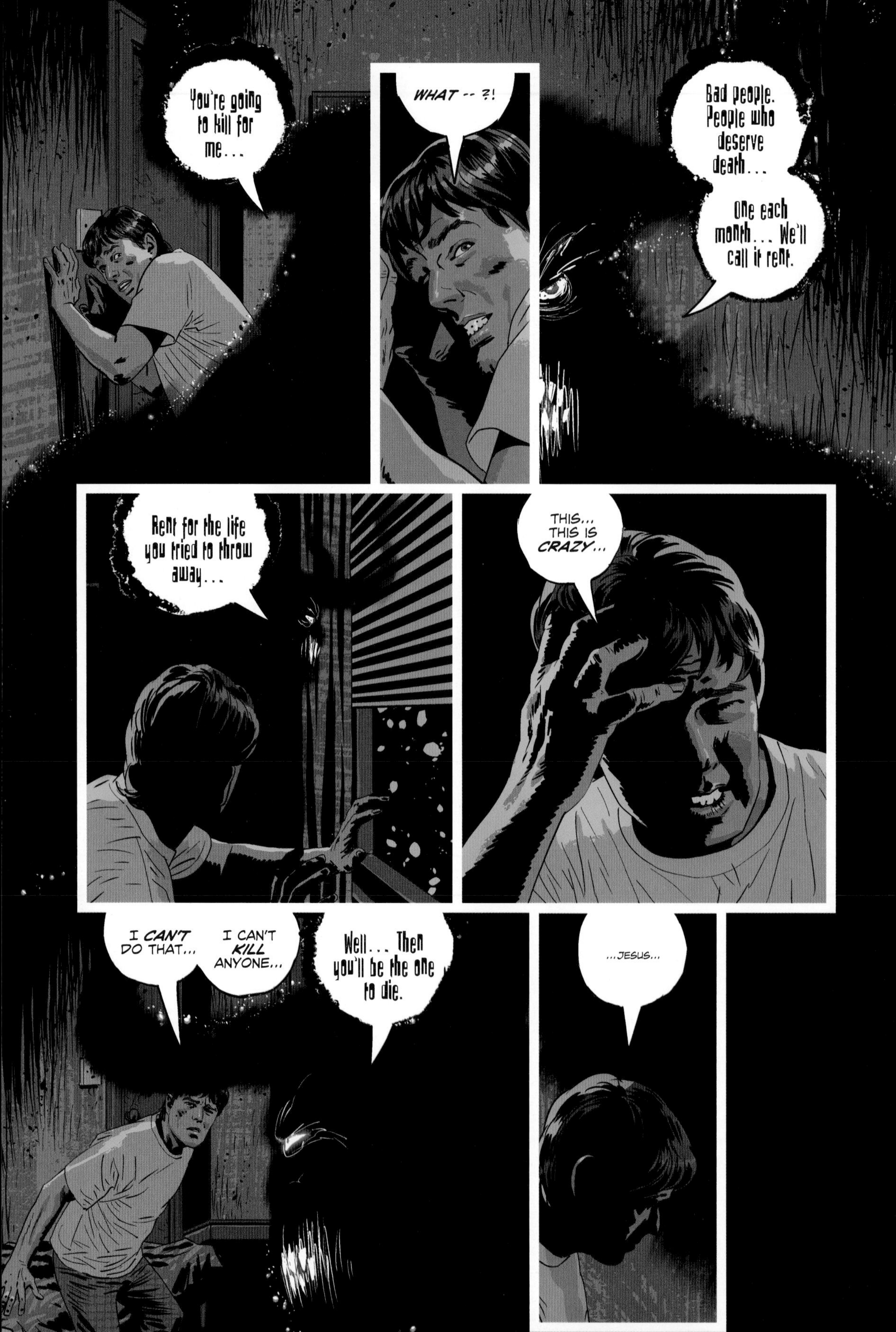
You're going to kill for me...
WHAT -- ?!
Bad people. People who deserve death...
One each month... We'll call it rent.
Rent for the life you tried to throw away...
THIS... THIS IS CRAZY...
I CAN'T DO THAT...
I CAN'T KILL ANYONE...
Well... Then you'll be the one to die.
...JESUS...

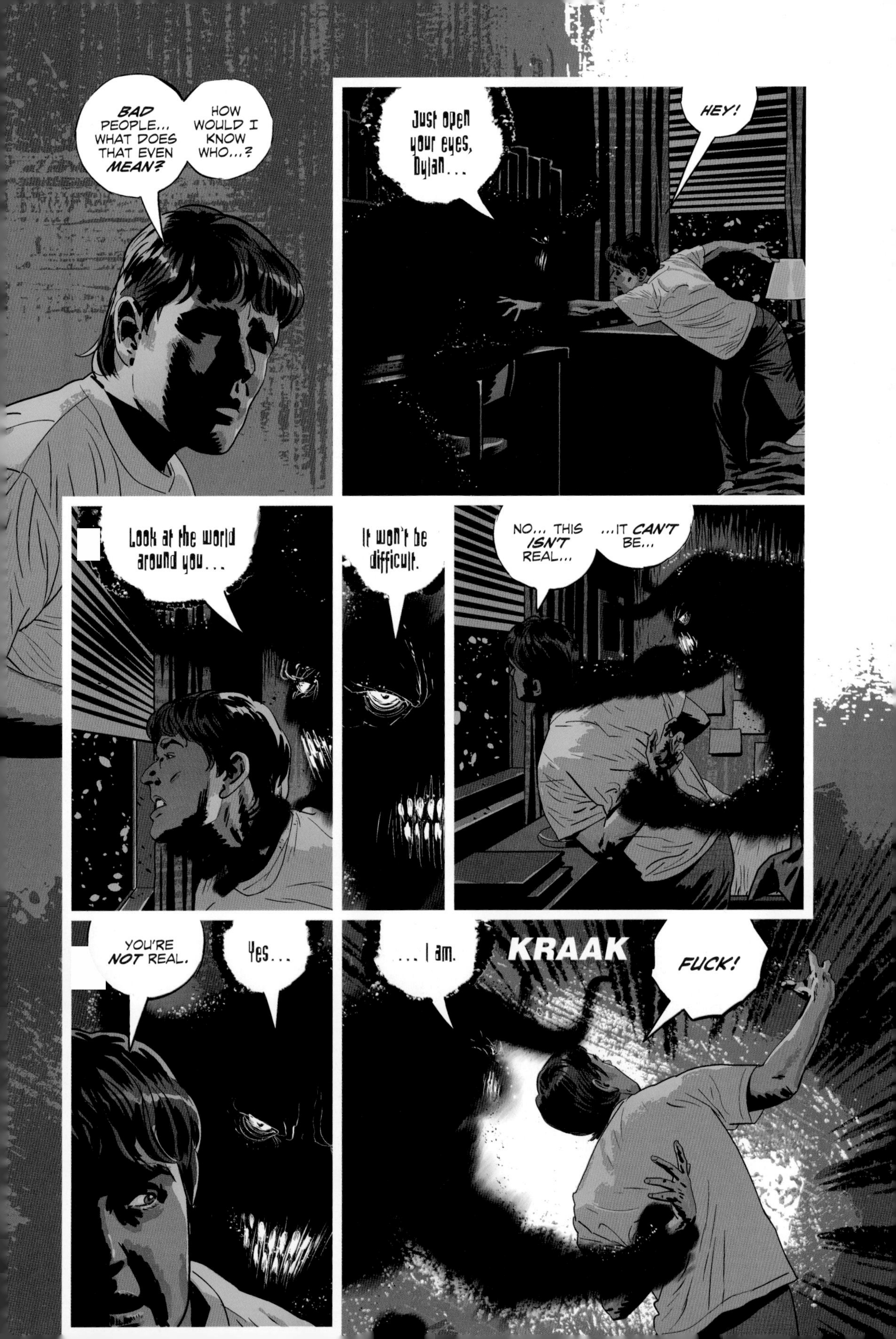
BAD PEOPLE... WHAT DOES THAT EVEN MEAN?
HOW WOULD I KNOW WHO...?
Just open your eyes, Dylan...
HEY!
Look at the world around you...
It won't be difficult.
NO... THIS ISN'T REAL...
...IT CAN'T BE...
YOU'RE NOT REAL.
Yes...
...I am.
KRAAK
FUCK!

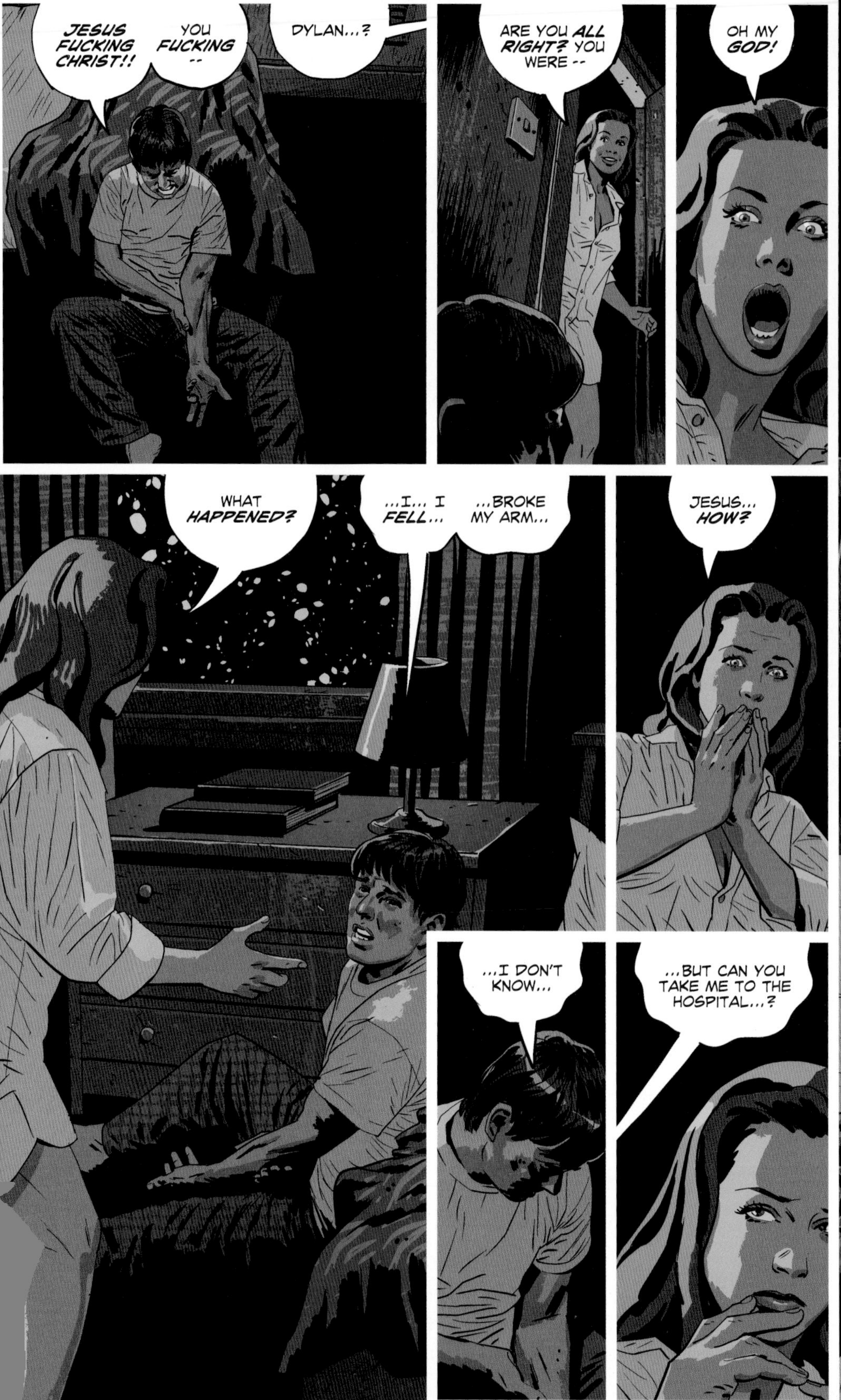
DYLAN...?
JESUS FUCKING CHRIST!!
YOU FUCKING --
ARE YOU ALL RIGHT? YOU WERE --
OH MY GOD!
WHAT HAPPENED?
...I... I FELL...
...BROKE MY ARM...
JESUS... HOW?
...I DON'T KNOW...
...BUT CAN YOU TAKE ME TO THE HOSPITAL...?

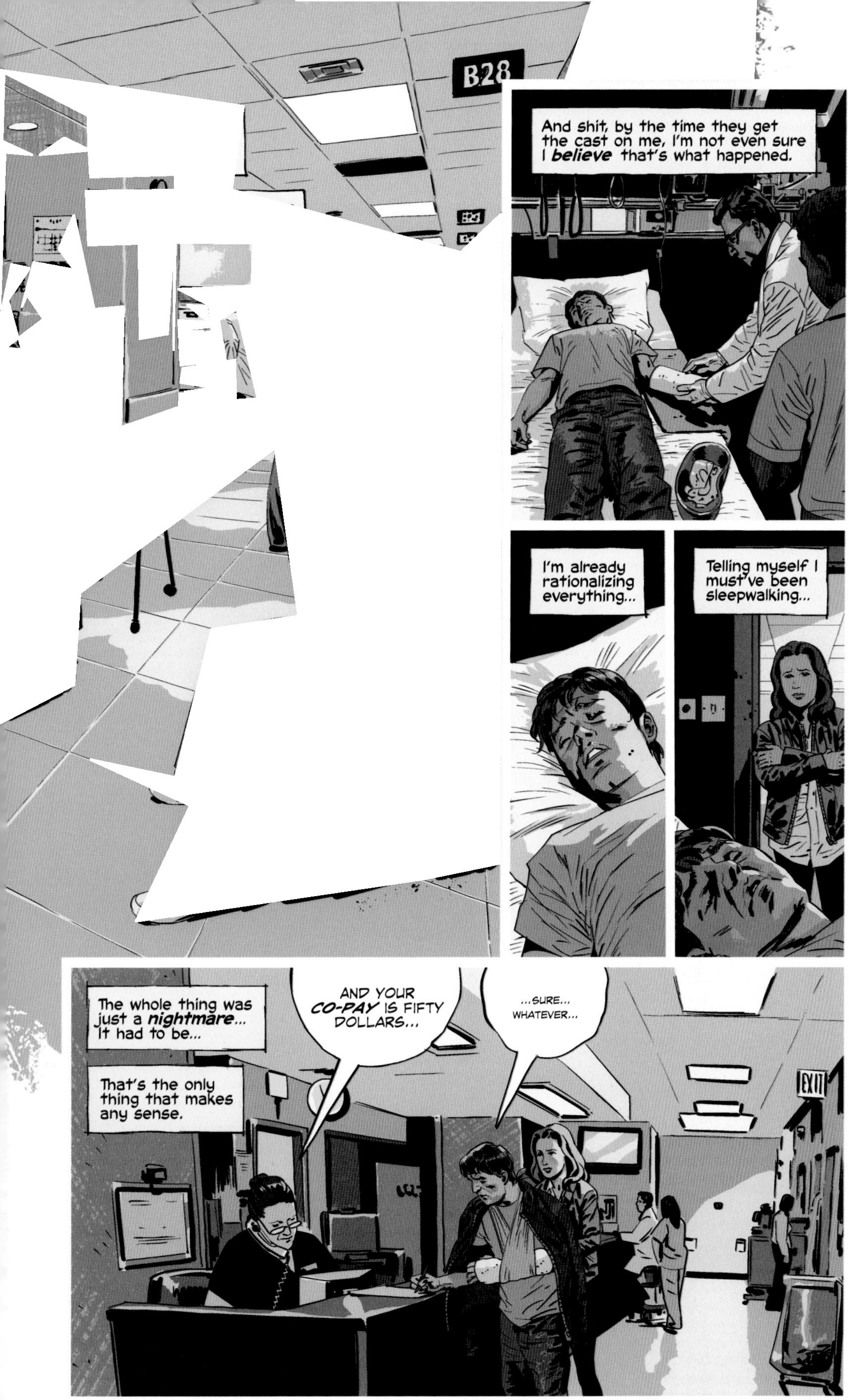
And shit, by the time they get the cast on me, I'm not even sure I ***believe*** that's what happened.
I'm already rationalizing everything...
Telling myself I must've been sleepwalking...
The whole thing was just a ***nightmare***... It had to be...
That's the only thing that makes any sense.
AND YOUR ***CO-PAY*** IS FIFTY DOLLARS...
...SURE... WHATEVER...
EXIT

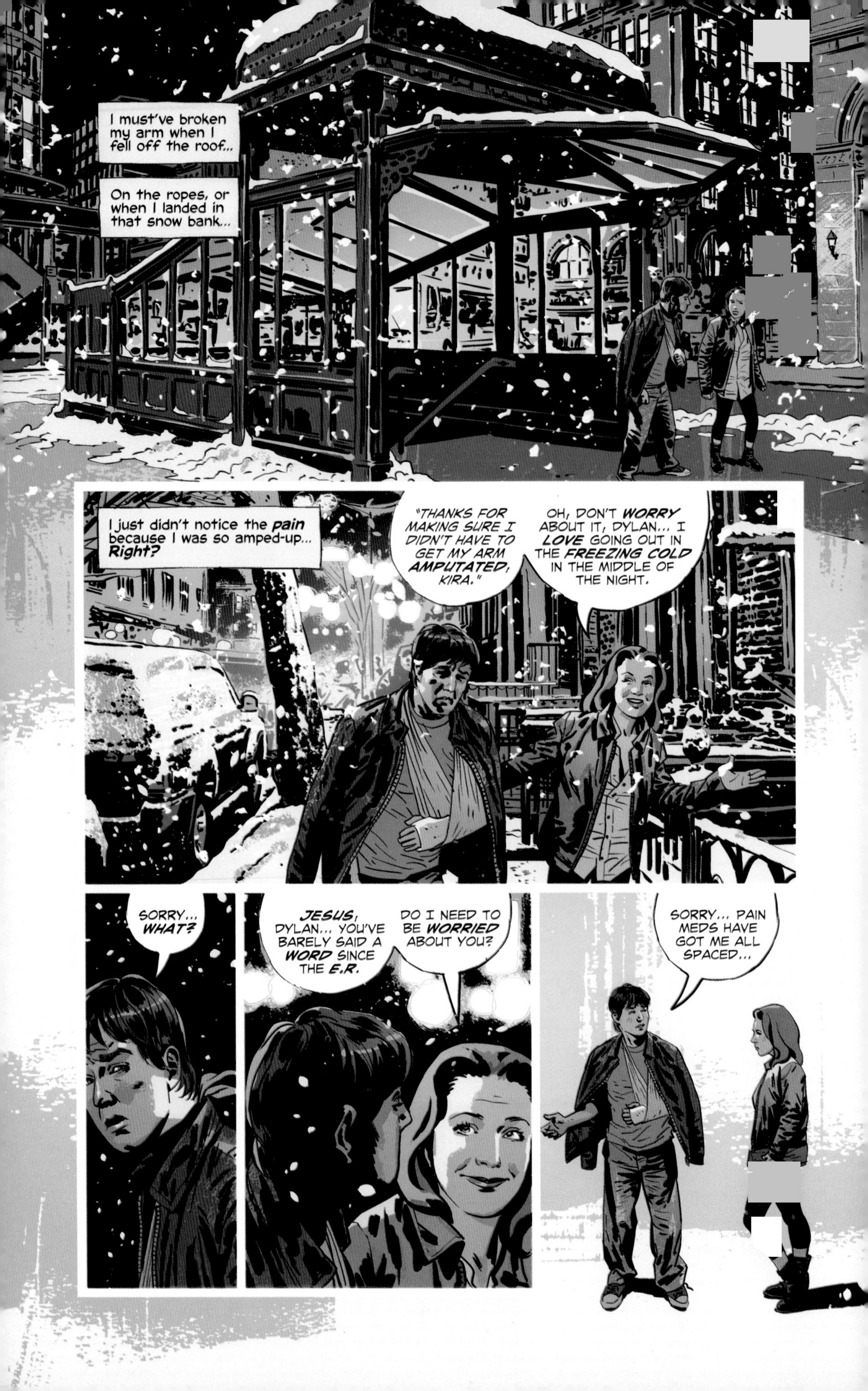
I must've broken my arm when I fell off the roof...
On the ropes, or when I landed in that snow bank...
I just didn't notice the pain because I was so amped-up... Right?
"THANKS FOR MAKING SURE I DIDN'T HAVE TO GET MY ARM AMPUTATED, KIRA."
OH, DON'T WORRY ABOUT IT, DYLAN... I LOVE GOING OUT IN THE FREEZING COLD IN THE MIDDLE OF THE NIGHT.
SORRY... WHAT?
JESUS, DYLAN... YOU'VE BARELY SAID A WORD SINCE THE E.R.
DO I NEED TO BE WORRIED ABOUT YOU?
SORRY... PAIN MEDS HAVE GOT ME ALL SPACED...

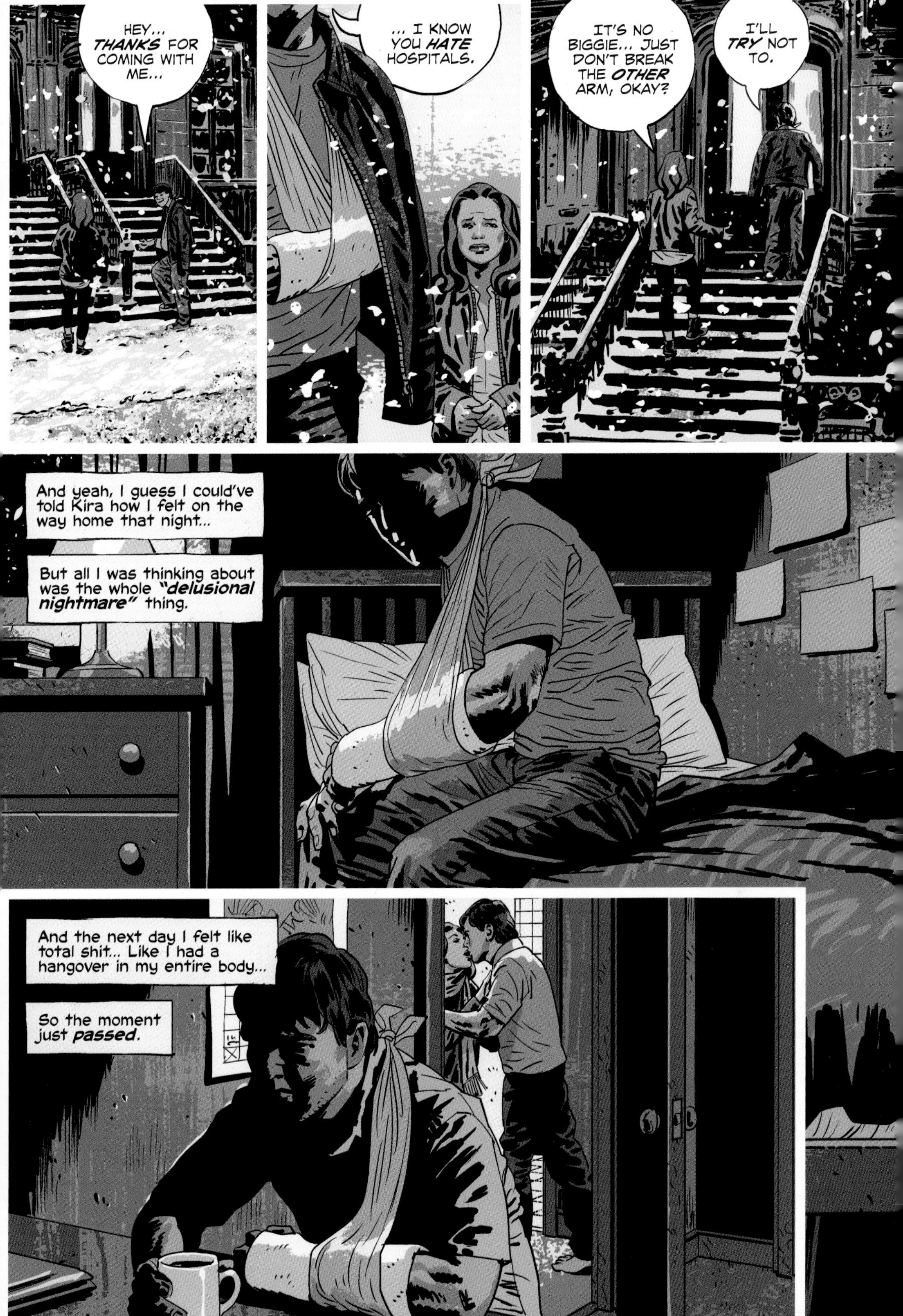
HEY... THANKS FOR COMING WITH ME...
... I KNOW YOU HATE HOSPITALS.
IT'S NO BIGGIE... JUST DON'T BREAK THE OTHER ARM, OKAY?
I'LL TRY NOT TO.
And yeah, I guess I could've told Kira how I felt on the way home that night...
But all I was thinking about was the whole "delusional nightmare" thing.
And the next day I felt like total shit... Like I had a hangover in my entire body...
So the moment just passed.

I spent the rest of the month trying to put that whole night out of my mind...

Which wasn't ***easy***, with my broken arm as a constant reminder.

But see, here's the thing... Demons ***do not*** exist.

I'm not some backwoods hick who believes in angels and the devil and shit like that.

So I know -- I ***know*** -- that what I saw that night ***had*** to be all in my head...

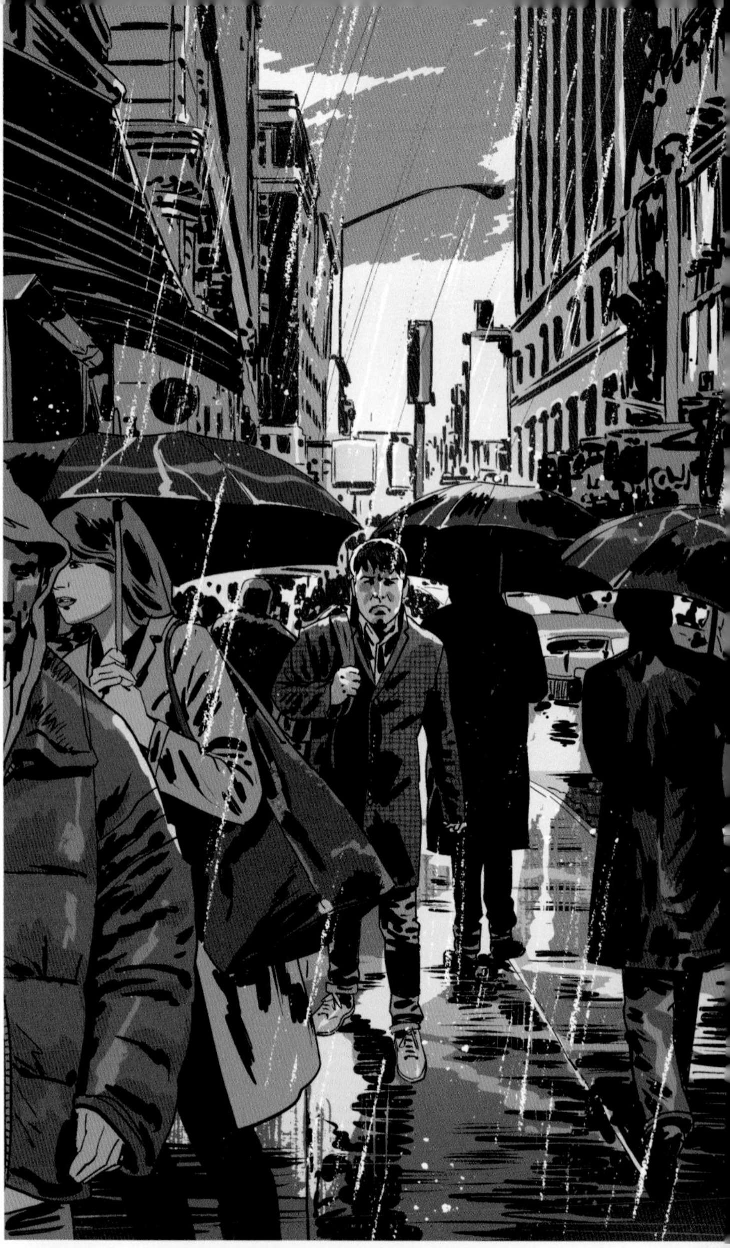

But still, it bugged me... Why was ***that*** the fever dream I had? Some ***demon*** telling me I had to kill people?

That's fucked up.

Even if it's just a delusion.

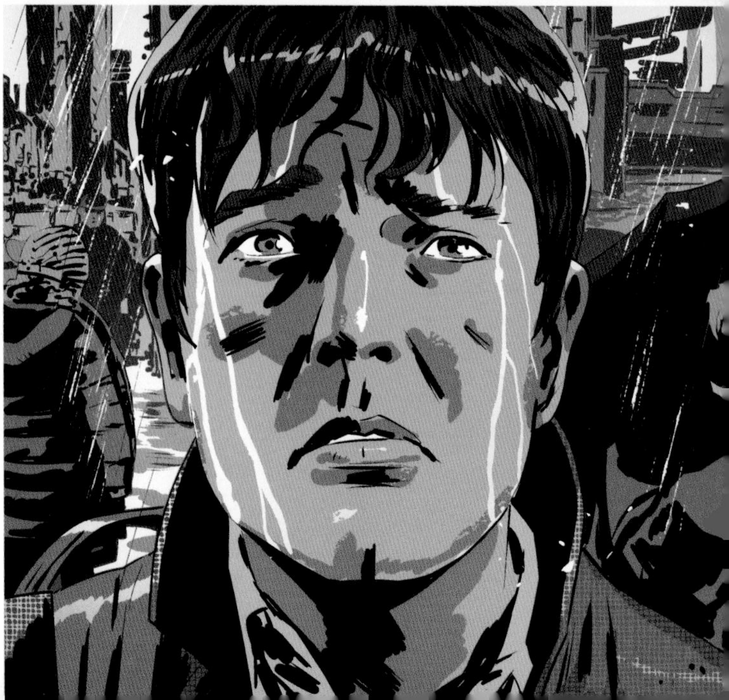

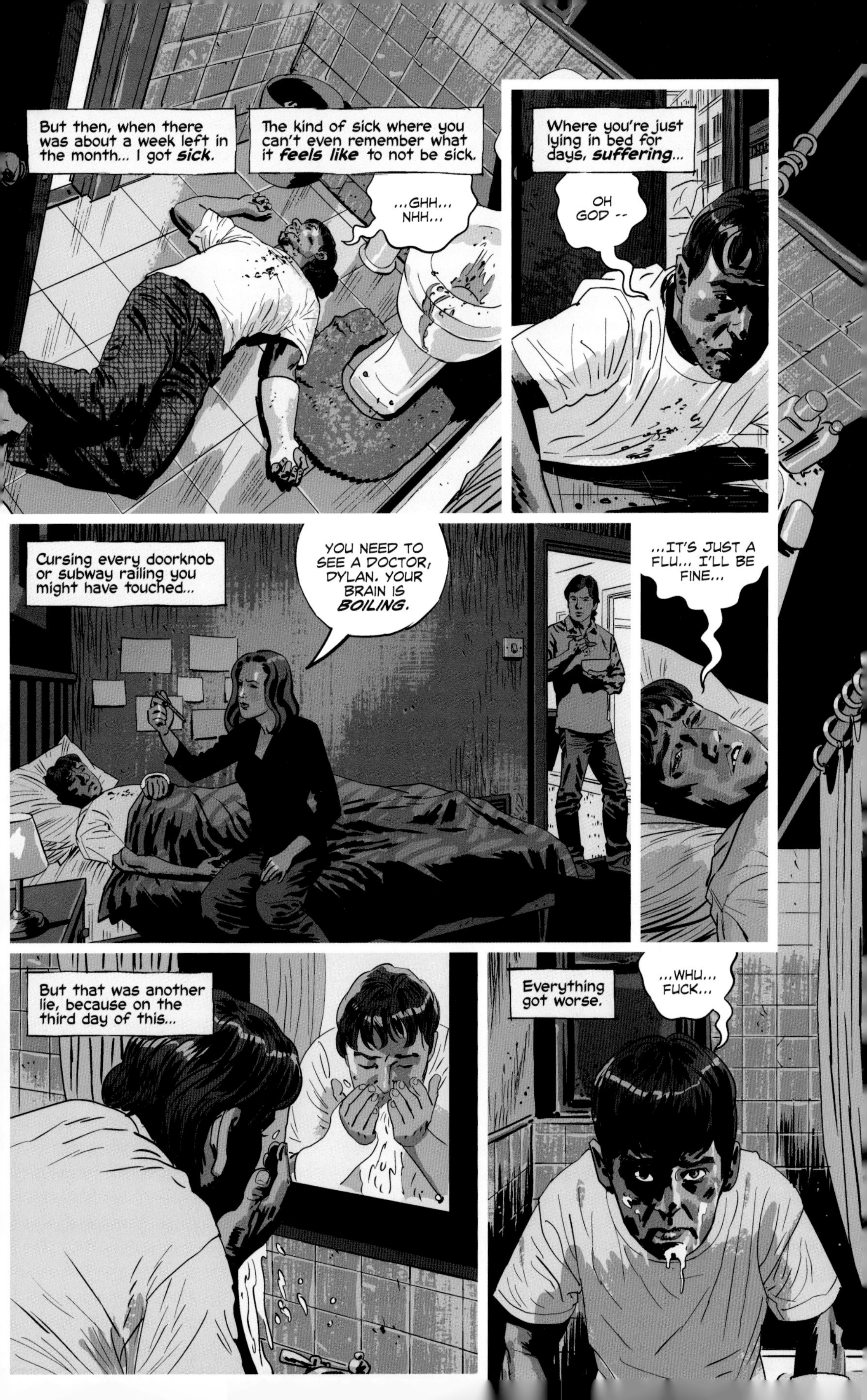

But then, when there was about a week left in the month... I got *sick.*
The kind of sick where you can't even remember what it *feels like* to not be sick.
...GHH... NHH...
Where you're just lying in bed for days, *suffering*...
OH GOD --
Cursing every doorknob or subway railing you might have touched...
YOU NEED TO SEE A DOCTOR, DYLAN. YOUR BRAIN IS *BOILING.*
...IT'S JUST A FLU... I'LL BE FINE...
But that was another lie, because on the third day of this...
Everything got worse.
...WHU... FUCK...

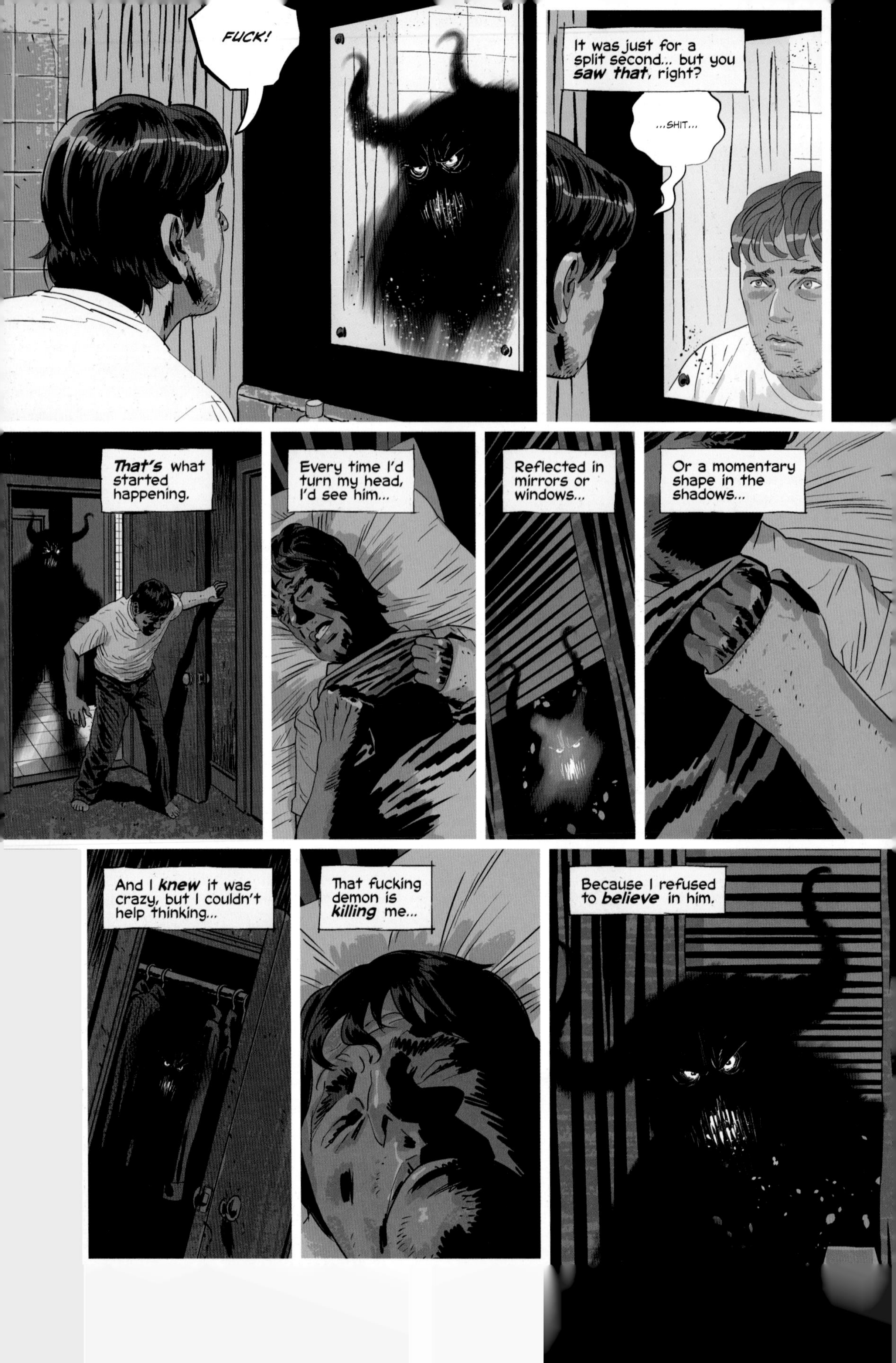
FUCK!
It was just for a split second... but you **saw that**, right?
...SHIT...
That's what started happening.
Every time I'd turn my head, I'd see him...
Reflected in mirrors or windows...
Or a momentary shape in the shadows...
And I **knew** it was crazy, but I couldn't help thinking...
That fucking demon is **killing** me...
Because I refused to **believe** in him.

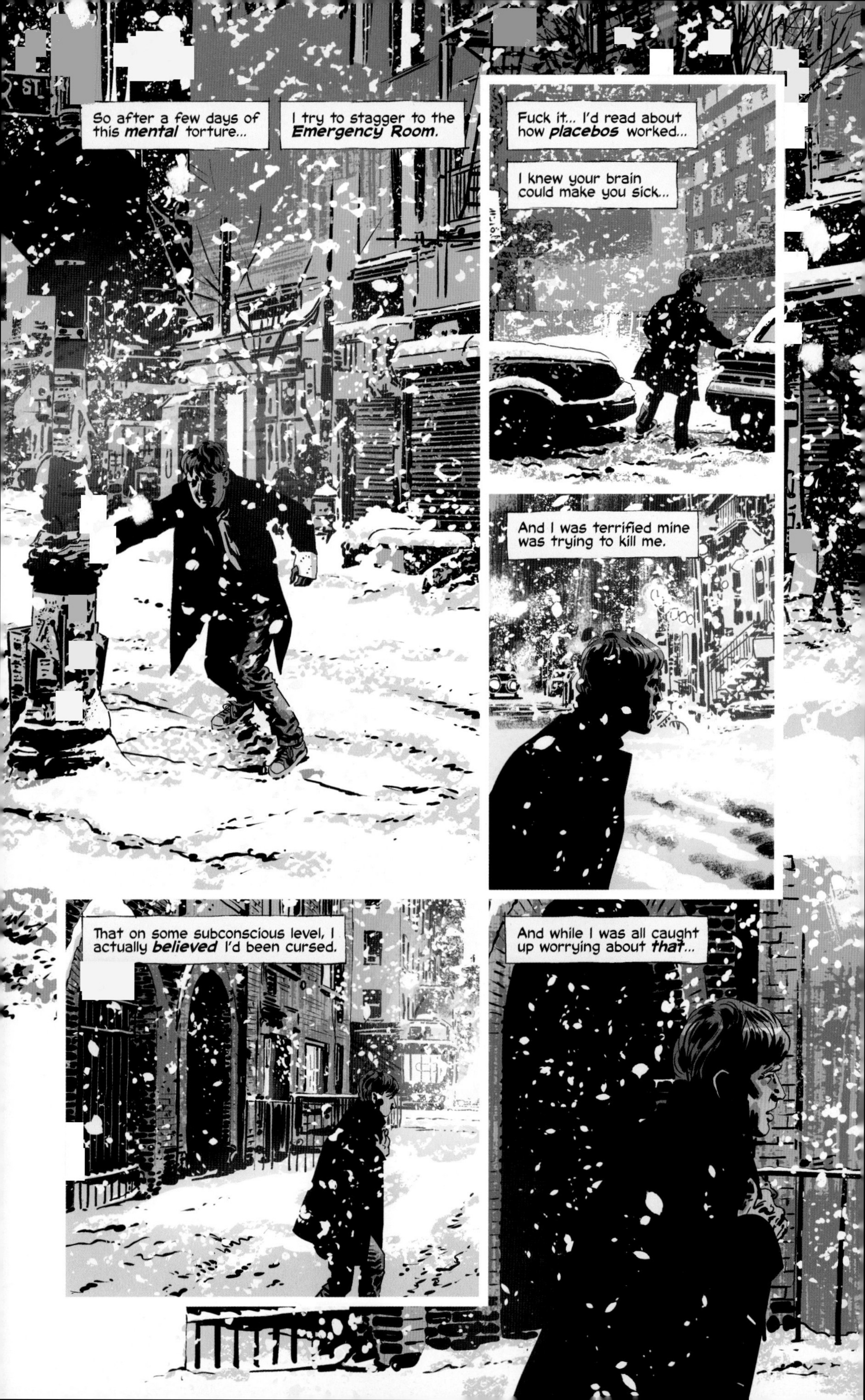
So after a few days of this mental torture...
I try to stagger to the Emergency Room.
Fuck it... I'd read about how placebos worked...
I knew your brain could make you sick...
And I was terrified mine was trying to kill me.
That on some subconscious level, I actually believed I'd been cursed.
And while I was all caught up worrying about that...

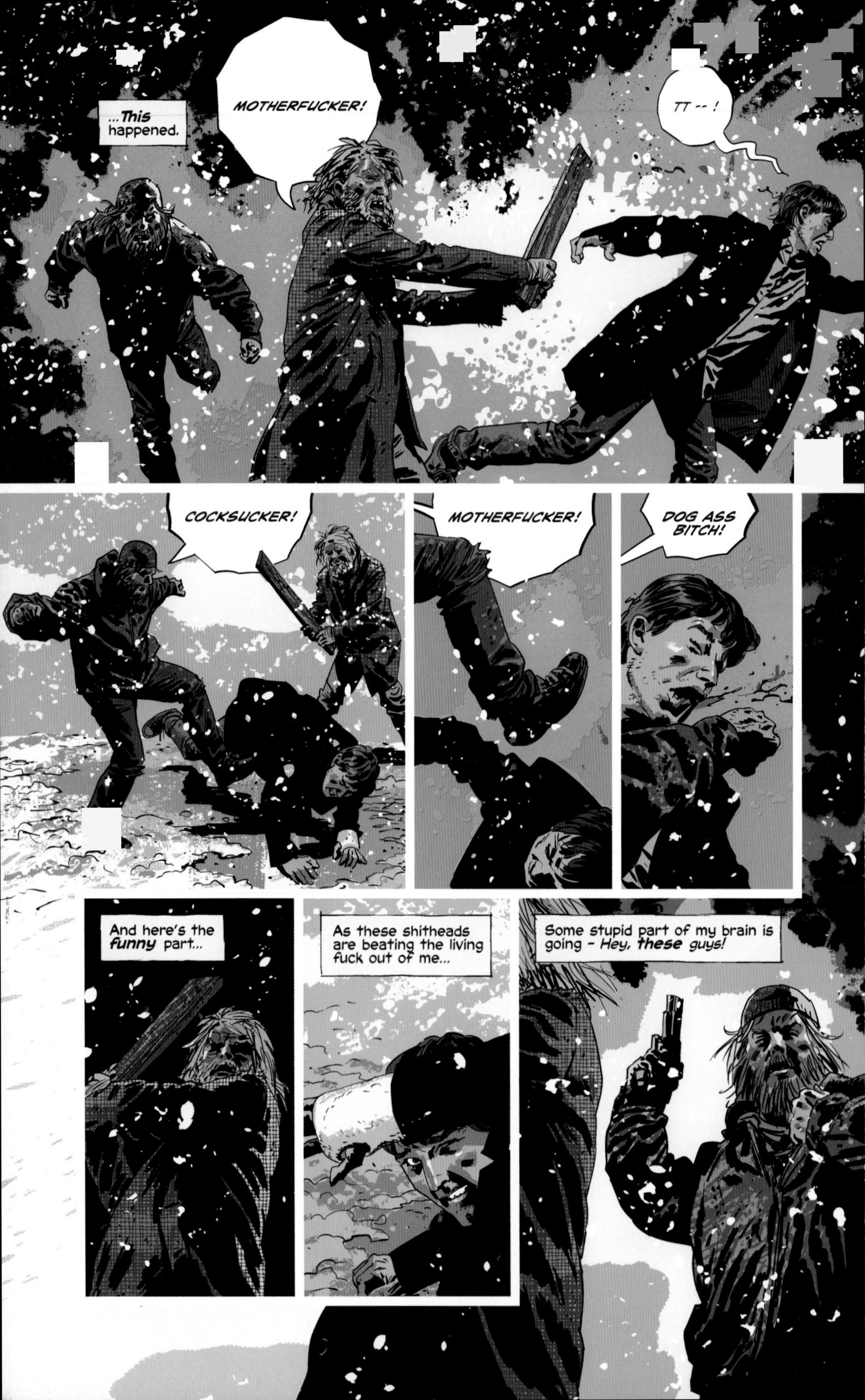
...This happened.
MOTHERFUCKER!
TT -- !
COCKSUCKER!
MOTHERFUCKER!
DOG ASS BITCH!
And here's the *funny* part...
As these shitheads are beating the living fuck out of me...
Some stupid part of my brain is going - *Hey,* ***these*** *guys!*

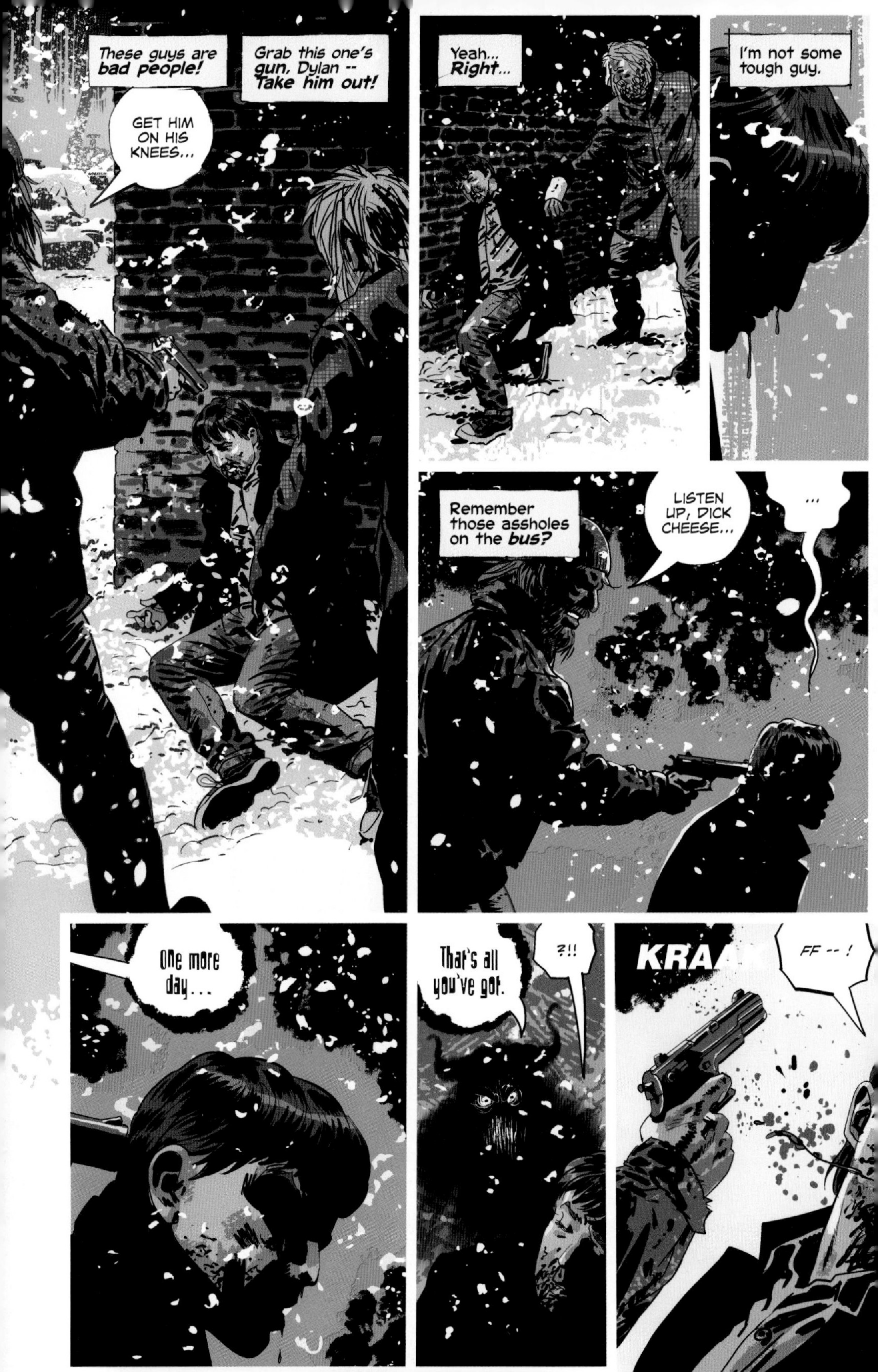
These guys are bad people!
GET HIM ON HIS KNEES...
Grab this one's gun, Dylan -- Take him out!
Yeah... Right...
I'm not some tough guy.
Remember those assholes on the bus?
LISTEN UP, DICK CHEESE...
...
One more day...
That's all you've got.
?!!
KRAA
FF -- !

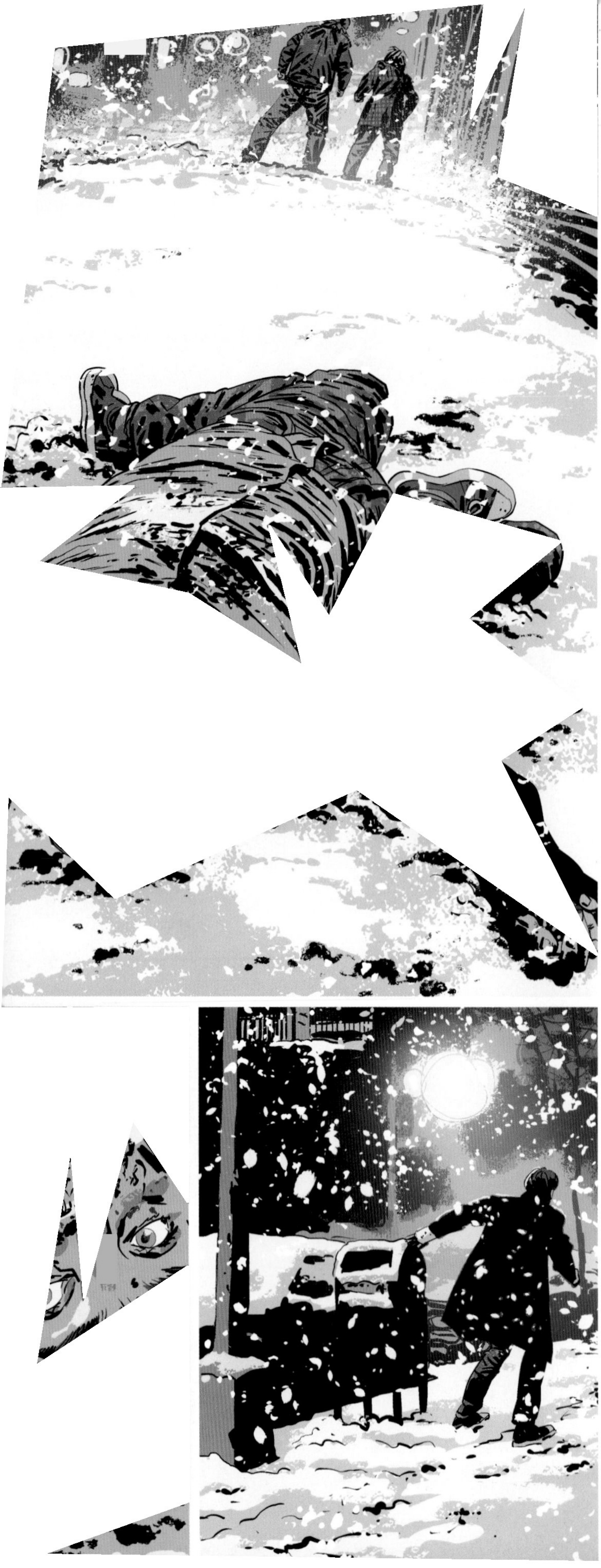

I'd like to tell you I lay there for a long time thinking about everything over and over again...

But the truth is, it only took a minute before I thought... *The hell with this, I'll do it.*

Because I wasn't sure what was happening to me... But I ***didn't*** want to die.

And the ***second*** I gave in... The second I told myself I was actually going to commit a ***homicide***... I felt better.

How fucked up is that?

Now I just had to find someone who deserved to die and kill them...

How hard could ***that*** be?

The best story ever written - well, ***one*** of the best stories - I mean, I'm not sure it's better than Kafka or Nabokov, but still...

One of the best stories ever is ***The Tale of the Hunchback***, from the ***Thousand and One Nights.***

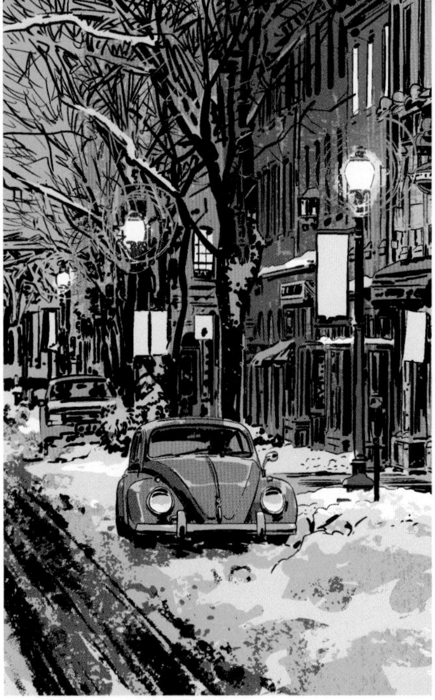

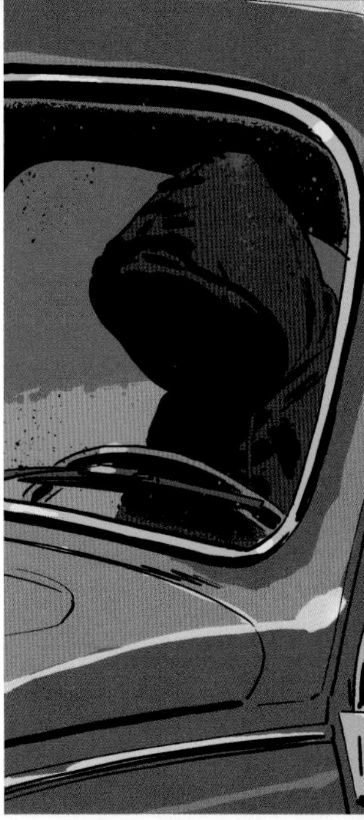

In the story, the Emperor's favorite ***jester***, a hunchback, accidentally ***chokes*** to death on a fish bone at the home of a tailor and his wife.

Terrified of the wrath of the Emperor, they dump his body on a doctor, who accidentally trips over him in the dark and thinks ***he*** killed him.

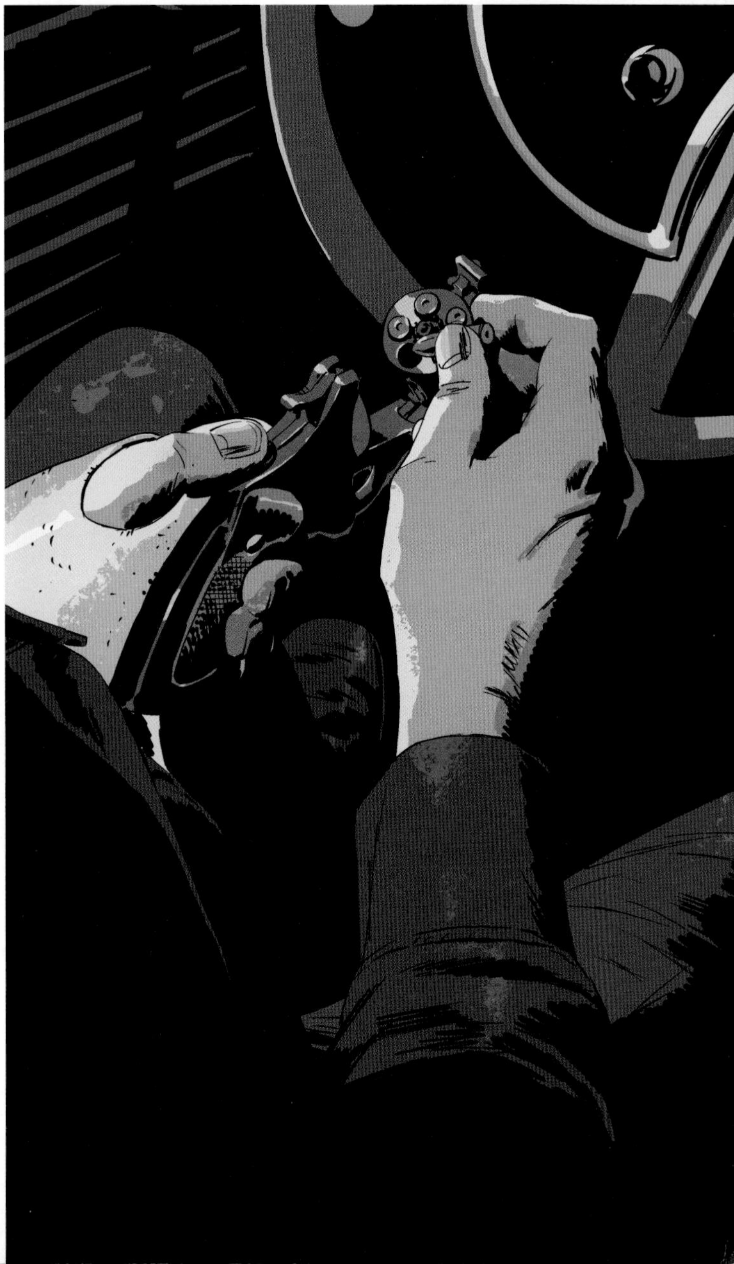

Then the ***doctor*** gets rid of the body, tricking someone else into thinking ***they*** killed the hunchback...

This passing of the corpse just continues, over and over again... Until someone is finally ***caught*** with the dead body by the city guard.

But when this man is about to be executed for the murder of the Emperor's jester, the story unwinds the other way...

One by one, the men and women who think ***they*** killed this poor hunchback step forward to confess...

Unable to let anyone else be punished for their crime.

And in typical fairy tale fashion, the Emperor is so amused by all this, that he pardons them...

And then, even better, the hunchback turns out to not actually be ***dead*** and they're all ***rewarded*** with riches and titles.

They spent the entire night passing around a supposedly dead body, and they all end up ***wealthy*** for it...

Because they made some old man laugh.

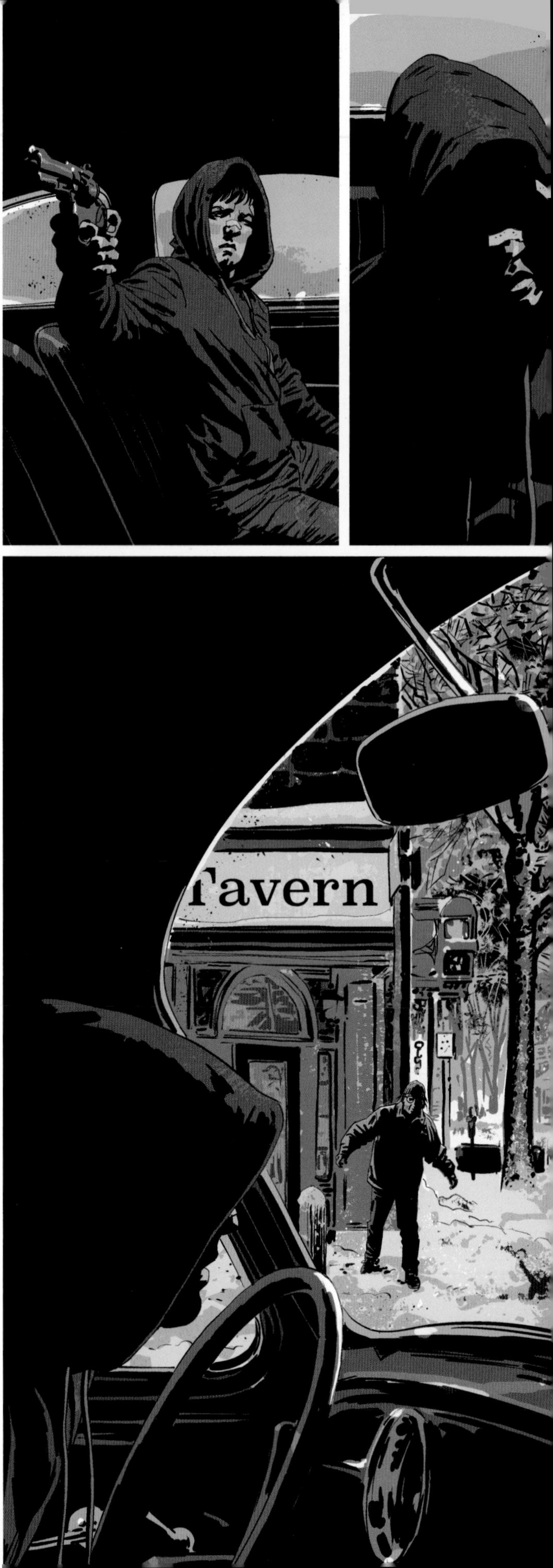
Tavern

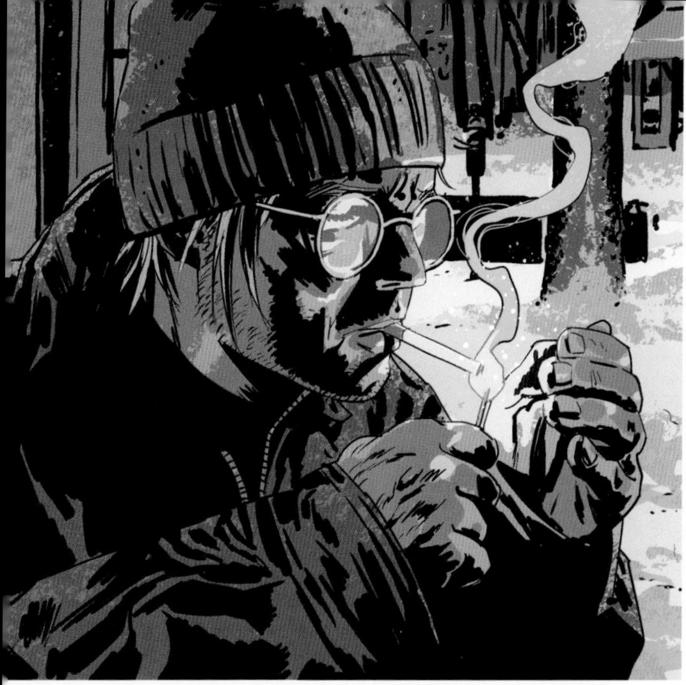

So ***why*** is this the best story ever?

Not just because it's inventive, or because even though it's fucking ancient it still totally makes you laugh.

No, it's because it tells us a very simple ***truth*** about people...

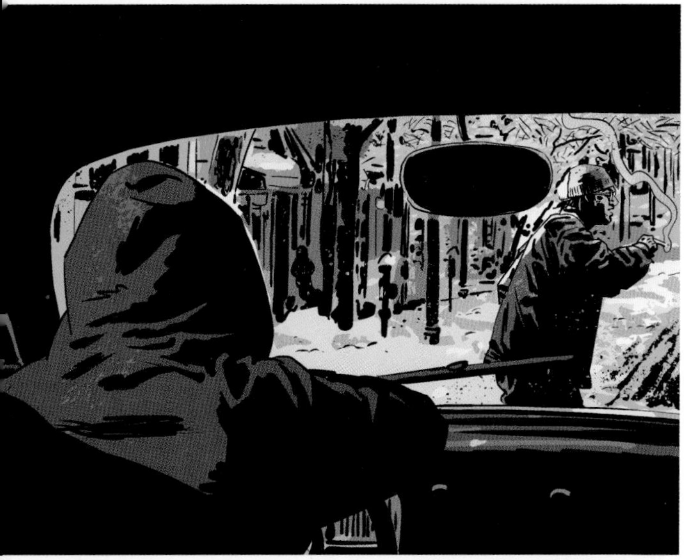

They all want to ***get away*** with it.

Whatever ***crime*** they've committed, whatever they've done... They want to blame it on ***somebody else*** and run the fuck ***away***.

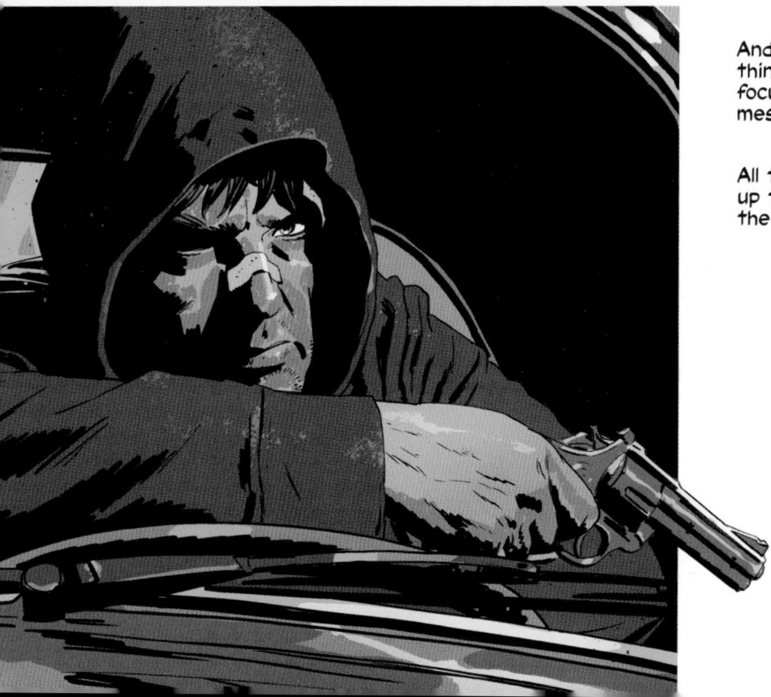

And I know what you're thinking - that I should be focusing on the ***positive*** message instead.

All those people stepping up to do the right thing in the end... But I don't know.

That implies this is a story about being unable to live with ***guilt***, but I don't think that's what it is.

I mean, look at what happens... These are awful people, who all think they've ***murdered*** this poor hunchback...

And they get fucking ***rewarded***... For trying to get away with it.

I think the part where they all try to do the right thing is a lie, put in there to reassure little kids...

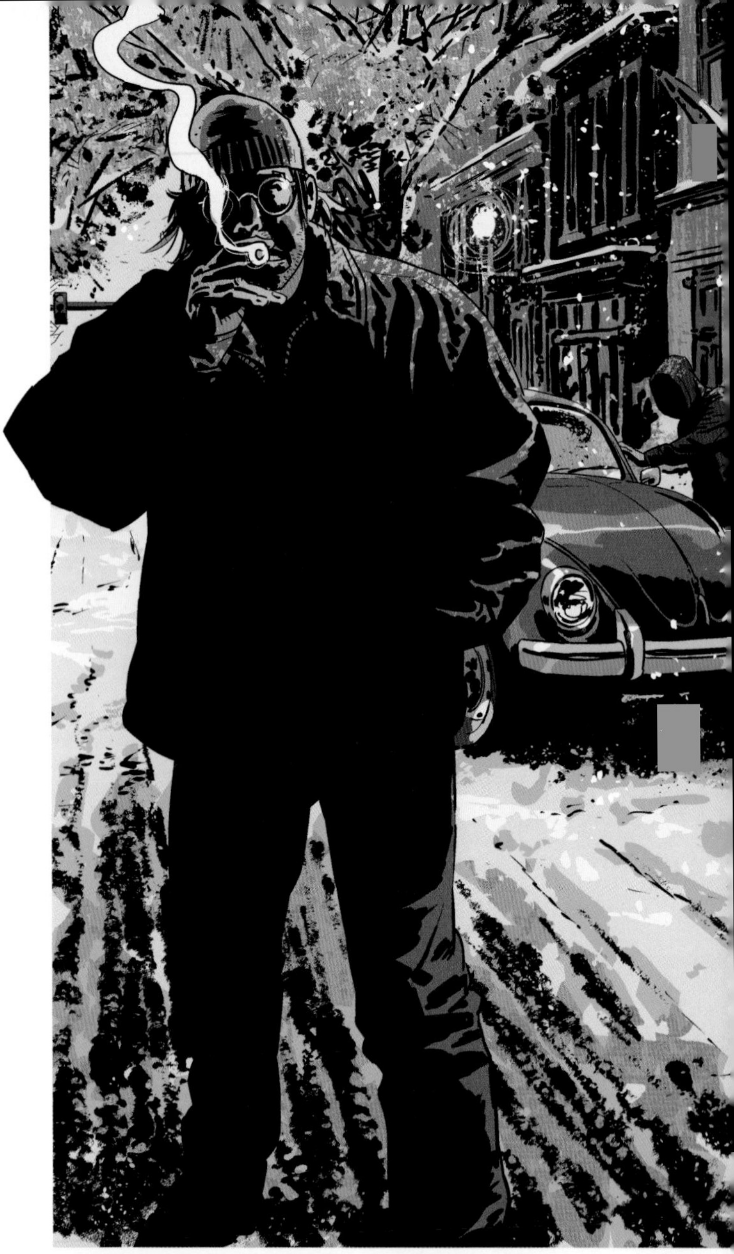

So they can drift off to sleep believing that people are good underneath everything, no matter what.

But I think whoever first wrote this story knew the truth...

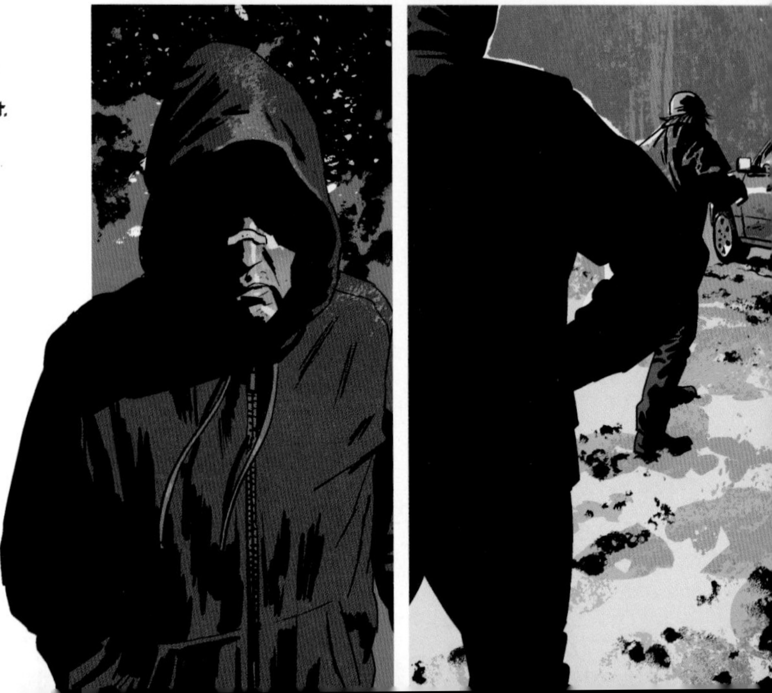

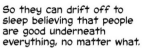

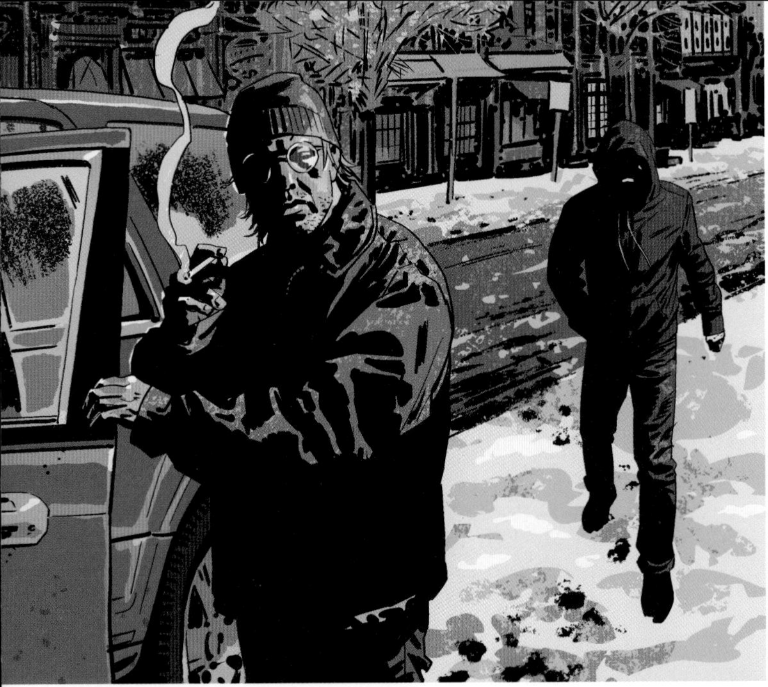

That in ***real life***, the bad sleep well... And guilt doesn't trouble them.

Hell, real bad men? They don't even live in the ***same world*** as we do...

When they look around themselves, they see a whole other reality...

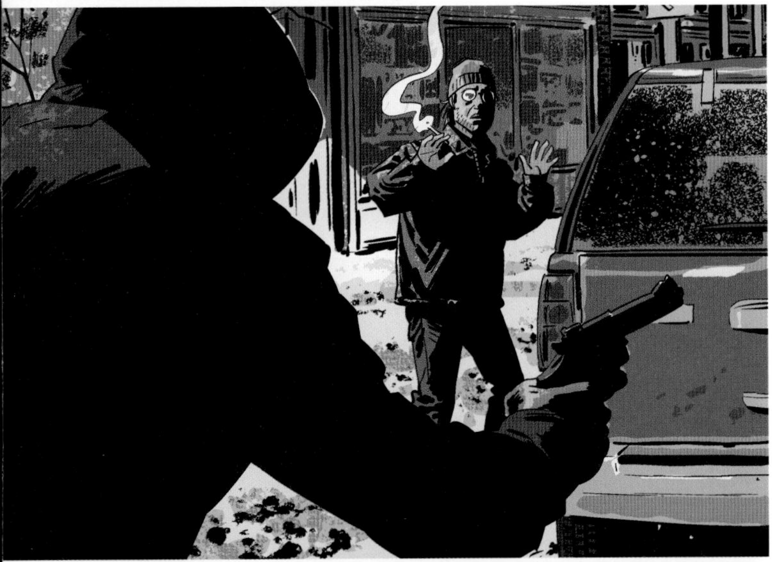

They see ***sheep***, and they're looking through the eyes of ***wolves.***

I know it's true, because ***I'm*** a wolf now, too...

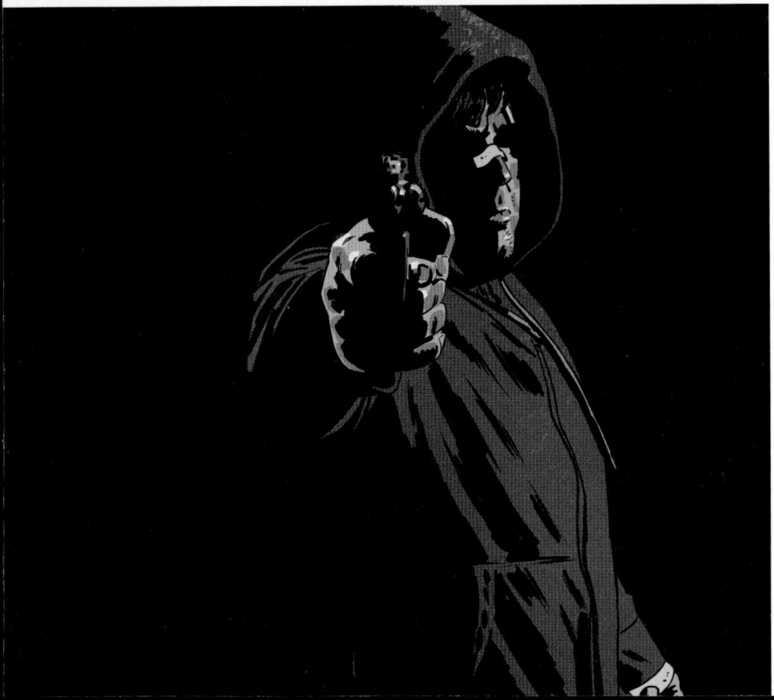

Aw crap - I fucking did it ***again***, didn't I?

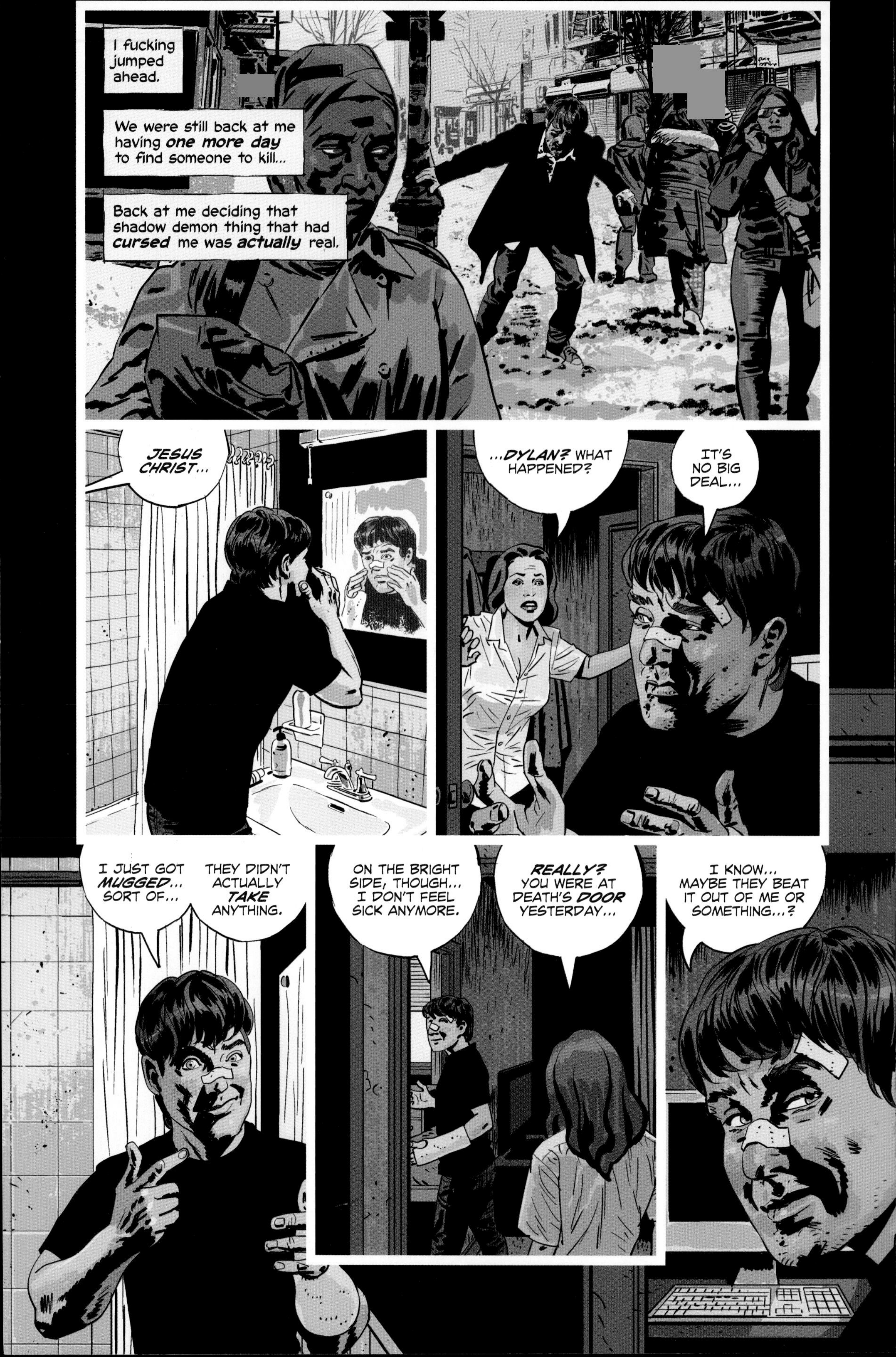
I fucking jumped ahead.
We were still back at me having ***one more day*** to find someone to kill...
Back at me deciding that shadow demon thing that had ***cursed*** me was ***actually*** real.
JESUS CHRIST...
...***DYLAN?*** WHAT HAPPENED?
IT'S NO BIG DEAL...
I JUST GOT ***MUGGED***... SORT OF...
THEY DIDN'T ACTUALLY ***TAKE*** ANYTHING.
ON THE BRIGHT SIDE, THOUGH... I DON'T FEEL SICK ANYMORE.
REALLY? YOU WERE AT DEATH'S ***DOOR*** YESTERDAY...
I KNOW... MAYBE THEY BEAT IT OUT OF ME OR SOMETHING...?

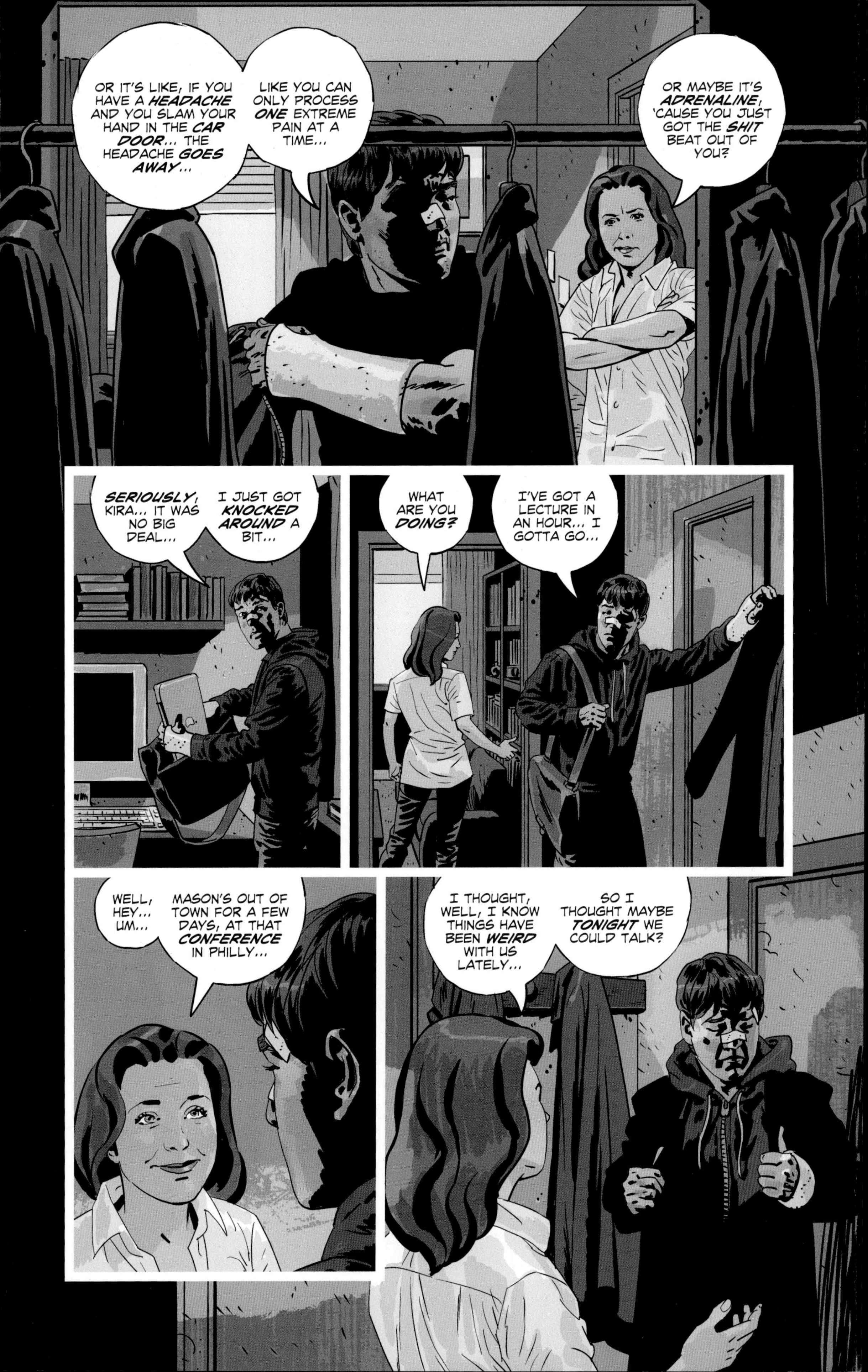
OR IT'S LIKE, IF YOU HAVE A HEADACHE AND YOU SLAM YOUR HAND IN THE CAR DOOR... THE HEADACHE GOES AWAY...
LIKE YOU CAN ONLY PROCESS ONE EXTREME PAIN AT A TIME...
OR MAYBE IT'S ADRENALINE, 'CAUSE YOU JUST GOT THE SHIT BEAT OUT OF YOU?
SERIOUSLY, KIRA... IT WAS NO BIG DEAL...
I JUST GOT KNOCKED AROUND A BIT...
WHAT ARE YOU DOING?
I'VE GOT A LECTURE IN AN HOUR... I GOTTA GO...
WELL, HEY... UM...
MASON'S OUT OF TOWN FOR A FEW DAYS, AT THAT CONFERENCE IN PHILLY...
I THOUGHT, WELL, I KNOW THINGS HAVE BEEN WEIRD WITH US LATELY...
SO I THOUGHT MAYBE TONIGHT WE COULD TALK?

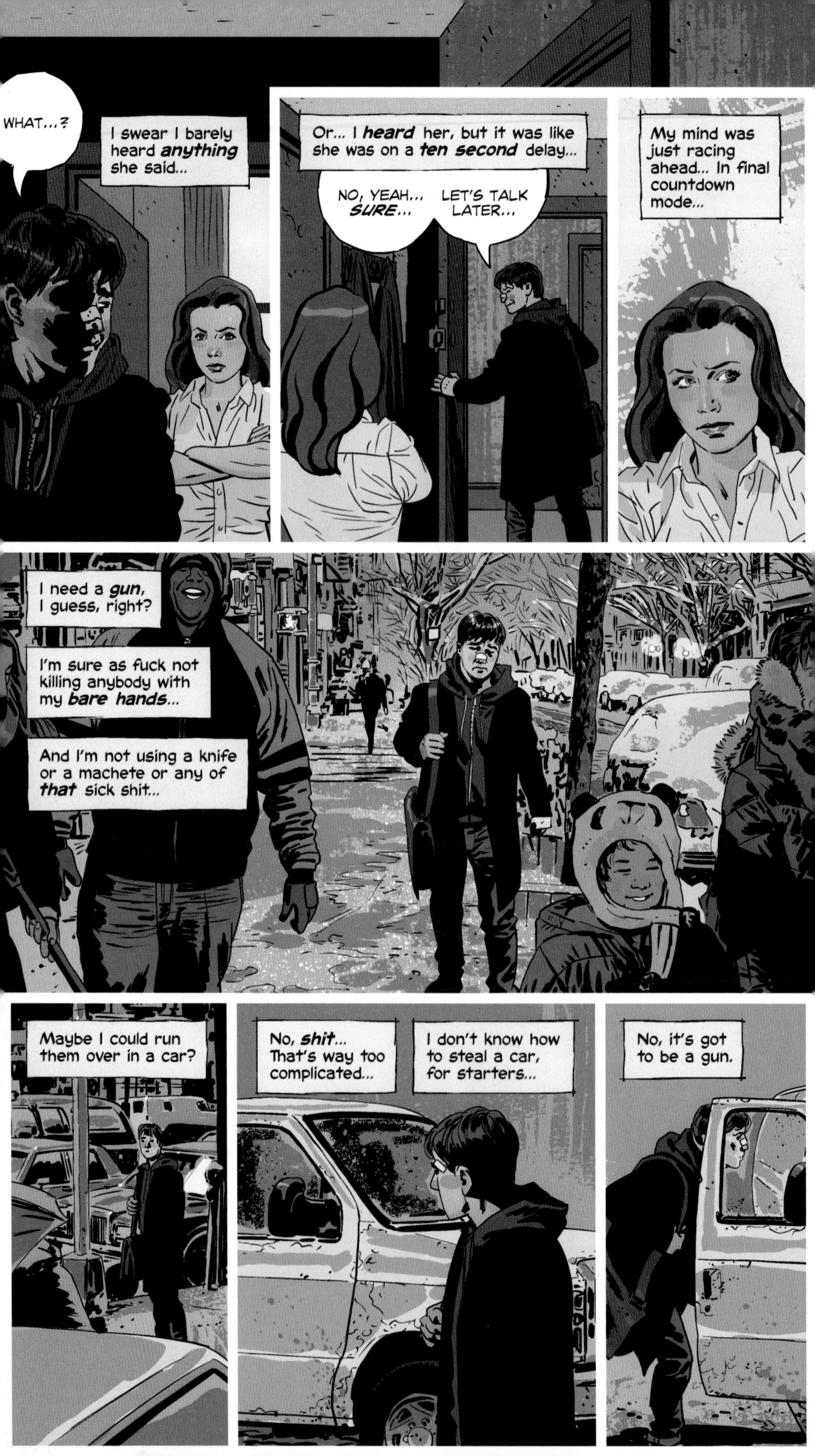
WHAT...?
I swear I barely heard anything she said...
Or... I heard her, but it was like she was on a ten second delay...
NO, YEAH... SURE...
LET'S TALK LATER...
My mind was just racing ahead... In final countdown mode...
I need a gun, I guess, right?
I'm sure as fuck not killing anybody with my bare hands...
And I'm not using a knife or a machete or any of that sick shit...
Maybe I could run them over in a car?
No, shit... That's way too complicated...
I don't know how to steal a car, for starters...
No, it's got to be a gun.

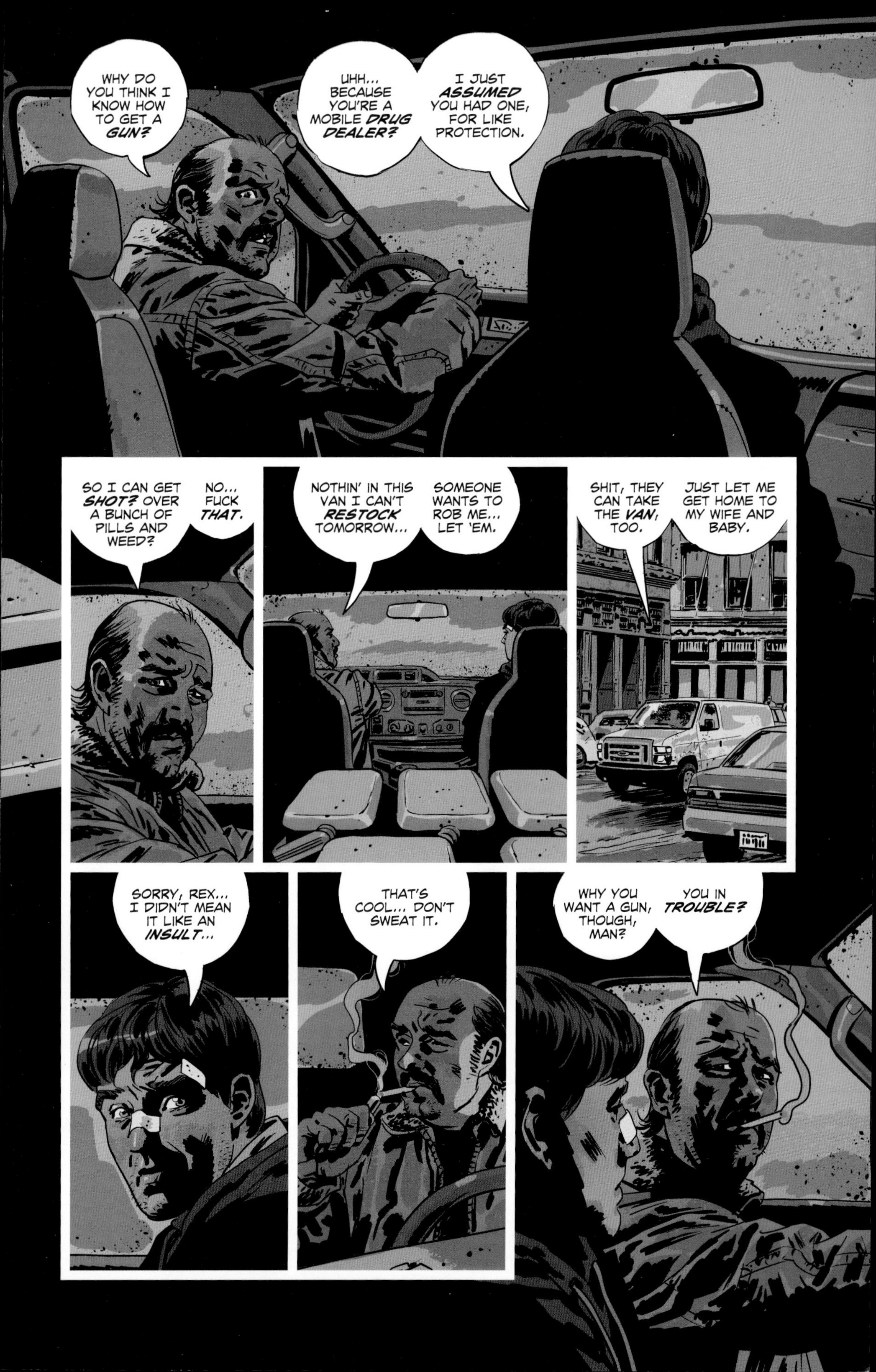
WHY DO YOU THINK I KNOW HOW TO GET A GUN?
UHH... BECAUSE YOU'RE A MOBILE DRUG DEALER?
I JUST ASSUMED YOU HAD ONE, FOR LIKE PROTECTION.
SO I CAN GET SHOT? OVER A BUNCH OF PILLS AND WEED?
NO... FUCK THAT.
NOTHIN' IN THIS VAN I CAN'T RESTOCK TOMORROW...
SOMEONE WANTS TO ROB ME... LET 'EM.
SHIT, THEY CAN TAKE THE VAN, TOO.
JUST LET ME GET HOME TO MY WIFE AND BABY.
SORRY, REX... I DIDN'T MEAN IT LIKE AN INSULT...
THAT'S COOL... DON'T SWEAT IT.
WHY YOU WANT A GUN, THOUGH, MAN?
YOU IN TROUBLE?

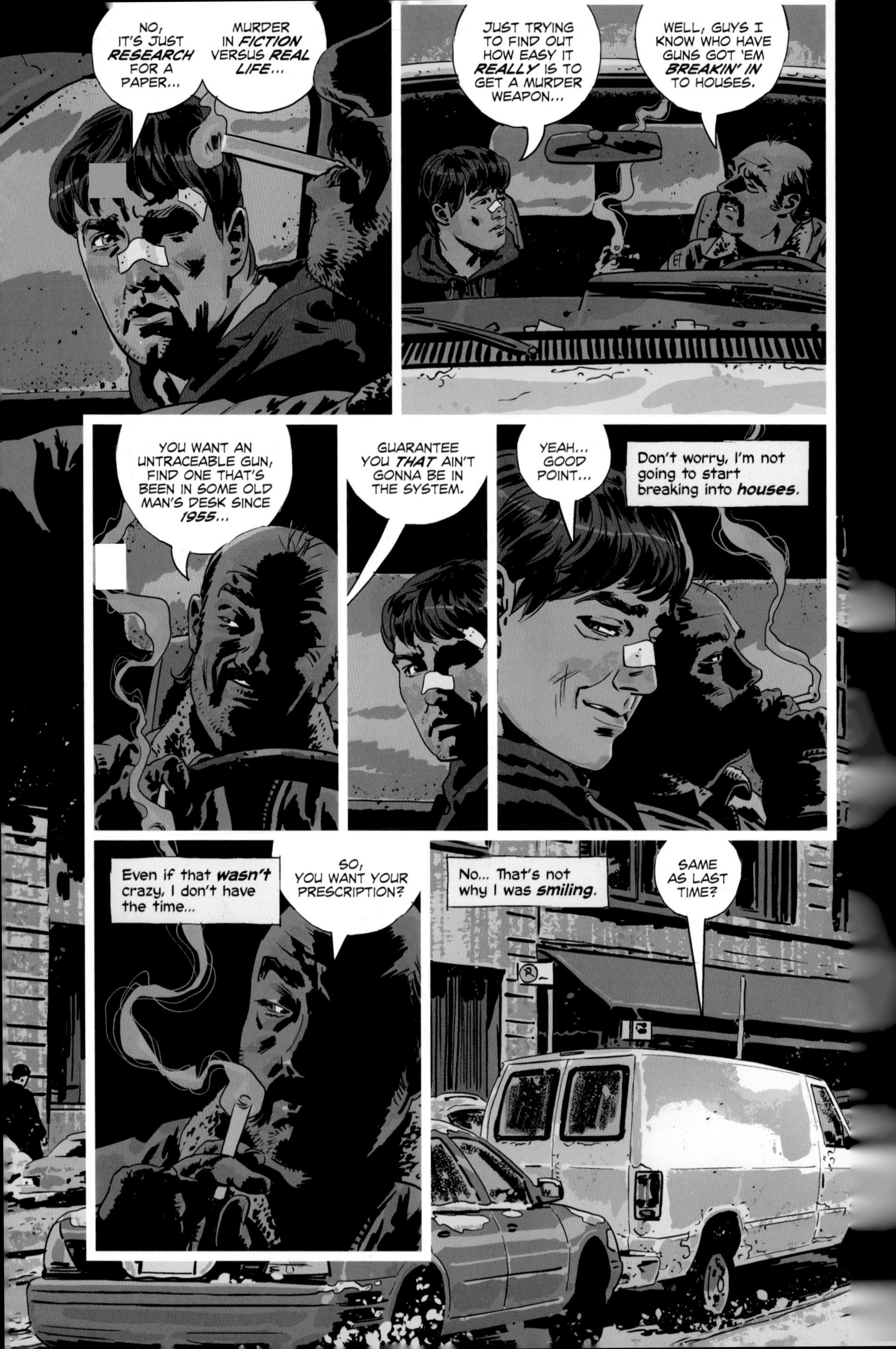
NO, IT'S JUST RESEARCH FOR A PAPER...
MURDER IN FICTION VERSUS REAL LIFE...
JUST TRYING TO FIND OUT HOW EASY IT REALLY IS TO GET A MURDER WEAPON...
WELL, GUYS I KNOW WHO HAVE GUNS GOT 'EM BREAKIN' IN TO HOUSES.
YOU WANT AN UNTRACEABLE GUN, FIND ONE THAT'S BEEN IN SOME OLD MAN'S DESK SINCE 1955...
GUARANTEE YOU THAT AIN'T GONNA BE IN THE SYSTEM.
YEAH... GOOD POINT...
Don't worry, I'm not going to start breaking into houses.
Even if that wasn't crazy, I don't have the time...
SO, YOU WANT YOUR PRESCRIPTION?
No... That's not why I was smiling.
SAME AS LAST TIME?

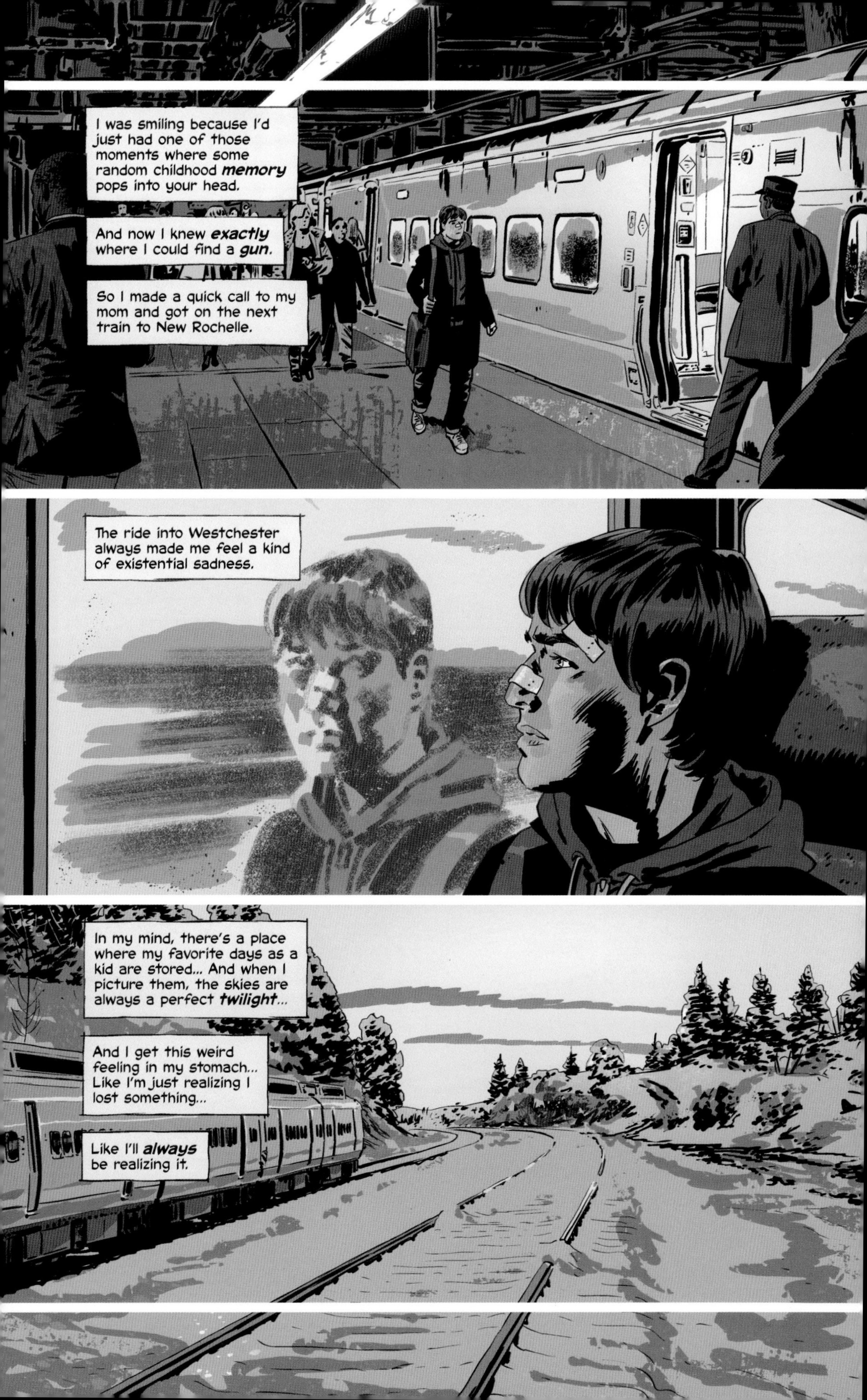
I was smiling because I'd just had one of those moments where some random childhood **memory** pops into your head.
And now I knew **exactly** where I could find a **gun**.
So I made a quick call to my mom and got on the next train to New Rochelle.
The ride into Westchester always made me feel a kind of existential sadness.
In my mind, there's a place where my favorite days as a kid are stored... And when I picture them, the skies are always a perfect **twilight**...
And I get this weird feeling in my stomach... Like I'm just realizing I lost something...
Like I'll **always** be realizing it.

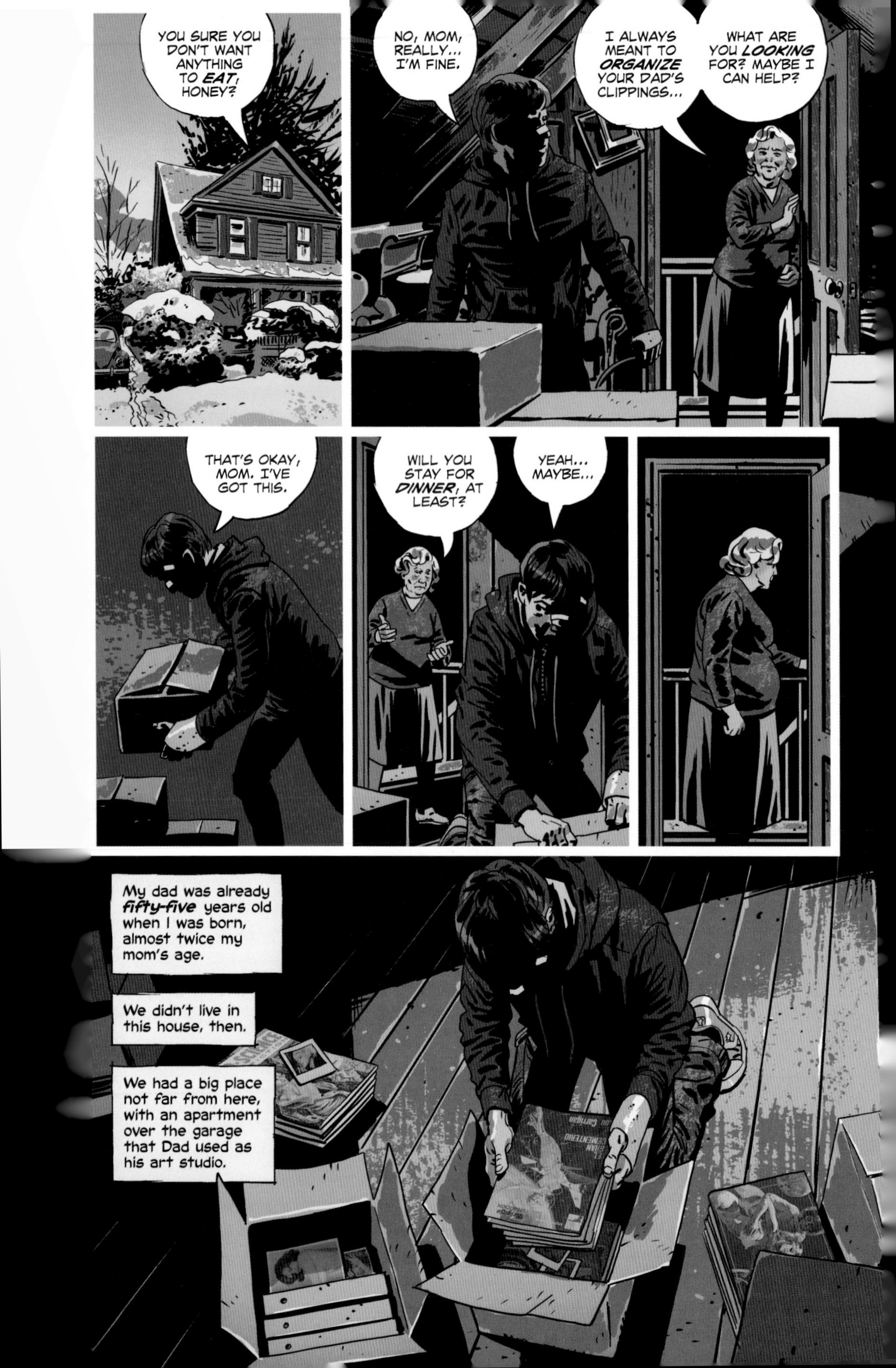

YOU SURE YOU DON'T WANT ANYTHING TO EAT, HONEY?
NO, MOM, REALLY... I'M FINE.
I ALWAYS MEANT TO ORGANIZE YOUR DAD'S CLIPPINGS...
WHAT ARE YOU LOOKING FOR? MAYBE I CAN HELP?
THAT'S OKAY, MOM. I'VE GOT THIS.
WILL YOU STAY FOR DINNER, AT LEAST?
YEAH... MAYBE...
My dad was already fifty-five years old when I was born, almost twice my mom's age.
We didn't live in this house, then.
We had a big place not far from here, with an apartment over the garage that Dad used as his art studio.

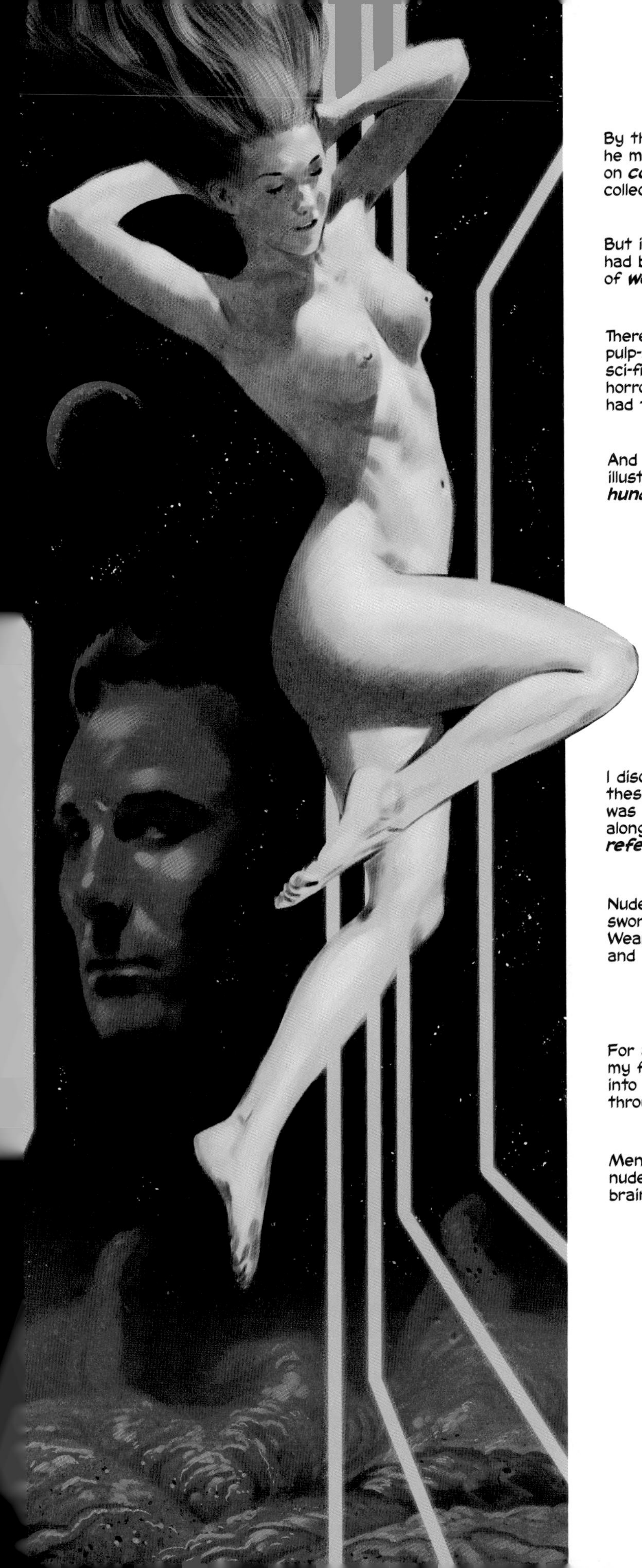

By the time I came around, he made most of his money on ***commissions*** to private collectors...

But in the 60s and 70s, Dad had been one of the ***kings*** of ***weird porn***...

There were all these pulp-style magazines, with sci-fi and fantasy and horror stories, but they all had tons of ***sex*** in them.

And my dad's illustrations were in ***hundreds*** of them.

I discovered a few boxes of these old magazines when I was like five or six years old... along with a bunch of Dad's ***reference photos***.

Nude models holding prop swords or laser guns. Wearing a space helmet and nothing else.

For a few months after that, my friends and I would sneak into the garage and dig through all of them...

Mentally cataloging every nude lady our little kid brains could absorb.

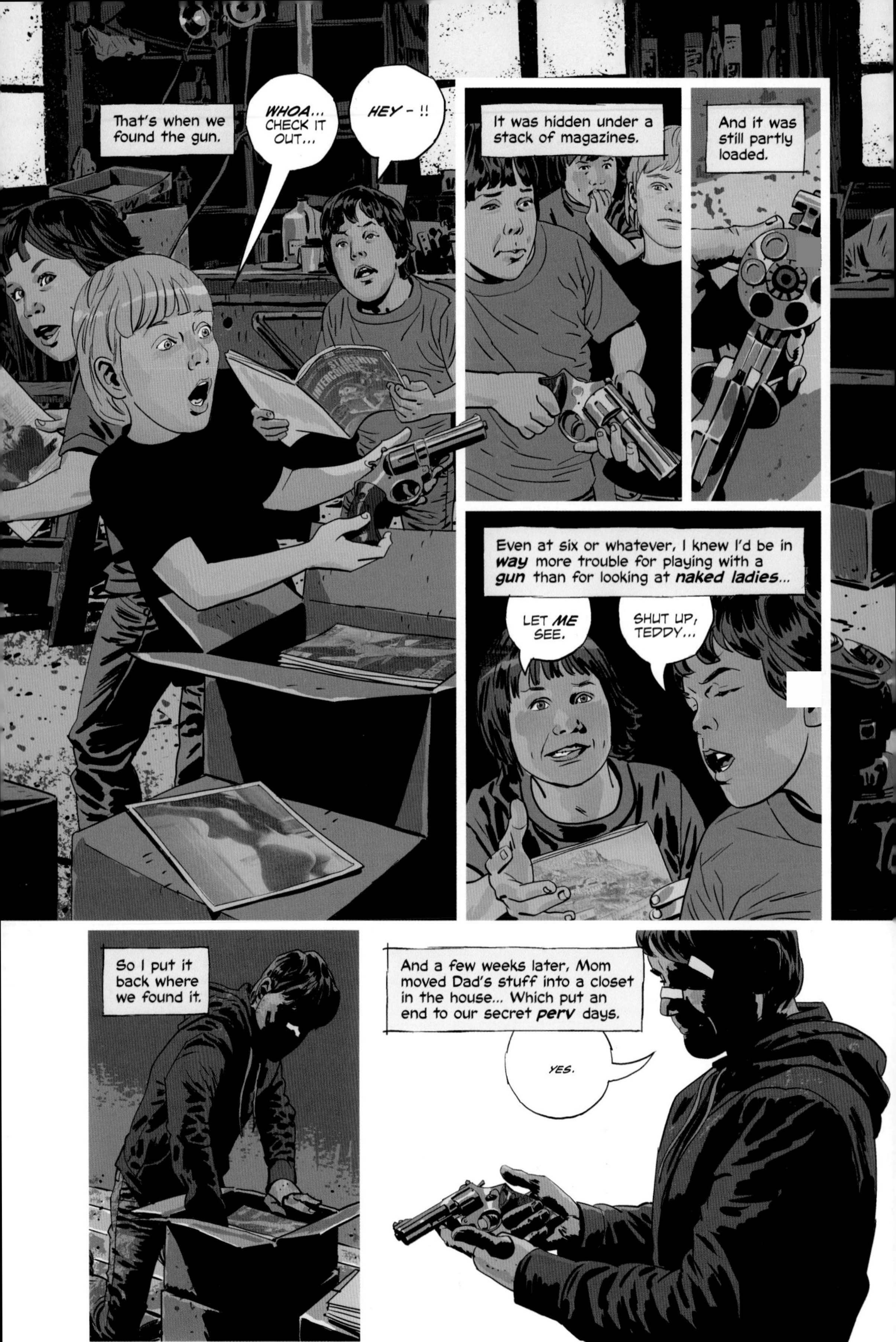
That's when we found the gun.
WHOA... CHECK IT OUT...
HEY - !!
It was hidden under a stack of magazines.
And it was still partly loaded.
Even at six or whatever, I knew I'd be in way more trouble for playing with a gun than for looking at naked ladies...
LET ME SEE.
SHUT UP, TEDDY...
So I put it back where we found it.
And a few weeks later, Mom moved Dad's stuff into a closet in the house... Which put an end to our secret perv days.
YES.

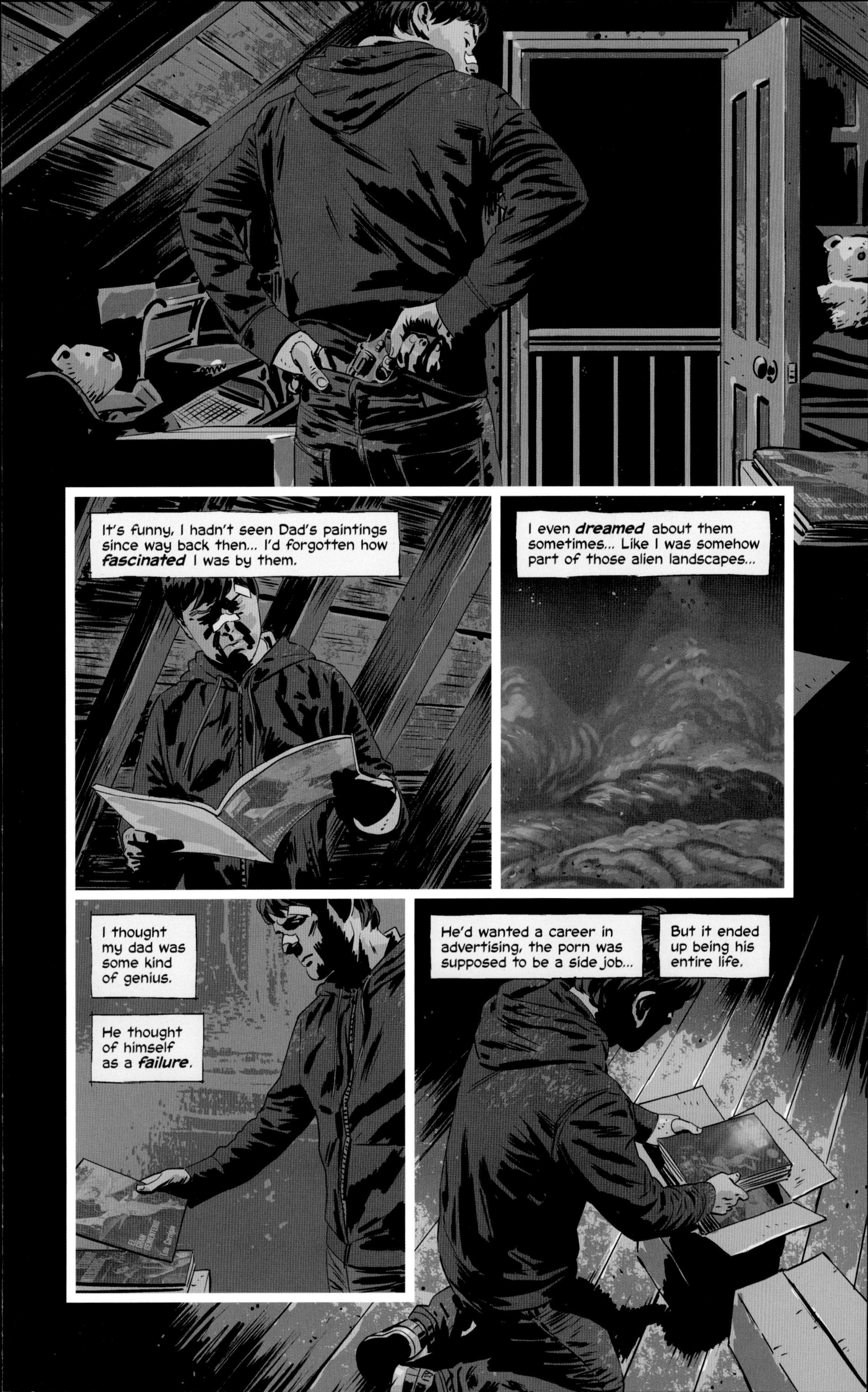
It's funny, I hadn't seen Dad's paintings since way back then... I'd forgotten how *fascinated* I was by them.
I even *dreamed* about them sometimes... Like I was somehow part of those alien landscapes...
I thought my dad was some kind of genius.
He thought of himself as a *failure*.
He'd wanted a career in advertising, the porn was supposed to be a side job...
But it ended up being his entire life.

One night a few months before he killed himself, he got really *drunk* and told me all about it...

...LIFE SCREWS OVER *EVERYBODY* SOMEHOW...

...AIN'T NOTHIN' YOU CAN *DO* ABOUT IT, KIDDO...

...SOMETIMES YOU'RE JUST THE ONE THAT GETS *PICKED*...

...YOUR DREAM GETS CRUSHED...

It's that last bit of memory that slides everything into place.

...NOTHIN' YOU CAN DO...

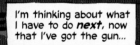

I'm thinking about what I have to do *next*, now that I've got the gun...

And I'm looking at my dad's art, remembering how unfair the world is...

And right then... I know who I can *kill* tonight.

HEY MOM... CAN I BORROW YOUR *CAR?*

I WANT TO TAKE SOME OF THIS STUFF BACK TO THE CITY...

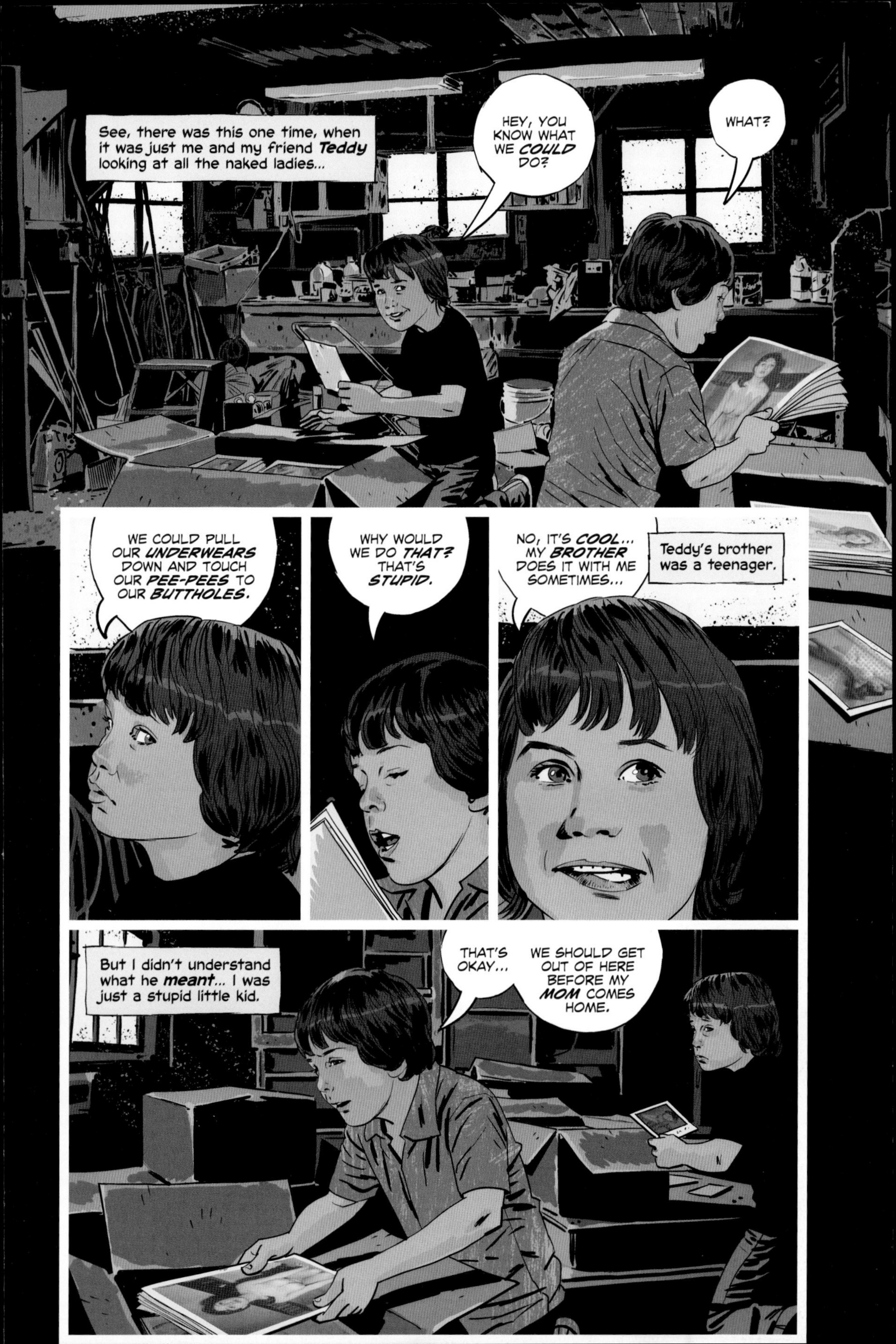
See, there was this one time, when it was just me and my friend *Teddy* looking at all the naked ladies...
HEY, YOU KNOW WHAT WE *COULD* DO?
WHAT?
WE COULD PULL OUR *UNDERWEARS* DOWN AND TOUCH OUR *PEE-PEES* TO OUR *BUTTHOLES*.
WHY WOULD WE DO *THAT?* THAT'S *STUPID*.
NO, IT'S *COOL*... MY *BROTHER* DOES IT WITH ME SOMETIMES...
Teddy's brother was a teenager.
But I didn't understand what he *meant*... I was just a stupid little kid.
THAT'S OKAY...
WE SHOULD GET OUT OF HERE BEFORE MY *MOM* COMES HOME.

I actually forgot about the whole thing, until high school.

By then, me and Teddy were in different crowds. He was with the stoners and tweakers, and I was on the swim team.

Then halfway through tenth grade, Teddy dropped out.

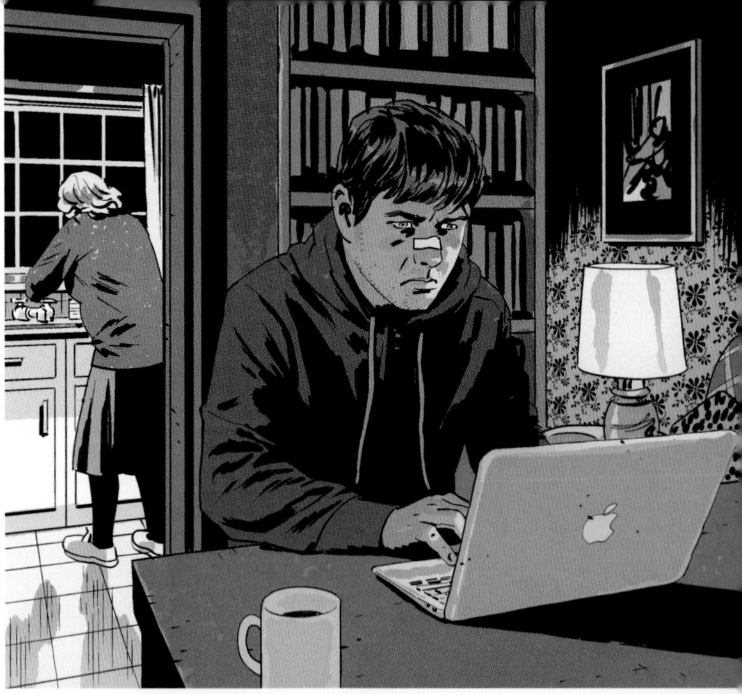

We'd hear crazy stories about him... How he was all strung out on ***heroin***... Living on the streets.

It seemed so punk rock.

But that winter, Teddy ***froze to death*** sleeping in a doorway in Alphabet City.

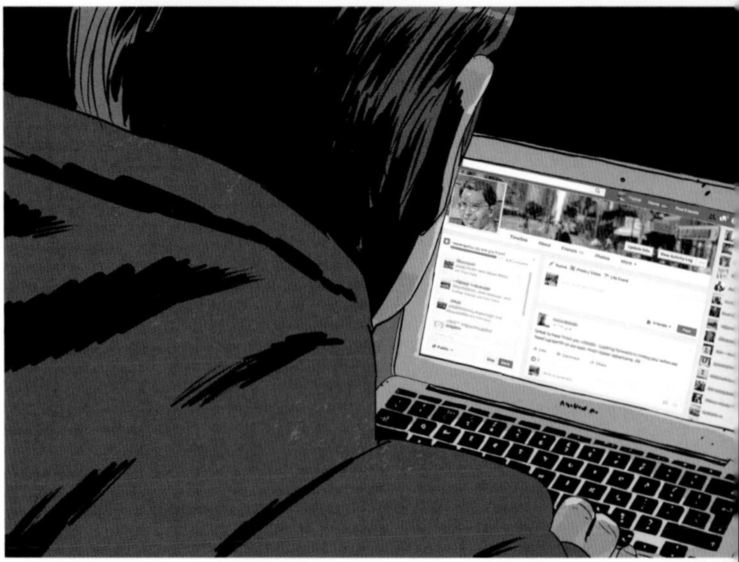

And for a while after that, he was all anybody at school talked about.

Suddenly every guy had been Teddy's best friend, and every girl had secretly had a crush on him, so they could cry about it in the halls.

That's when I thought about that day in the ***garage*** again...

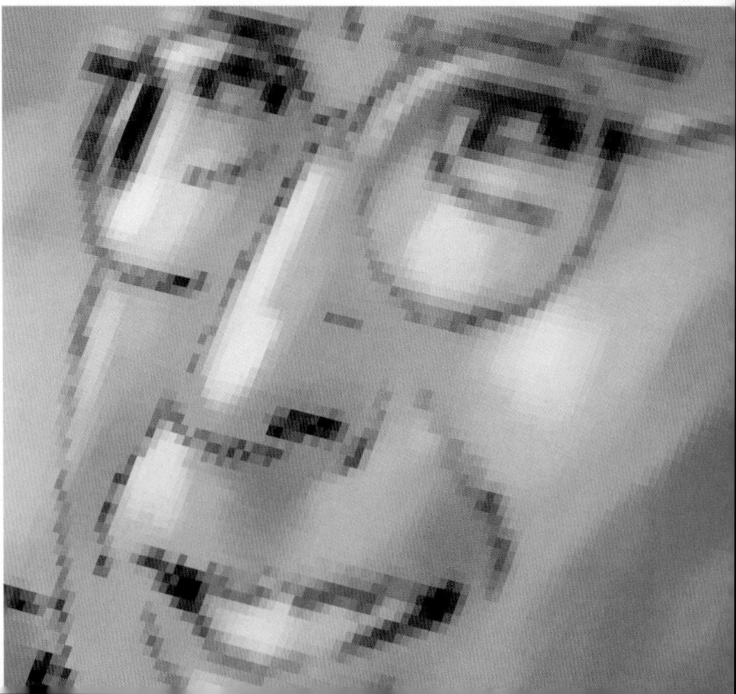

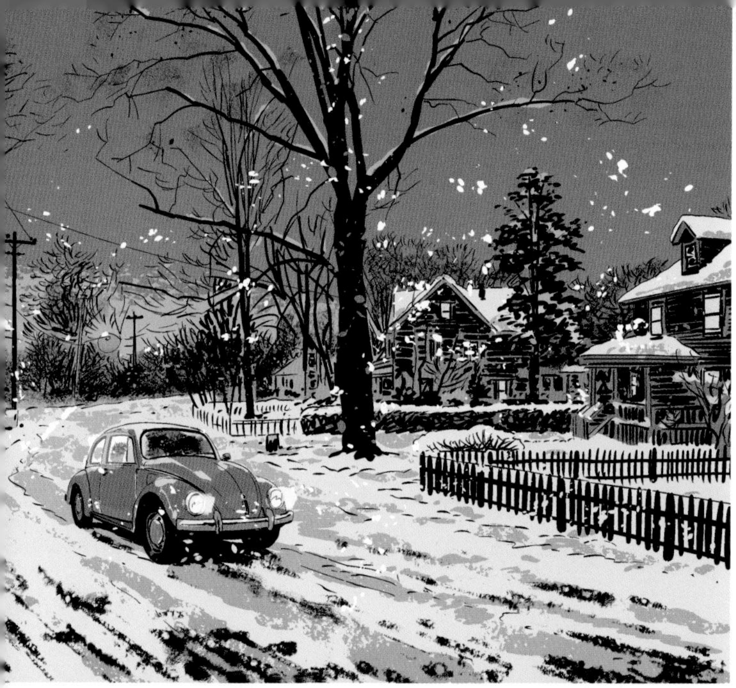

And by then I knew what the poor kid had been telling me.

That his older brother was ***molesting*** him.

And he was so young and naïve that he didn't even get that it was ***bad.***

But later, obviously, he got that.

Later it destroyed him.

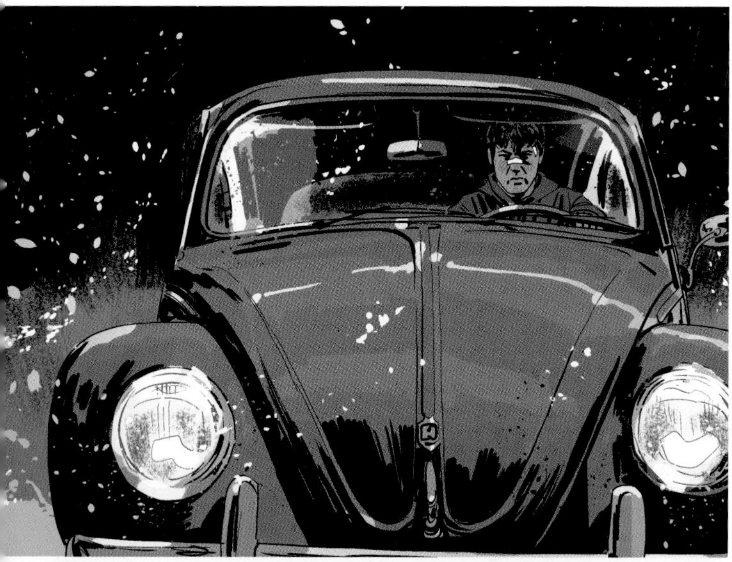

So, why didn't I go ***tell*** anyone about this back then?

Because who's gonna believe some ***tenth grader*** about something that happened when they were a little fucking kid?

Nobody, that's who.

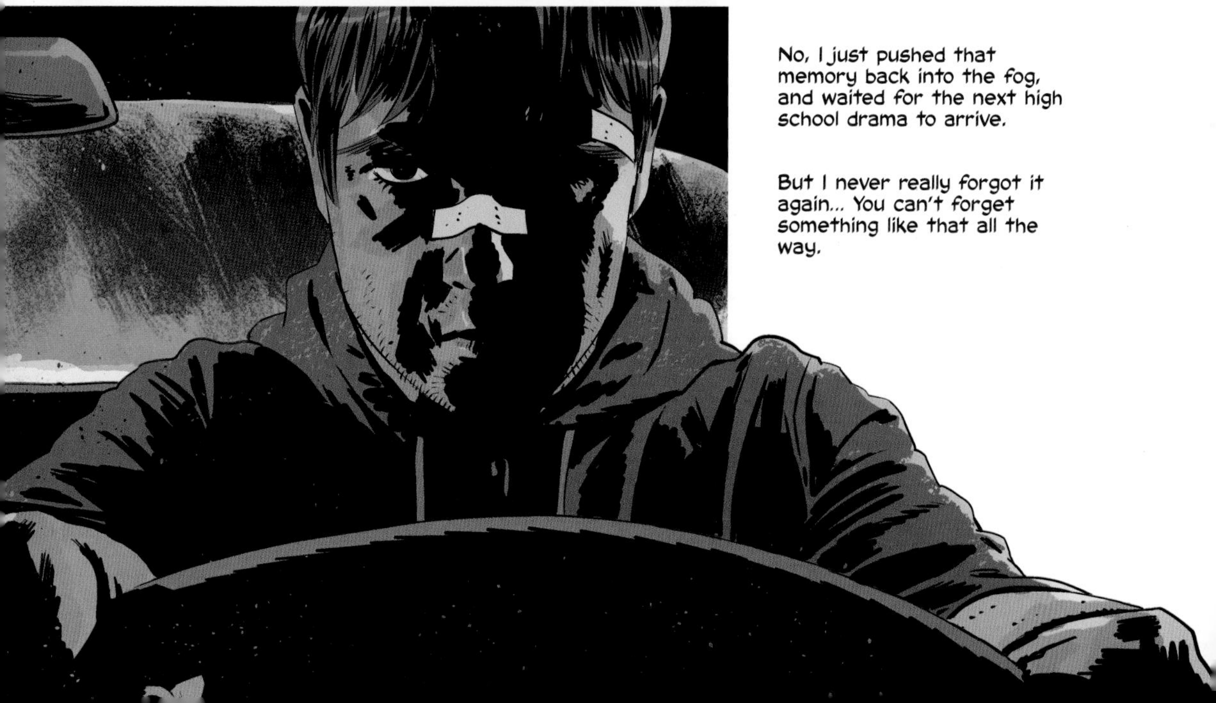

No, I just pushed that memory back into the fog, and waited for the next high school drama to arrive.

But I never really forgot it again... You can't forget something like that all the way.

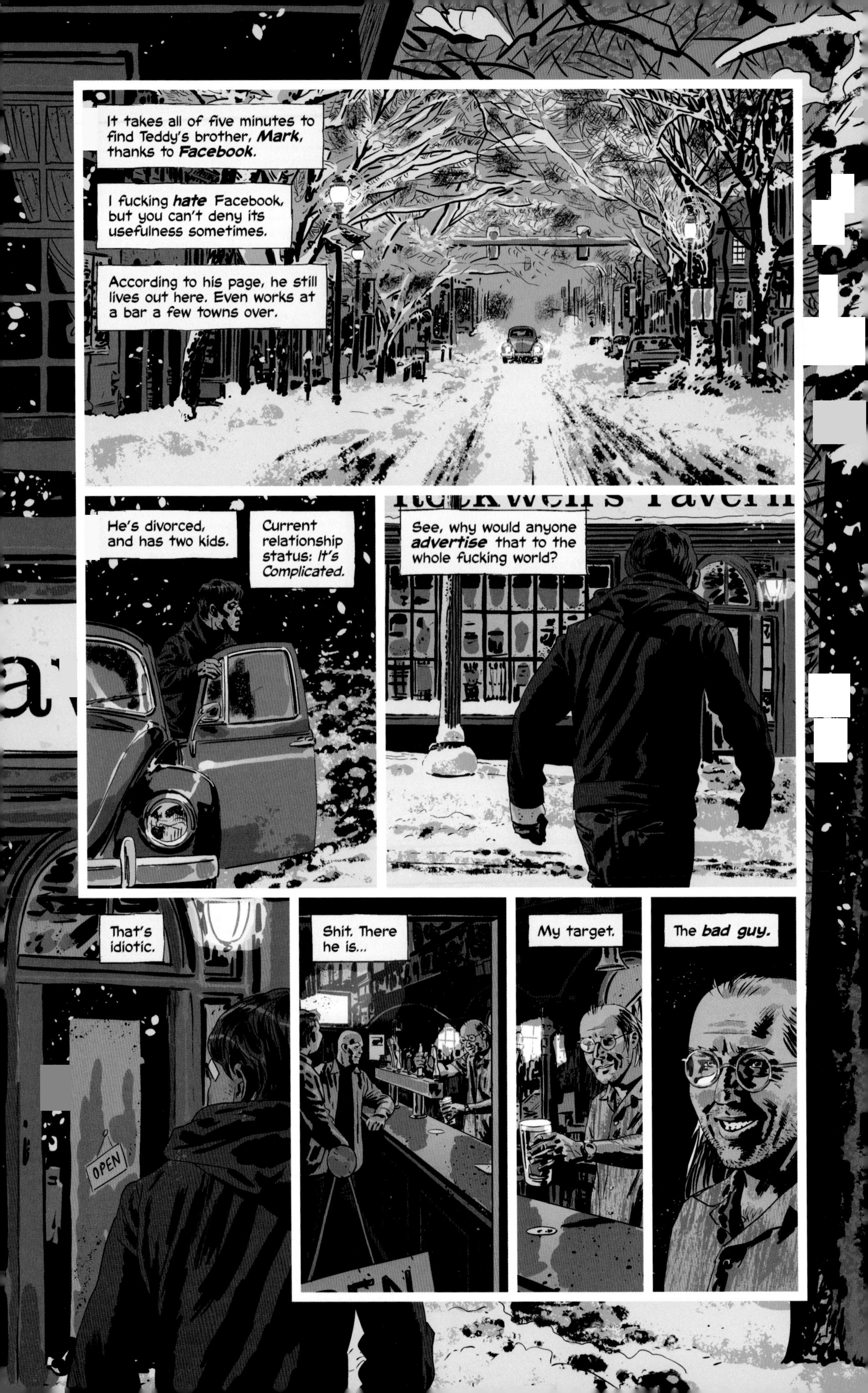
It takes all of five minutes to find Teddy's brother, ***Mark***, thanks to ***Facebook***.
I fucking ***hate*** Facebook, but you can't deny its usefulness sometimes.
According to his page, he still lives out here. Even works at a bar a few towns over.
He's divorced, and has two kids.
Current relationship status: *It's Complicated.*
See, why would anyone ***advertise*** that to the whole fucking world?
That's idiotic.
OPEN
Shit. There he is...
My target.
The ***bad guy.***

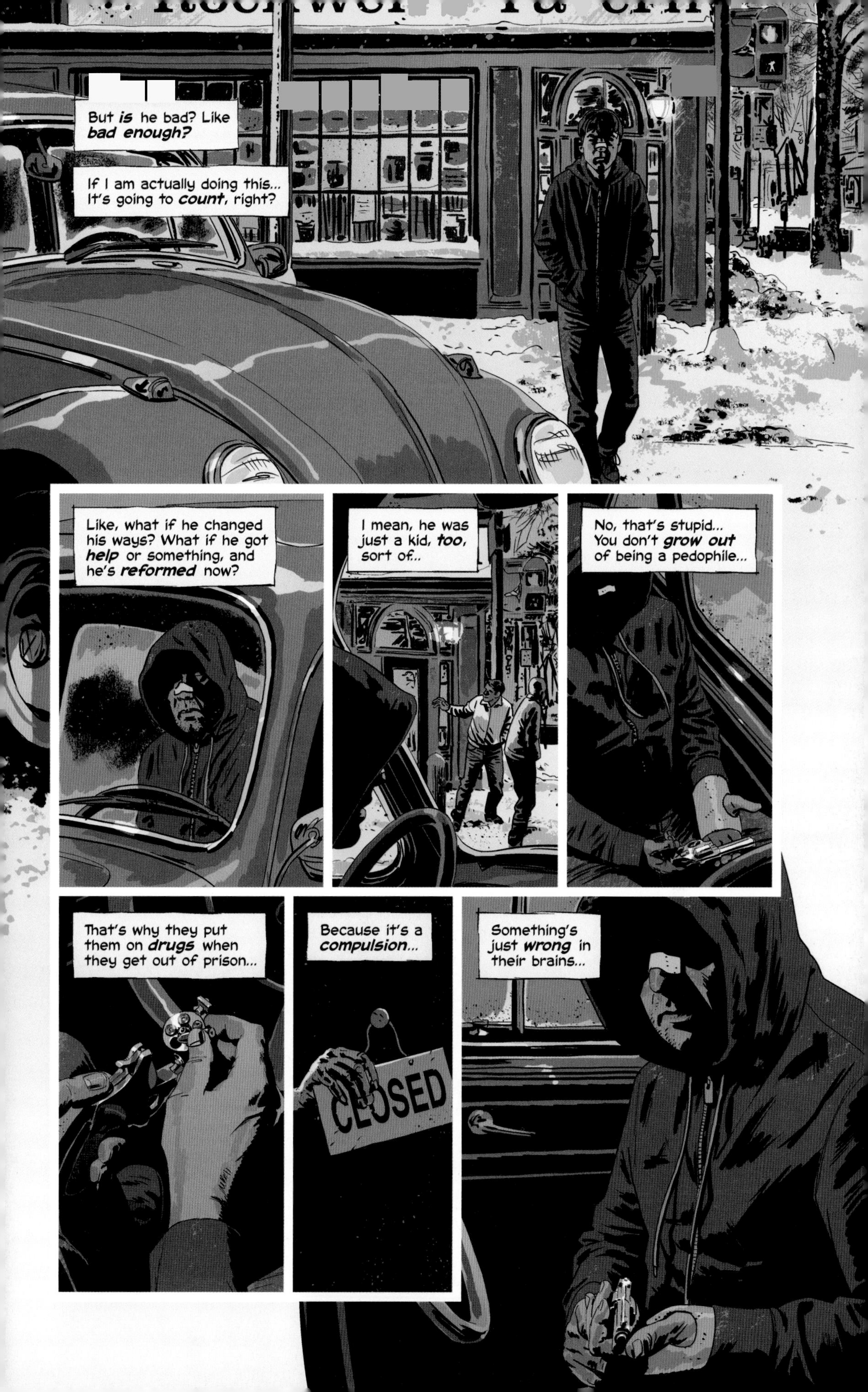
But *is* he bad? Like *bad enough?*
If I am actually doing this... It's going to *count*, right?
Like, what if he changed his ways? What if he got *help* or something, and he's *reformed* now?
I mean, he was just a kid, *too*, sort of...
No, that's stupid... You don't *grow out* of being a pedophile...
That's why they put them on *drugs* when they get out of prison...
Because it's a *compulsion*...
CLOSED
Something's just *wrong* in their brains...

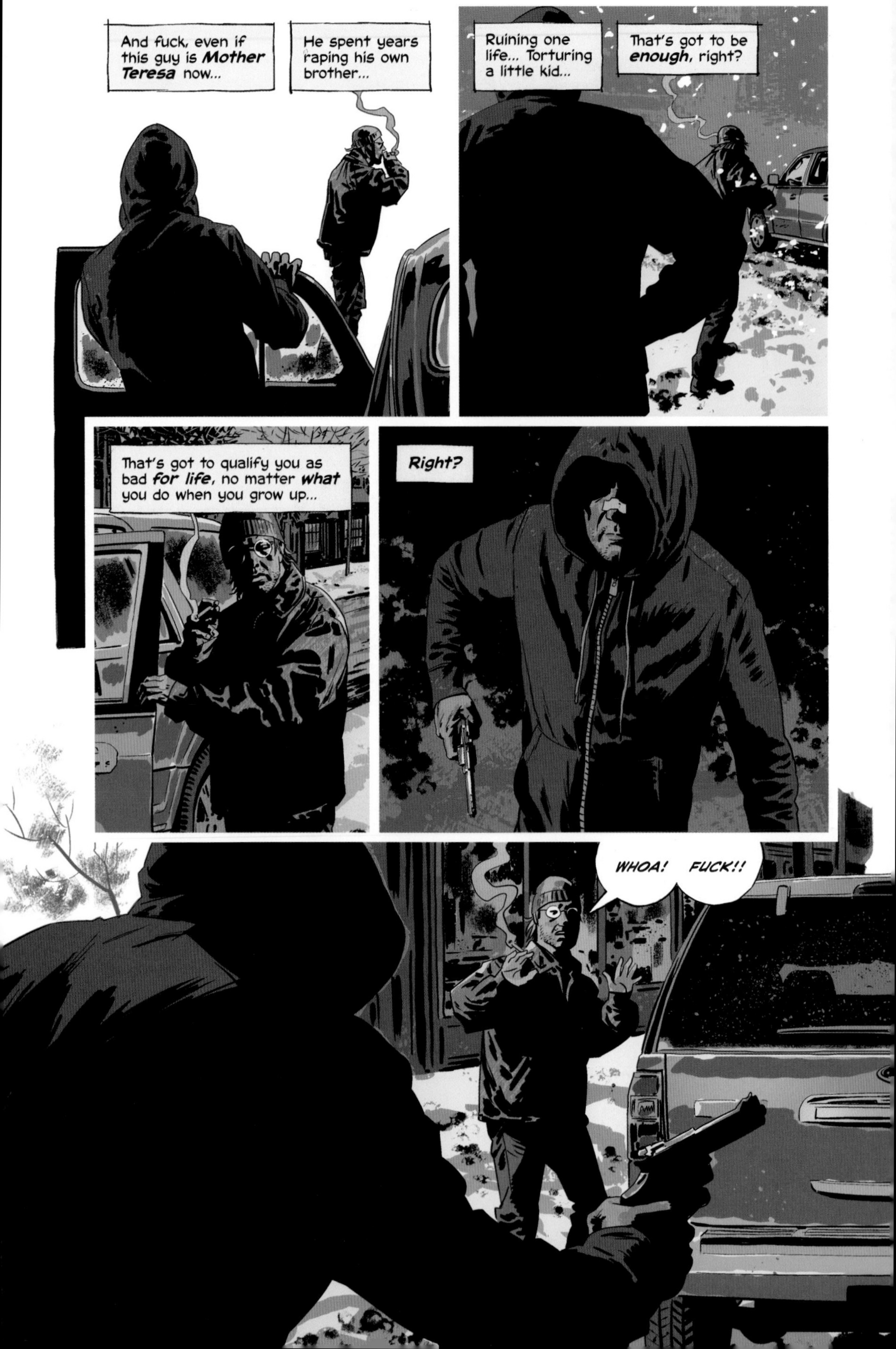
And fuck, even if this guy is ***Mother Teresa*** now...
He spent years raping his own brother...
Ruining one life... Torturing a little kid...
That's got to be ***enough***, right?
That's got to qualify you as bad ***for life***, no matter ***what*** you do when you grow up...
Right?
WHOA! FUCK!!

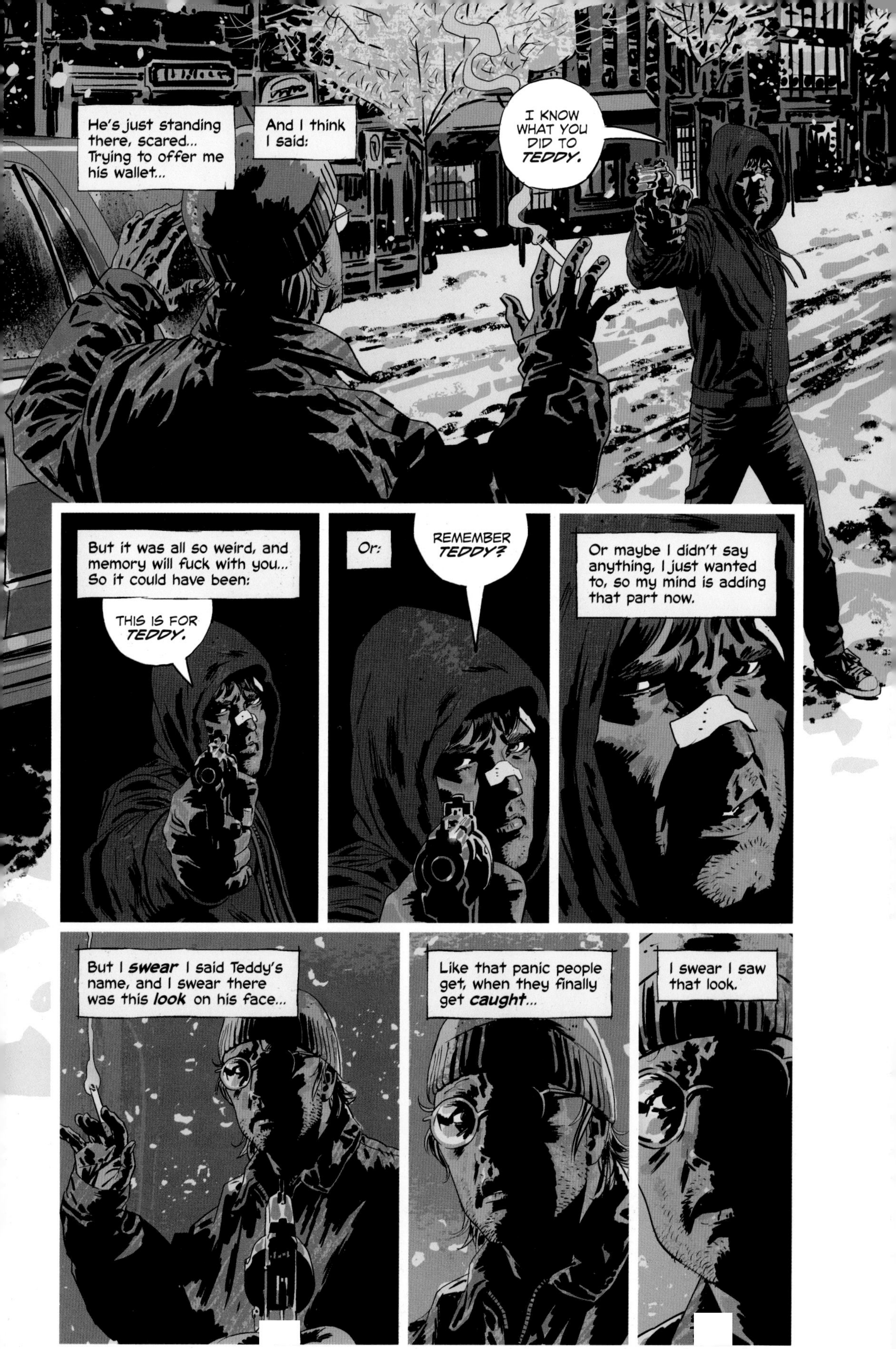
He's just standing there, scared... Trying to offer me his wallet...
And I think I said:
I KNOW WHAT YOU DID TO *TEDDY.*
But it was all so weird, and memory will fuck with you... So it could have been:
THIS IS FOR *TEDDY.*
Or:
REMEMBER *TEDDY?*
Or maybe I didn't say anything, I just wanted to, so my mind is adding that part now.
But I ***swear*** I said Teddy's name, and I swear there was this ***look*** on his face...
Like that panic people get, when they finally get ***caught***...
I swear I saw that look.

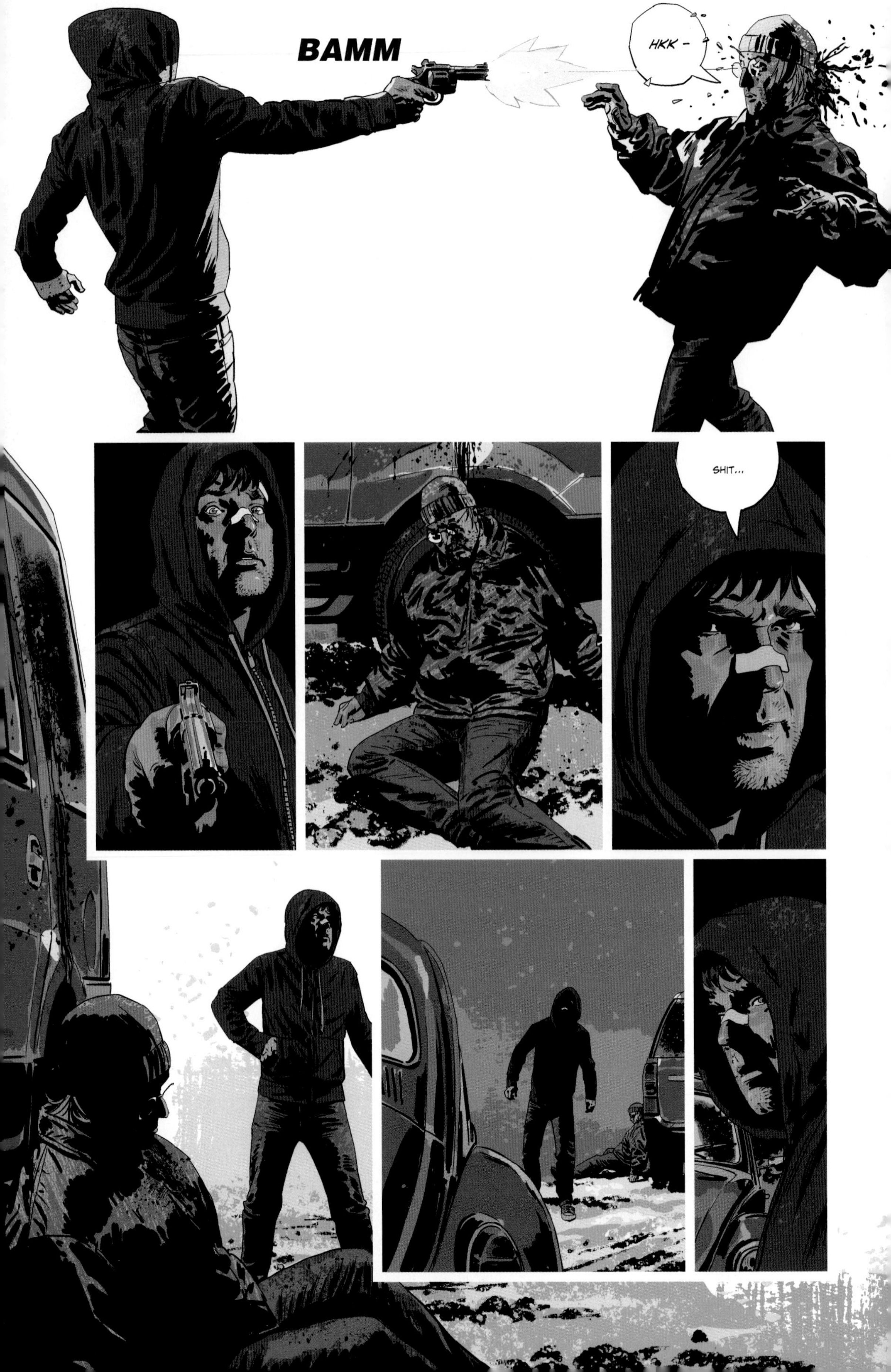
BAMM
HKK -
SHIT...

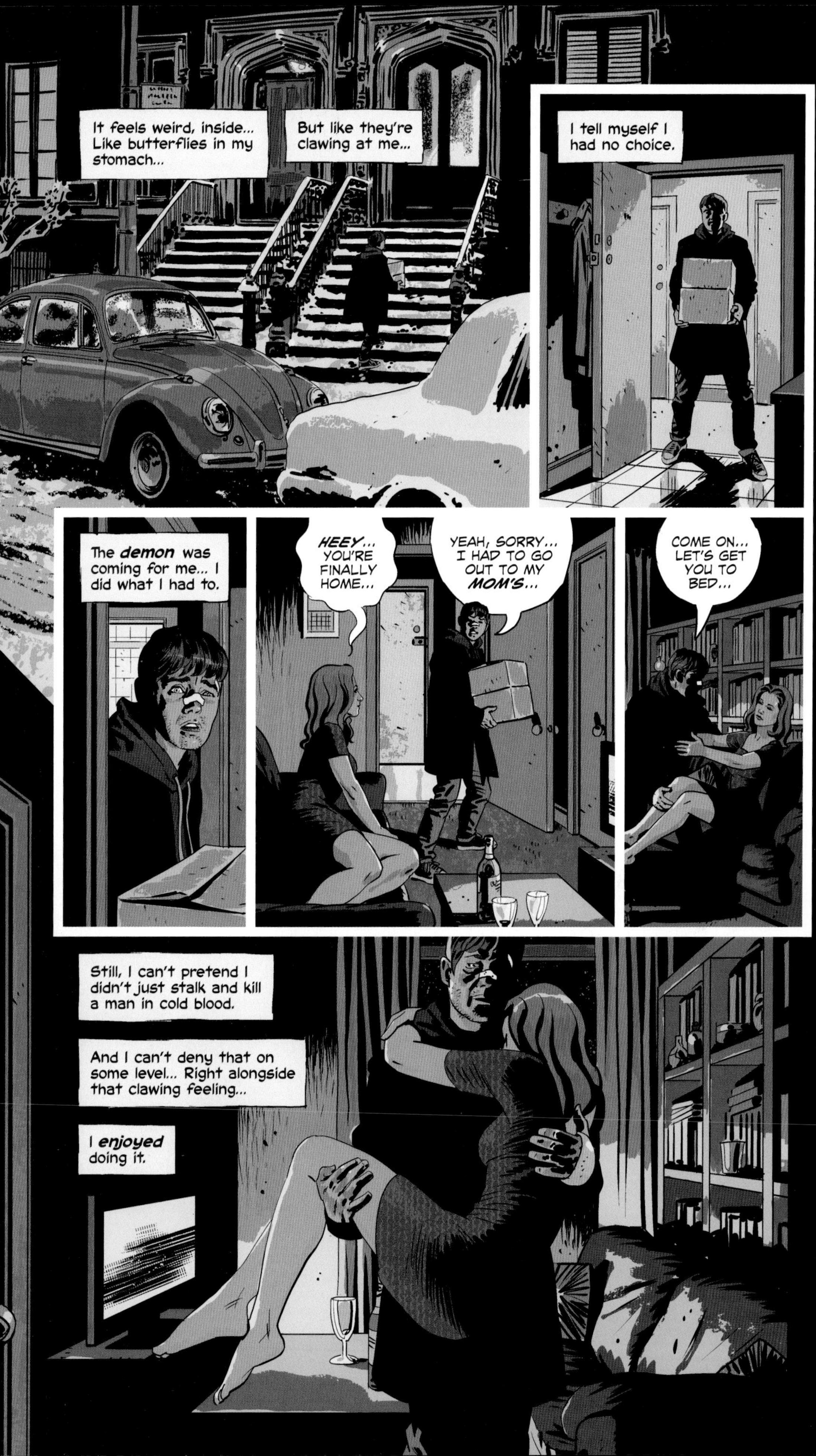
It feels weird, inside... Like butterflies in my stomach...
But like they're clawing at me...
I tell myself I had no choice.
The *demon* was coming for me... I did what I had to.
HEEY... YOU'RE FINALLY HOME...
YEAH, SORRY... I HAD TO GO OUT TO MY *MOM'S*...
COME ON... LET'S GET YOU TO BED...
Still, I can't pretend I didn't just stalk and kill a man in cold blood.
And I can't deny that on some level... Right alongside that clawing feeling...
I *enjoyed* doing it.

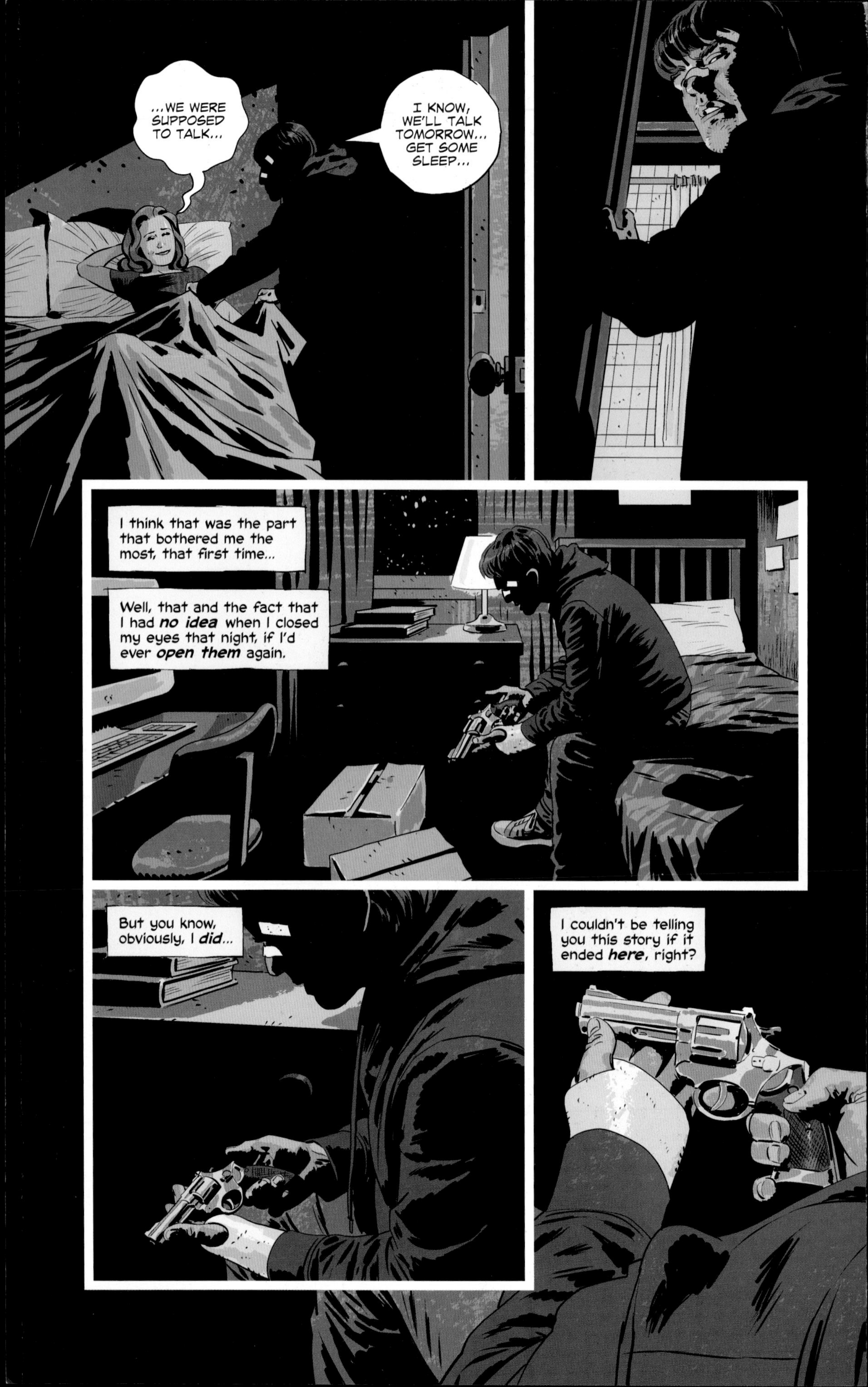
...WE WERE SUPPOSED TO TALK...
I KNOW, WE'LL TALK TOMORROW... GET SOME SLEEP...
I think that was the part that bothered me the most, that first time...
Well, that and the fact that I had *no idea* when I closed my eyes that night, if I'd ever *open them* again.
But you know, obviously, I *did*...
I couldn't be telling you this story if it ended *here*, right?

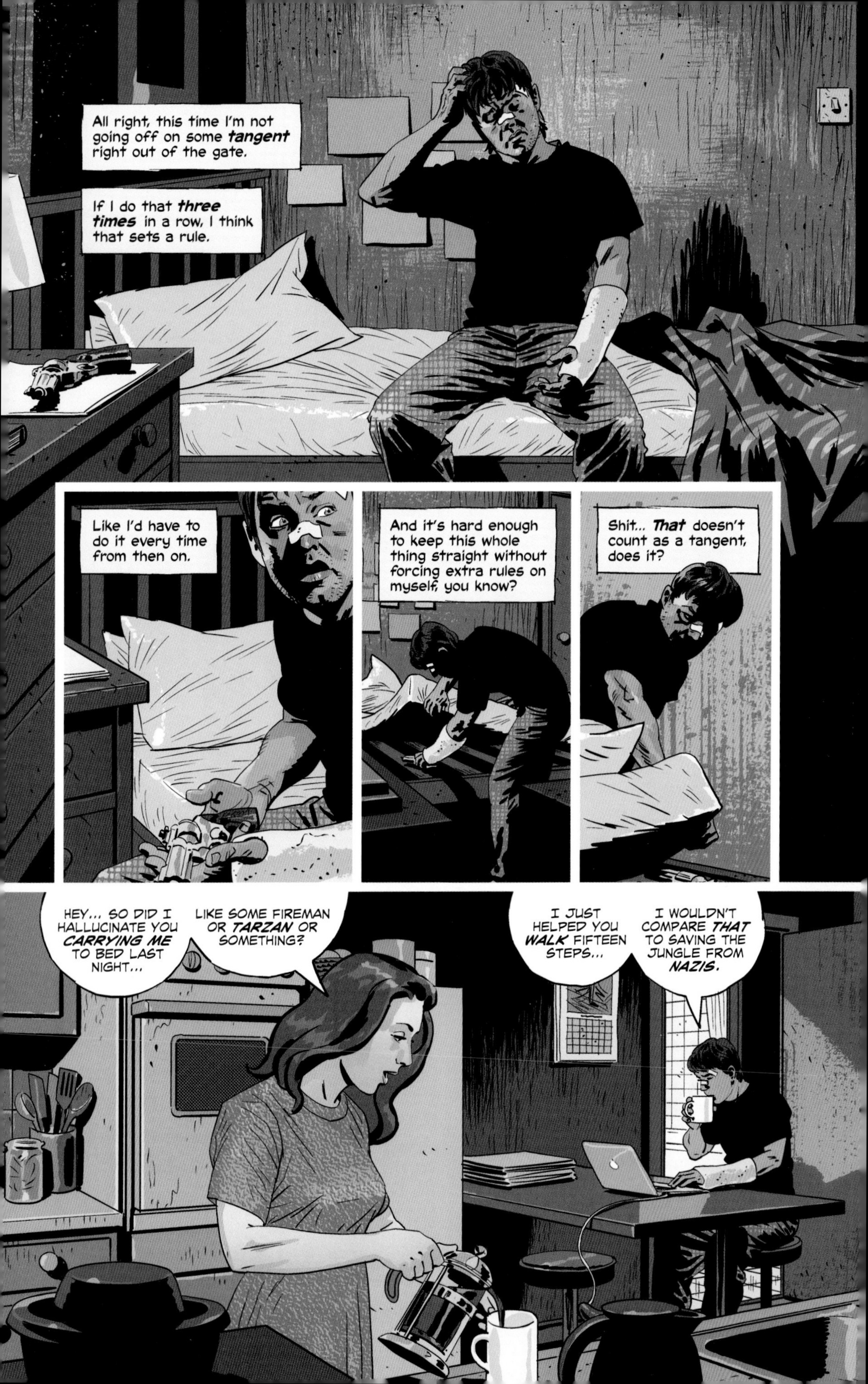
All right, this time I'm not going off on some *tangent* right out of the gate.
If I do that *three times* in a row, I think that sets a rule.
Like I'd have to do it every time from then on.
And it's hard enough to keep this whole thing straight without forcing extra rules on myself, you know?
Shit... *That* doesn't count as a tangent, does it?
HEY... SO DID I HALLUCINATE YOU *CARRYING ME* TO BED LAST NIGHT...
LIKE SOME FIREMAN OR *TARZAN* OR SOMETHING?
I JUST HELPED YOU *WALK* FIFTEEN STEPS...
I WOULDN'T COMPARE *THAT* TO SAVING THE JUNGLE FROM *NAZIS*.

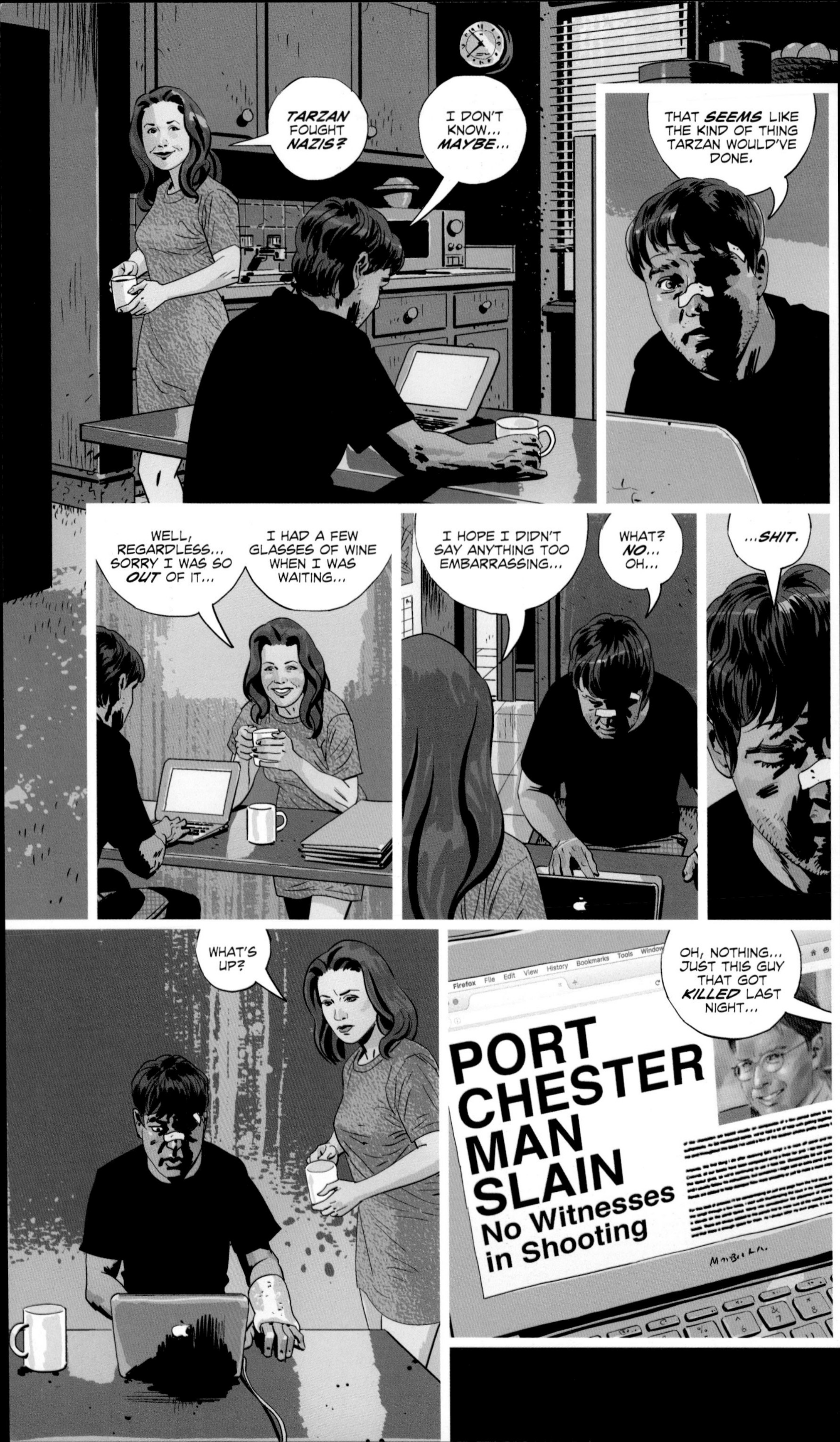
TARZAN FOUGHT NAZIS?
I DON'T KNOW... MAYBE...
THAT SEEMS LIKE THE KIND OF THING TARZAN WOULD'VE DONE.
WELL, REGARDLESS... SORRY I WAS SO OUT OF IT...
I HAD A FEW GLASSES OF WINE WHEN I WAS WAITING...
I HOPE I DIDN'T SAY ANYTHING TOO EMBARRASSING...
WHAT? NO... OH...
...SHIT.
WHAT'S UP?
Firefox File Edit View History Bookmarks Tools Window
OH, NOTHING... JUST THIS GUY THAT GOT KILLED LAST NIGHT...
PORT CHESTER MAN SLAIN
No Witnesses in Shooting

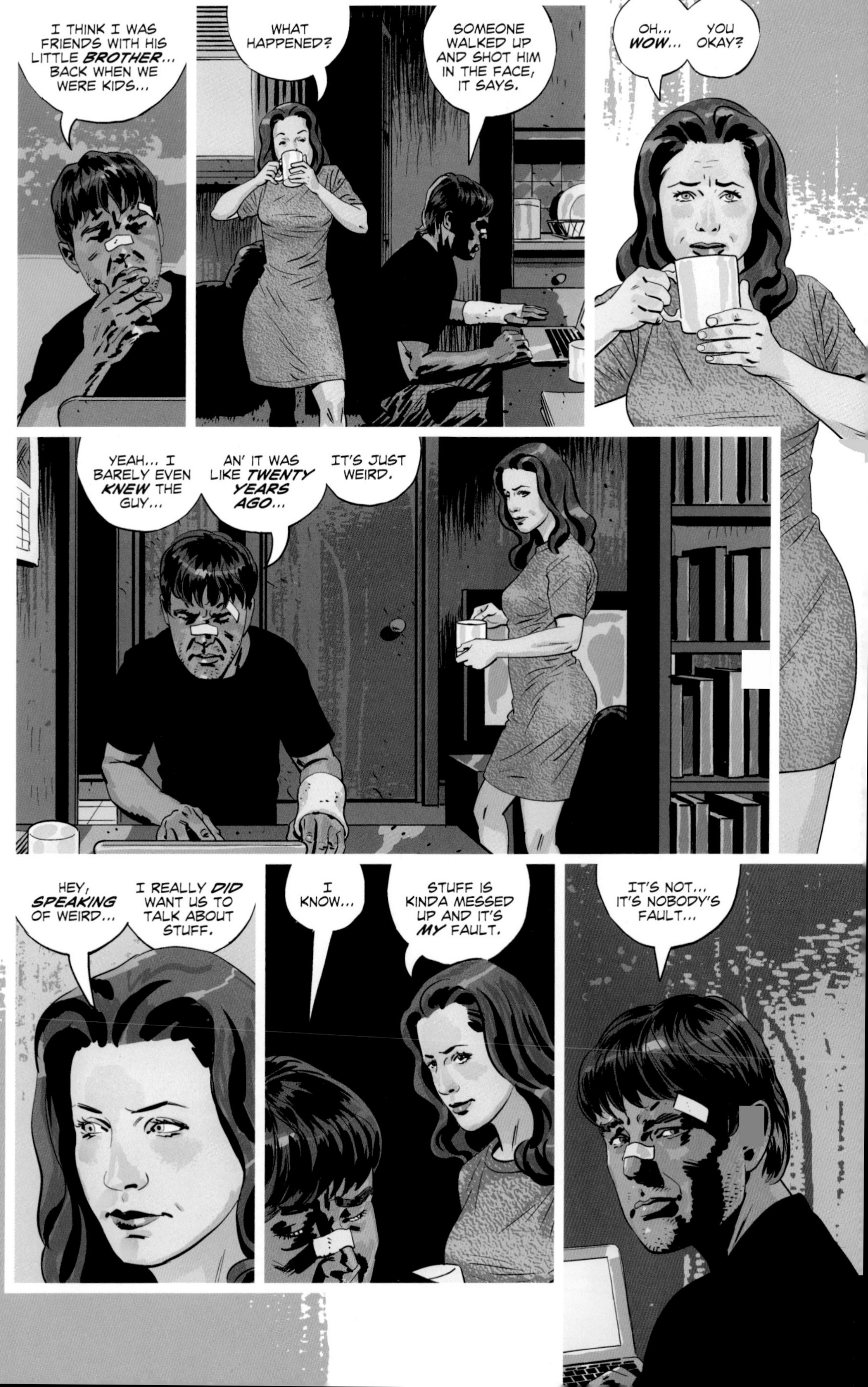
I THINK I WAS FRIENDS WITH HIS LITTLE BROTHER... BACK WHEN WE WERE KIDS...
WHAT HAPPENED?
SOMEONE WALKED UP AND SHOT HIM IN THE FACE, IT SAYS.
OH... WOW...
YOU OKAY?
YEAH... I BARELY EVEN KNEW THE GUY...
AN' IT WAS LIKE TWENTY YEARS AGO...
IT'S JUST WEIRD.
HEY, SPEAKING OF WEIRD...
I REALLY DID WANT US TO TALK ABOUT STUFF.
I KNOW...
STUFF IS KINDA MESSED UP AND IT'S MY FAULT.
IT'S NOT... IT'S NOBODY'S FAULT...

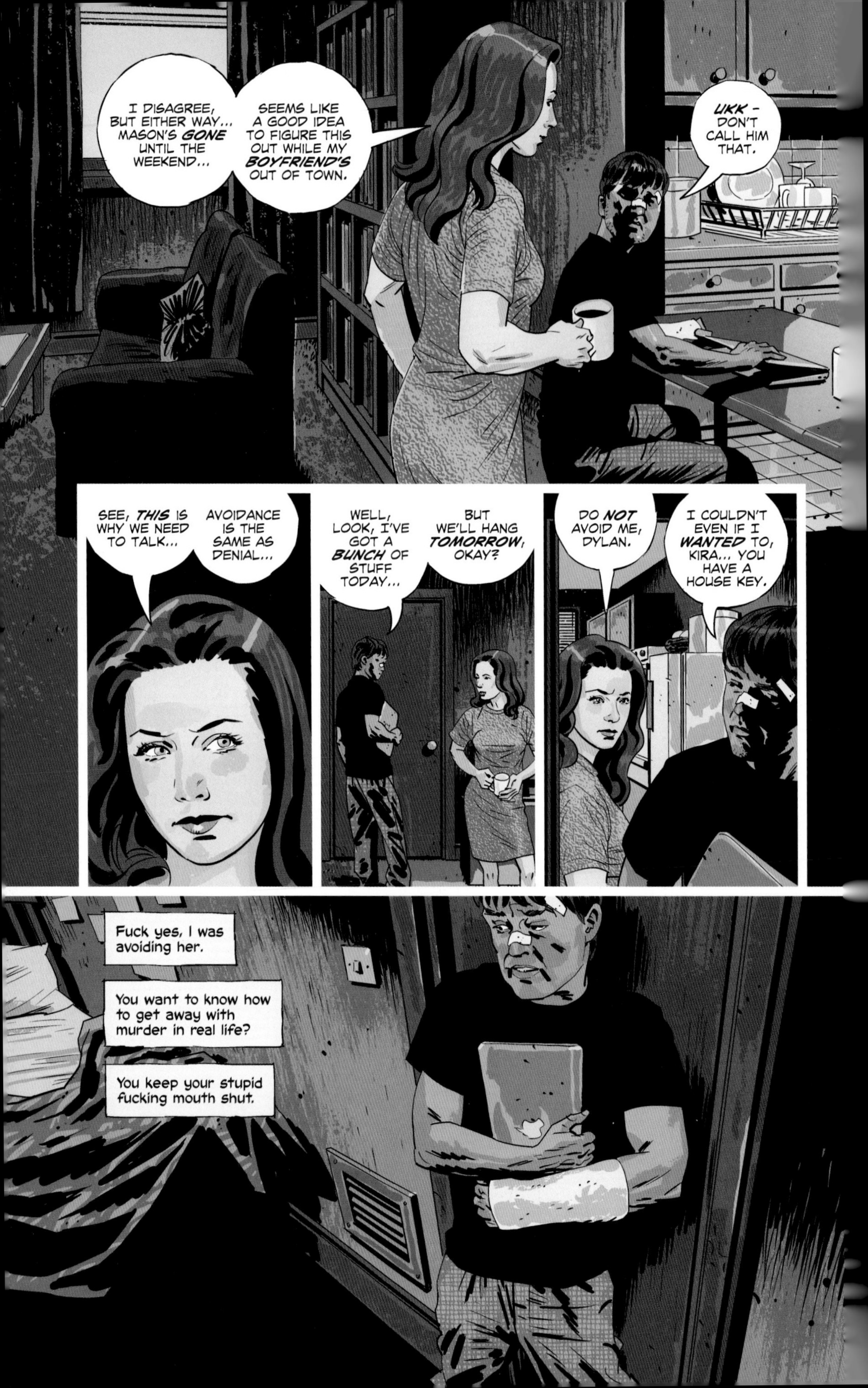
I DISAGREE, BUT EITHER WAY... MASON'S GONE UNTIL THE WEEKEND...
SEEMS LIKE A GOOD IDEA TO FIGURE THIS OUT WHILE MY BOYFRIEND'S OUT OF TOWN.
UKK - DON'T CALL HIM THAT.
SEE, THIS IS WHY WE NEED TO TALK...
AVOIDANCE IS THE SAME AS DENIAL...
WELL, LOOK, I'VE GOT A BUNCH OF STUFF TODAY...
BUT WE'LL HANG TOMORROW, OKAY?
DO NOT AVOID ME, DYLAN.
I COULDN'T EVEN IF I WANTED TO, KIRA... YOU HAVE A HOUSE KEY.
Fuck yes, I was avoiding her.
You want to know how to get away with murder in real life?
You keep your stupid fucking mouth shut.

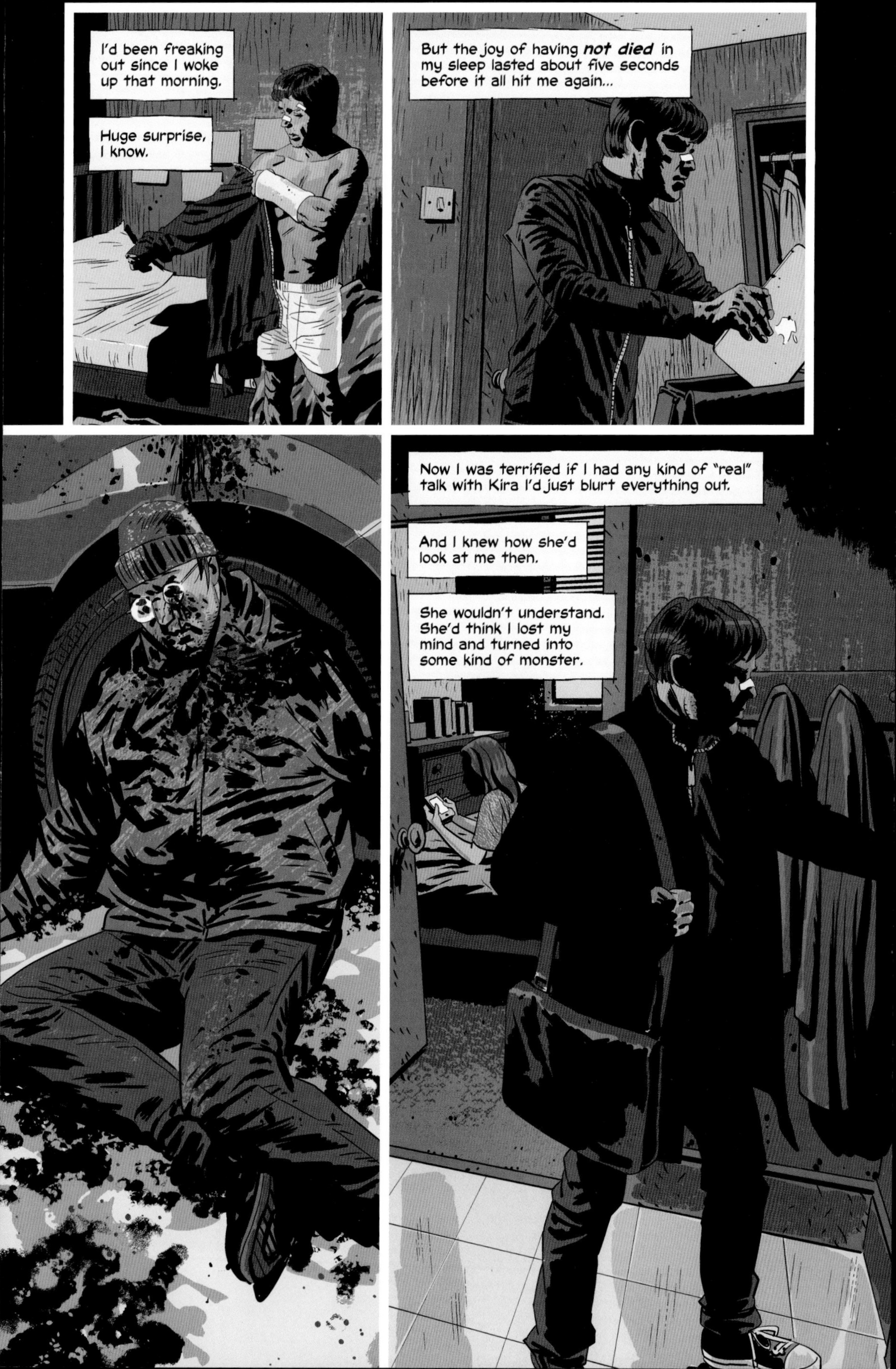
I'd been freaking out since I woke up that morning.
Huge surprise, I know.
But the joy of having ***not died*** in my sleep lasted about five seconds before it all hit me again...
Now I was terrified if I had any kind of "real" talk with Kira I'd just blurt everything out.
And I knew how she'd look at me then.
She wouldn't understand. She'd think I lost my mind and turned into some kind of monster.

Then she'd turn me in, for my own good.

She'd be crying when she called the police, but she ***would*** call them... And shit, maybe she'd be ***right*** to.

That's what I was thinking just then.

Or... that's what ***half*** of me was thinking. And the ***other half*** was arguing with it.

See, I kept having this sick feeling that I might have ***killed someone*** for no reason.

Like, think about it for a second. There had to be at least ***some*** possibility that I hallucinated that demon... Didn't there? And if I did, if it wasn't actually real, that meant my head was ***fucked***, right?

Which meant the way I remembered that day with Teddy could be ***wrong***, too... Right?

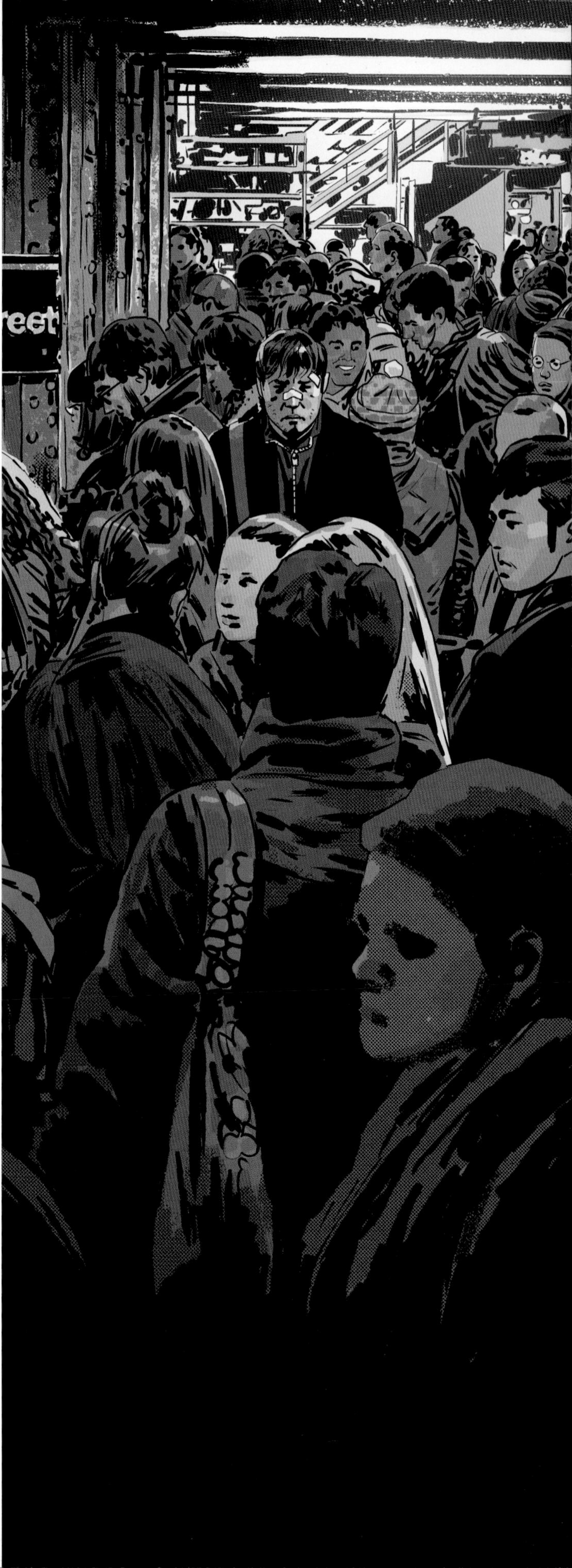

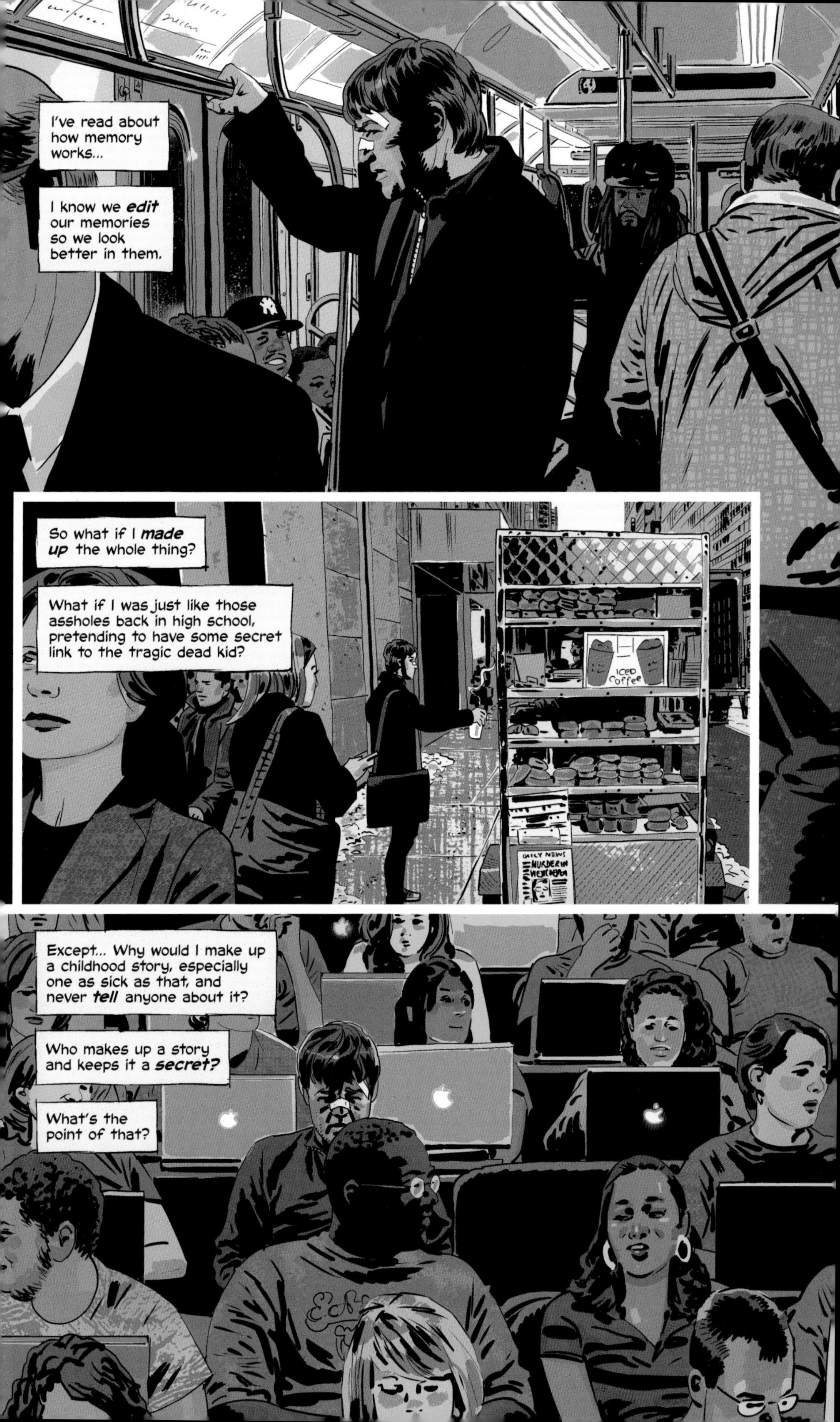
I've read about how memory works...
I know we *edit* our memories so we look better in them.
So what if I *made up* the whole thing?
What if I was just like those assholes back in high school, pretending to have some secret link to the tragic dead kid?
ICED Coffee
DAILY NEWS
MURDER IN WESTCHESTER
Except... Why would I make up a childhood story, especially one as sick as that, and never *tell* anyone about it?
Who makes up a story and keeps it a *secret?*
What's the point of that?

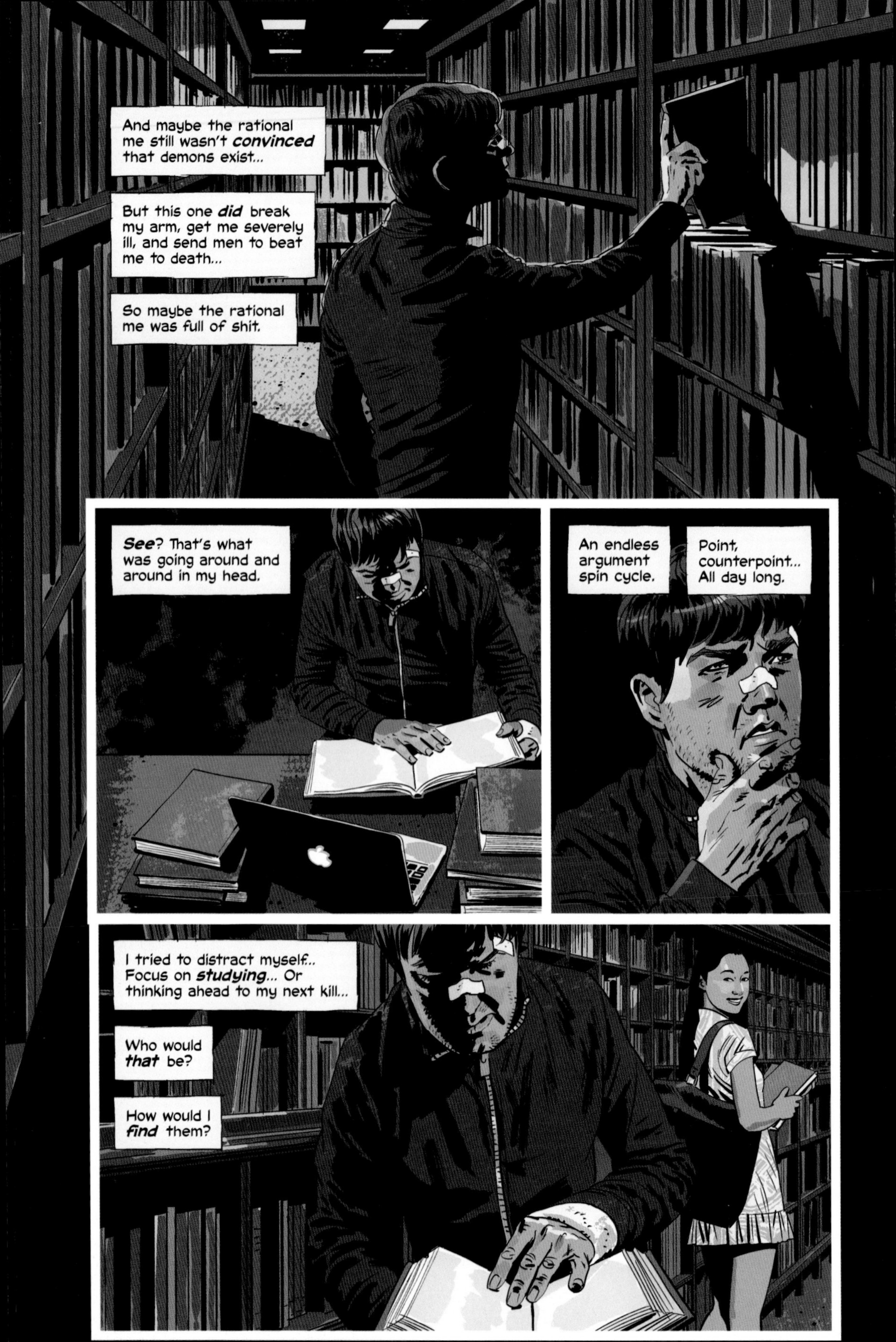
And maybe the rational me still wasn't *convinced* that demons exist...
But this one *did* break my arm, get me severely ill, and send men to beat me to death...
So maybe the rational me was full of shit.
See? That's what was going around and around in my head.
An endless argument spin cycle.
Point, counterpoint... All day long.
I tried to distract myself.. Focus on *studying*... Or thinking ahead to my next kill...
Who would *that* be?
How would I *find* them?

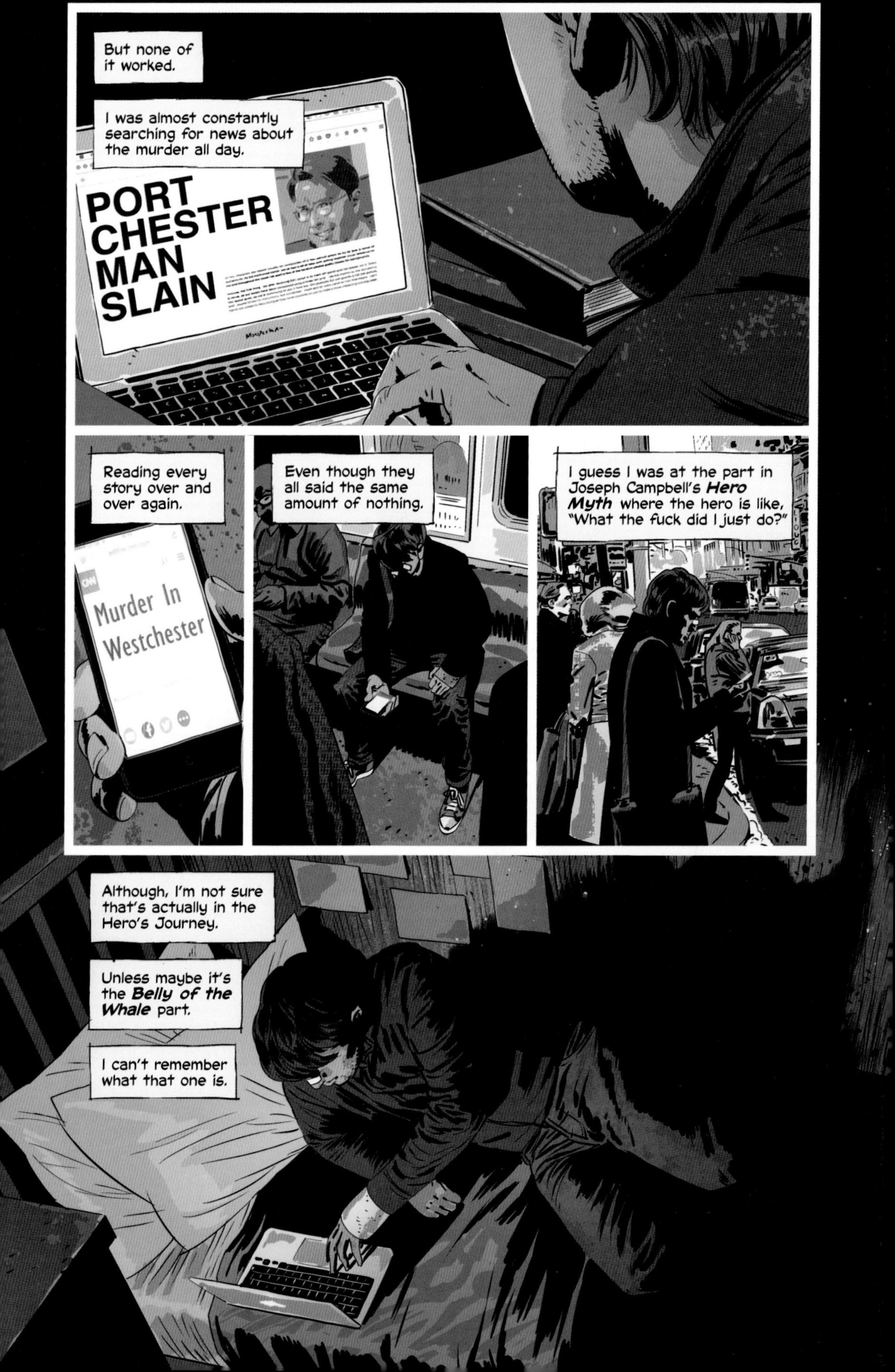
But none of it worked.
I was almost constantly searching for news about the murder all day.
PORT CHESTER MAN SLAIN
Reading every story over and over again.
Murder In Westchester
Even though they all said the same amount of nothing.
I guess I was at the part in Joseph Campbell's ***Hero Myth*** where the hero is like, "What the fuck did I just do?"
Although, I'm not sure that's actually in the Hero's Journey.
Unless maybe it's the ***Belly of the Whale*** part.
I can't remember what that one is.

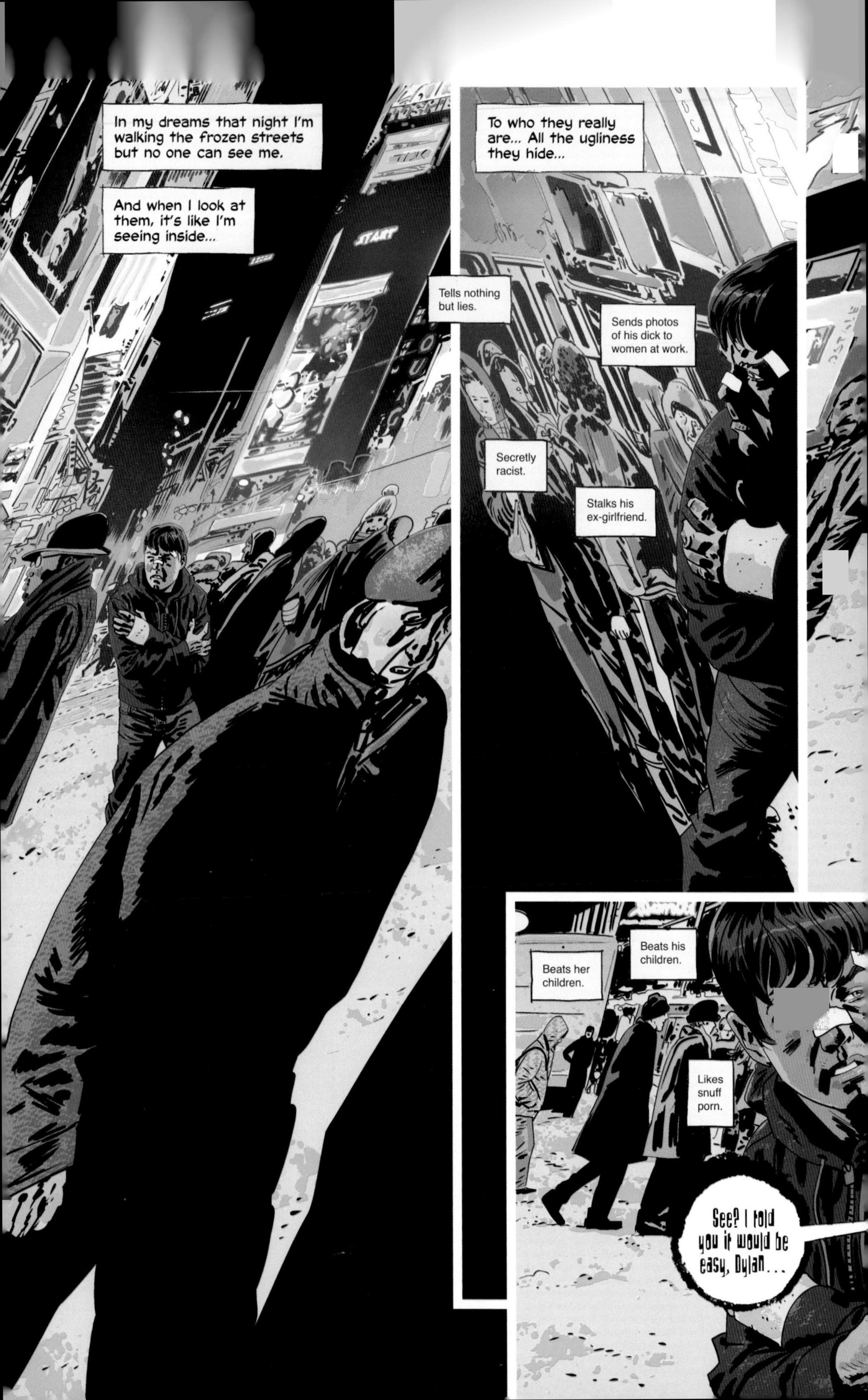
In my dreams that night I'm walking the frozen streets but no one can see me.
And when I look at them, it's like I'm seeing inside...
To who they really are... All the ugliness they hide...
Tells nothing but lies.
Sends photos of his dick to women at work.
Secretly racist.
Stalks his ex-girlfriend.
Beats her children.
Beats his children.
Likes snuff porn.
See? I told you it would be easy, Dylan...

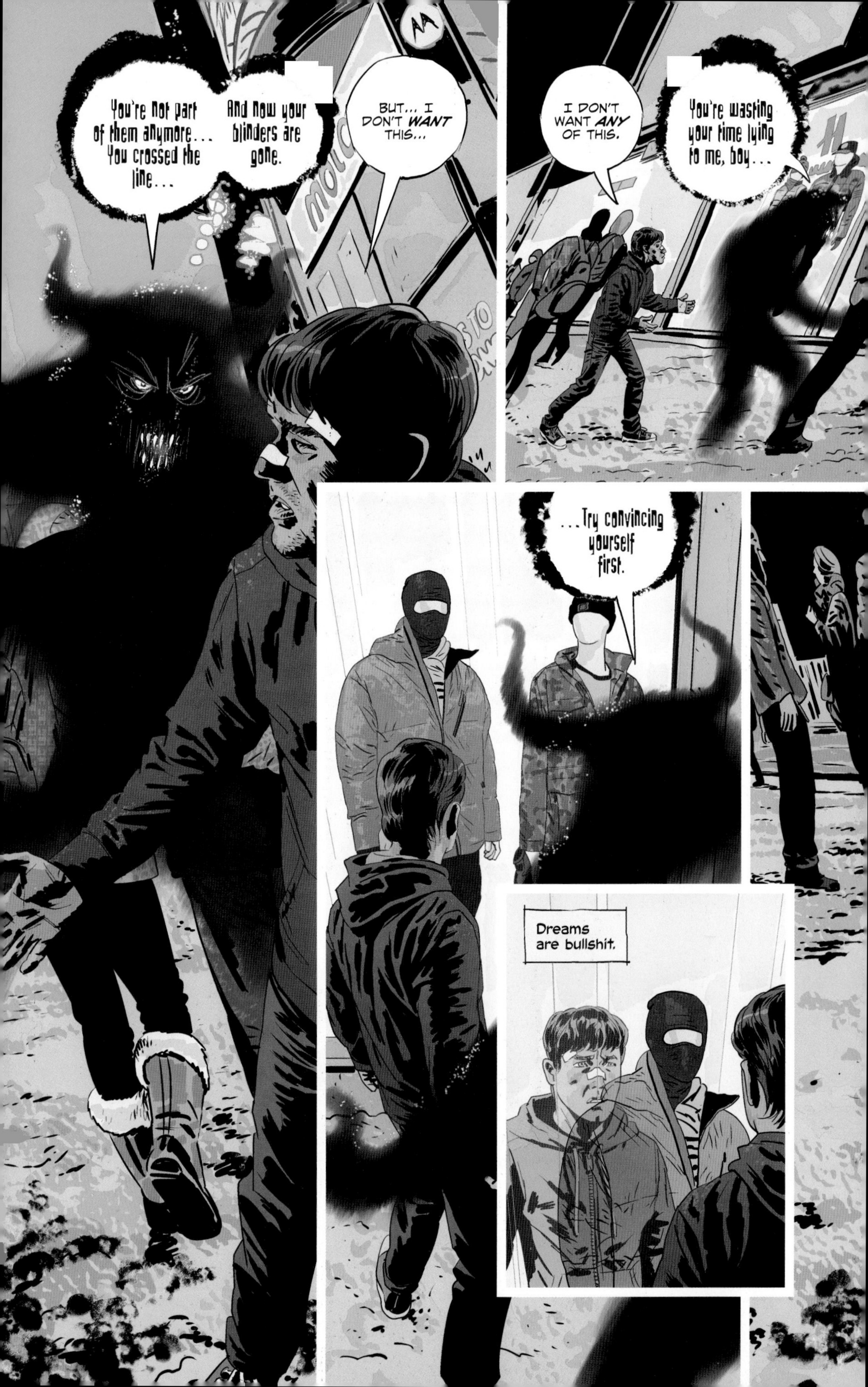
You're not part of them anymore... You crossed the line...
And now your blinders are gone.
BUT... I DON'T WANT THIS...
I DON'T WANT ANY OF THIS.
You're wasting your time lying to me, boy...
...Try convincing yourself first.
Dreams are bullshit.

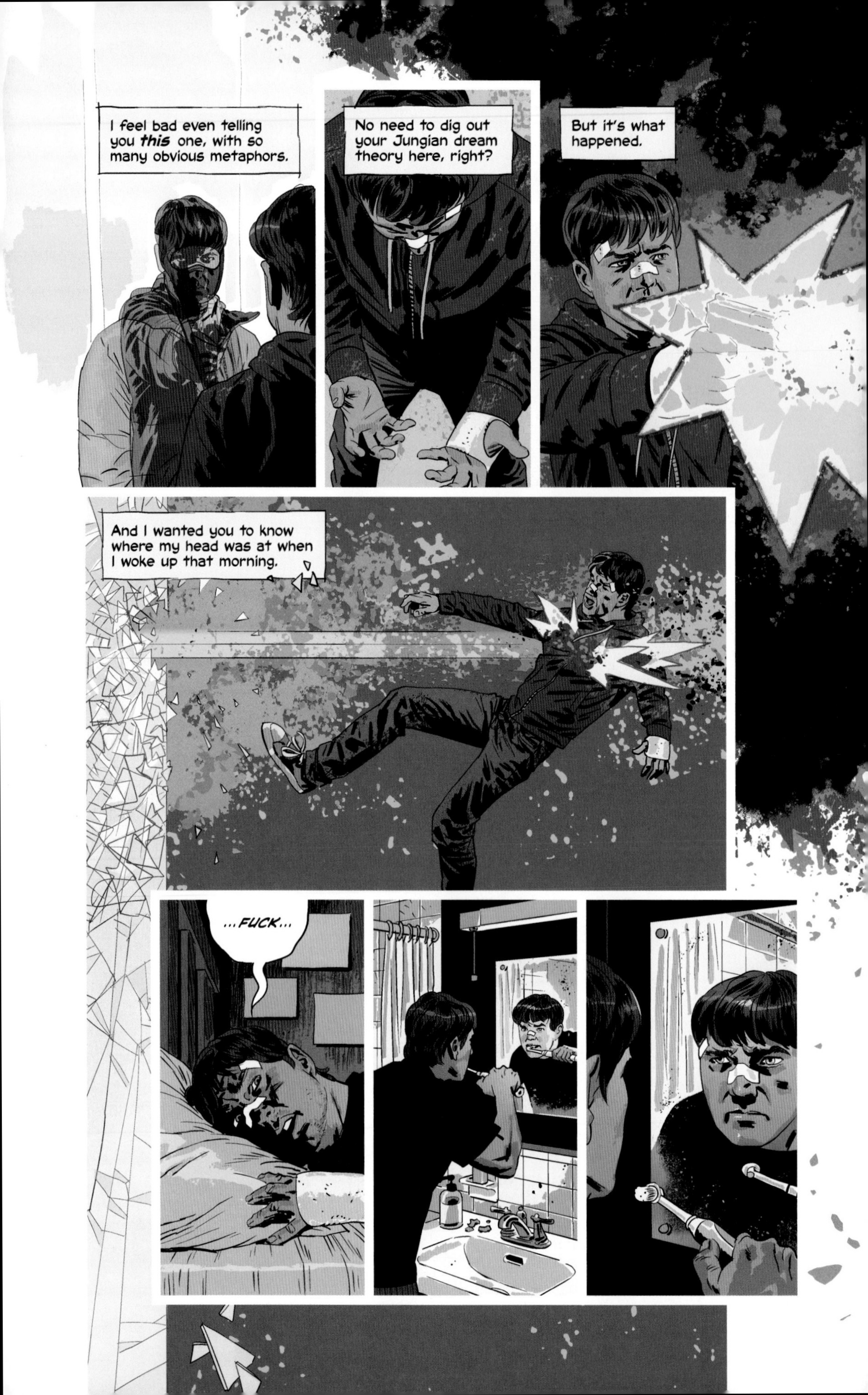
I feel bad even telling you *this* one, with so many obvious metaphors.
No need to dig out your Jungian dream theory here, right?
But it's what happened.
And I wanted you to know where my head was at when I woke up that morning.
...FUCK...

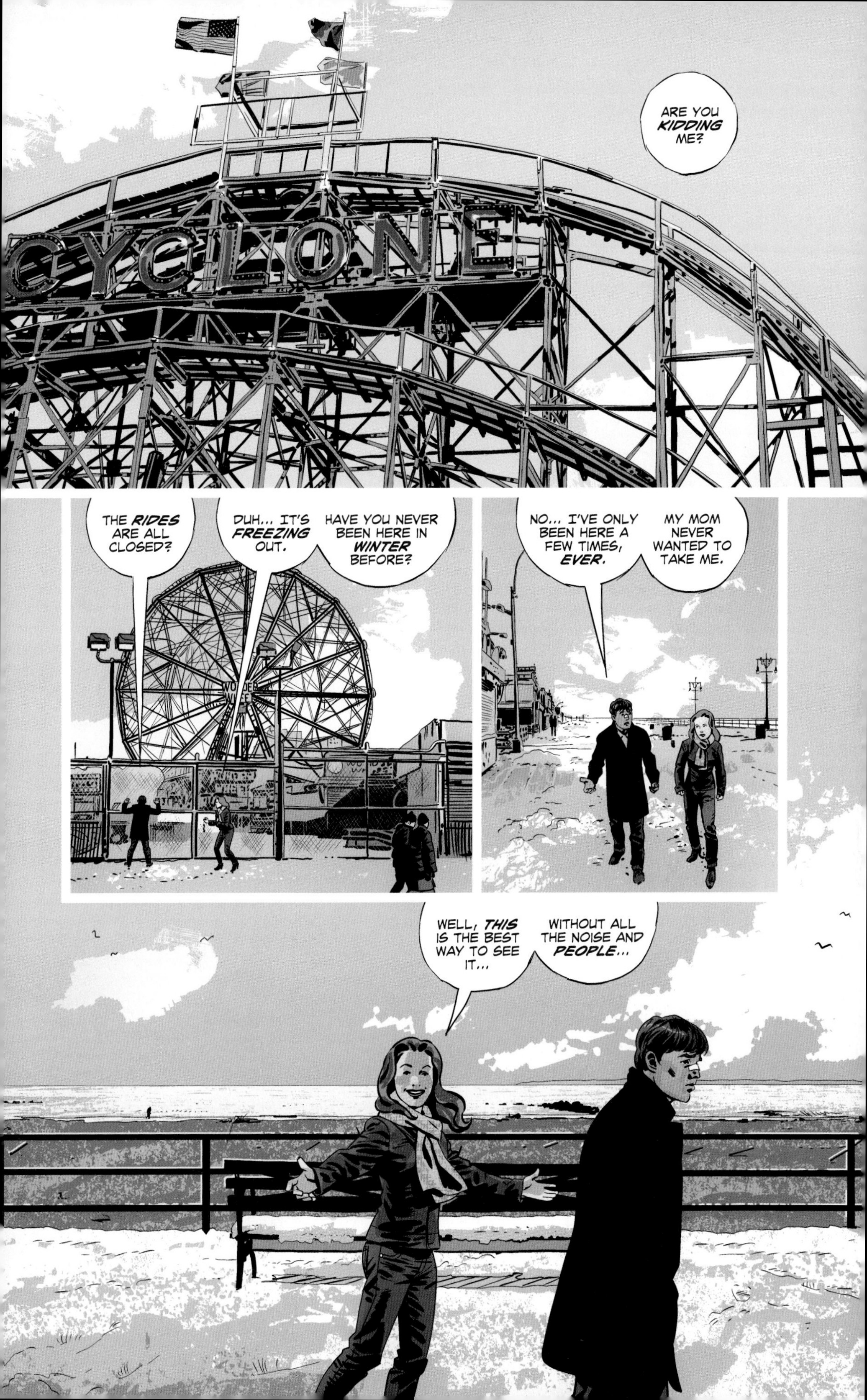
ARE YOU KIDDING ME?
CYCLONE
THE RIDES ARE ALL CLOSED?
DUH... IT'S FREEZING OUT.
HAVE YOU NEVER BEEN HERE IN WINTER BEFORE?
NO... I'VE ONLY BEEN HERE A FEW TIMES, EVER.
MY MOM NEVER WANTED TO TAKE ME.
WELL, THIS IS THE BEST WAY TO SEE IT...
WITHOUT ALL THE NOISE AND PEOPLE...

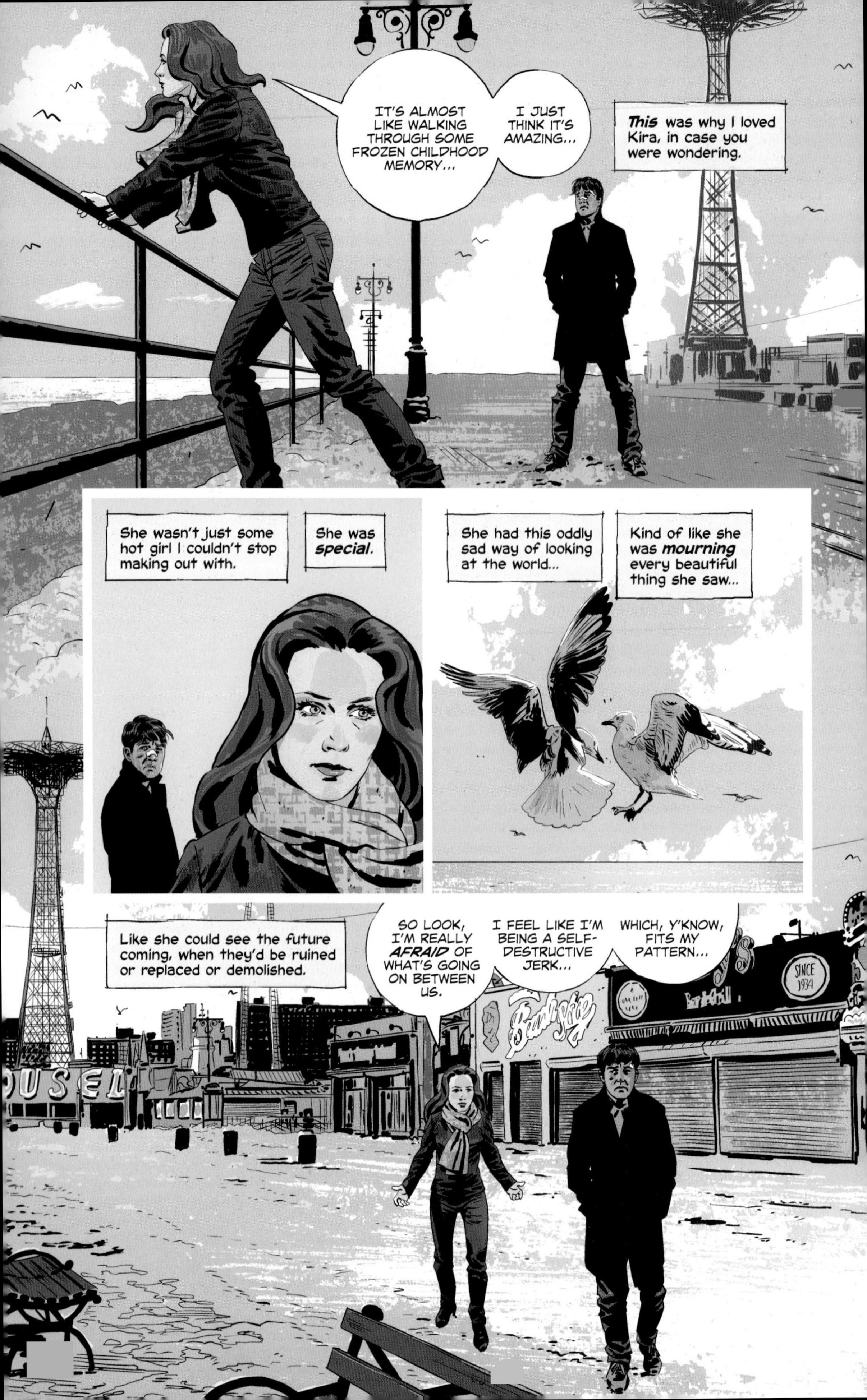

IT'S ALMOST LIKE WALKING THROUGH SOME FROZEN CHILDHOOD MEMORY...
I JUST THINK IT'S AMAZING...
This was why I loved Kira, in case you were wondering.
She wasn't just some hot girl I couldn't stop making out with.
She was special.
She had this oddly sad way of looking at the world...
Kind of like she was mourning every beautiful thing she saw...
Like she could see the future coming, when they'd be ruined or replaced or demolished.
SO LOOK, I'M REALLY AFRAID OF WHAT'S GOING ON BETWEEN US.
I FEEL LIKE I'M BEING A SELF-DESTRUCTIVE JERK...
WHICH, Y'KNOW, FITS MY PATTERN...
SINCE 1934

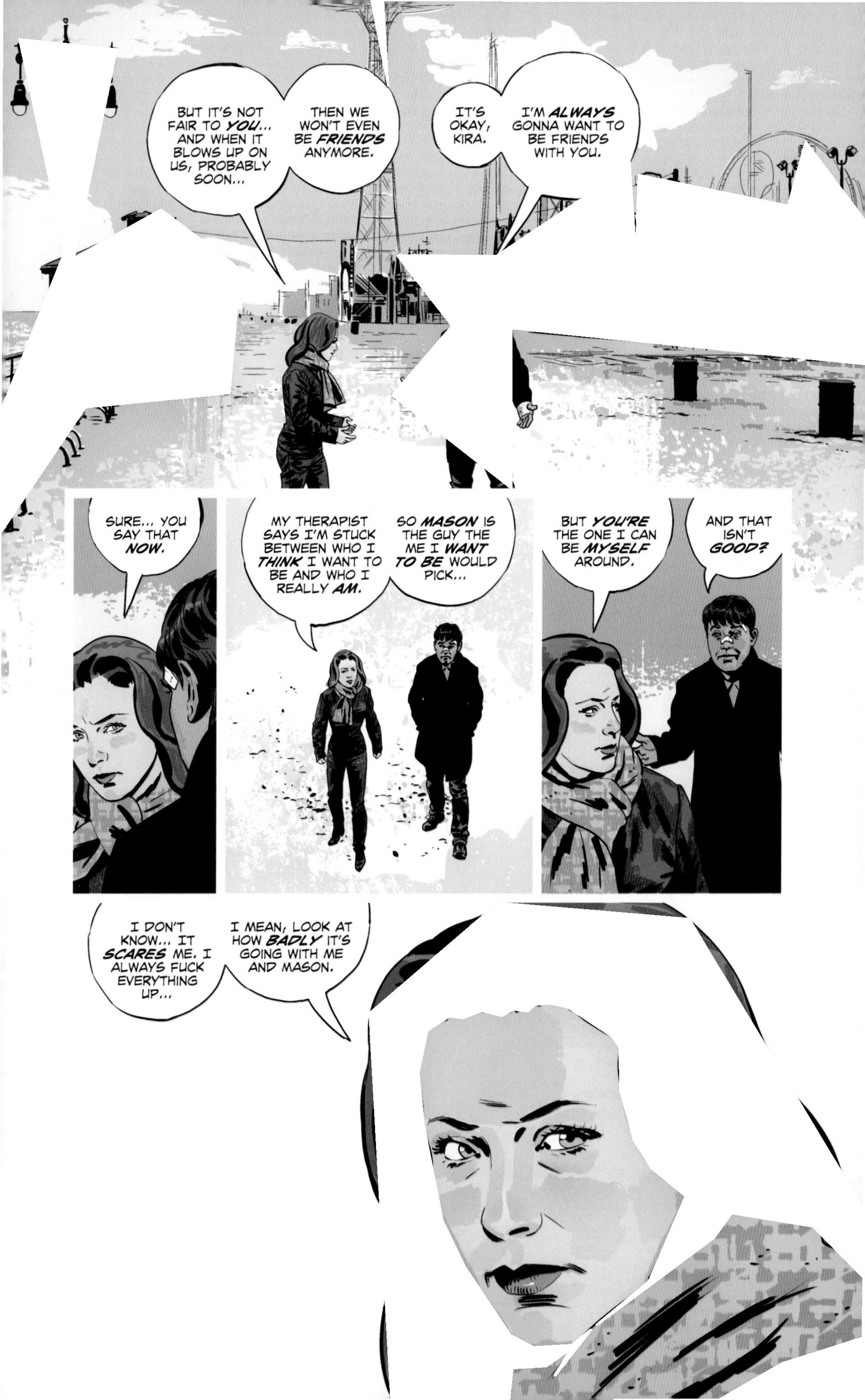
BUT IT'S NOT FAIR TO YOU... AND WHEN IT BLOWS UP ON US, PROBABLY SOON...
THEN WE WON'T EVEN BE FRIENDS ANYMORE.
IT'S OKAY, KIRA.
I'M ALWAYS GONNA WANT TO BE FRIENDS WITH YOU.
SURE... YOU SAY THAT NOW.
MY THERAPIST SAYS I'M STUCK BETWEEN WHO I THINK I WANT TO BE AND WHO I REALLY AM.
SO MASON IS THE GUY THE ME I WANT TO BE WOULD PICK...
BUT YOU'RE THE ONE I CAN BE MYSELF AROUND.
AND THAT ISN'T GOOD?
I DON'T KNOW... IT SCARES ME. I ALWAYS FUCK EVERYTHING UP...
I MEAN, LOOK AT HOW BADLY IT'S GOING WITH ME AND MASON.

I guess the advantage of me being Kira's best friend is, I know where she's coming from.

I know her history... I know where her patterns ***begin***.

See, Kira's mom always ***changed*** with every guy she married, like a chameleon trying to hide herself behind her husband's image.

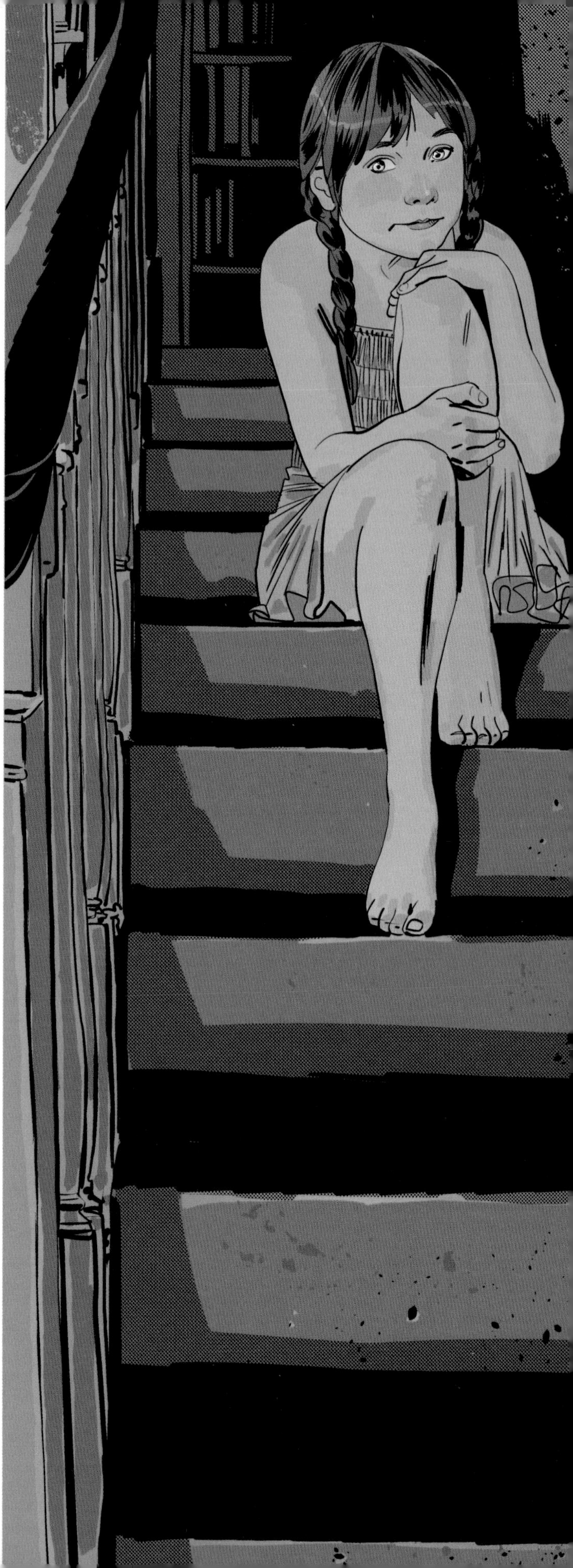

Husband #2 was into ***sailing***, so they were out at ***Martha's Vineyard*** every summer, spending half the day on the water.

Husband #4 was a ***Republican***, so Mom started preaching about immigrants and how global warming was a hoax.

But the guy before him, ***Husband #3***, he was the interesting one... Because this guy was a ***swinger***.

So when Kira was just getting to the age where you think about ***sex*** a lot, she had a front row seat to a few dozen ***orgies***.

She was supposed to be up in her bedroom with her headphones on, but the adults were all so ***drunk*** or high on ***X*** that none of them even noticed her...

Just peering down from the top of the stairs.

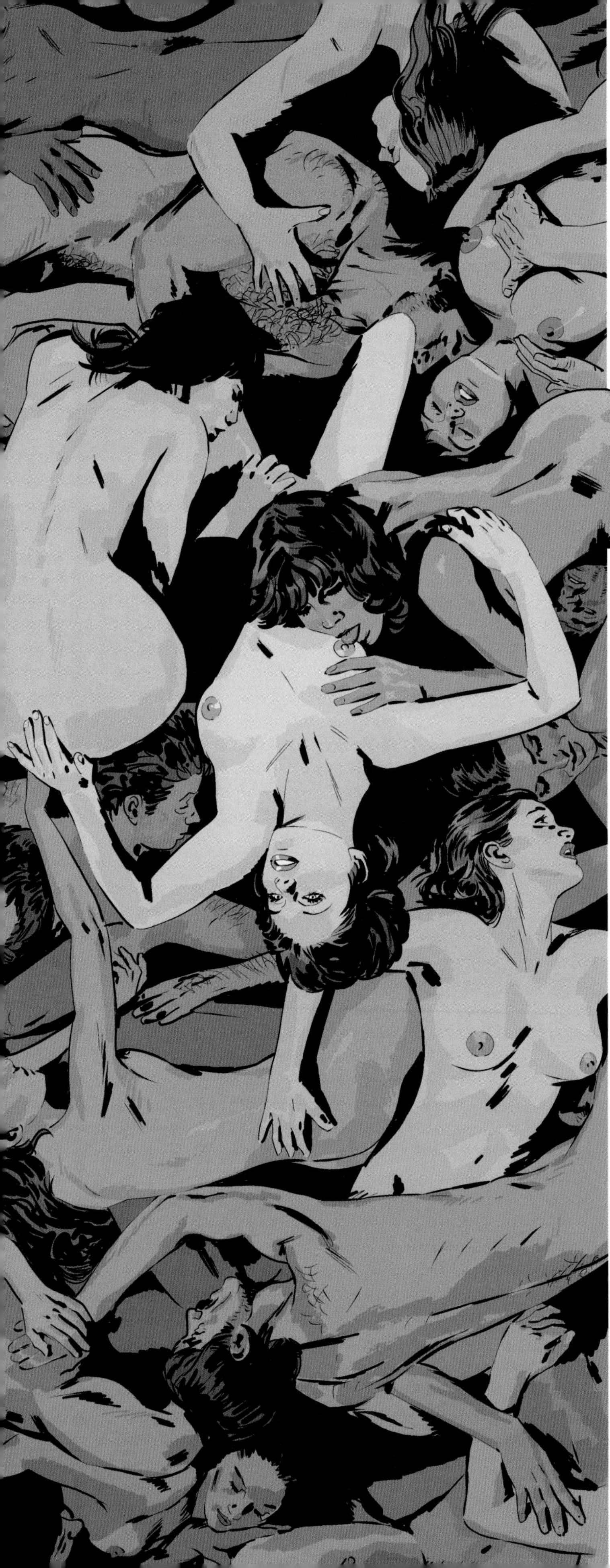

And you'd think the usual clichés would apply here, right?

Watching your mom have ***sex*** with two guys at once, or going down on some lady you sort of recognize from ***church***... It should gross you out.

It should give you nightmares.

But for Kira it was different.

Everyone looked so ***happy***, she said.

And they were being so nice to each other.

And in the center of it, surrounded by all this skin and sex... Her mother looked ***incandescent***.

Of course, ***that*** marriage ended after three years, when Husband #3 started having orgies with his ***secretary*** instead...

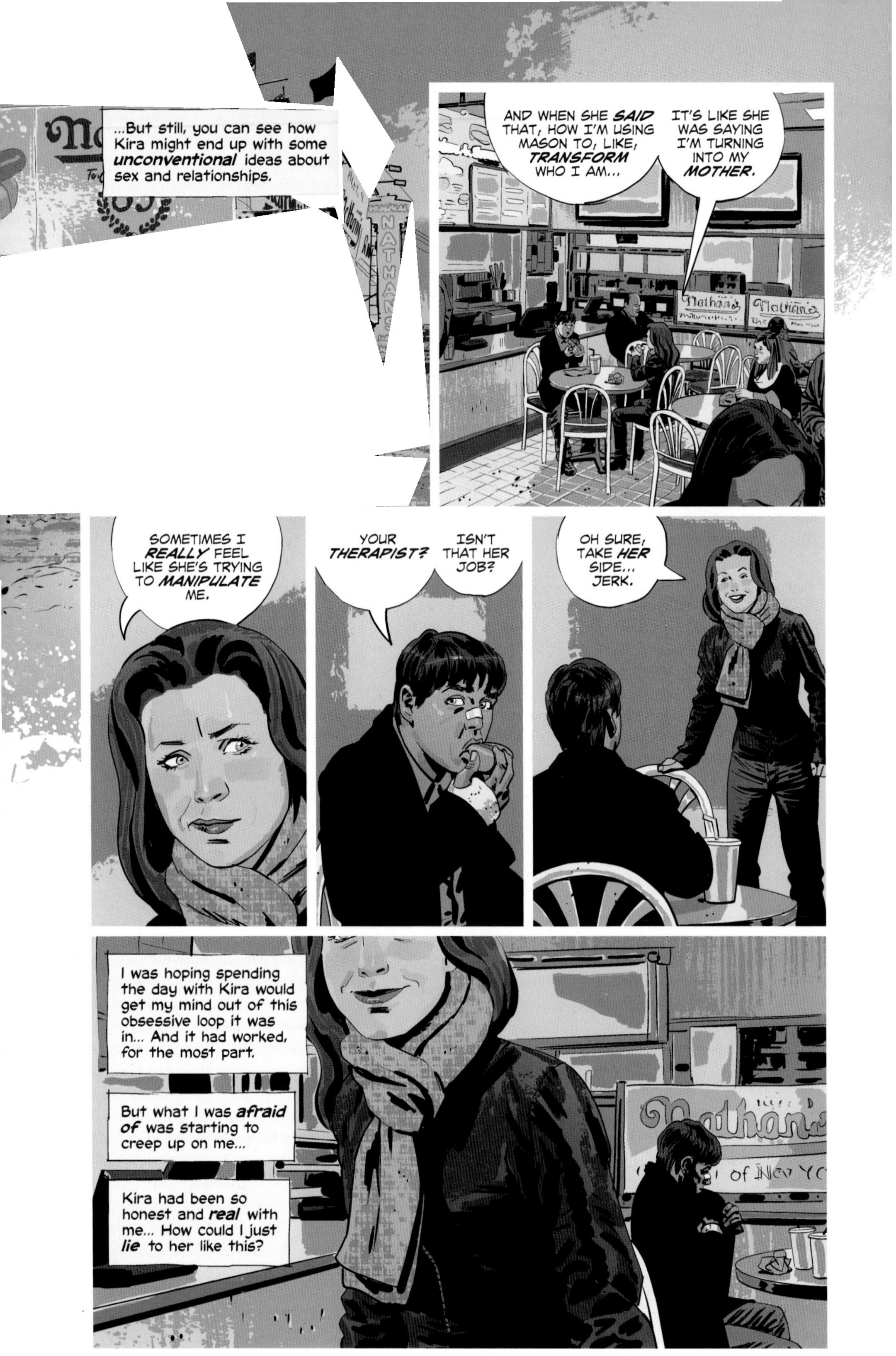

...But still, you can see how Kira might end up with some *unconventional* ideas about sex and relationships.
AND WHEN SHE *SAID* THAT, HOW I'M USING MASON TO, LIKE, *TRANSFORM* WHO I AM...
IT'S LIKE SHE WAS SAYING I'M TURNING INTO MY *MOTHER*.
SOMETIMES I *REALLY* FEEL LIKE SHE'S TRYING TO *MANIPULATE* ME.
YOUR *THERAPIST?*
ISN'T THAT HER JOB?
OH SURE, TAKE *HER* SIDE... JERK.
I was hoping spending the day with Kira would get my mind out of this obsessive loop it was in... And it had worked, for the most part.
But what I was *afraid of* was starting to creep up on me...
Kira had been so honest and *real* with me... How could I just *lie* to her like this?

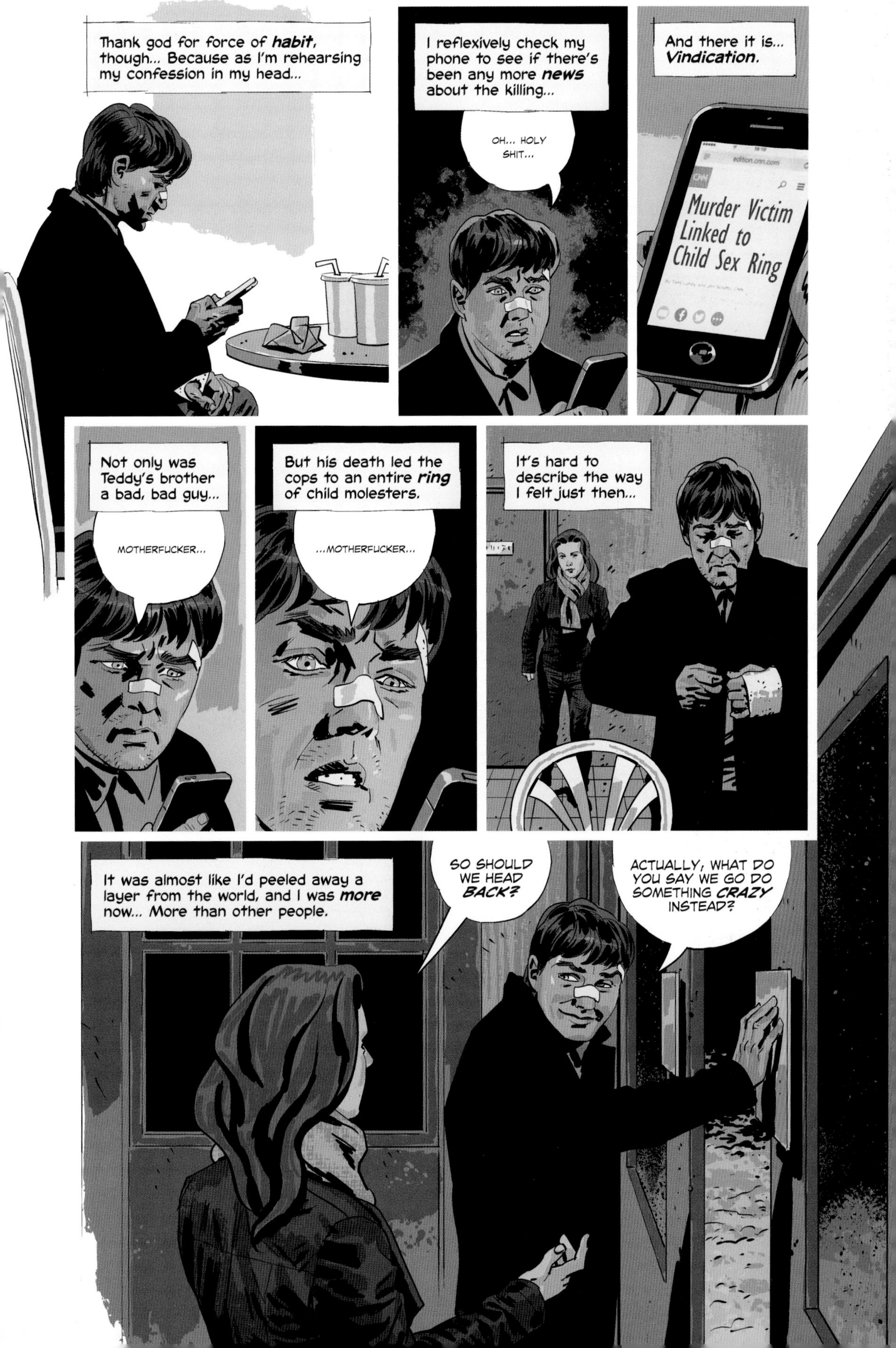
Thank god for force of *habit*, though... Because as I'm rehearsing my confession in my head...
I reflexively check my phone to see if there's been any more *news* about the killing...
OH... HOLY SHIT...
And there it is... *Vindication*.
edition.cnn.com
Murder Victim Linked to Child Sex Ring
Not only was Teddy's brother a bad, bad guy...
MOTHERFUCKER...
But his death led the cops to an entire *ring* of child molesters.
...MOTHERFUCKER...
It's hard to describe the way I felt just then...
It was almost like I'd peeled away a layer from the world, and I was *more* now... More than other people.
SO SHOULD WE HEAD *BACK?*
ACTUALLY, WHAT DO YOU SAY WE GO DO SOMETHING *CRAZY* INSTEAD?

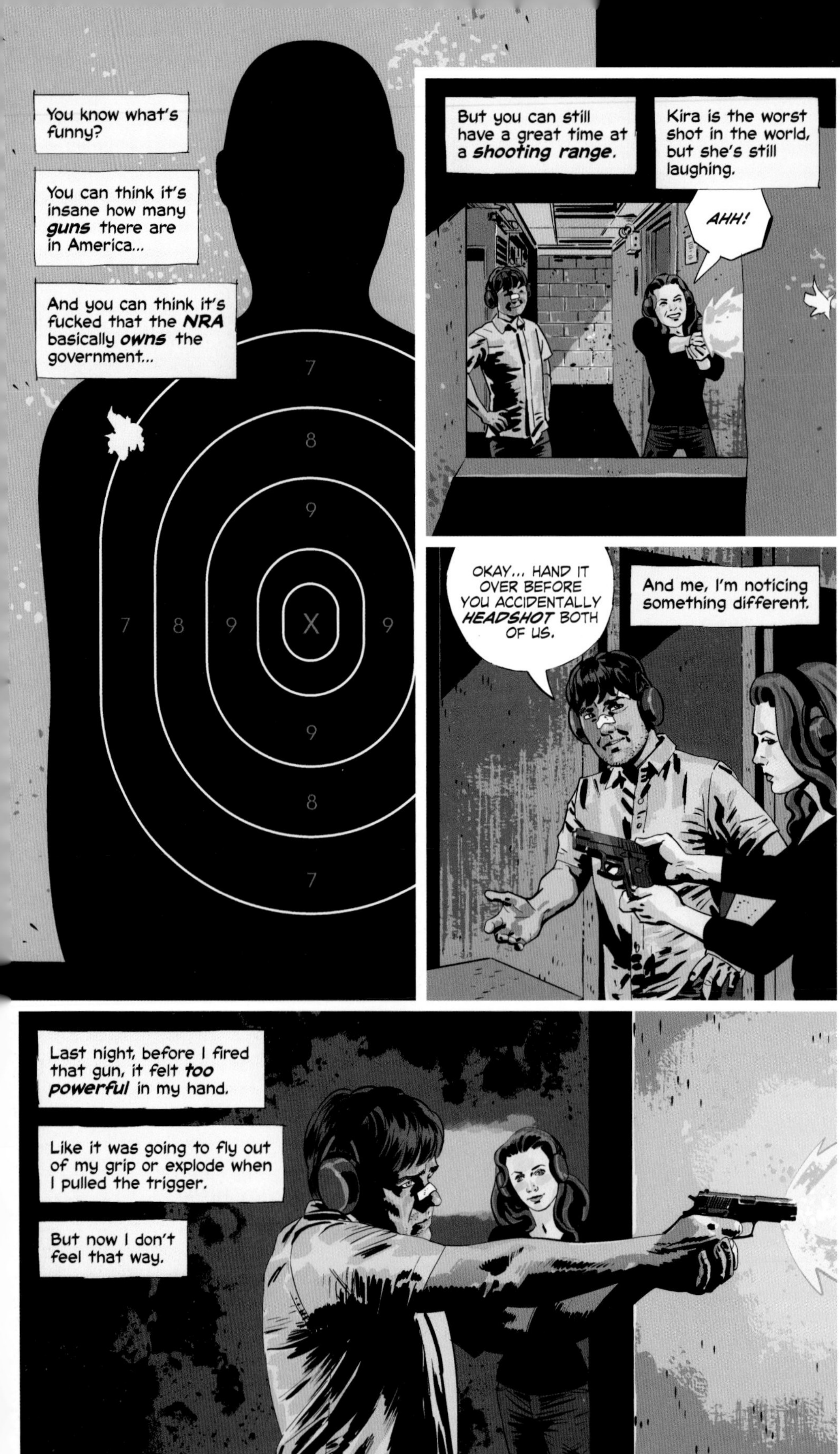
You know what's funny?
You can think it's insane how many guns there are in America...
And you can think it's fucked that the NRA basically owns the government...
7
8
9
X
7 8 9
9
9
8
7
But you can still have a great time at a shooting range.
Kira is the worst shot in the world, but she's still laughing.
AHH!
OKAY... HAND IT OVER BEFORE YOU ACCIDENTALLY HEADSHOT BOTH OF US.
And me, I'm noticing something different.
Last night, before I fired that gun, it felt too powerful in my hand.
Like it was going to fly out of my grip or explode when I pulled the trigger.
But now I don't feel that way.

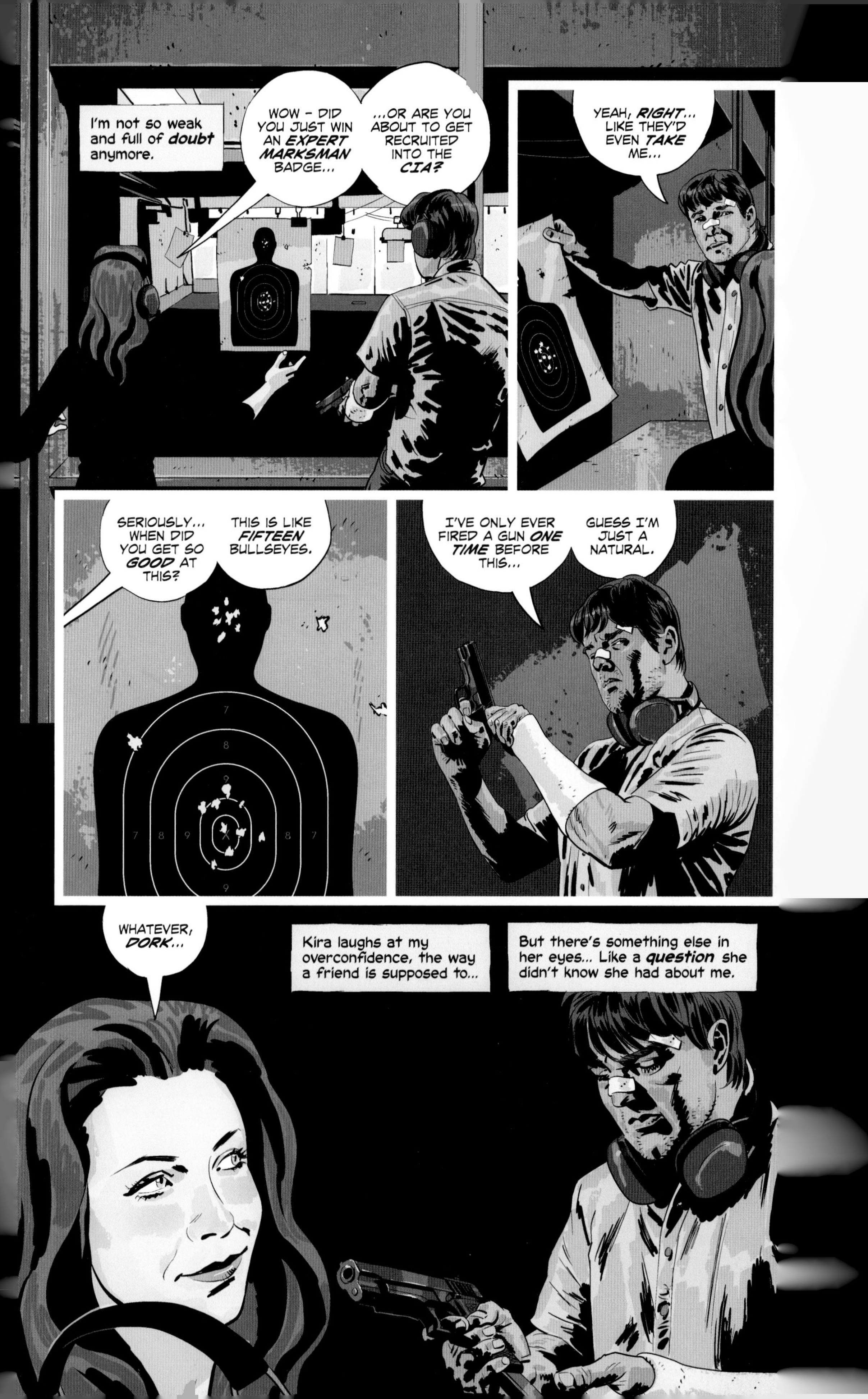
I'm not so weak and full of doubt anymore.
WOW – DID YOU JUST WIN AN EXPERT MARKSMAN BADGE...
...OR ARE YOU ABOUT TO GET RECRUITED INTO THE CIA?
YEAH, RIGHT... LIKE THEY'D EVEN TAKE ME...
SERIOUSLY... WHEN DID YOU GET SO GOOD AT THIS?
THIS IS LIKE FIFTEEN BULLSEYES.
I'VE ONLY EVER FIRED A GUN ONE TIME BEFORE THIS...
GUESS I'M JUST A NATURAL.
WHATEVER, DORK...
Kira laughs at my overconfidence, the way a friend is supposed to...
But there's something else in her eyes... Like a question she didn't know she had about me.

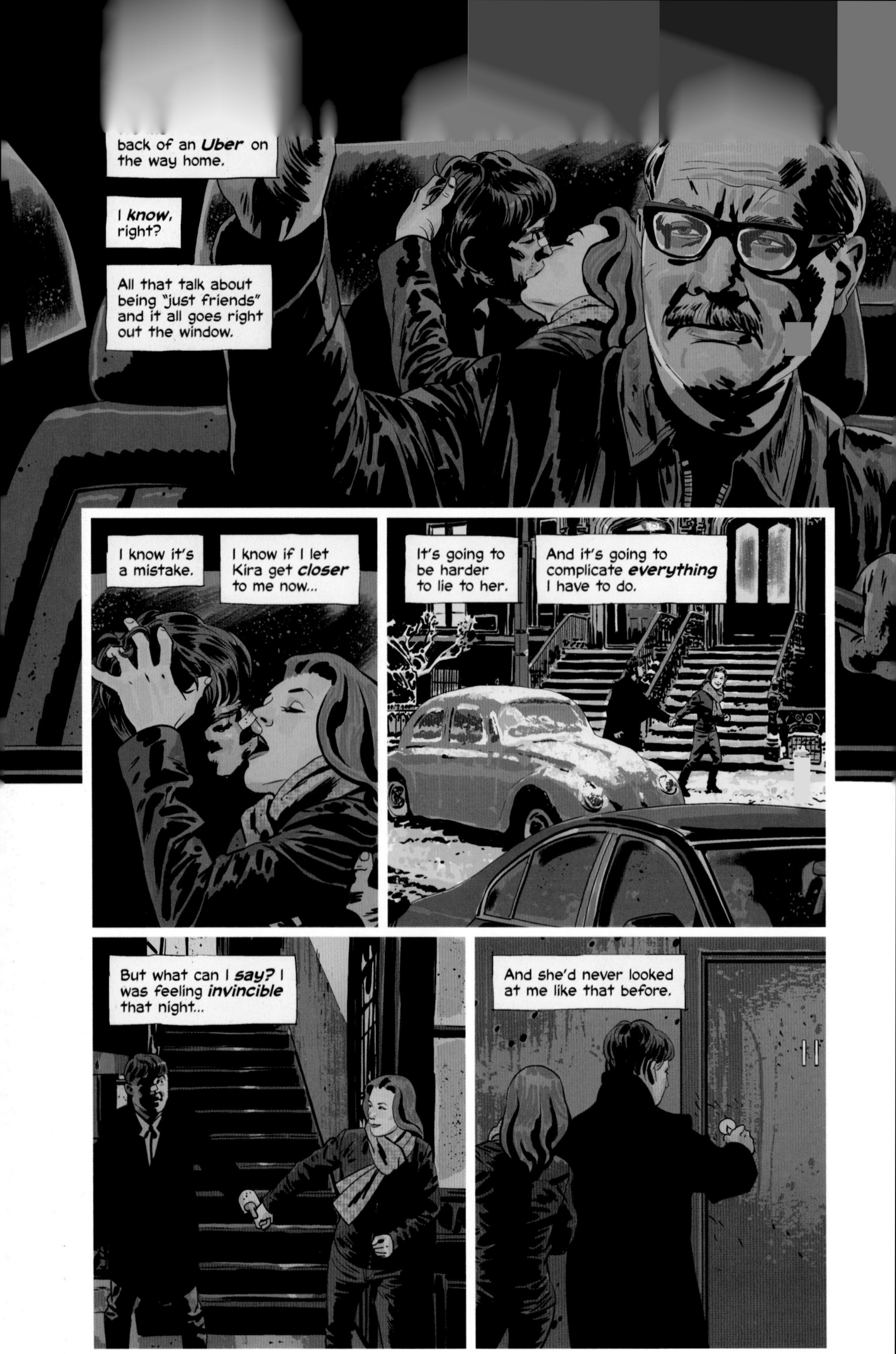
back of an Uber on the way home.
I know, right?
All that talk about being "just friends" and it all goes right out the window.
I know it's a mistake.
I know if I let Kira get closer to me now...
It's going to be harder to lie to her.
And it's going to complicate everything I have to do.
But what can I say? I was feeling invincible that night...
And she'd never looked at me like that before.

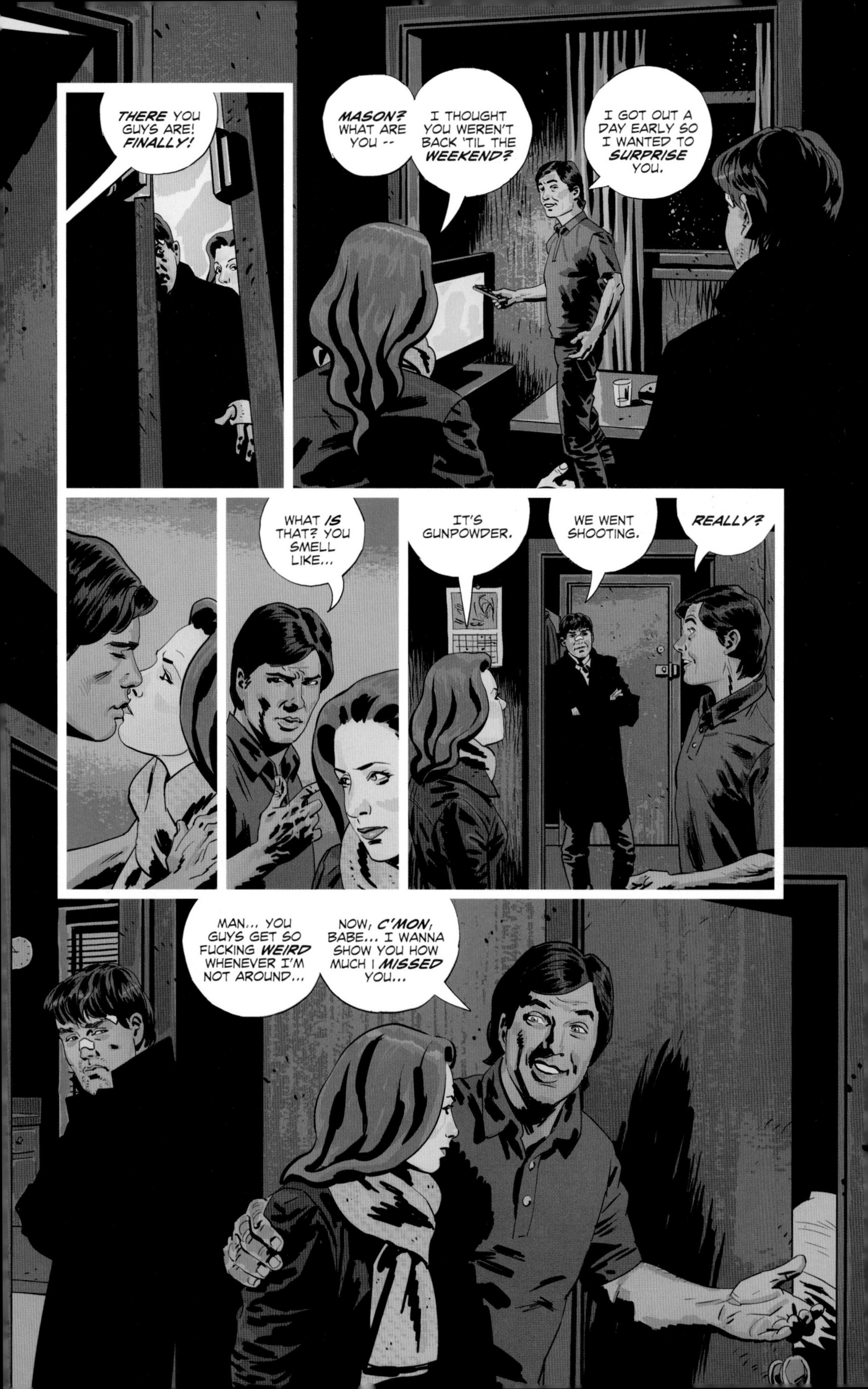
THERE YOU GUYS ARE! FINALLY!
MASON? WHAT ARE YOU --
I THOUGHT YOU WEREN'T BACK 'TIL THE WEEKEND?
I GOT OUT A DAY EARLY SO I WANTED TO SURPRISE YOU.
WHAT IS THAT? YOU SMELL LIKE...
IT'S GUNPOWDER.
WE WENT SHOOTING.
REALLY?
MAN... YOU GUYS GET SO FUCKING WEIRD WHENEVER I'M NOT AROUND...
NOW, C'MON, BABE... I WANNA SHOW YOU HOW MUCH I MISSED YOU...

If this had happened a month ago, I'd have wanted to scream. But that night, I actually felt a little relieved.

It still *burned*, don't get me wrong. She *had* to break up with him, like soon...

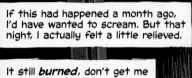

But I didn't really want our lives blowing up that exact second.

And to be totally honest, my mind was *already* preoccupied.

I had work to do, after all.

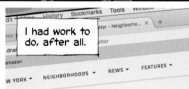

History   Bookmarks   Tools   Window

...tter - Neighborho...

W YORK ▾   NEIGHBORHOODS ▾   NEWS ▾   FEATURES ▾

E BLOTTER

DOWNTOWN BROOKLYN ▸
Man Knocks Down 82-Year-Old Woman Steals 4K Necklace, NYPD says

LOWER EAST SIDE ▸
Woman Fends Off Subway Attack

FINANCIAL DISTRICT ▸
Man Hit with Bat by Attackers Yelling Anti-Gay Slurs, Police say

LOWER EAST SIDE ▸

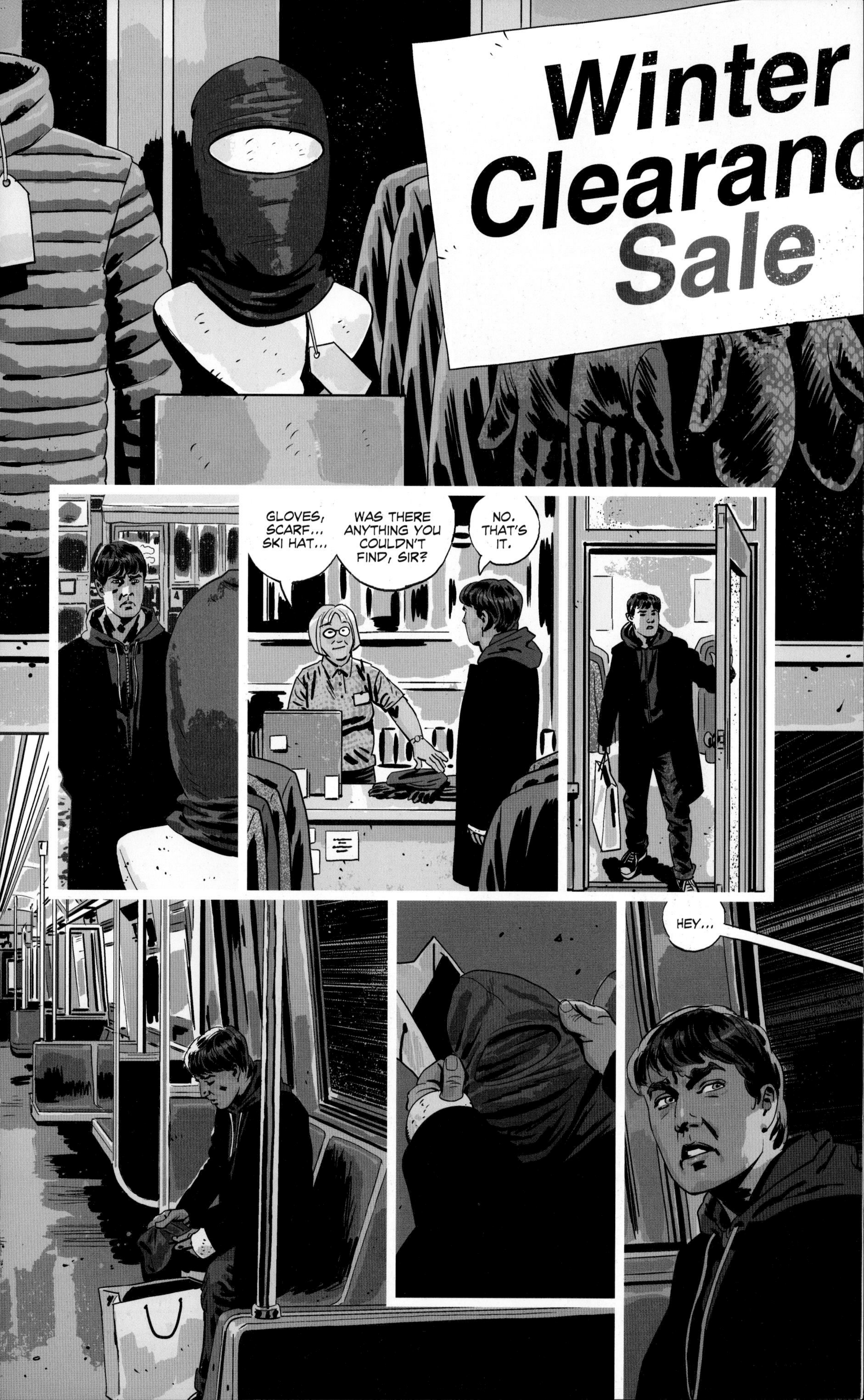

Winter
Clearanc
Sale
GLOVES, SCARF... SKI HAT...
WAS THERE ANYTHING YOU COULDN'T FIND, SIR?
NO. THAT'S IT.
HEY...

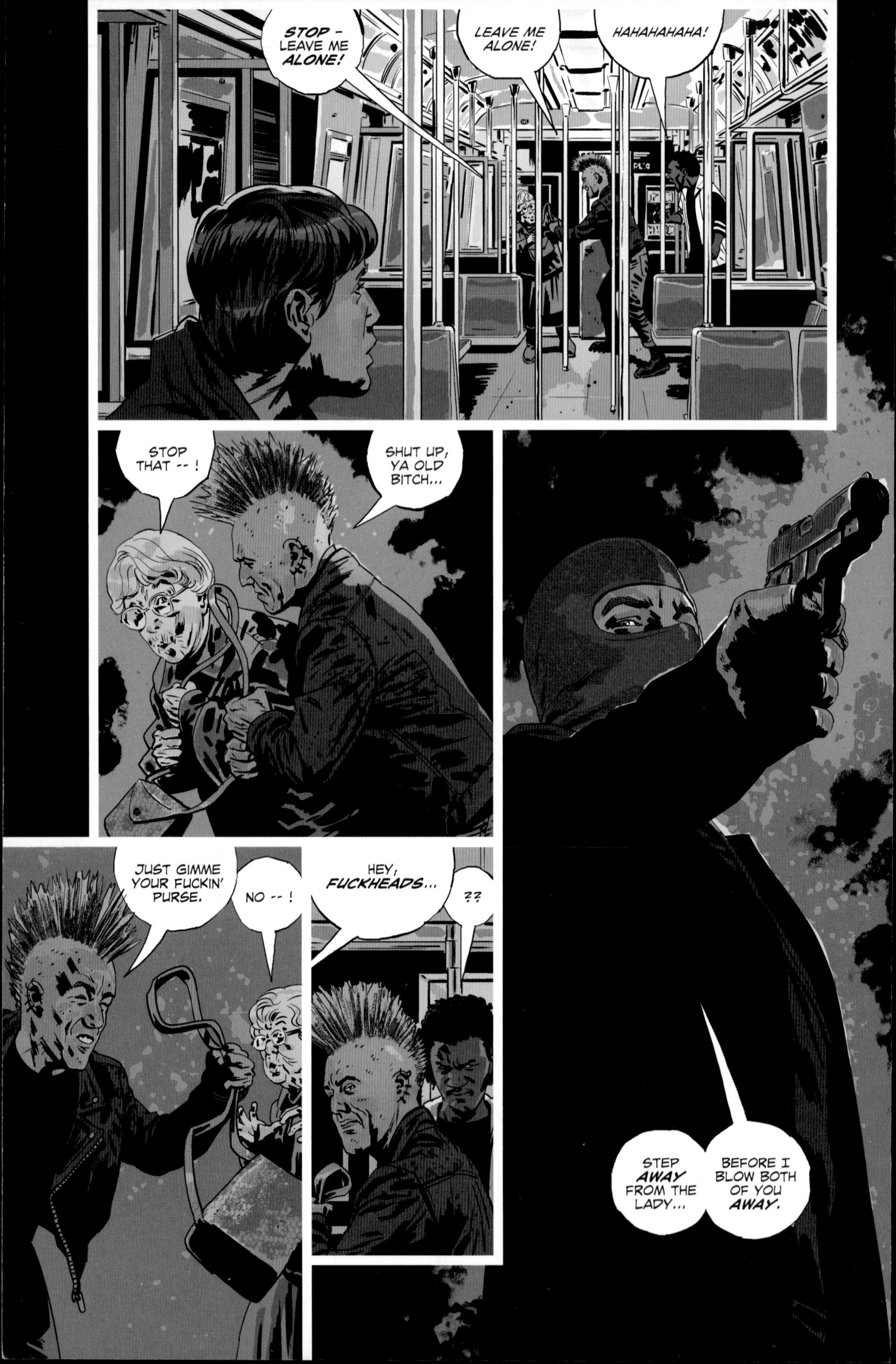
STOP - LEAVE ME ALONE!
LEAVE ME ALONE!
HAHAHAHAHA!
STOP THAT -- !
SHUT UP, YA OLD BITCH...
JUST GIMME YOUR FUCKIN' PURSE.
NO -- !
HEY, FUCKHEADS...
??
STEP AWAY FROM THE LADY...
BEFORE I BLOW BOTH OF YOU AWAY.

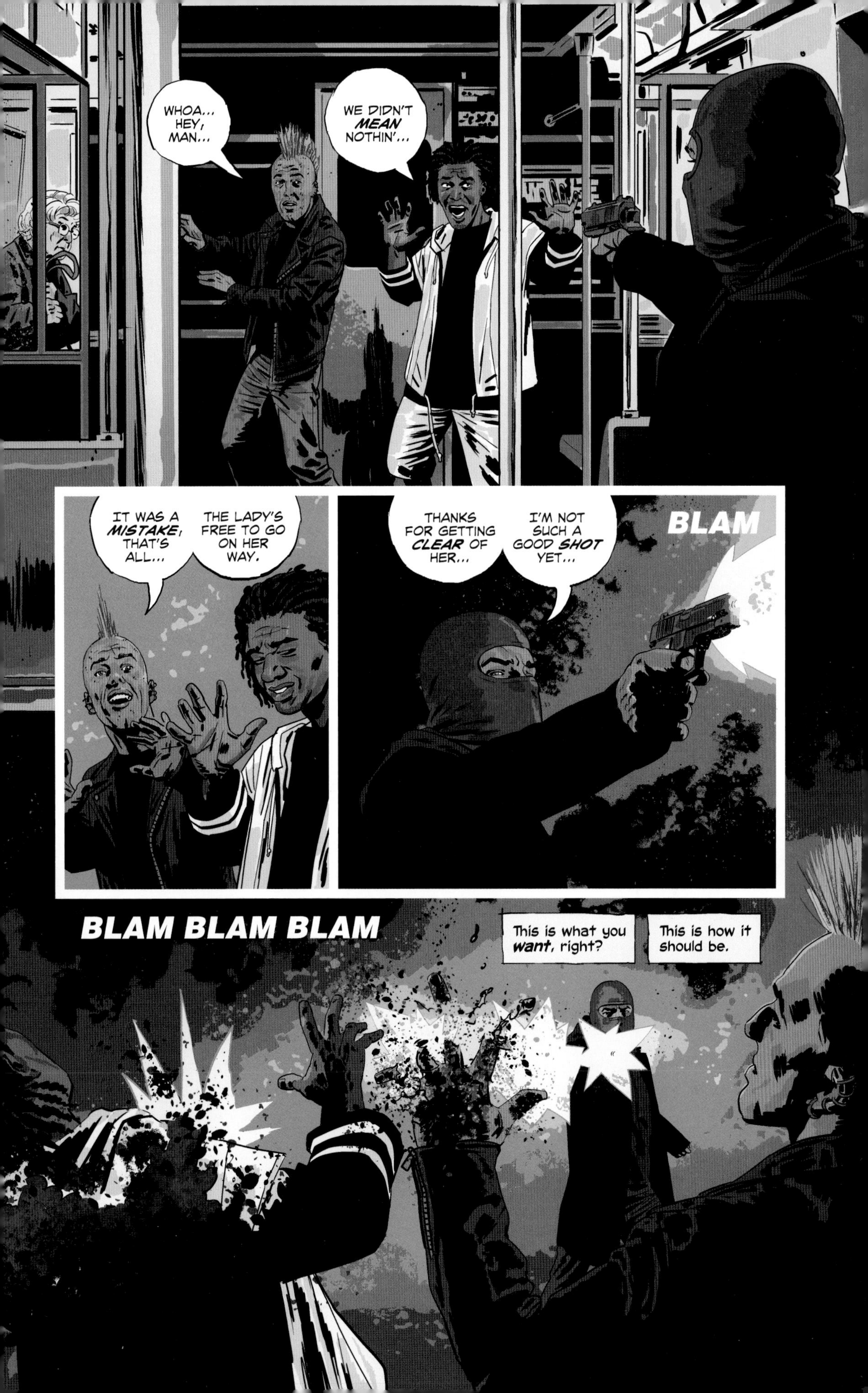
WHOA... HEY, MAN...
WE DIDN'T *MEAN* NOTHIN'...
IT WAS A *MISTAKE*, THAT'S ALL...
THE LADY'S FREE TO GO ON HER WAY.
THANKS FOR GETTING *CLEAR* OF HER...
I'M NOT SUCH A GOOD *SHOT* YET...
BLAM
BLAM BLAM BLAM
This is what you *want*, right?
This is how it should be.

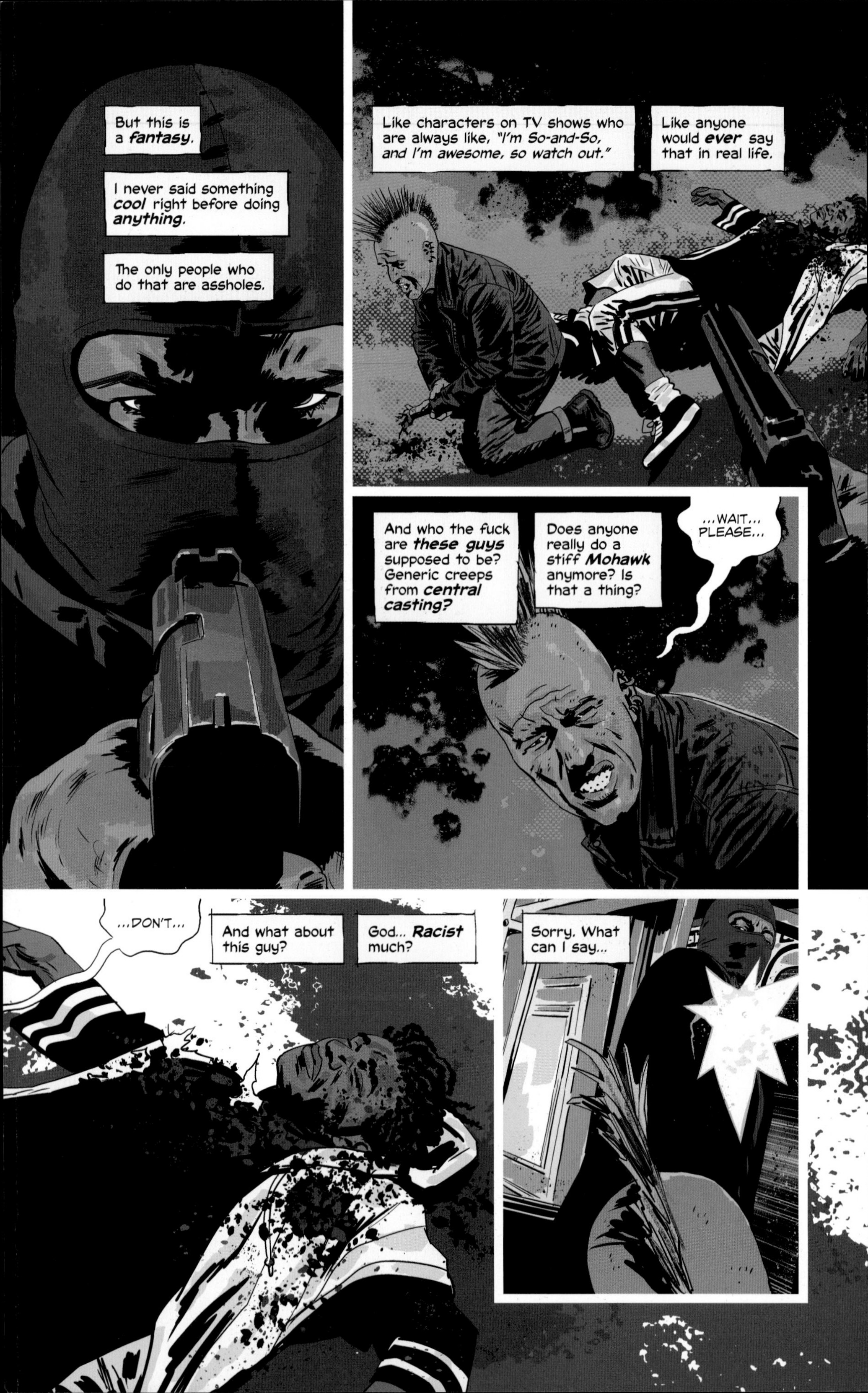

But this is a *fantasy*.
I never said something *cool* right before doing *anything*.
The only people who do that are assholes.
Like characters on TV shows who are always like, *"I'm So-and-So, and I'm awesome, so watch out."*
Like anyone would *ever* say that in real life.
And who the fuck are *these guys* supposed to be? Generic creeps from *central casting?*
Does anyone really do a stiff *Mohawk* anymore? Is that a thing?
...WAIT... PLEASE...
...DON'T...
And what about this guy?
God... *Racist* much?
Sorry. What can I say...

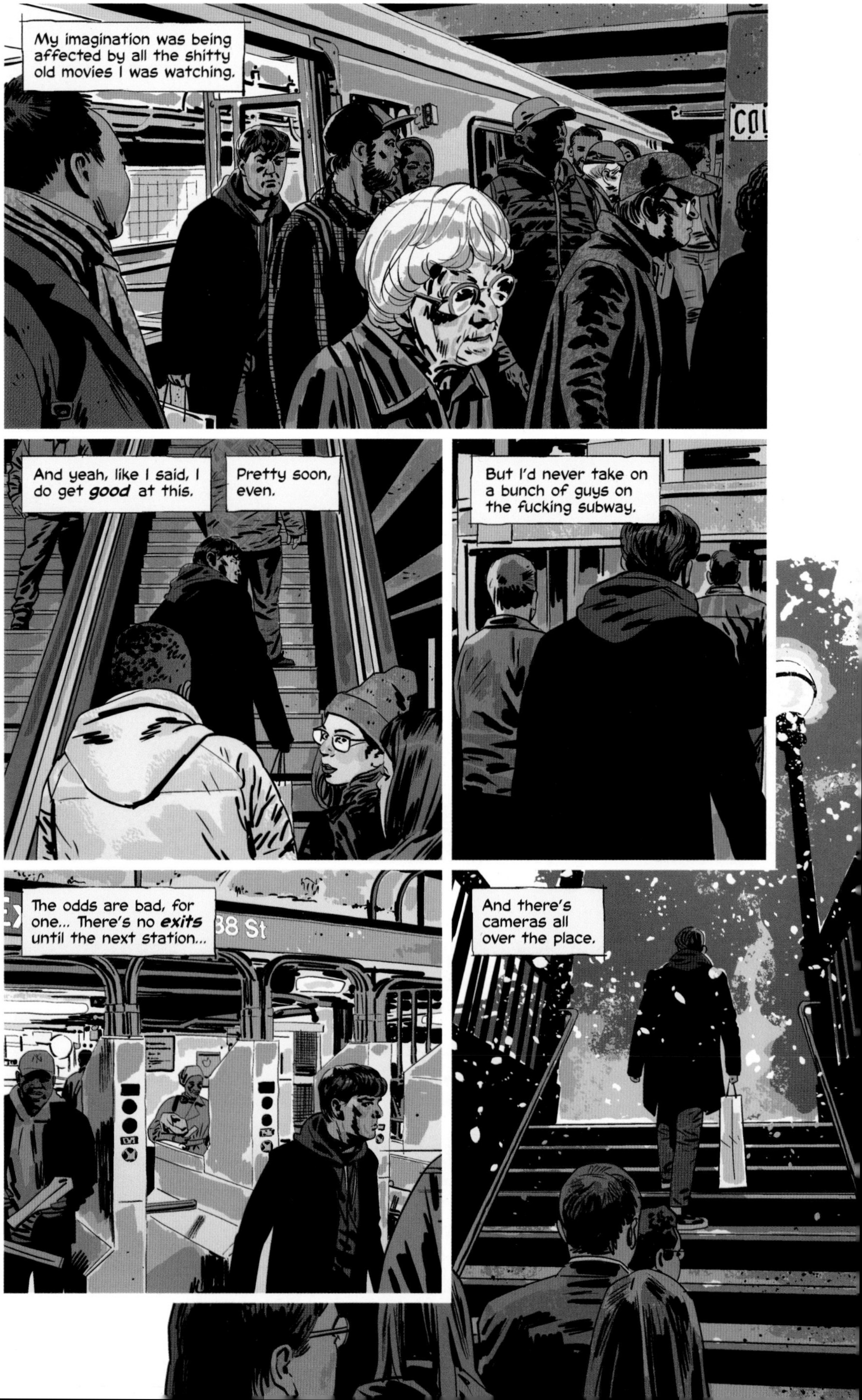
My imagination was being affected by all the shitty old movies I was watching.
COL
And yeah, like I said, I do get *good* at this.
Pretty soon, even.
But I'd never take on a bunch of guys on the fucking subway.
The odds are bad, for one... There's no *exits* until the next station...
38 St
And there's cameras all over the place.

It's so easy for the guys in those old vigilante movies to find their targets... They just walk around waiting to get mugged.

Or they listen for screams and arrive just in time.

In real life, it's not like that.

I've ridden the subway a million times and the worst thing I've ever seen was some asshole hitting on a woman who has headphones on.

No pickpocketings or robberies or beatings.

No one trying to push anyone onto the tracks as the train speeds into the station.

I know this shit happens, because it's in the ***Police Blotter***, but being there when it actually goes down is just random.

Hell, even the police usually arrive ***after*** the muggings and murders and every other awful thing people do to each other...

Except for when the police are the ones ***committing*** the crimes.

And I'm not going to follow cops around waiting for them to start shooting people for being ***black***.

I don't even have a car, for one thing.

And it's not like the ***racist*** cops advertise themselves. They don't wear ***Klan sheets*** to work.

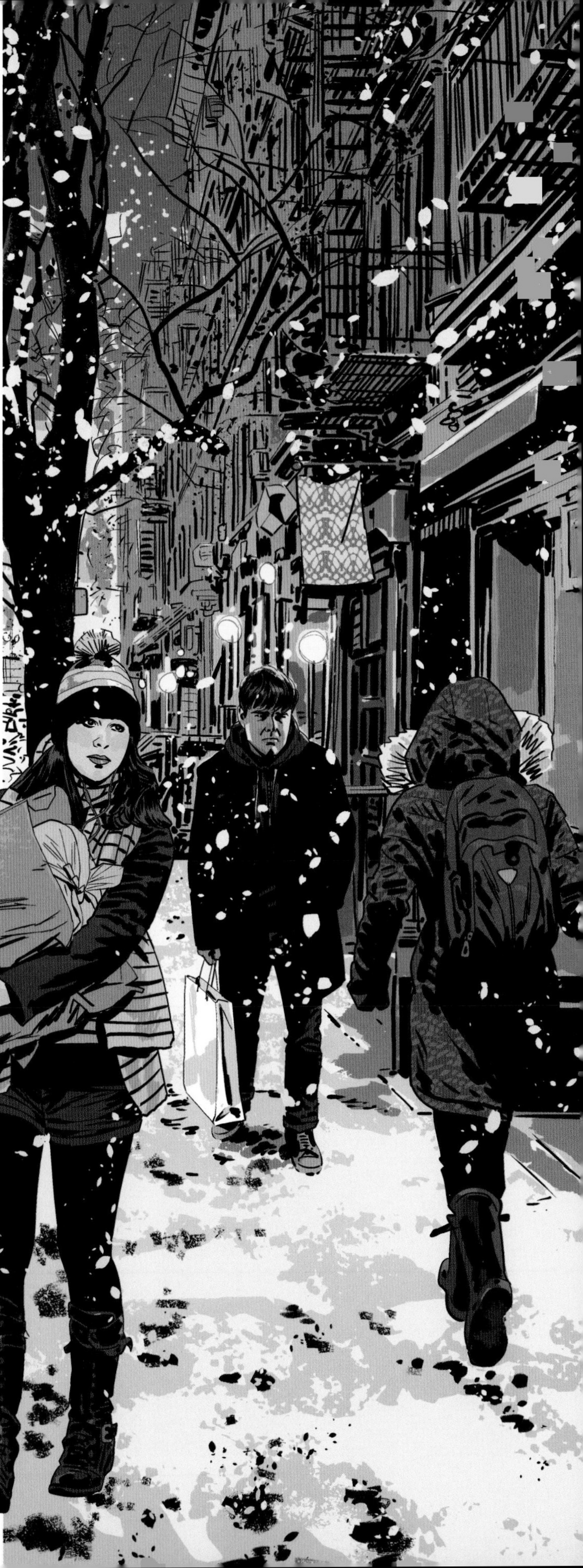

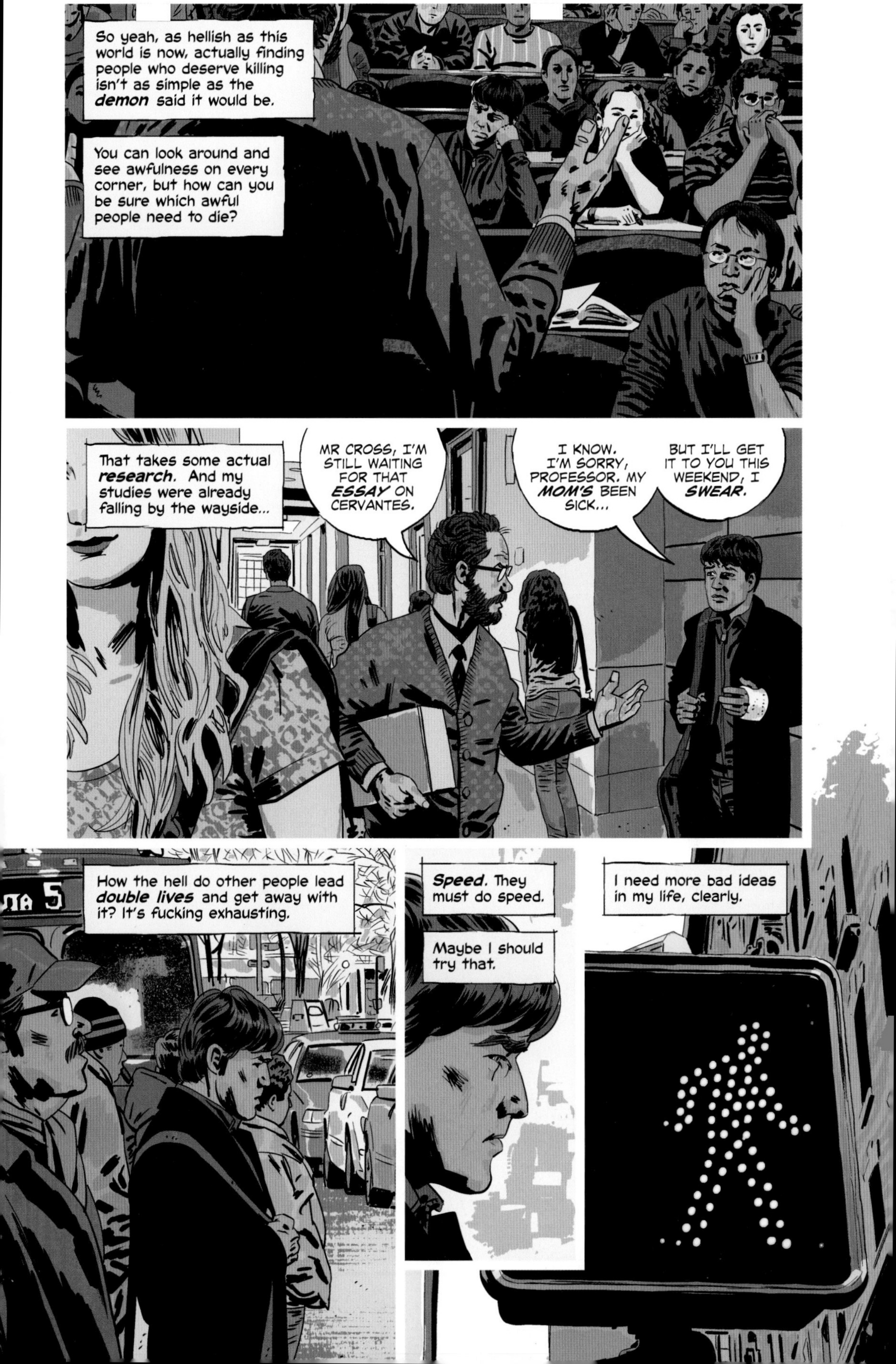
So yeah, as hellish as this world is now, actually finding people who deserve killing isn't as simple as the *demon* said it would be.
You can look around and see awfulness on every corner, but how can you be sure which awful people need to die?
That takes some actual *research*. And my studies were already falling by the wayside...
MR CROSS, I'M STILL WAITING FOR THAT *ESSAY* ON CERVANTES.
I KNOW. I'M SORRY, PROFESSOR. MY *MOM'S* BEEN SICK...
BUT I'LL GET IT TO YOU THIS WEEKEND, I *SWEAR*.
How the hell do other people lead *double lives* and get away with it? It's fucking exhausting.
Speed. They must do speed.
Maybe I should try that.
I need more bad ideas in my life, clearly.

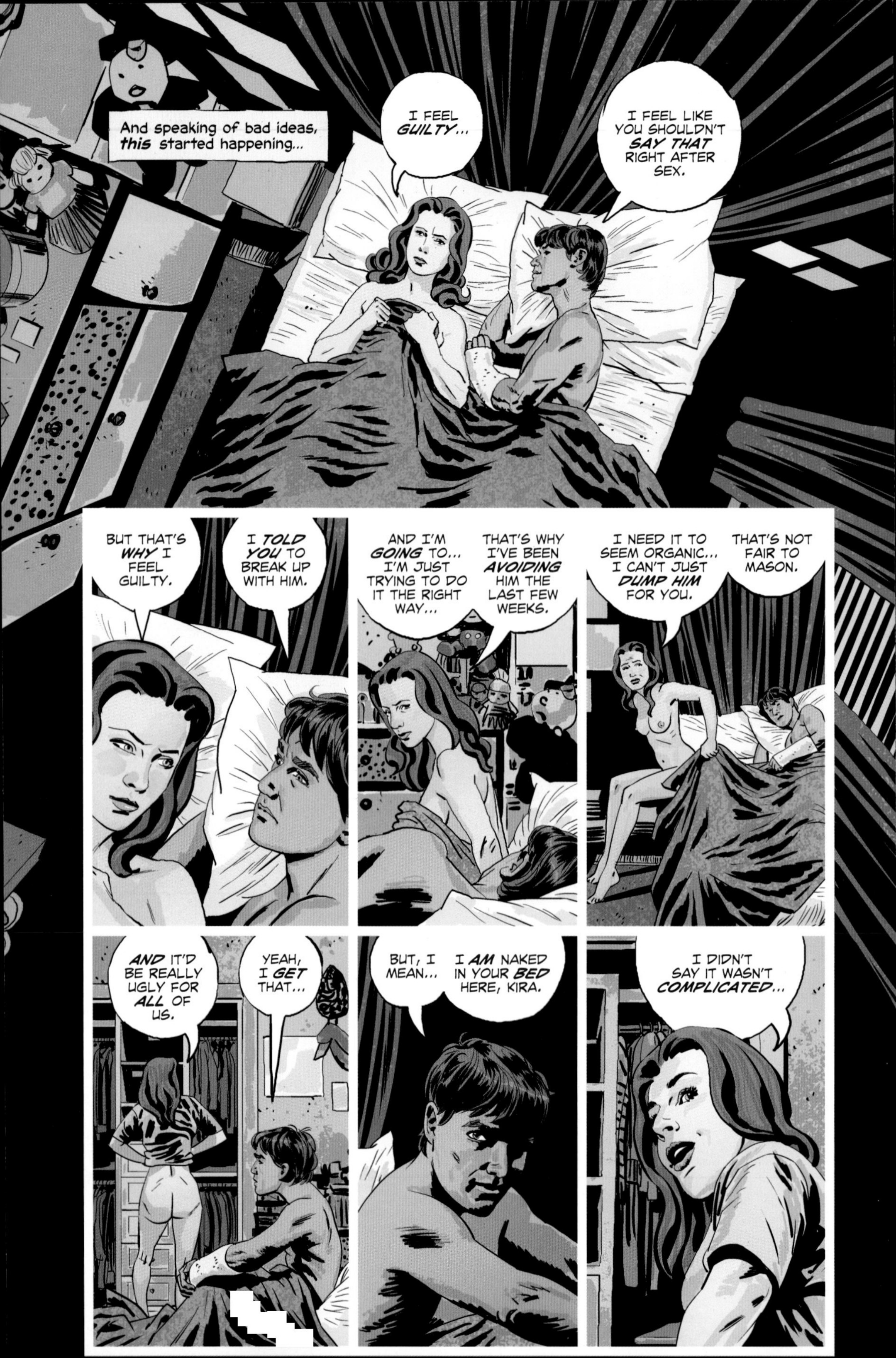

And speaking of bad ideas, this started happening...
I FEEL GUILTY...
I FEEL LIKE YOU SHOULDN'T SAY THAT RIGHT AFTER SEX.
BUT THAT'S WHY I FEEL GUILTY.
I TOLD YOU TO BREAK UP WITH HIM.
AND I'M GOING TO... I'M JUST TRYING TO DO IT THE RIGHT WAY...
THAT'S WHY I'VE BEEN AVOIDING HIM THE LAST FEW WEEKS.
I NEED IT TO SEEM ORGANIC... I CAN'T JUST DUMP HIM FOR YOU.
THAT'S NOT FAIR TO MASON.
AND IT'D BE REALLY UGLY FOR ALL OF US.
YEAH, I GET THAT...
BUT, I MEAN...
I AM NAKED IN YOUR BED HERE, KIRA.
I DIDN'T SAY IT WASN'T COMPLICATED...

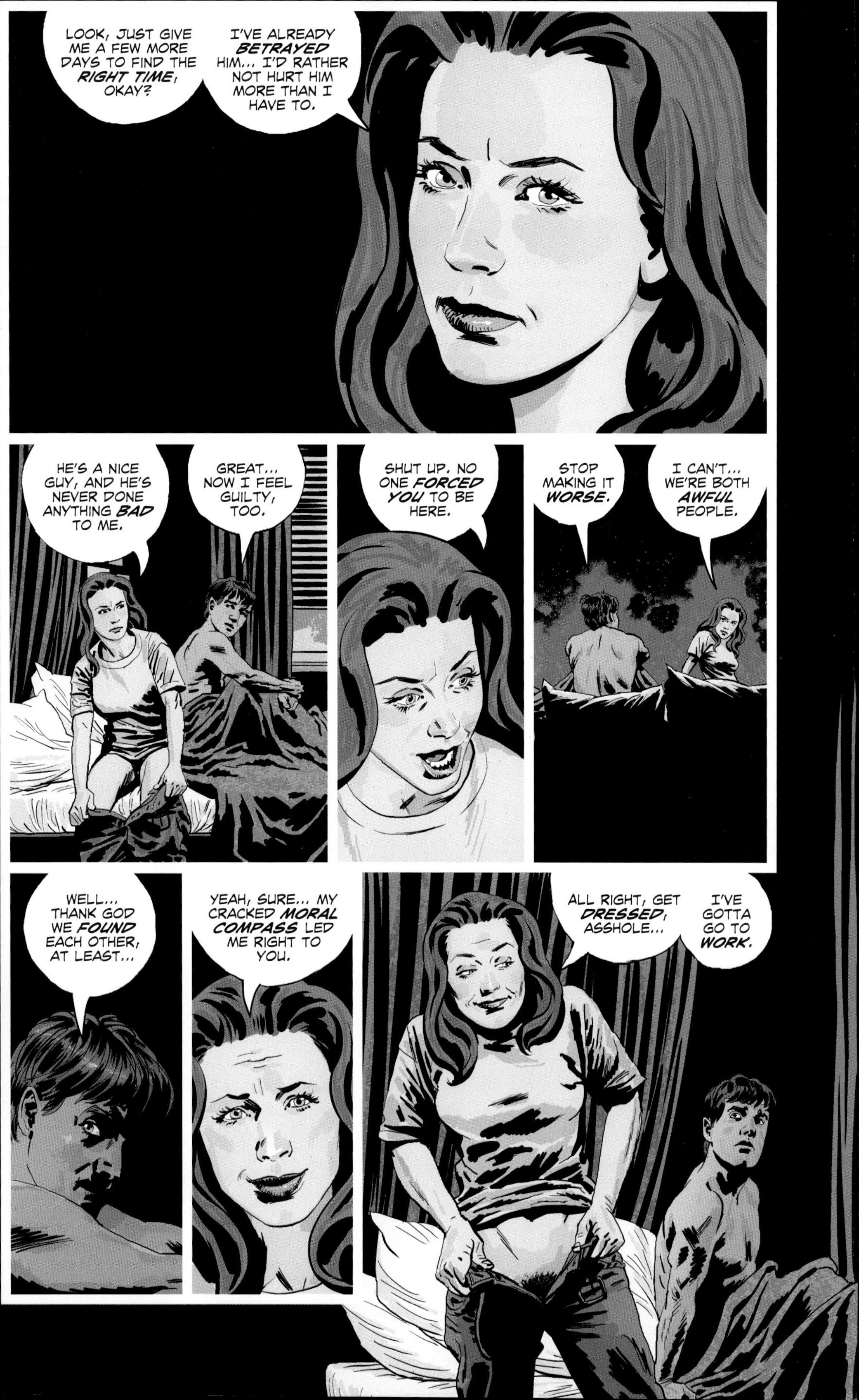
LOOK, JUST GIVE ME A FEW MORE DAYS TO FIND THE RIGHT TIME, OKAY?
I'VE ALREADY BETRAYED HIM... I'D RATHER NOT HURT HIM MORE THAN I HAVE TO.
HE'S A NICE GUY, AND HE'S NEVER DONE ANYTHING BAD TO ME.
GREAT... NOW I FEEL GUILTY, TOO.
SHUT UP. NO ONE FORCED YOU TO BE HERE.
STOP MAKING IT WORSE.
I CAN'T... WE'RE BOTH AWFUL PEOPLE.
WELL... THANK GOD WE FOUND EACH OTHER, AT LEAST...
YEAH, SURE... MY CRACKED MORAL COMPASS LED ME RIGHT TO YOU.
ALL RIGHT, GET DRESSED, ASSHOLE...
I'VE GOTTA GO TO WORK.

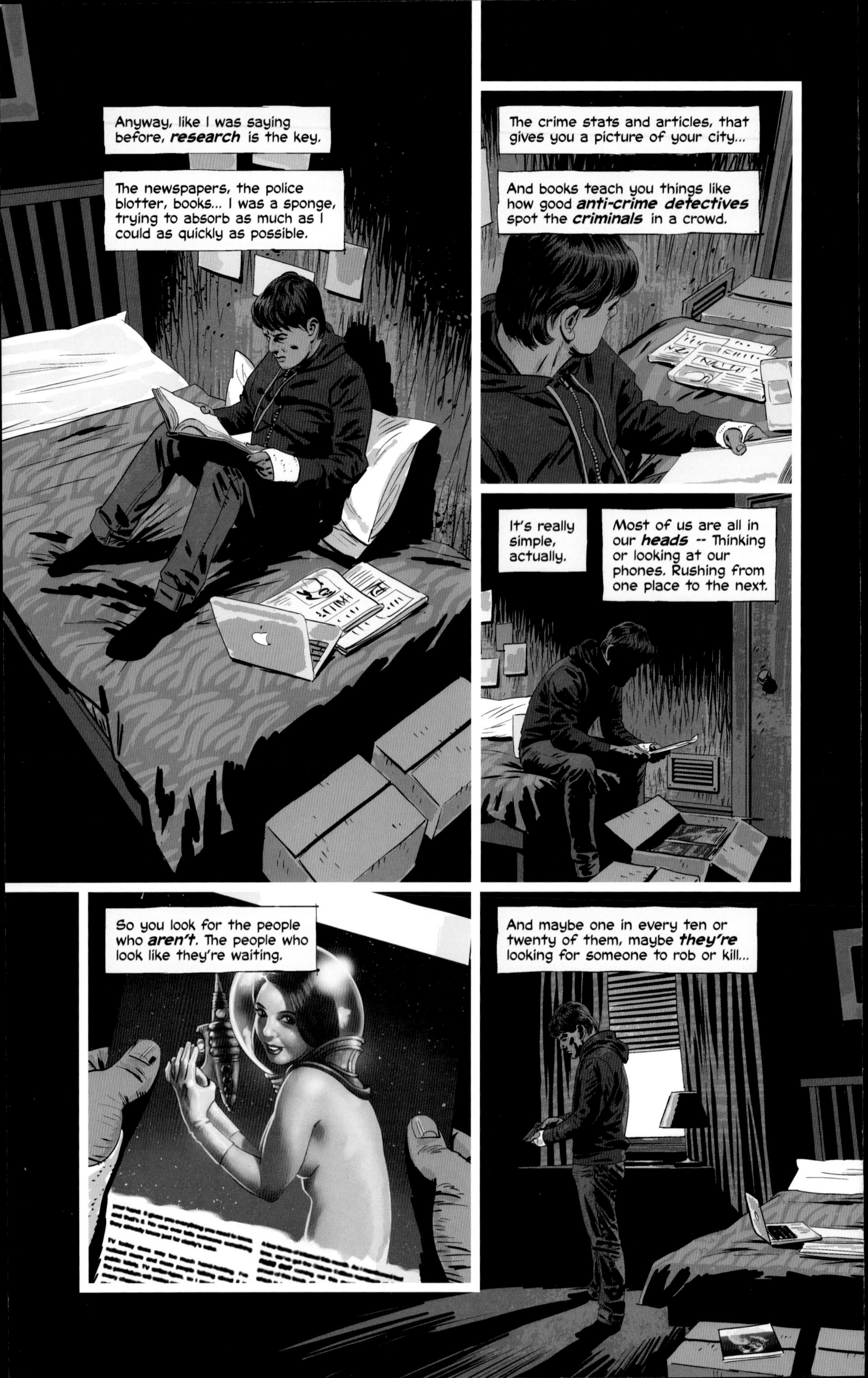
Anyway, like I was saying before, ***research*** is the key.
The newspapers, the police blotter, books... I was a sponge, trying to absorb as much as I could as quickly as possible.
The crime stats and articles, that gives you a picture of your city...
And books teach you things like how good ***anti-crime detectives*** spot the ***criminals*** in a crowd.
It's really simple, actually.
Most of us are all in our ***heads*** -- Thinking or looking at our phones. Rushing from one place to the next.
So you look for the people who ***aren't***. The people who look like they're waiting.
And maybe one in every ten or twenty of them, maybe ***they're*** looking for someone to rob or kill...

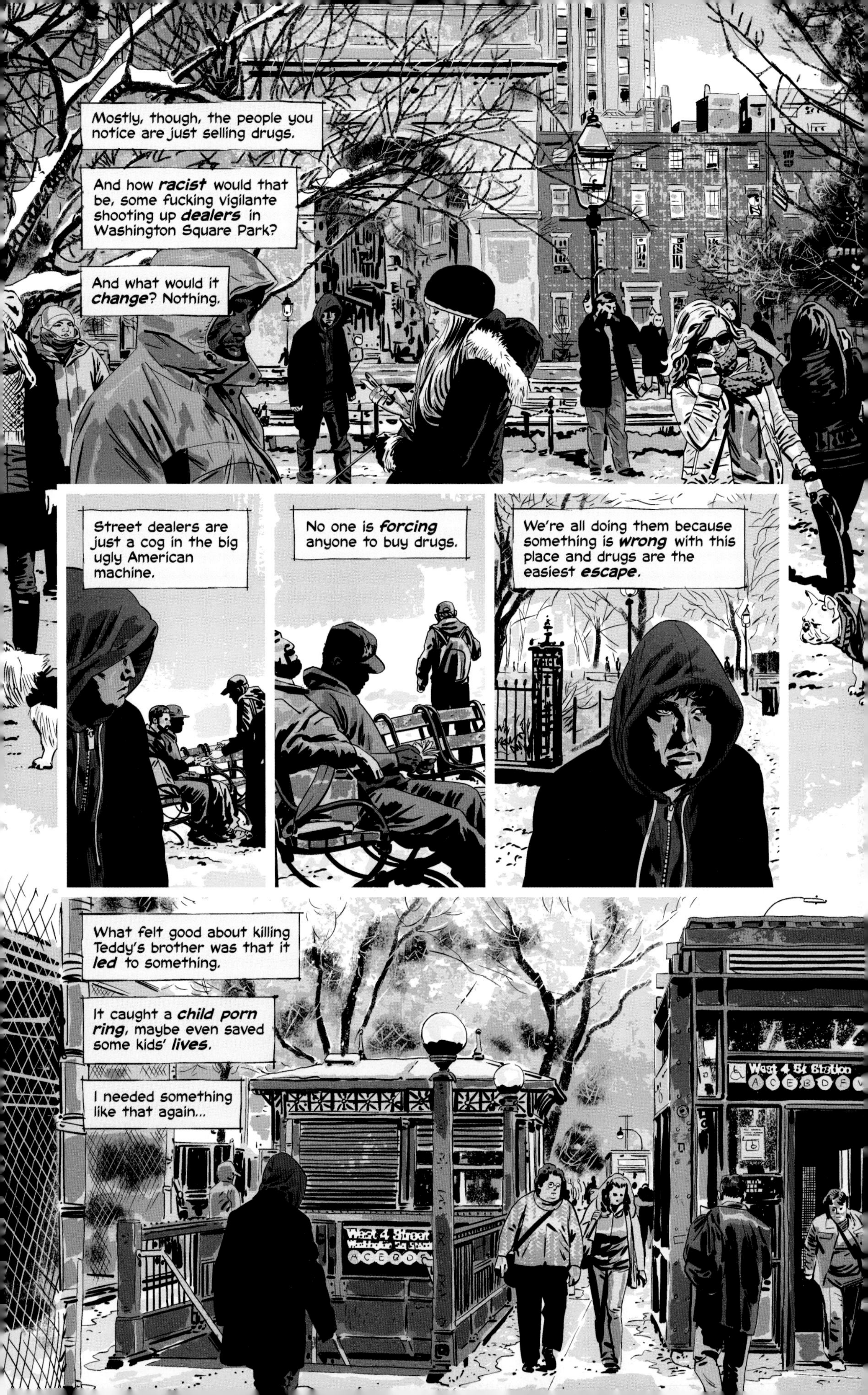

Mostly, though, the people you notice are just selling drugs.
And how *racist* would that be, some fucking vigilante shooting up *dealers* in Washington Square Park?
And what would it *change*? Nothing.
Street dealers are just a cog in the big ugly American machine.
No one is *forcing* anyone to buy drugs.
We're all doing them because something is *wrong* with this place and drugs are the easiest *escape*.
What felt good about killing Teddy's brother was that it *led* to something.
It caught a *child porn ring*, maybe even saved some kids' *lives*.
I needed something like that again...
West 4 St Station
West 4 Street

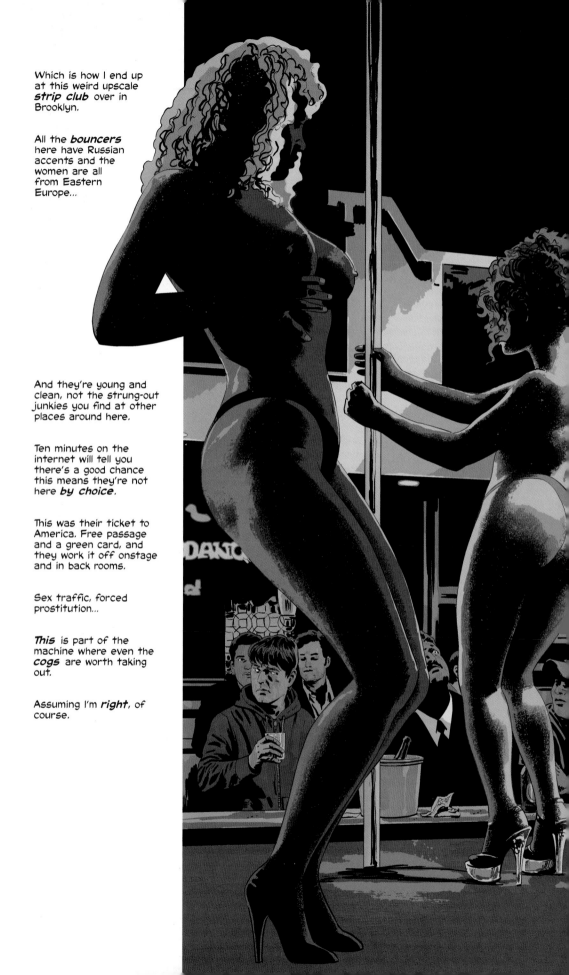

Which is how I end up at this weird upscale **strip club** over in Brooklyn.

All the **bouncers** here have Russian accents and the women are all from Eastern Europe...

And they're young and clean, not the strung-out junkies you find at other places around here.

Ten minutes on the internet will tell you there's a good chance this means they're not here **by choice**.

This was their ticket to America. Free passage and a green card, and they work it off onstage and in back rooms.

Sex traffic, forced prostitution...

This is part of the machine where even the **cogs** are worth taking out.

Assuming I'm **right**, of course.

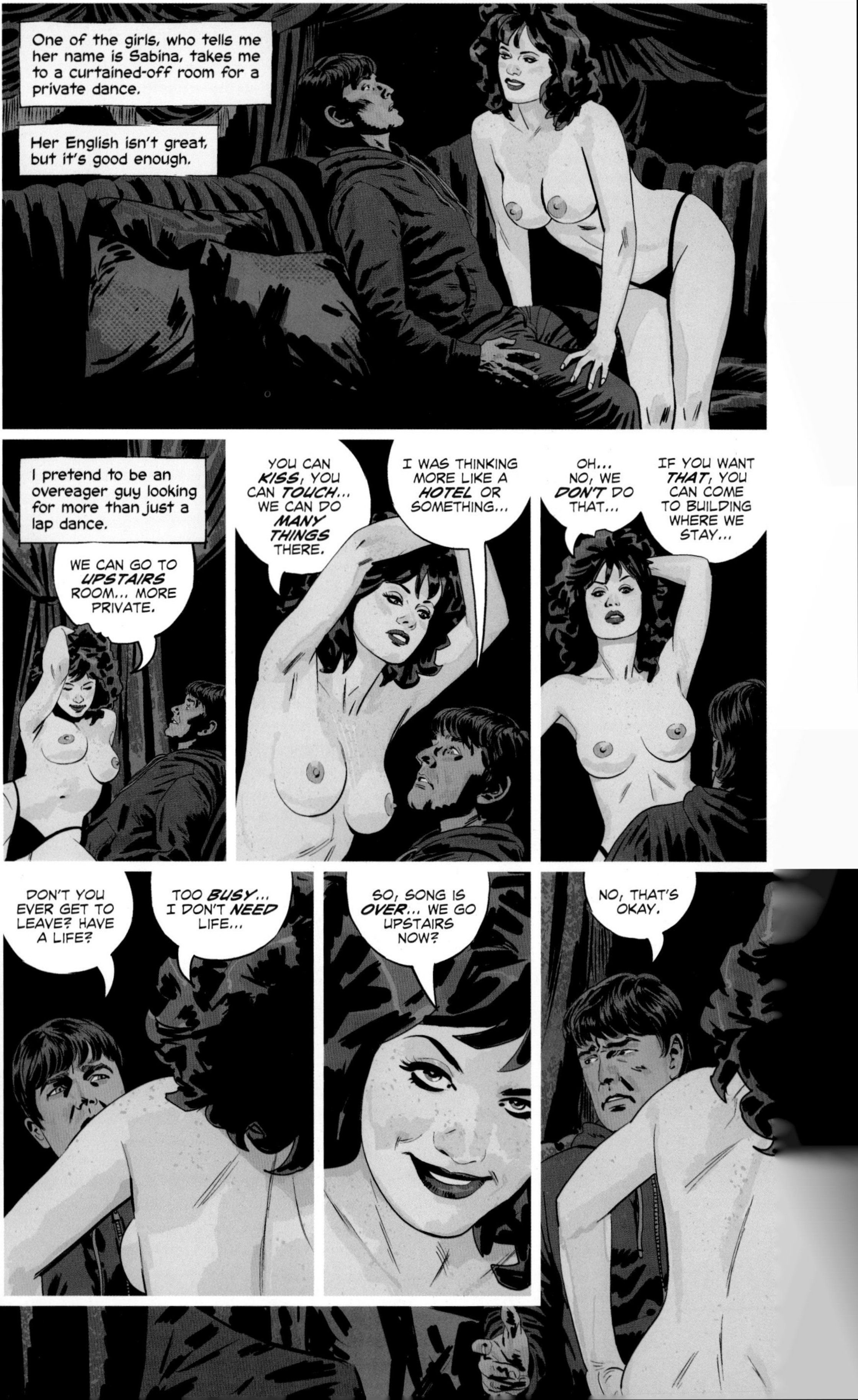
One of the girls, who tells me her name is Sabina, takes me to a curtained-off room for a private dance.
Her English isn't great, but it's good enough.
I pretend to be an overeager guy looking for more than just a lap dance.
WE CAN GO TO UPSTAIRS ROOM... MORE PRIVATE.
YOU CAN KISS, YOU CAN TOUCH... WE CAN DO MANY THINGS THERE.
I WAS THINKING MORE LIKE A HOTEL OR SOMETHING...
OH... NO, WE DON'T DO THAT...
IF YOU WANT THAT, YOU CAN COME TO BUILDING WHERE WE STAY...
DON'T YOU EVER GET TO LEAVE? HAVE A LIFE?
TOO BUSY... I DON'T NEED LIFE...
SO, SONG IS OVER... WE GO UPSTAIRS NOW?
NO, THAT'S OKAY.

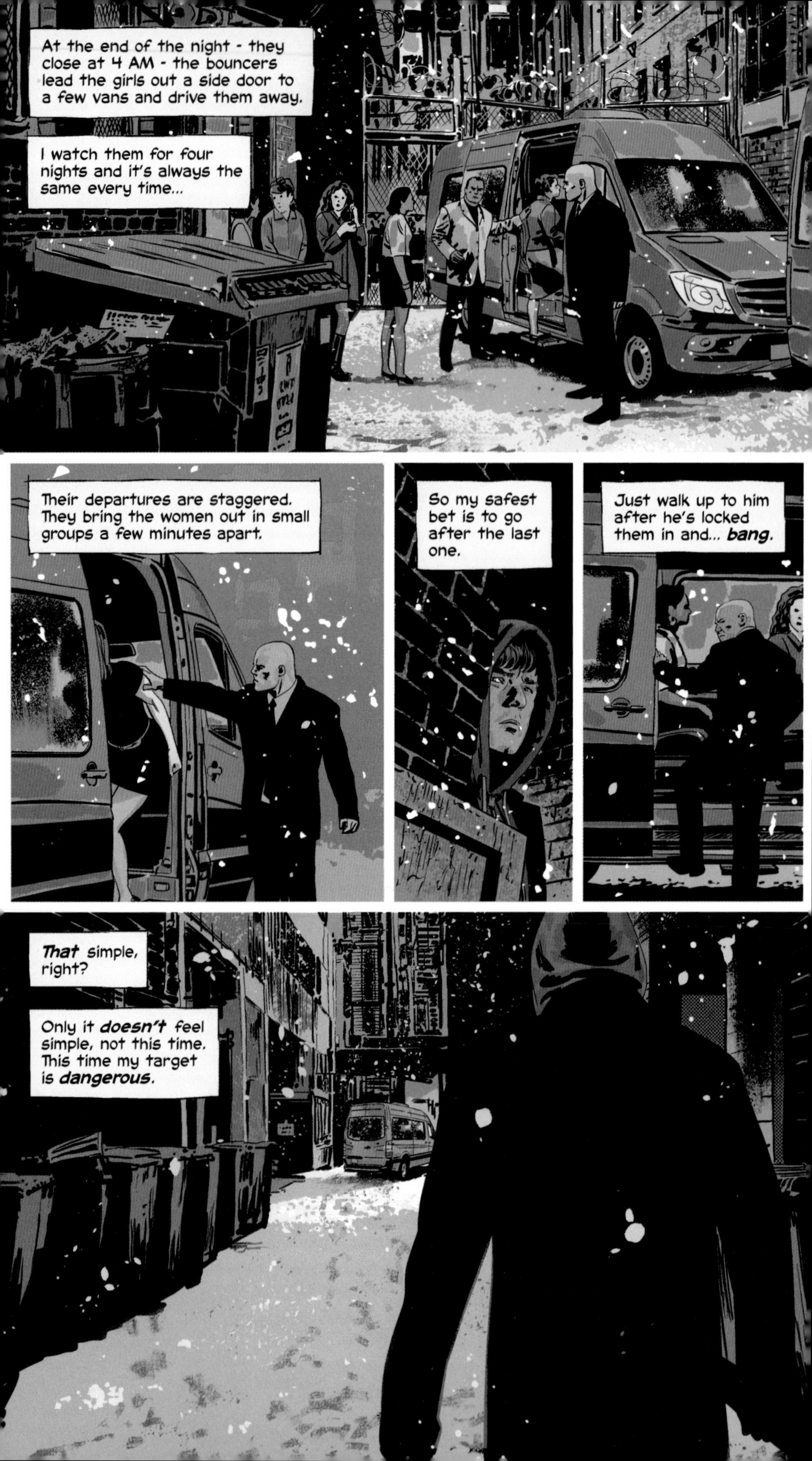
At the end of the night - they close at 4 AM - the bouncers lead the girls out a side door to a few vans and drive them away.
I watch them for four nights and it's always the same every time...
Their departures are staggered. They bring the women out in small groups a few minutes apart.
So my safest bet is to go after the last one.
Just walk up to him after he's locked them in and... **bang.**
That simple, right?
Only it ***doesn't*** feel simple, not this time. This time my target is ***dangerous***.

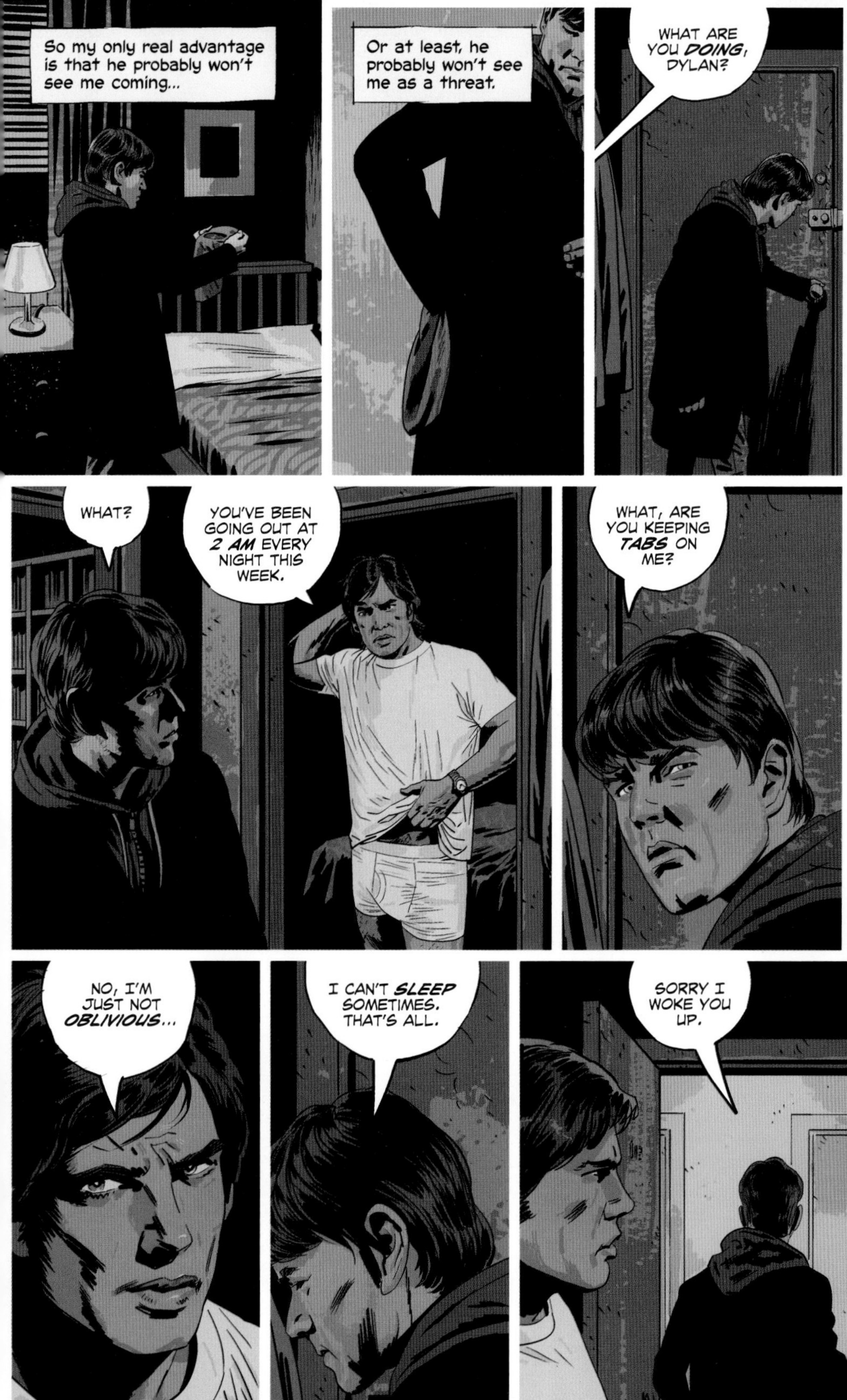
So my only real advantage is that he probably won't see me coming...
Or at least, he probably won't see me as a threat.
WHAT ARE YOU DOING, DYLAN?
WHAT?
YOU'VE BEEN GOING OUT AT 2 AM EVERY NIGHT THIS WEEK.
WHAT, ARE YOU KEEPING TABS ON ME?
NO, I'M JUST NOT OBLIVIOUS...
I CAN'T SLEEP SOMETIMES. THAT'S ALL.
SORRY I WOKE YOU UP.

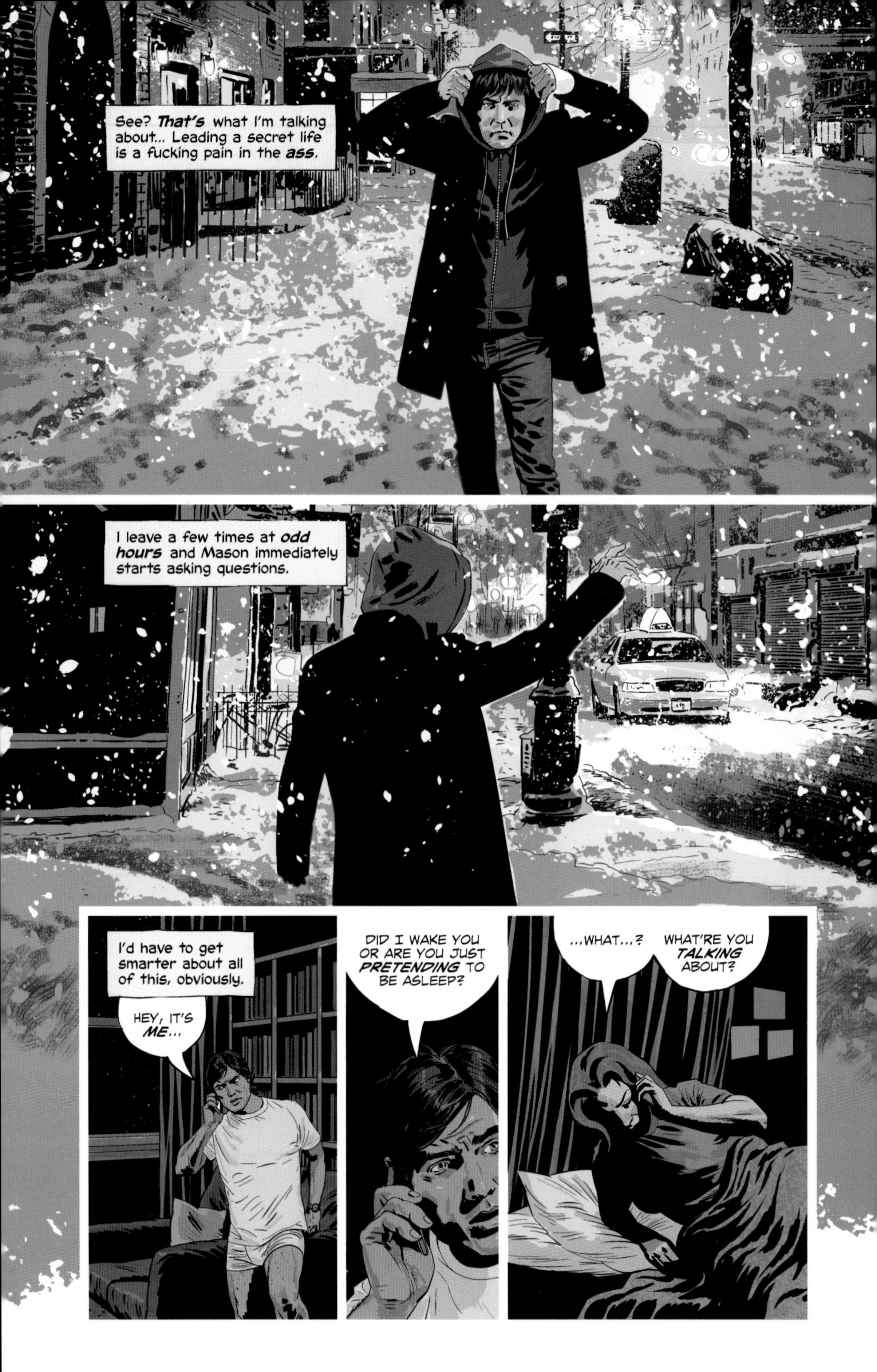

See? That's what I'm talking about... Leading a secret life is a fucking pain in the ass.
I leave a few times at odd hours and Mason immediately starts asking questions.
I'd have to get smarter about all of this, obviously.
HEY, IT'S ME...
DID I WAKE YOU OR ARE YOU JUST PRETENDING TO BE ASLEEP?
...WHAT...?
WHAT'RE YOU TALKING ABOUT?

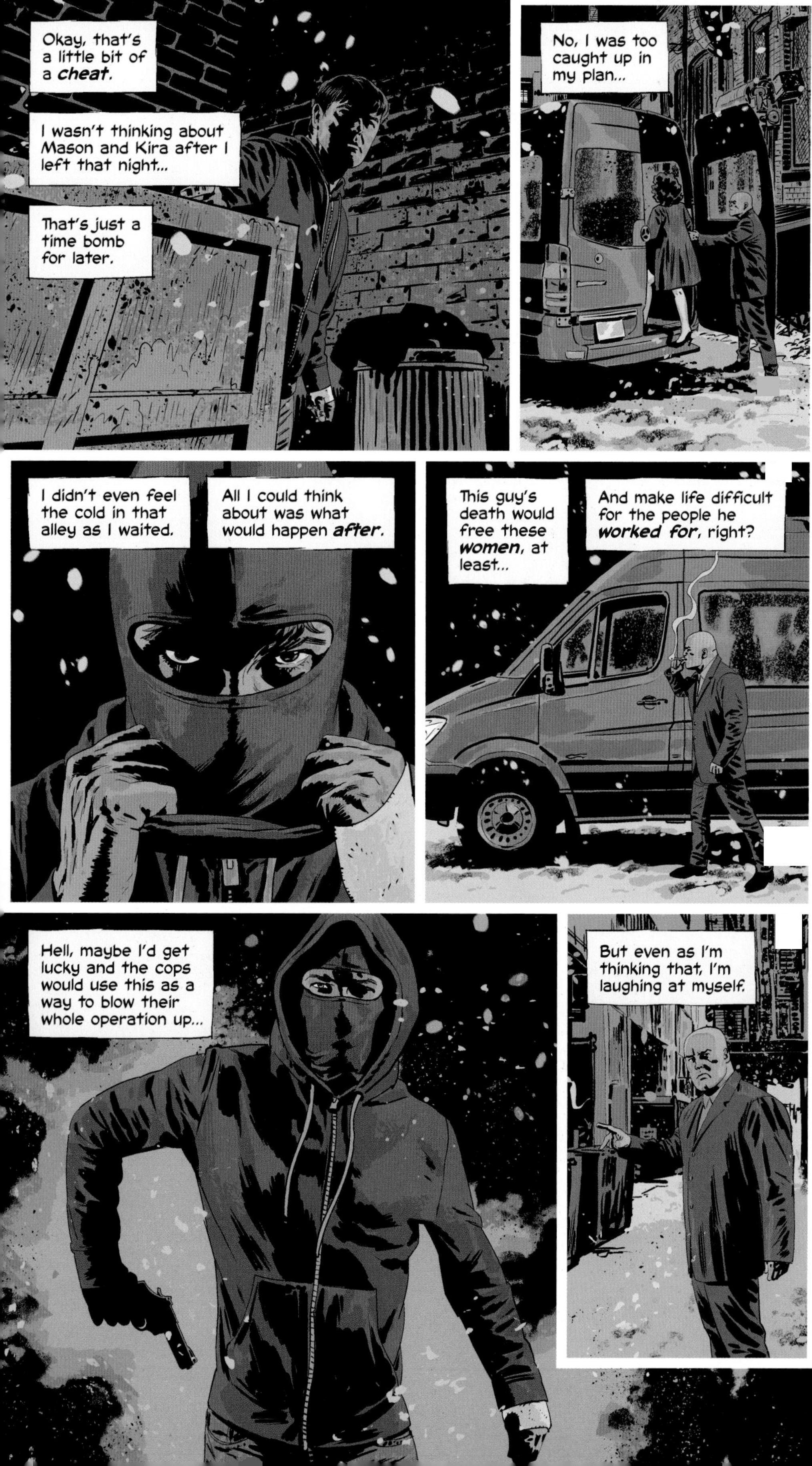
Okay, that's a little bit of a ***cheat***.
I wasn't thinking about Mason and Kira after I left that night...
That's just a time bomb for later.
No, I was too caught up in my plan...
I didn't even feel the cold in that alley as I waited.
All I could think about was what would happen ***after***.
This guy's death would free these ***women***, at least...
And make life difficult for the people he ***worked for***, right?
Hell, maybe I'd get lucky and the cops would use this as a way to blow their whole operation up...
But even as I'm thinking that, I'm laughing at myself.

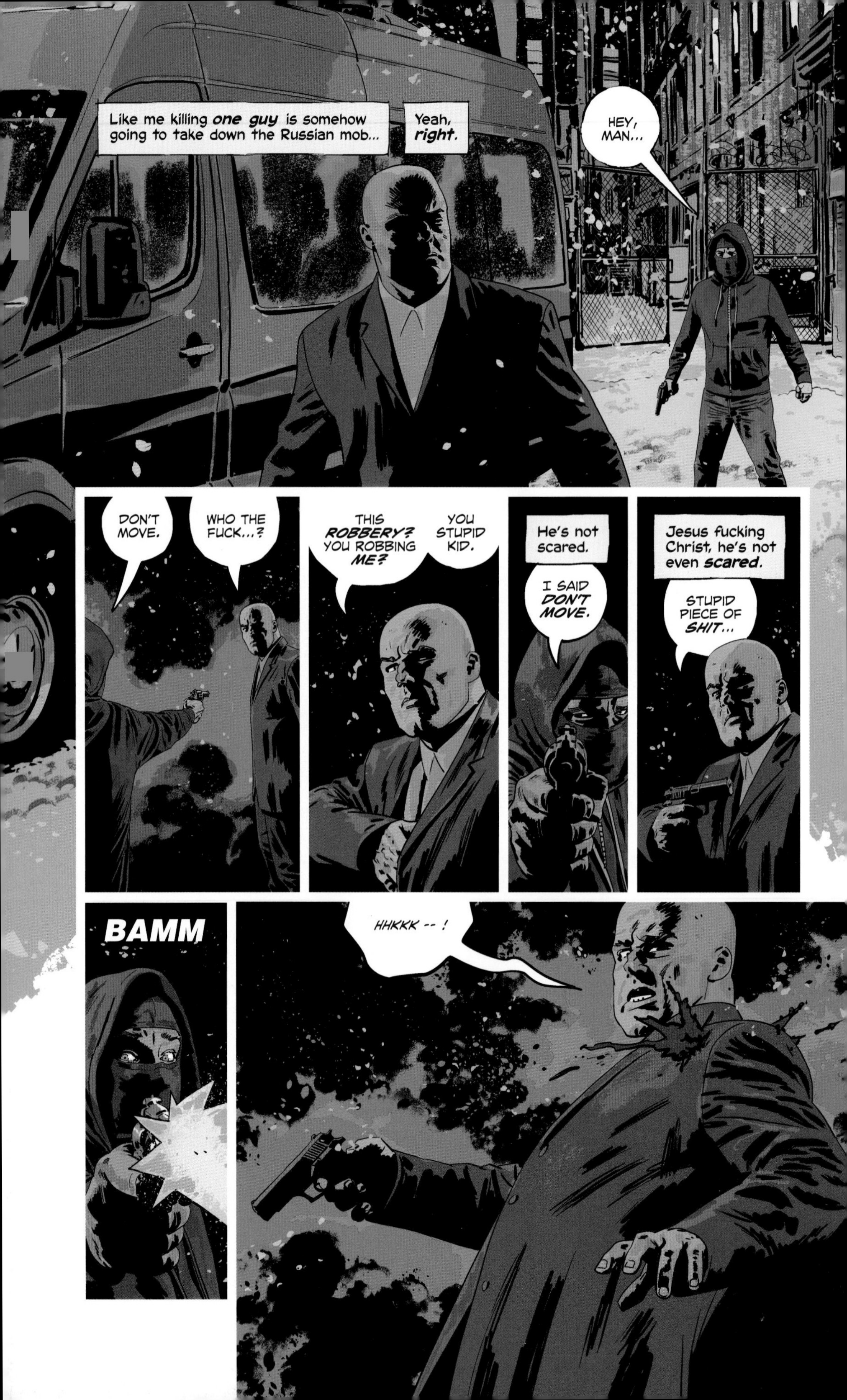
Like me killing *one guy* is somehow going to take down the Russian mob...
Yeah, *right*.
HEY, MAN...
DON'T MOVE.
WHO THE FUCK...?
THIS *ROBBERY?* YOU ROBBING *ME?*
YOU STUPID KID.
He's not scared.
I SAID *DON'T MOVE.*
Jesus fucking Christ, he's not even *scared*.
STUPID PIECE OF *SHIT*...
BAMM
HHKKK -- !

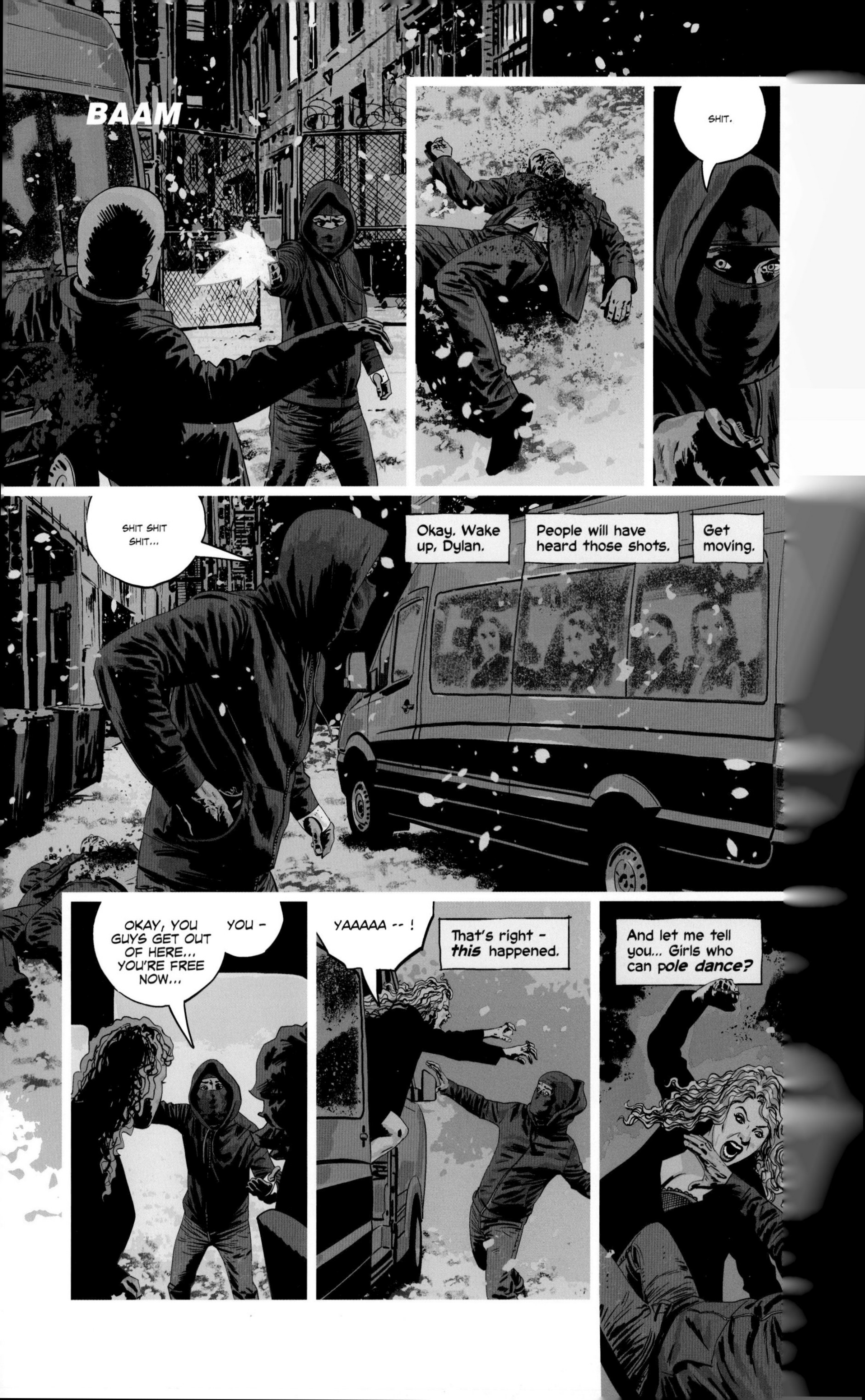
BAAM
SHIT.
SHIT SHIT SHIT...
Okay. Wake up, Dylan.
People will have heard those shots.
Get moving.
OKAY, YOU GUYS GET OUT OF HERE... YOU'RE FREE NOW...
YOU -
YAAAAA -- !
That's right - *this* happened.
And let me tell you... Girls who can pole *dance?*

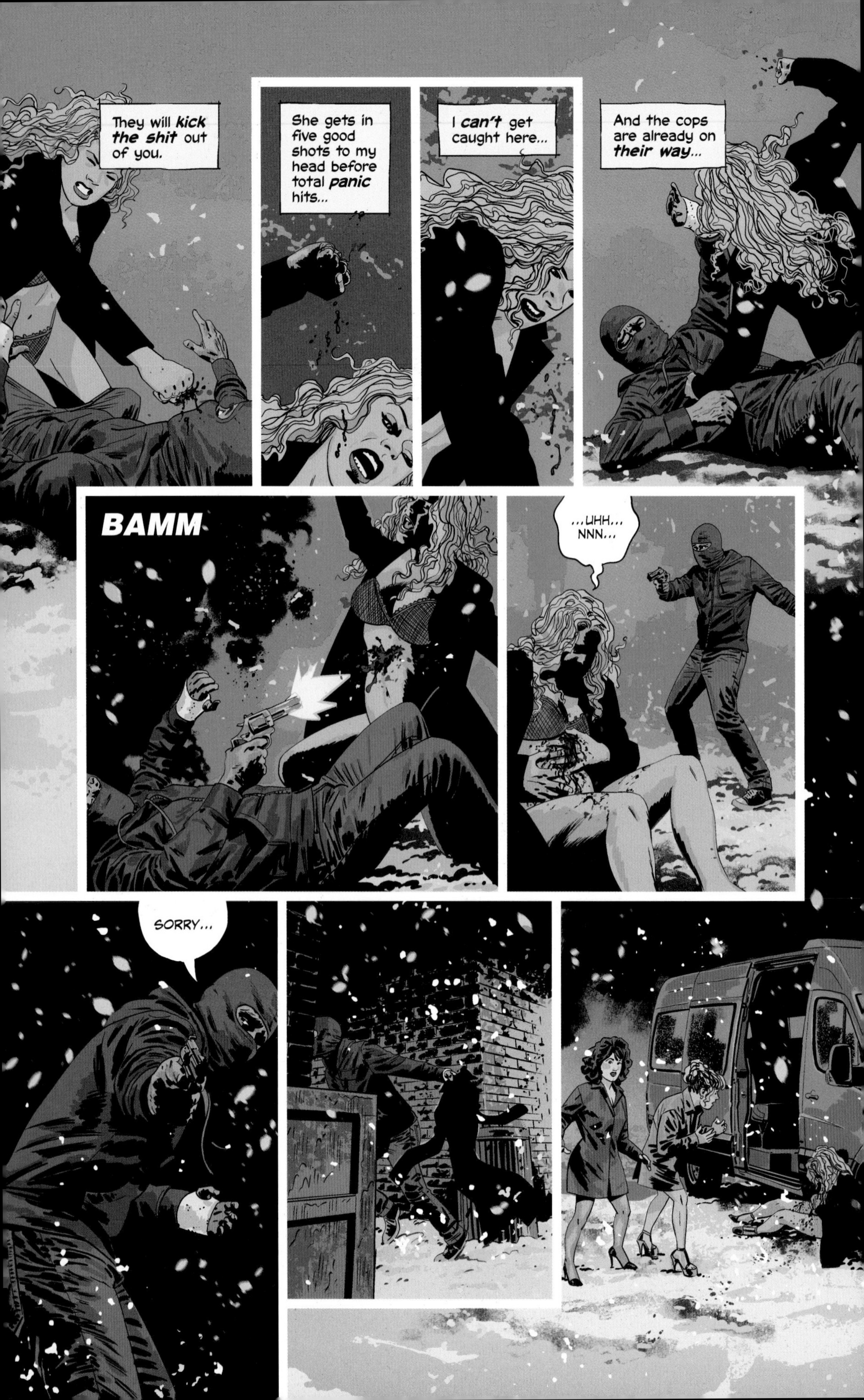

They will *kick the shit* out of you.
She gets in five good shots to my head before total *panic* hits...
I *can't* get caught here...
And the cops are already on *their way*...
BAMM
...UHH... NNN...
SORRY...

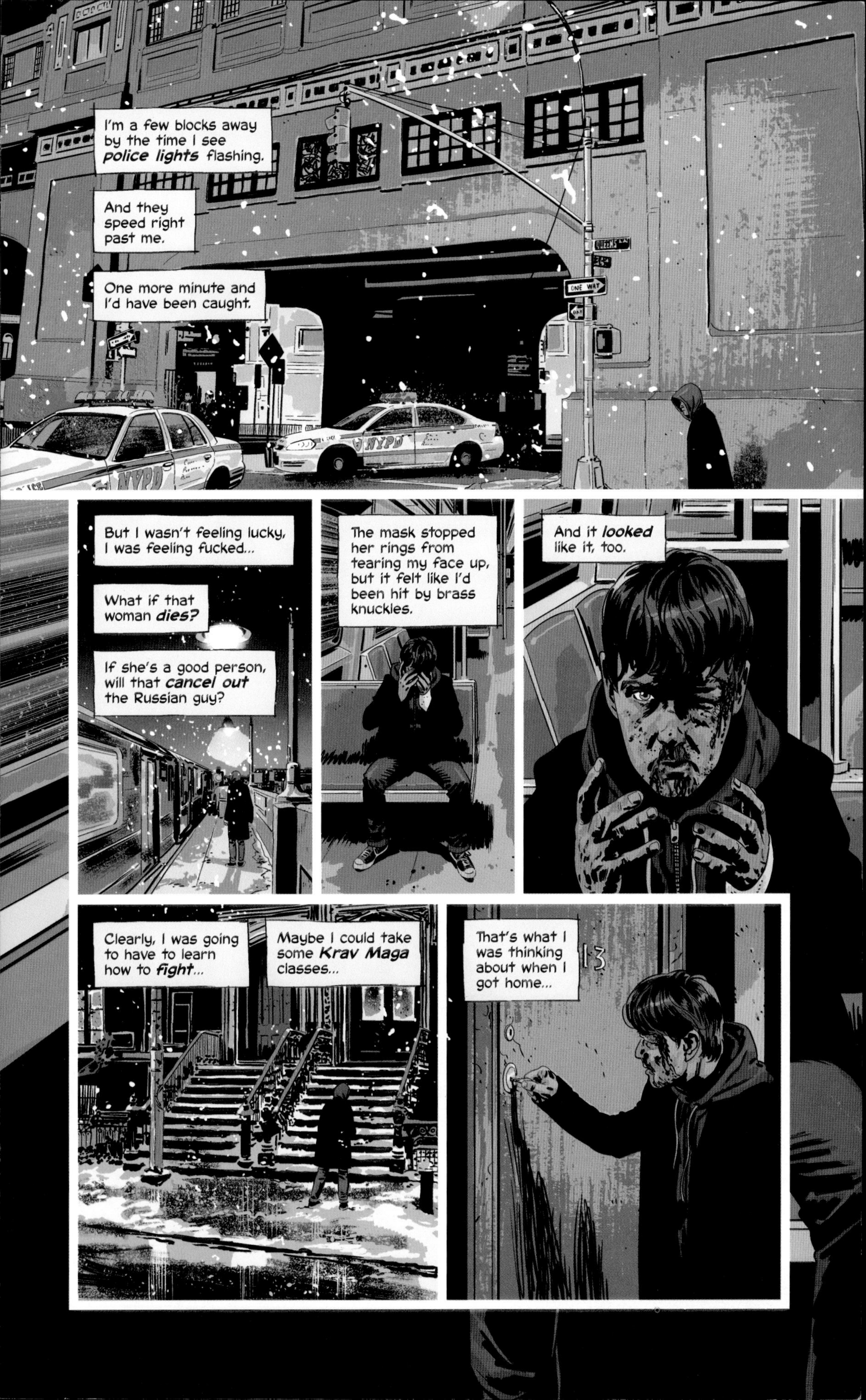
I'm a few blocks away by the time I see *police lights* flashing.
And they speed right past me.
One more minute and I'd have been caught.
QUEENS
ONE WAY
NYPD
NYPD
But I wasn't feeling lucky, I was feeling fucked...
What if that woman *dies?*
If she's a good person, will that *cancel out* the Russian guy?
The mask stopped her rings from tearing my face up, but it felt like I'd been hit by brass knuckles.
And it *looked* like it, too.
Clearly, I was going to have to learn how to *fight*...
Maybe I could take some *Krav Maga* classes...
That's what I was thinking about when I got home...
13

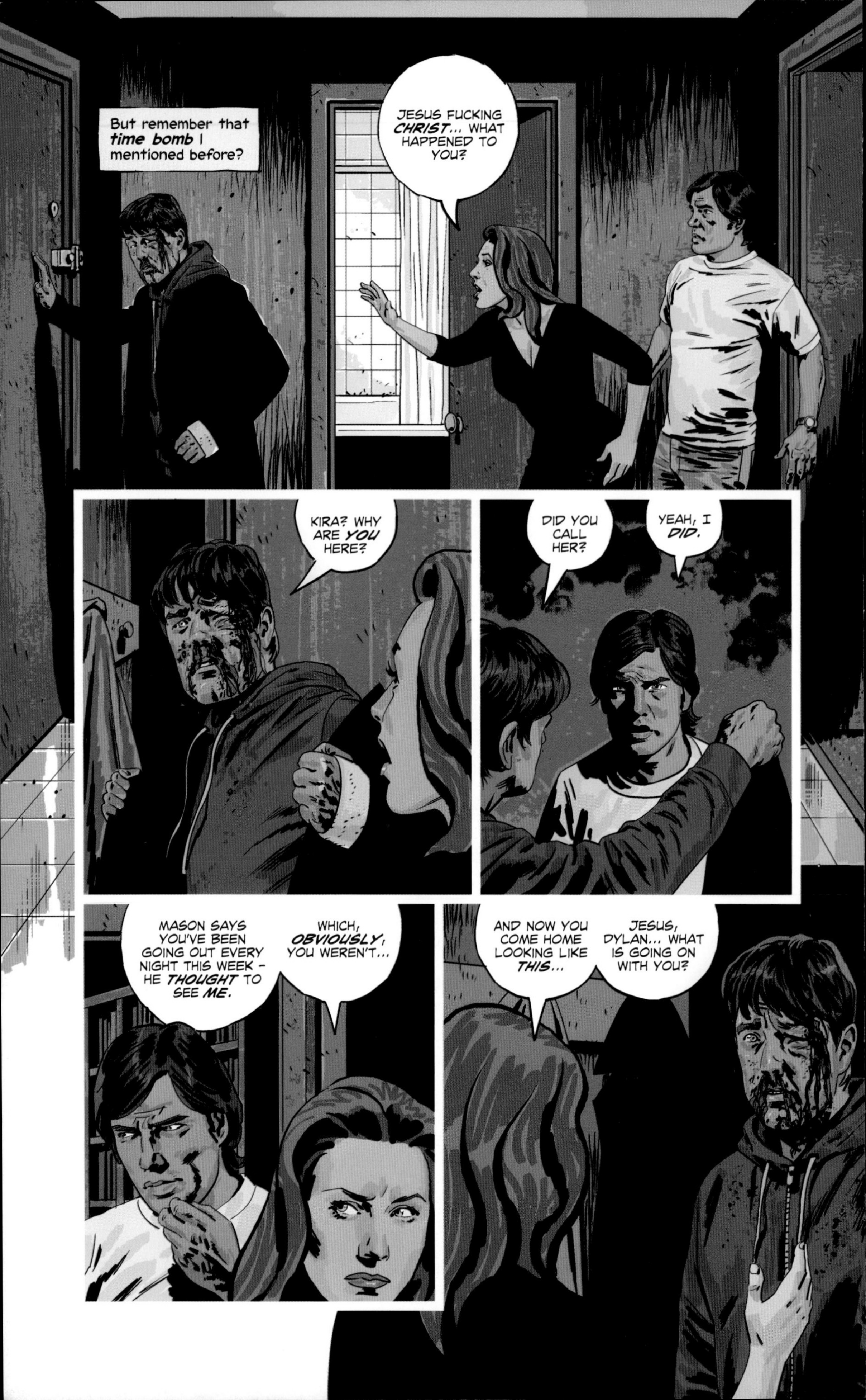
But remember that *time bomb* I mentioned before?
JESUS FUCKING *CHRIST*... WHAT HAPPENED TO YOU?
KIRA? WHY ARE *YOU* HERE?
DID YOU CALL HER?
YEAH, I *DID.*
MASON SAYS YOU'VE BEEN GOING OUT EVERY NIGHT THIS WEEK – HE *THOUGHT* TO SEE *ME.*
WHICH, *OBVIOUSLY*, YOU WEREN'T...
AND NOW YOU COME HOME LOOKING LIKE *THIS*...
JESUS, DYLAN... WHAT IS GOING ON WITH YOU?

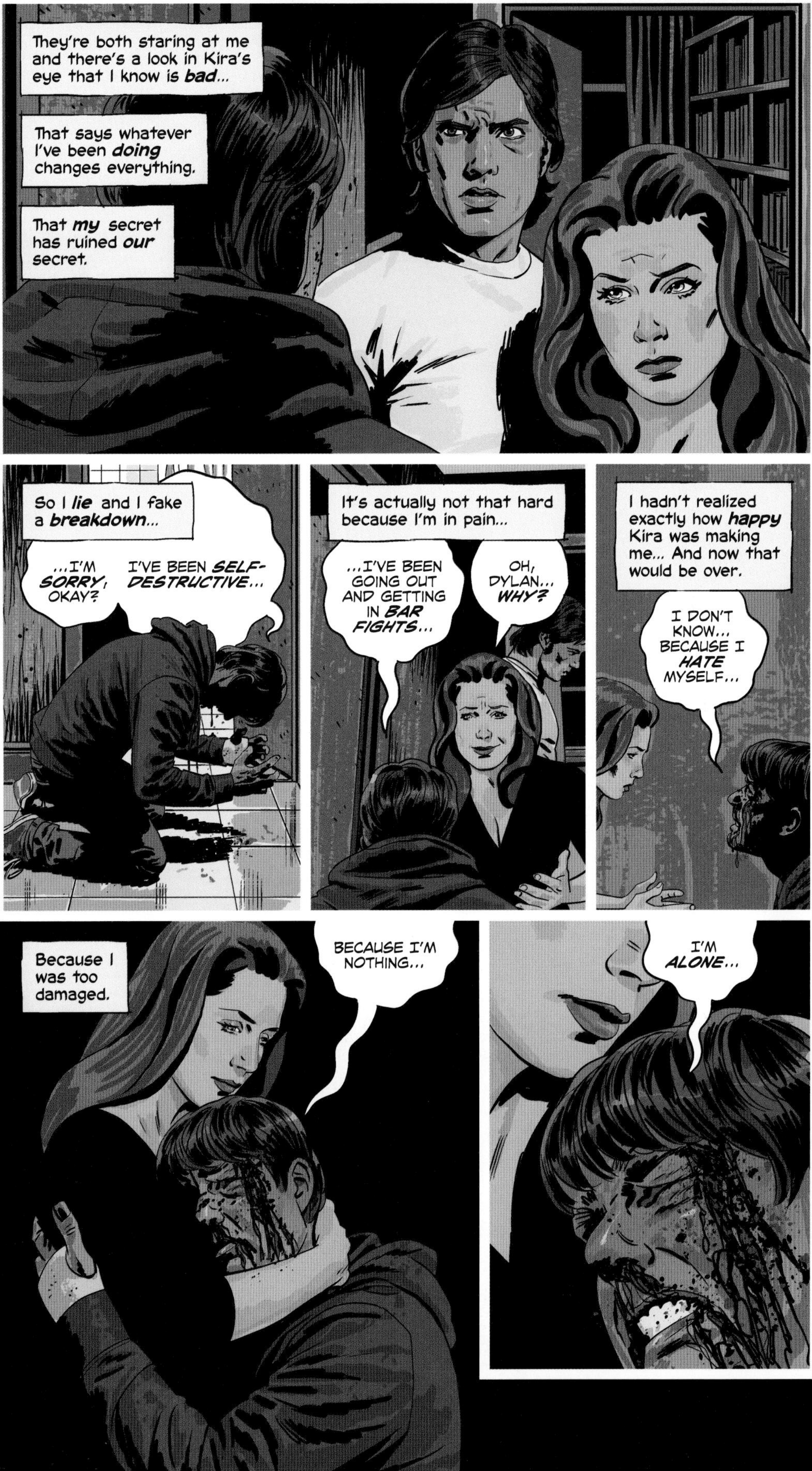
They're both staring at me and there's a look in Kira's eye that I know is *bad*...
That says whatever I've been *doing* changes everything.
That *my* secret has ruined *our* secret.
So I *lie* and I fake a *breakdown*...
...I'M *SORRY*, OKAY?
I'VE BEEN *SELF-DESTRUCTIVE*...
It's actually not that hard because I'm in pain...
...I'VE BEEN GOING OUT AND GETTING IN *BAR FIGHTS*...
OH, DYLAN... *WHY?*
I hadn't realized exactly how *happy* Kira was making me... And now that would be over.
I DON'T KNOW... BECAUSE I *HATE* MYSELF...
Because I was too damaged.
BECAUSE I'M NOTHING...
I'M *ALONE*...

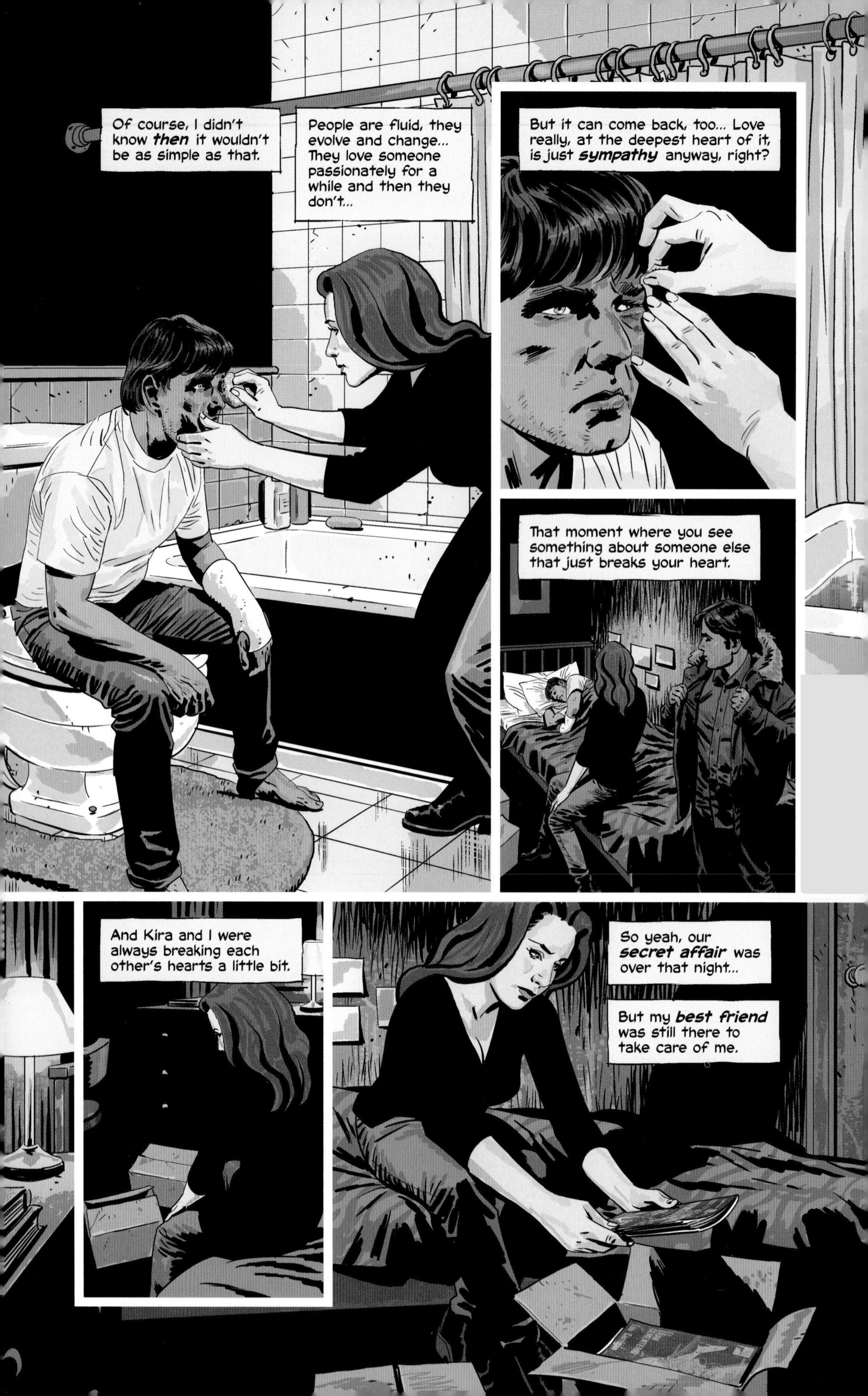
Of course, I didn't know *then* it wouldn't be as simple as that.
People are fluid, they evolve and change... They love someone passionately for a while and then they don't...
But it can come back, too... Love really, at the deepest heart of it, is just *sympathy* anyway, right?
That moment where you see something about someone else that just breaks your heart.
And Kira and I were always breaking each other's hearts a little bit.
So yeah, our *secret affair* was over that night...
But my *best friend* was still there to take care of me.

And the rest of our story was just beginning...

HE HAD A *MASK*, LIKE FOR WINTER?

COULDN'T SEE HIS FACE.

BUT HIS VOICE... HE SOUNDED LIKE A *BOY* MORE THAN A MAN.

...YOU STAYED...?

I WANTED TO BE SURE YOU WERE OKAY.

WHAT IS ALL THIS *ART?* IT'S SO WEIRD.

THOSE ARE MY *DAD'S* ILLUSTRATIONS.

I USED TO LOOK AT THEM ALL THE TIME WHEN I WAS A *KID.*

NO WONDER YOU'RE SUCH A *WEIRDO.*

TAKES ONE TO KNOW ONE.

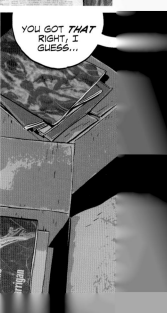

YOU GOT *THAT* RIGHT, I GUESS...

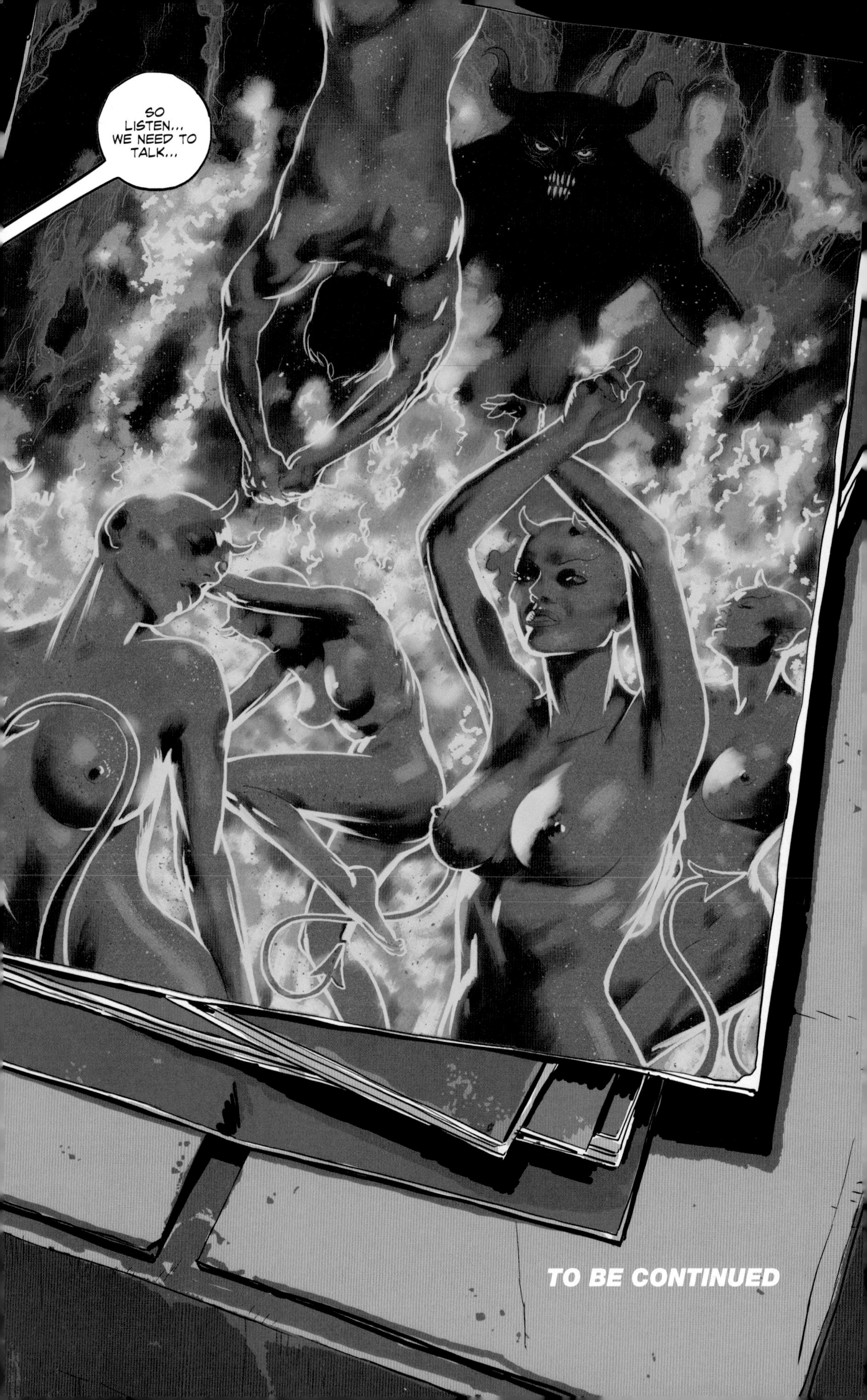
SO LISTEN... WE NEED TO TALK...
TO BE CONTINUED

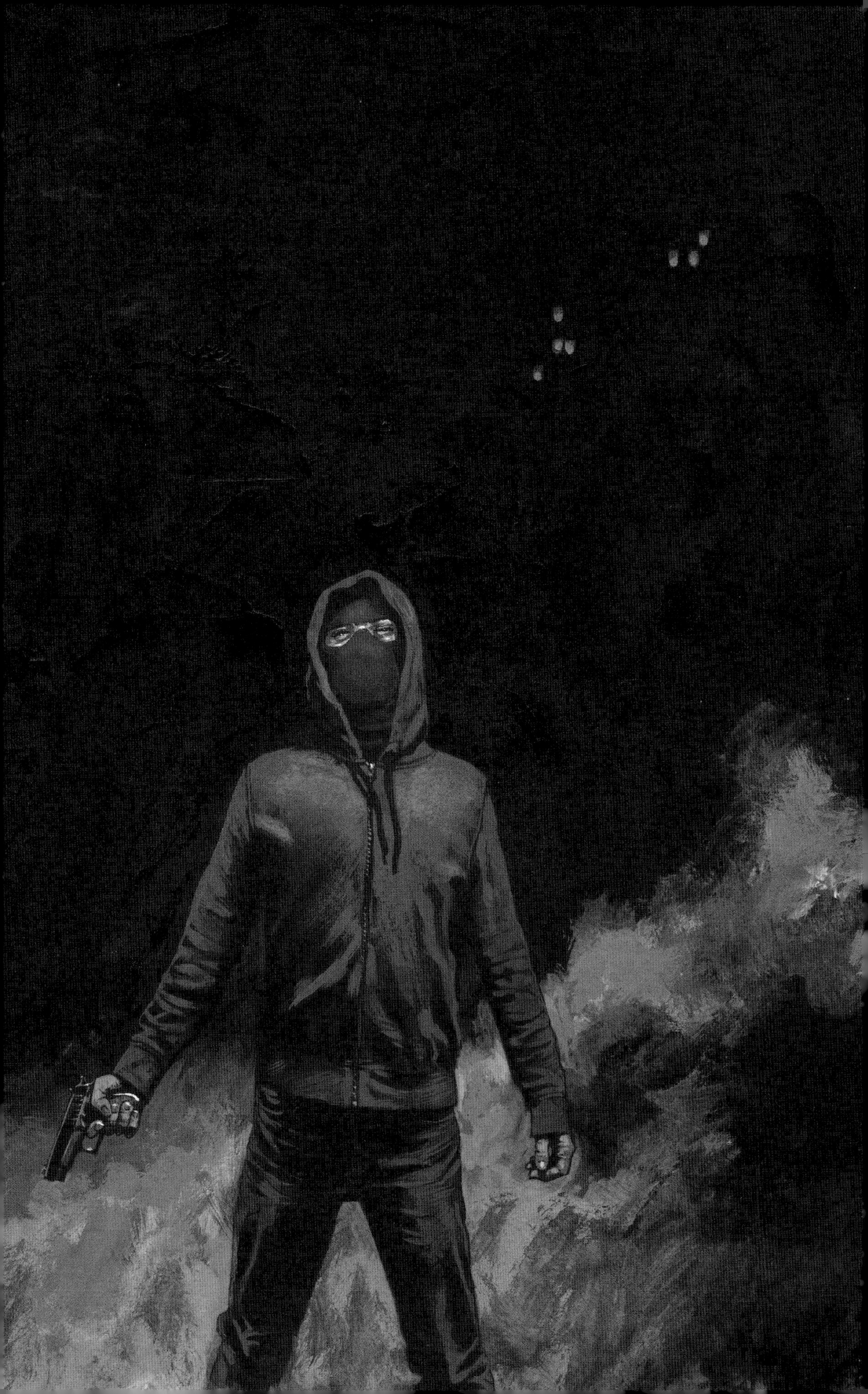

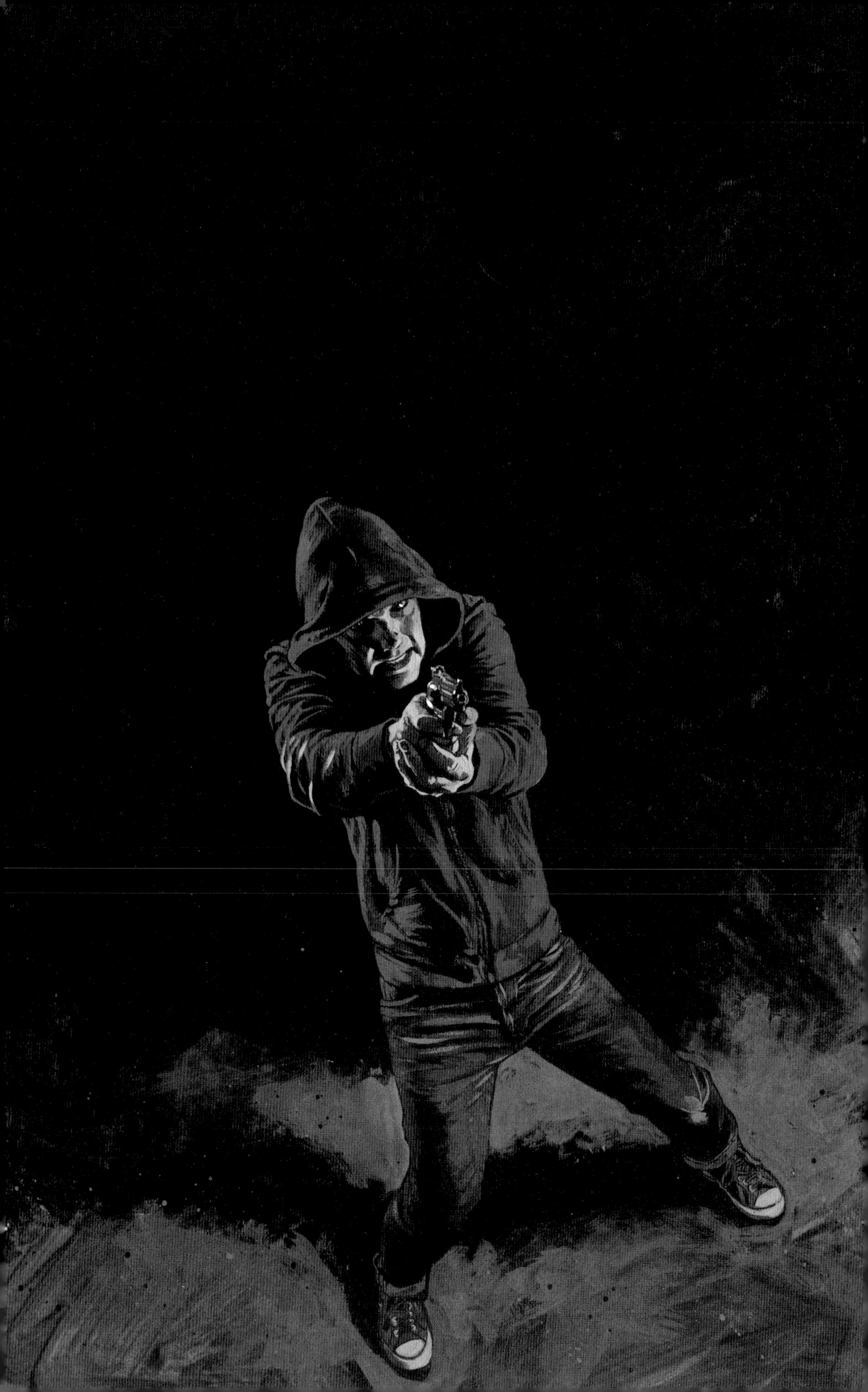

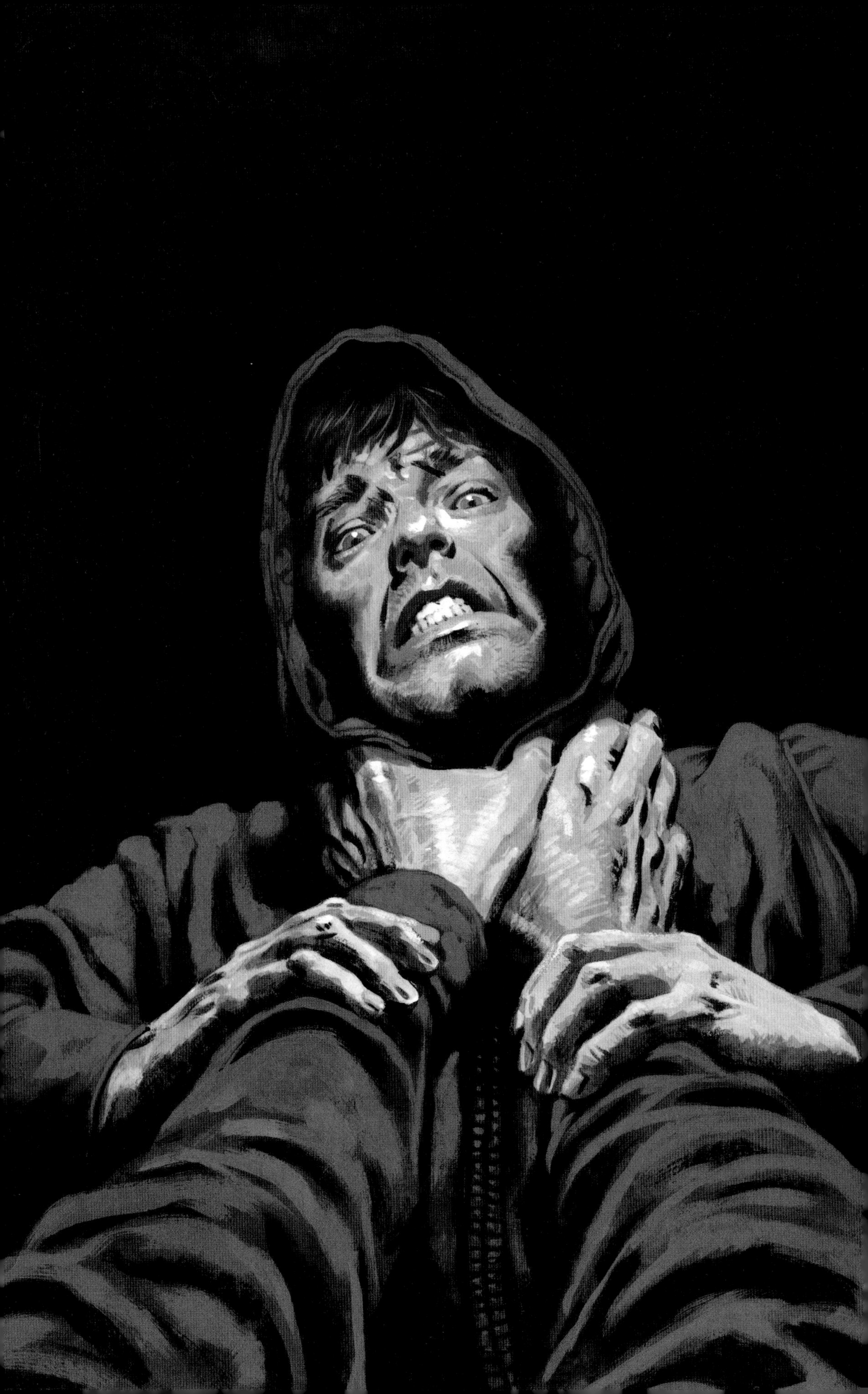

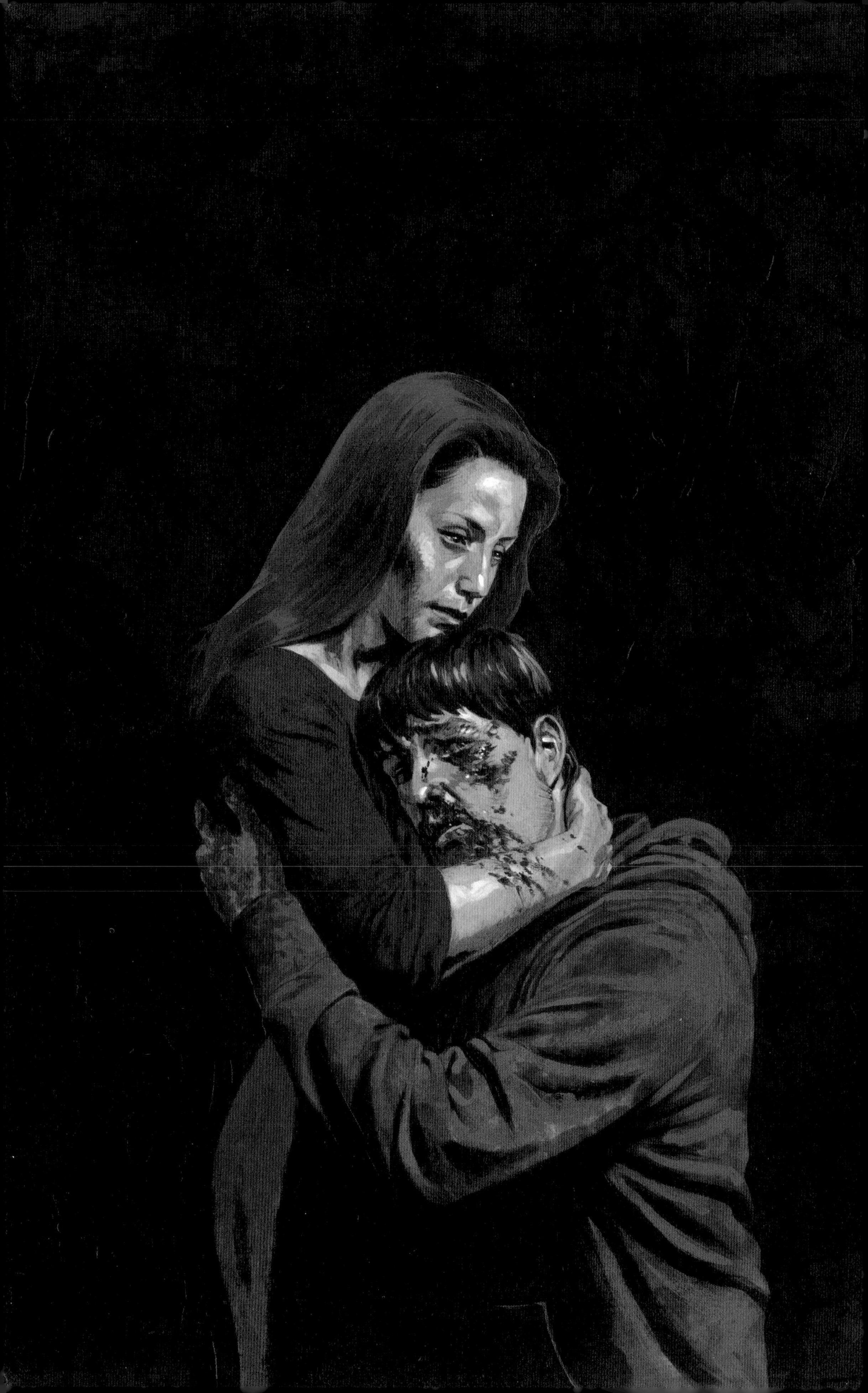